VARANGER

FORGE BOOKS BY CECELIA HOLLAND

FOR CHILDREN

A TOM DOHERTY ASSOCIATES BOOK
New York

VARANGER

CECELIA HOLLAND

VARANGER

Copyright © 2008 by Cecelia Holland

A Forge Book
Published by Tom Doherty Associates, LLC
175 Fifth Avenue
New York, NY 10010

www.tor-forge.com

Forge® is a registered trademark of Tom Doherty Associates, LLC.

The Library of Congress has catalogued the hardcover edition as follows:

Holland, Cecelia, 1943–
    Varanger / Cecelia Holland.—1st hardcover ed.
       p. cm.
    "A Tom Doherty Associates book."
    ISBN 978-0-7653-0558-9
    1. Vikings—Fiction. 2. Vikings—Russia—Fiction. 3. Fur traders—Fiction.
4. Byzantine Empire—Fiction. I. Title.
  PS3558.O348V37   2008
  813'.54—dc22

                            2007044246

ISBN 978-0-7653-1233-4 (trade paperback)

First Edition: April 2008
First Trade Paperback Edition: October 2010

Printed in the United States of America

0 9 8 7 6 5 4 3 2 1

For JP AND JL,
the sons of my heart

VARANGER

CHAPTER ONE

"Your brother's an odd one," Thorfinn said, counting the money.

"In a fight, he's the best," Conn said. "On any water." He was used to people thinking Raef was his brother. He thought they were better than brothers. "Don't play dice with him."

Thorfinn looked up from the pile of coins in his hand. His hat was tucked under his arm and his bald head shone as if waxed. "He cheats?"

"Oh, no," Conn said. "Or at least I've never caught him. But he doesn't lose." He looked away up the shelving river beach, where Raef had gone toward a swarm of waiting peddlers; he was standing in front of an old woman selling smoked fish. Tall and gangly, slightly stooped, Raef himself looked a little like a long narrow fish. Conn turned back to Thorfinn. "I'll take his."

Thorfinn dug into the leather sack and counted up more coins; the money was in different kinds, so he was looking at each one carefully. "Anyway. You two got me through that mess up in the lake, and I heard what you did at Hjorunga Bay. I take it you're wintering here in Holmgard? The river's already icing up, here."

Conn said, "We might." He had no idea what lay ahead of him; he had never been this far east before. Or this far north, which was the trouble now. This city lay in the middle of a frozen fen; there was a foot of snow on the ground here already and more to come, by the feel of the wind. He put out his hand for Raef's money and Thorfinn gave it to him.

"If you decide to go elsewhere, do it soon, before the winter takes hold. If you stay here, you're welcome at my hall. Just ask in the market, you'll find it. I keep a good hall, plenty of drink and meat, and a hot fire always." Thorfinn pursed his lips, his pale eyes calculating. "Take care here. Don't mess with the local girls. And watch out for the Tishats."

"The what?"

"One of their words." Thorfinn made a little vague gesture toward the town on the riverbank. "The commander of the city guard. Big, ugly bastard named Pavo. Scalplock down to his ass, hands like mauls. Everybody steps out of his way."

Conn felt the hair tingle up on the back of his neck. He thought, Not me.

Thorfinn was watching him, his eyes narrow, a little smile curling the corners of his mouth. His gray hair hung in a fringe below the smooth dome of his head. His beard was still mostly dark, but streaked with gray, like strings of frost. "There's something you can do for me, later today, if you would. I have to go up to the council oak, and present myself to the chief. If you'd go with me, I'll see you're well repaid."

Conn nodded. "Raef and I, we'll come."

"Good." Thorfinn laid a fatherly hand on his shoulder. "I'll send Einar for you when the moment comes. Thanks. And tonight we'll tell stories and pass a cup beside my hearth." The hand on Conn's shoulder rose and fell solidly. "Thanks, Conn." He went on down toward his boat, in the shallows where the slaves had it half unloaded.

Raef was walking up the beach again, eating a smoked fish. "Did you get mine?" He held out another of the fish, stiff, greasy and golden, with horrible eyes, stinking of smoke.

Conn declined the fish and handed him half the coins. Their sea chests stood on the icy sand by his feet and in unison they stooped and lifted them up to their shoulders. Conn led the way up the shore toward the city, Raef on his heels, munching steadily through the fish.

The town sprawled across the bank in the low sun, taking up most of a snowy bench along the river, the place studded with big oak trees. An earthworks hemmed it all against the river. Conn noticed that the base of the earthworks was paved with stones, like the Danewirk. He wondered who they held outside, here, who their enemies were.

Within the crescent of the earthworks, most of the buildings were sunk down into the ground, the ridgelines of their roofs coated with a filthy glaze of old snow. One end of each roof was overhung with a cloud of smoke. The hazy sky was colorless as iron, the sun used up burning a hole through the middle, so it gave no warmth and little light. Conn felt the coming of the winter like a roof shutting down over him; in a few days getting out of here at all would be hard. At his elbow, Raef put the last of his fish into his belt pouch and sorted through the money in his hand.

"This is a new one." He held up the smallest coin, turning it to show Conn the faces on either side, all wreathed in strange runes. "I've never seen this one before."

"Don't lose it," Conn said. "It's gold. It's more than a penny. You can't buy anything with it, it's too much."

Raef tucked the coin into the pouch on his belt. The ground was rising slightly underfoot, the snow on either side trampled to black muck, the boards of the walkway booming hollow. Ahead, a hammer banged. They were coming up to a forge. In front of a fat brick cone of a furnace, a clot of men stood around watching the smith pound away at a chunk of red iron. The smell of the hot iron reached Conn's nose and he tasted it in his throat; he thought of the blade it would be and his hands tingled. He thought regretfully of the sword he had lost at Hjorunga Bay.

The boardwalk was leading them into the city, which was smaller than Hedeby, maybe fifty roofs, with stretches of open snowfield and naked trees between, pens for animals. They passed a shambles, with scraped hides nailed to the walls. It felt good to be walking, after so long on the boat, and the town spread out around him wide as the whole world, a web of smells and sounds and new sights.

A woman with a red-patterned shawl around her head came

toward him, holding a basket of bread, and calling in a long voice. A baby slept wrapped into the cloak on her back. A row of slaves trudged along the boardwalk, hauling familiar bales of cloth and wool: part of the cargo Raef and Conn had just brought in here from the west. Under a gaunt tree a little way off a man knelt down, fumbling with something on the ground.

Near the center of the space within the earthworks, they came into a broad, crowded market. All around the edge people were selling baskets of bread and fish and nuts, while other people roamed around before them looking everything over. Most of them were using the other language, which he had heard already coming through Ladoga, out on the Swedish Sea. The cackle of voices was like geese flocking and the swarms of people never stopped moving.

A few little club-headed horses stood under the leafless broad-spreading branches of a massive oak tree at the center of the space, and several men were sitting or standing just in front of it, passing around a jug. Likely this was the council oak Thorfinn had mentioned. Conn stopped a big-bosomed girl selling warm meat pies from a tray in her arms, and dickered with her awhile, enjoying her soft roundness, before he took the pie and enjoyed that.

Raef said, "What did Thorfinn say? Did you ask him where we can go next?"

Conn licked meat juice from his fingers. "He has a place here. We can stay with him, he says, all winter if we have to. I'd as soon go south, I hate long nights." He turned and looked after the soft roundness of the pie girl walking off.

Raef gave a little shake of his head. "Last night was damned cold."

"He wants us to stand behind him, later, he has to present himself here. I said we would. We can certainly stay the night at his hall."

"Let's stow these chests there, then."

They were leaving the market behind, drifting down a broad

lane through a stand of sunken houses, the sharp ridged rooflines
taller than they were; the log trusses were carved in patterns like
vines. Under the eaves were stacks of firewood, rows of barrels,
sleeping dogs. All the doors faced south. Steps led down into the
houses. All around the snow was trampled into crisscrossing
tracks, like a web. They passed one little house made all of wood,
even the roof, the door hanging open; Conn looked in as they went
by, saw the firepit in the middle, and decided it was a bathhouse.

Before the next set of steps a woman bundled in a shawl stooped
to sweep the snow off the hard ground with a handful of straw. Hung
between the trusses above her doorway was a swag of yellow cloth.
Beside the wall lay a garden turned over for the winter, blanketed
with more straw, all covered now with a hat of snow.

Conn felt the cold of the oncoming winter in that thick blanket
of straw. In the way these houses crawled down into the ground to
stay warm. He shifted the weight of his sea chest, in which he had
nothing save one cloak and an extra pair of shoes. "There's got to
be some way to get south of here."

Raef said, "Not if the river freezes up. I'd say, two more
nights like last night, we might not have gotten this far."

"Ah, you stonehead. Always down." Conn cuffed his arm.
"There must be some way out of here. If we stay with Thorfinn
we'll have to ship out with him in the spring."

"He'll go west," Raef said. "I don't want to go backwards." In
the last few years he had grown much the taller of the two of them,
but he was lean as bone and jittery as a reed in the wind, and he
stooped, as if to stay at Conn's height. He veered off suddenly toward the nearest tree, where a wooden post stood tilted back
against the trunk. Four faces were carved into the top, each looking a different way. A broken bowl lay on the ground before it.
"So that's what it is," he said.

"Some kind of god," Conn said.

Raef took a little piece of the fish out of his belt pouch and
bent and put it down at the foot of the post. Conn crowed at him.

"You are spook-ridden as a Christian, you know that."

Raef shrugged. "It's their place," he said.

"Sure. Look, there's Einar."

He yelled, and by the string of horses, whose line ended at this tree, several other men yelled back. One of them strode forward, lanky yellowheaded Einar, who had sat on the bench behind him on Thorfinn's boat, and who talked too much, and who now gladly greeted them, and slung his arm around Conn's neck.

"What're you doing? What're you doing? Come drink with us."

"Later," Conn said, disentangling himself from Einar. He was glad to see that the strangers with Einar all looked dansker. "We're supposed to stand up with you for Thorfinn. Where's his place, anyway?"

"Right over there—" Einar tottered a few strides away, pointing. "That one with the red sun on the door." He slapped Conn across the back. "You'll be there, too? That's good. We can use you. Helgi will be glad, too. I'm really glad Thorfinn thought of that. Come back, once you've stowed your gear, there. We've got a whole cask of this kind of mead these people cook up. It'll put the fire in you. Bring a cup."

"Maybe," Conn said. He started off toward the door of the red sun.

———⊷———

Raef had been in Holmgard for only a few hours and already he was itching to move on. Since he left the far western island where he had grown up, he had been moving, driven like an ember in the wind; he had no idea what he was looking for but the need to find it would not let him rest. When he was sailing, at least, he knew he was going onward, but now he was stuck here, probably for the whole winter, and it already seemed too small to him.

Thorfinn's hall was deep in the ground, but its rooftree stood higher than Raef's head, and when they went down the front steps it was like walking into a cave. On either end of the long dark space a fire burned in a stone hearth, and smoke filled the top half of the room; there was no other light, and it all stank of sweat and old food and piss. The sleeping benches along each wall and three big cloth looms took up most of the space. Raef knew why so many people were out in the street in spite of the cold. He and Conn left their sea chests on an empty bench as close to the door as possible and went back up to the ground.

"I'm still hungry, where's that pie girl?"

"Over there's a cooker."

They went back into the market; up ahead on their right was an open brazier and a man squatting behind it turning strips of meat laid across a grill. An old woman selling bread had set up next to him and people were waiting in a crowd two and three deep in front of them. Raef stood with his head down, jingling the coins in his hands. Conn dickered with the Sclava behind the grill, pointing and gesturing, and got them each some chunks of greasy meat piled on a piece of bread.

"Do you want to go find Einar?"

"Not yet. He's hard on the ears, Einar."

Raef laughed. He stuffed his mouth with the bread and the sour, stringy meat, warm and good.

They went down to the river again; Thorfinn had moved his boat on down the shore, where several other boats were drawn up almost to the top of the bank. The peddlers had gone. Where Thorfinn's boat had been before, three stacks of wool and cloth stood on the beach and a steady stream of slaves came and heaved them up on their shoulders and bore them away into the city.

Raef walked down to the river's edge, muddied and scummy from the constant coming and going of men. The farther bank was marsh, flat to the horizon except for an occasional elm tree; oaks would not grow on such soggy ground. Another boat was just rowing up from the lake beyond the next bend, to the south, not a clinker-built Western longship like Thorfinn's but a single hollowed log, its sides built higher with planks, wallowing in the water, oars at either end.

The sand under his feet crunched with ice; he saw petals of ice in the shallows, even now, with the sun as high as it was going to get here for the next four or five months. In places where the water was still, he thought he saw a thin film on the surface, the flakes of ice knitting together like a cold garment. The sky was yellow, not just from the smoke of the city fires. It would be dark soon, and the noon hardly by.

The log boat pulled in, and Conn found the captain and they stood talking awhile. The captain was going straight south again in the morning, but he already had a full crew. Raef stood staring at the log boat, wondering if he even wanted to sail on something so miserable.

The captain's voice boomed. "If any of my men decide to stay here, I'll take you on. But don't depend on that. And I'm only going to the other side of the lake." He turned back to his log boat, bellowing to his crew to work faster.

Raef followed Conn up toward the boardwalk; the wind down the river was cutting sharp and low clouds were moving in from the northwest. Conn said, "What do you think of that log? That's our only chance, I think. If we don't leave that way, we won't be getting out of here."

"I hate those boats. They're worse than rafts. They handle like dead bodies." They passed the forge again, where a few men still gathered around its fire.

"There's Thorfinn," Conn said.

Raef looked up; their old captain stood up ahead of them on the boardwalk, watching them come, and he waved his arm impatiently at them to come faster. The peaked hat perched on his dome of a head made him look even taller than he was. Raef hung back a little, not liking such a summons. Einar and Helgi were already standing by Thorfinn, and two of the other men who had been with them earlier. Conn was walking on ahead of Raef now, striding easily up to join them, belonging among them at once.

When Raef reached them Thorfinn was saying, "I don't expect any trouble. Just stand behind me and look like warriors." He glanced briefly at Raef, making sure he was coming, and led them off.

"My name's Bjorn." The older of the two strangers put his hand out. "This is Vagn." He indicated the dark scrawny boy beside him, who grunted, looking elsewhere. Raef shook the outstretched hand, and said his name; he noticed a Christian cross on a thong around Bjorn's neck.

They went up into the marketplace. The whole crowd there had collected around the great oak tree in the middle, watching a knot of men beneath the spread leafless branches. Thorfinn led his crew into the midst of the loose mass of people; Raef, going along on Conn's heels, saw the pie girl, selling her wares briskly. Conn stopped, because Thorfinn had stopped, near the front edge of the ring of onlookers around the oak tree. Over their shoulders Raef could see the council there.

There were twenty or thirty men standing or sitting around in the thin shade of the winter-naked branches, but it was easy to pick out the important ones, the nine at the center, with their gold chains and splendid fur cloaks trimmed with more gold and the fawning people around them. None of them were dansker. They sat on benches under the oak tree. One held a staff, trimmed with gold, of course, which he swayed back and forth importantly, and rapped often on the ground.

Another man sat in the back, a little to one side, as if he were not really with them, but his eyes moved constantly around him, seeing everything, and Raef knew he was the chief. He sat with his hands in his lap, doing nothing. He had long fair hair under an ornate cap, a square blond beard.

The crowd watching was mostly Sclava, the local people, men

in long tunics and women in shawls and aprons. The Sclava maidens were prettier than most, he thought, fair and blue-eyed, their skin smooth as the skin of a fruit. The older women, as everywhere, were worn and wrinkled and used up. Something white flickered in the corner of his eye; over there a man with a white cloth on his head stood watching from the other side of the crowd, visible among the dark clothes of the people around him like a quartz in a stream.

"Thorfinn Hrolfsson," a strange voice bellowed, from under the oak tree. The man with the gold-handled staff stepped forward and banged the butt of his stick on the ground. He spoke dansker, not well. "Come forward to this council!"

Thorfinn straightened himself, pulling his sleeves down, glanced around him at his men, and walked out into the open before the council. The men under the tree—they were all Sclava, Raef saw, like the golden-haired man in the fancy cap—stopped their mingling together to watch him come; in the back, the man in the fancy cap leaned forward to see him better. Before them, Thorfinn bowed down from the waist, and said his name.

He spoke dansker to them, although Raef knew he spoke Sclava well enough. He said, "I have come back with many goods for the markets of Holmgard. And I ask permission to be allowed to stay here the winter, and do some buying and selling, as I have done since my father's time."

Behind the rest of the council the fair-haired man in the cap stood up suddenly. When he did the other Sclava all fell still and turned to watch him. In a respectful hush, he stepped forward, coming around the side of the benches, past the man with the staff. He had eyes so blue Raef could see them from across the crowd.

"Thorfinn," he said, his voice loud and strong. "There was talk you would not come this year. Some agreement with another fahrman. Is this going to make trouble for us?"

Thorfinn stood solid, on wide-planted feet. "I am here now, Dobrynya. That other thing, that's a matter for the Varanger."

"Varanger or no, we are all Rus', and while I am posadnik of
Novgorod I will not tolerate trouble in my city."

Thorfinn said, "I intend no trouble. I have bought and sold
here since my father's time. Since your father's time, Dobrynya.
And this is business of the Varanger, not you. Holmgard, not Novgorod." His voice was hard as a stone, but he was taking a purse
from his belt. Raef heard it jingle with coins. "In token of my
goodwill, then, I shall give you my tithes in advance."

Dobrynya drew back, looking angry at that, as if he saw it for
a bribe, but the man with the staff hurried eagerly forward, his
hand out. All the other men on the benches craned their necks to
watch, as the man with the staff took the purse, held it calculat-
ingly a moment in his palm, and turned back to nod to them. The
men under the oak tree clapped their hands.

"We welcome our good friend Thorfinn Hrolfsson," said the
man with the staff.

"Very well, then. I defer to the council," said Dobrynya. "Only,
Thorfinn, keep the peace, Holmgard, or Novgorod. We are all Rus'
here, remember."

Thorfinn bowed again and stepped back, in among the men of
his crew. Raef saw a light sheen of sweat on his neck, in spite of
the cold: he had been worried about this. The council lapsed back
into their own speech, and several people came up before them
and spoke with feeling, waving their hands.

Thorfinn said, "Let's go. I'll empty a cup with all of you, back
at my hall."

He turned on his heel and tramped off through the onlookers,
away from the council. Einar and Helgi followed after him, with
the other two men, Bjorn and Vagn; Raef and Conn trailed them
all. Conn said, "I'm not much interested in going back to that hall,
are you? Yet, anyway."

"There's daylight left," Raef said; he glanced up at the hazy
winter sky. Thorfinn was getting farther ahead of them with each
step. "What do you want to do?"

Conn said, "I want to find a woman."

"Hold on," Raef said. "Something's going on."

Thorfinn and his crew had left the crowd behind, and headed off through the empty market, but then suddenly from one side a swarm of men stepped out to block the way.

Thorfinn stopped in his tracks. Face-to-face with him stood a square-shaped man with hair and beard as red as a new brick, and a face all squinched up in the middle like a purse string drawn shut.

Conn said, "Come on. This is what he needs us for." He strode up to join the men around Thorfinn.

"Get out of my way, Magnus," Thorfinn's voice boomed.

Raef followed a little slower, staying off to one side, so that he could look this over. Now he understood why Thorfinn was worried. Whatever the right of their dispute, Magnus had two men to each of Thorfinn's. Some of them had swords. Raef glanced at Conn, saw him taking all this in; Conn folded his arms across his chest, his gaze on the red beard.

"You aren't even supposed to be here, Thorfinn," Magnus said. "We had an agreement, remember?"

Thorfinn set himself, his feet wide apart. "You broke the agreement, Magnus. I kept my end, but you never paid up."

Magnus laughed, as if that was a joke. "Well, maybe I clipped a few pennies. But a deal is a deal, isn't it? And I'm here now, Thorfinn." He lifted his gaze and stabbed it at Thorfinn's outnumbered crew, and his voice rang out hard and loud. "You men, there, I'll give you a chance. You can stay with Thorfinn, and suffer with him, or you can come to me, and be with the winners. The best of food and drink in my hall!" He leered at Thorfinn. "We'll see how many of you are left standing at the end of the winter, Thorfinn."

Then abruptly the golden Sclava lord, Dobrynya, was pushing in between them. He was a stout man but he moved lightly as a deer. Both Thorfinn and Magnus stepped back away from him; Magnus staggered in his haste and almost fell.

Dobrynya said, in a high strong voice, "I will warn you both again—I will allow no fighting in my city. We are all Rus' here, and I will throw any man out who fights. You, Thorfinn, this way, and Magnus, that way, and go now, all of you." Standing alone between them, magnificent in his bright clothes, he thrust his arms out at them, driving them apart. "Start now, or I will get Pavo and his whip."

Thorfinn turned on his heel and walked off toward his hall. Behind him, Raef heard the red beard say, "Dobrynya, this is a Varanger thing. Let us deal with it." He did not catch what Dobrynya said back. Beside him, Conn said to Thorfinn, "What is Varanger?"

"We are," Thorfinn said.

"Then who are the Rus'?"

Thorfinn crowded his shoulders together. "Everybody— Varanger and Sclava together. That's what Dobrynya calls us when he wants to wield power over us. Come on." He bustled them all along toward his hall.

CHAPTER TWO

"There are actually two cities here, in a way," said Thorfinn, later. He leaned his forearm on the scarred wooden table. Everybody was crowded into his hall, not only his crew but the whole household, and he sat with Conn and Raef near one hearth in a little alcove, which was warm, and quieter than the rest of the place. A rushlight glowed in a niche in the earthen wall, so they could see each other. "One city is Holmgard, our city, the Varanger. Novgorod is the city of the Sclava. Dobrynya would say, of the Rus'."

"What does that actually mean, Rus'?"

"That's a long story. It's a Sclava hearing of a Swedish word, I've heard. They had a king once, who was a Swede, whose name was Rurik, something like that. So they use that word to mean the whole kingdom here. But the real name for people like us is Varanger, because we are free men."

"Sounds like trouble to me," Conn said.

"It works out, mostly. We've been coming here a long time. My father was one of the first, in the early days, he came to trade and put up for the winter. In the spring, the pelts here are incomparable."

His hands moved, up and down and crosswise. "Holmgard is a wonderful place for us. From here you can get anywhere, back to the west, for instance. Or south along this river into the lake down there and out onto another river, and walk a little to a big river that runs a long way south, and you will come to some fine places, I'll tell you, good markets, soft people, lots of money." His eyes shifted; he contemplated these far places a moment in his mind's eye, a wistful smile on his face.

Abruptly he shrugged himself back into the moment. "Then there's Novgorod, the Sclava city. It was here first. Holmgard is in it like a mist in the woods in the morning. We Varanger always know Novgorod is here but to the Sclava Holmgard's a passing nuisance. The farmers here, the cattle and horses, the workmen, the gardens, that's all Novgorod."

"And the men under the oak tree," Raef said. "And this Pavo, with his whip."

Thorfinn leaned back a little, his hands on the table before him, fingers splayed apart. Raef could see he liked talking about this. "The Sclava aren't warriors. They like growing things and racing their horses and cooking their wotka and drinking it, and they've been sitting on this road here down to Miklagard for a while, picking off what they can out of what comes by and doing pretty well at that."

"What about Dobrynya?" Raef said.

Thorfinn made a face, his head tipping to one side and then the other. "That's the problem, as I see it, right now. The seed of Rurik still rules here. The Knyaz, as they call him, Volodymyr, down in Kiev, his father was one of us, but his mother was pure Sclava. Dobrynya is her brother, and he fostered Volodymyr. And made him Knyaz, when he wasn't the true heir. With the help of a lot of Varanger, this was. But Dobrynya calls us all Rus', and doesn't want to make distinctions." He rocked his head side to side again, fretful. "Some distinctions are important."

"Where does Magnus Redbeard come into this?" Conn asked.

"Magnus is a swindling bastard. Here's what happened between me and Magnus. He had me in a tight spot, I won't bother you how, but to get out of it I sold him my station here." Thorfinn's face worked; Conn saw that this gnawed at him like a worm in the belly. He turned and spat out into the hall. "Then the bastard didn't even pay me."

Conn took another head-whirling sip from the cup; what it held was not mead, but something past that, an icy liquid fire with an oily aftertaste and a kick that exploded up somewhere behind his eyes. He glanced around at Raef; their eyes met, and his cousin gave a little nod.

Conn turned around toward Thorfinn. "I have to go outside—save me a swallow or two."

"Wait," Thorfinn said. He shuffled around on the bench. "I said you would not regret helping me. You will need these." He stood; the bench he sat on had a lid, which he opened, revealing a deep box. From this he took a dusty fur cloak and handed it to Conn, and then after some shuffling through the chest found another for Raef. "Go on," he said. "I'll see you later. There's plenty of the wotka." He shut the bench and sat down on it again, slumping on one elbow over the table, and reaching for the cup.

Conn shook out the fur cloak, a black bearskin, sending up a haze of dust. He said, "I don't know about this." But he took the cloak with him, slung over his shoulder.

With Raef on his heels he went out into the darkness, walked around the hall toward the horse pens, and made water. The horses had all gone in under the lean-to shelter at the north end of Thorfinn's hall. The sun had just set and the night was clear and cold enough to set his teeth ringing together almost at once. The ground crunched underfoot with new frost. He swung the cloak around him, glad now for its musty depths. With Raef beside him he went off through the city again.

"What do you think?" he said presently.

"I want to get out of here," Raef said. "Thorfinn's on the short end of this, and it's too cold." He glanced behind them. "Here comes Einar."

Conn looked back; tall, yammer-mouthed Einar was striding up toward them, bundled in a heavy hooded cloak. The scrawny rat-faced boy trailed after—Conn had heard his name and forgotten it, not a dansker name. Einar strode up toward him.

"So, what do you think, what do you think? Is Thorfinn more trouble than he's worth? He's lucky Dobrynya even let him stay here." The scrawny boy had stopped a few feet behind him.

Conn grunted at him, annoyed. Einar slapped his hands together. "Remember what Magnus said, he'll take us on. He'll pay us as well as Thorfinn will, I think." He looked from side to side, as if a whole crowd watched them. "We could do that, don't you think?"

Conn said, "I don't like jumping from one ship to another." Thorfinn he knew was an honest man.

Einar spun around suddenly, yelling. "Vagn, get out of here! Stop following me!" He stooped for a chunk of ice and flung it at the rat-faced boy, who darted off into the dark.

"Isn't he one of Thorfinn's men?" Raef said.

"No," Einar said. "He's nobody and belongs to nobody. He's not even dansker. Probably he escaped from a slave pen somewhere. Thorfinn just took him on today for another body to stand against Magnus. Which is how desperate Thorfinn is."

Conn started off again; it was too cold not to be moving. They went up through the maze of pens, between the steep thatched eaves of houses, past a tree with another carved wooden post beneath it. A lanky dog was wolfing down something left in front of it. The moon was rising and the air grew steadily brighter. They came into the market, broad and empty, the oak tree a great black tangle in the center.

"Up there," Einar said. "There's a house that sells wotka. When there's a branch over the door, that's what it means." He nudged them, and Conn veered that way, past the oak tree. Where there was good drink, he had learned, there often were good women too.

Raef gave a yell of warning. Conn wheeled around, his dream of good women flying out of his head; half a dozen men were charging at him out of the cover of the oak tree.

He had no weapon but his knife and he left it in his belt. Raef was just behind him, Einar back of him. The first of the dark mass of bodies hurtled down on him, one step ahead of the others, swinging a club. Conn stooped down, the lumpy head of the club sweeping by his shoulder, and lunging forward he sank both his bare hands into the man's fur coat. The swing of the club had the attacker already off-balance. Leaning hard against his weight

Conn swung him around the same way he was already going, pivoted him off his feet, and slung him back into the path of the others rushing at him.

When he let go of the fur coat he slipped down to one knee. He cast off the musty bearskin cloak. Raef shouted, beside him. The attackers had stumbled over their leader, but they came now through the dark toward him and Raef, spread out, in a rush. Conn got his feet under him and drove upward, rammed his shoulder into the body before him and flung it backward. He glimpsed Raef battling somebody with a long staff; beyond, Einar was down. A fist bounced off Conn's shoulder. Somebody nearby screamed in pain.

Off to one side, above him, there was a bellowing voice. He couldn't heed that. Legs braced, he was wrestling chest-to-chest with somebody struggling to get one arm up and free and Conn knew there was a knife at the end of that arm and he was clutching and wrenching at it, trying to pin it fast to the other man's body, hot breath in his face, and a stink of onions, and he swung one leg around and tripped the thrashing body down flat on its back.

He stumbled away a step, and from behind him something struck his shoulder like an arrow. He yelped, feeling the burn of a wound, saw the light behind him, and wheeled around.

Somebody there had a torch—somebody on a horse; and between the torch and him was another horseman, his arm cocked up. As Conn gathered himself to jump out of the way the arm swung forward and through the hazy torchlit air came a thin black uncoiling lash reaching straight for his eyes.

He flung himself sideways onto the ground. The whip cracked in his ears like a great branch snapping in a high wind. He hit the frozen snow and rolled away and at a safe distance bounced up onto his feet again, facing the man with the whip.

"No fighting!" this man roared; he was too big for the horse, sat there with his feet thrust down halfway to the ground; the torchlight showed only the beak of his nose and the jut of his long jaw.

Conn's shoulder throbbed. "Get them, then—they started it!"

He thrust his hand out, pointing; he could see Magnus's men sneaking away into the darkness. Einar had gotten up on one knee, breathing hard, and Raef stood beside him, holding the long staff. Two other men on horseback had come up behind them.

The torchbearer had come closer, to put them all into his light. The big man was coiling his whip. At first Conn thought he was wearing a cap with a long tail but then he saw it was his hair, bound up on the top of his head into a single braided hank that dangled down past his ear almost to his shoulder. And they had let Magnus's men go. Conn strode straight at him; the idea of being whipped burned worse than the wound. "Get them! What, are you afraid of them? Did Magnus pay you to let them go?"

"They're moving. You get moving too," the big man said, in bad dansker. "Or I will put another stripe on you."

Conn went up to the head of his horse, stood looking straight up at him. "I'd like to see you try."

The big man jerked his head back, angry, and his arm swung, uncoiling the whip; Conn jumped straight at him, up on the horse, and wrapping his arms around the big man's body he threw himself sideways.

Off-balanced, the horse went down with a crash. Conn's left arm hit the ground hard, and he lost the feeling in it, but he had hold of the big man still. He squirmed on top, punched the big man in the chest, and got one foot on the other man's arm. Under him the big Sclava surged strongly up, kicking out, bucking him off. Conn bashed him in the chest again, grabbing for the scalplock.

Under him the massive body twisted, heaving up sideways off the ground. Conn slugged him in the face, aiming for his nose, and snatched again for the flying hank of hair, and then from somewhere else something huge and hard smashed against his head and knocked him instantly cold.

Raef had never seen Conn beaten before. When his cousin crashed to the ground, he gaped a moment, still as stone; the big Sclava scrambled up off the snow and roared up onto his feet, his arms over his head, his voice like thunder. Almost under his feet Conn sprawled on the ground, unmoving.

Raef went quickly over and knelt beside him. Pressed his hand flat to his cousin's chest, his own breath stopped in his lungs, his own heart stalled in his throat, until he felt under his hand the solid thump-thump-thump of Conn's life beating. A shudder of relief went through him. Under his hand, now, Conn stirred a little, also.

The big man was roaring, "Everybody get out of here. You, get him out of here, or I'll whip him on the ground." Raef stood up, hauled his cousin's arm up over his shoulder, and started away toward Thorfinn's cave.

The torchlight faded; those people were going away. Einar had already bolted. Raef stopped and looked around, thinking about Magnus's men maybe lurking somewhere. He began to shiver, and Conn still hung almost limp against him, breathing hard. The distance to Thorfinn's hall seemed forever. Then the outcast boy Vagn appeared in front of him, holding out Conn's bearskin.

"Here. He dropped this."

"Where's Magnus's crew?"

"They took off running," Vagn said. "They're probably back in Magnus's hall by now."

Raef slung the cloak awkwardly around Conn's body, pulling the hood up, and wedging the flaps in against his own side, to keep them closed. "That was Pavo, I take it."

"Pavo," Vagn said. He nodded toward Conn, inside the cloak, who was trying to stand on his own feet and not succeeding. "He was winning, I thought."

Raef said nothing; carrying most of Conn's weight he crossed the broad marketplace. The dark was blustery with wind, and down on the way to the river something was banging, as if some hopeless creature tried to get inside. With a mutter below words Conn began to walk, still leaning on Raef.

"Pavo cheats, you know," Vagn said, behind them.

"I saw that," Raef said. Slowly they were picking a way through the horse pens toward Thorfinn's red sun door. The wind swept into his face, steely with the new snow. His feet were like blocks of ice that he dragged forward. Conn stumbled and Raef clutched him and they both nearly went down together, staggering in the wind and snow.

Thorfinn's door was just ahead, standing a little open, a dim patch of light coming through. He could hear Einar's voice inside, high and excited. Conn whispered, "I can walk," and Raef let him go and watched him creep down the steps by himself.

On the top step, Raef turned toward Vagn.

"Are you coming in?"

"I can't." The boy backed up a step. "They'll kill me."

"I'll watch out for you," Raef said.

The boy was backing away. "Thorfinn already paid me," he said, and went off into the dark.

"It felt as if he hit me with a rock," Conn said.

"Something like that," Raef said. "He got something from his belt, the back of his belt."

Thorfinn said, "I warned you, but you didn't listen to me. He can beat anybody. You found that out—no, I don't care if he cheats, he beat you, which is what matters."

Conn gritted his teeth together. His head throbbed and he felt a little dizzy and sick to his stomach. "He let Magnus's men jump us. Then he let them go."

Thorfinn leaned back on his seat. "Perhaps. He's as weak for a little gold as any man, Pavo. Or maybe he just decided you needed knocking down."

Conn lowered his eyes; worse even than the pulsing of his
head was knowing he had lost a fight. He felt as if all the world
were staring at him, thinking maybe he wasn't as good as they had
thought before. In the hall behind them everybody else had gone
to bed; he wanted to lie down and sleep but he knew to sleep when
he felt this way might kill him. He turned his eyes toward the
ruddy blear of the fire, his heart a burning coal.

"So," Thorfinn said. "I guess you're staying here for the winter?"

Conn said, "Until I beat Pavo." On the bench beside him Raef
stirred in a sudden twitch of alarm and stared at him.

Thorfinn said, "What?" He laughed, as if Conn had made a
joke, or as if Thorfinn wished it were. "Well, then, I may have you
here a long while." He turned toward a shelf on the wall next to him.

"I'm going to bed," Raef said, harsh, and left.

"Do you play chess?" Thorfinn put a board down on the table
between him and Conn and set a leather sack onto it, carefully
opening out the drawstring.

Conn put his elbow on the table and set his head in his hand.
"Not much. But I'll try." The table was whirling around before his
eyes. His head was swelling where Pavo had hit him. He fixed his
attention on the chess pieces, as Thorfinn took them from the sack
and lined up in front of him, and tried to remember how to play.

⊶

Conn's head stopped spinning after a while, and he slept, and
woke the next day considerably steadier. His eyes were clear now
and even the great swollen bruise hurt less. He got something to
eat and helped stoke the fire; the wood stack inside the hall was
nearly gone, and he and Raef set about bringing in more.

He could hear the storm howling in the thatch; from old times
he knew what to expect. When he wrenched open the door he
faced a wall of snow packed into the entry all the way up to the

lintel. He sent a slave for shovels and with Raef began to claw into
the snow. The south-facing door and the deep eave of the house
had sheltered the doorway from the worst of the storm but the
drift filled the space nonetheless. Just outside the door, he turned
to his left, and with the shovel dug away the snow up to ground
level, and then up under the eave, where the woodpiles were. Raef
followed him, packing the snow into the low side of the eave, and
they passed logs back hand-to-hand through this tunnel under the
eave to the slaves in the doorway.

Conn's teeth were chattering when they were done, and he
went hurriedly down into the hall again. Raef was already standing
almost in the fire; the slaves were stacking up the wood against the
wall.

Conn went over to the nearer hearth, rubbing the feeling back
into his hands. Down the hall he could see Einar and Helgi at the
other fire, burning wood they hadn't fought the frost gods for.
Thorfinn was nowhere, the curtain over his alcove drawn. The air
was smoky and raw in Conn's throat but at least now his hands and
feet were warming up.

He said, "We've got to keep the smokeholes open."

Raef grunted something; nearby a slave, short and brown,
said, "We do that, not idiots. Master." Raef laughed; he always had
a kind heart for slaves.

Conn glanced down the hall again. The wood they had brought
in almost filled the space between this hearth and the other, leaving only enough room for the looms where the women worked
and the space in front of the other hearth where Einar and Helgi
sat dicing.

Conn said, "You know, about Einar."

Raef gave a harsh short laugh, and said nothing. Conn stood
thinking about Einar, what he had said the night before when they
were walking toward the oak tree, and how he had gone down so
fast when Magnus's men attacked them. He glanced at Raef again
and saw his cousin's pale eyes watching him.

"Do you want help?" Raef said.

"No." Conn straightened, flexing his shoulders. "I'll do it." He went down the narrow lane through the hall, past the three big looms where the women sat working, to the other hearth.

Einar and Helgi were sitting on a blanket on the floor, throwing bones; Conn stood directly over Einar's shoulder, so he had to look up. The light from the hearth dappled his long yellow hair. He saw Conn's face and scrambled up onto his feet.

"I guess—" He glanced past Conn, saw Raef wasn't there, and seemed suddenly jauntier. He stuck his thumbs in his belt. "I guess you found out about Pavo, didn't you, there. How's your head today?" Helgi stood up beyond him and stood watching them, his face set. He was younger than Einar, and quieter.

Conn said, "You weren't much help, Einar." He stood solid and still, his hands at his sides.

Einar puffed himself up a little, twitching, looking from side to side, his face trying to smile. "They got the jump on us, pretty good, I thought, there, didn't they."

"On us," Conn said. He was staring at Einar, who would not meet his eyes. "I get the feeling it wasn't much of a surprise to you, now, was it?"

On the last words, he bounded forward; Einar scurried back a step but Conn got him by the left arm. When Einar swung a wild fist at him Conn twisted him around and pulled Einar's left wrist up between his shoulder blades.

Einar stiffened with a gasp, perched on his toes, trying to keep his arm in the socket. Predictably he kicked backward, and Conn lunged against him as he went off balance and drove him down on his knees, his arm still twisted behind him. Over Einar's head Conn faced Helgi.

"Are you in this?"

Helgi stepped delicately toward the hearth. "Do I look as if I'm in it?" He put out his hands to the fire.

"Do you know he's been taking Magnus's penny?" Conn said. He wrapped his free arm around Einar's neck.

Helgi's eyes widened slightly; he looked from Conn to Einar and back again. He said nothing.

Einar gasped. "I'm not. I'm not!"

"No," Conn said, into his ear. "Not anymore. From now on, you're mine, you take your orders from me. No penny, just orders. Understand?"

Einar said, "Yes." His breath rasped in his throat and there were tears in his eyes.

"You'd better," Conn said. He let go with a yank on Einar's arm that sent the other man sprawling, and went up the hall again toward Raef, at the other fire.

Raef had gotten a cup somewhere, which he held out silently, and Conn took it and drank. The kick of the wotka matched the hot excitement of the fighting all through his body. He said, "That was good."

Raef took the cup back. "What are you trying to do?"

"If anybody is going to be first here," Conn said, "it's going to be me."

He had thought that before, not in his mind, but in his body; he realized he had thought that all his life.

"What about Pavo?" Raef said.

"I'll see about Pavo."

The curtain over Thorfinn's alcove swayed, and the fahrman came out, yawning and stretching, his shirt rumpled up over his hairy belly. He saw Raef and Conn standing there, watching him, and something in their faces seemed to startle him; he said, sharply, "What's going on?"

"Nothing," Conn said. "Tell me what you need me to do, here, I am already bored."

CHAPTER THREE

The storm blew furiously over them for a long while; each day Raef cut a mark into the wall with his knife, to keep track. He played dice with Helgi and Einar, winning himself new boots and a belt he liked with a silver buckle. Years before he had discovered that when he picked up dice, if he let his mind go empty, he knew before the roll how the spots would come up, which meant he could win whenever he wanted to. He had never told anybody else this and he made sure to lose as much as he won. What he lost was just money, which he didn't care about, except the little gold piece.

He took this out of his purse now and then and studied it, the face on either side, and the runes, and polished it with his thumb. It seemed to him that he should know something from this object.

The storm seemed endless. They all drank, told stories by the fires; they all slept a lot. The women clattered away at their looms. The hall stank of close bodies, piss, smoke. On the day after he cut the fifth mark on the wall the snow finally blew out. Nobody could bear, then, to be any more in the hall, and they crowded toward the door, pushing and cursing each other, until Thorfinn shouted them back and the slaves, for once working hard, bashed and shoveled up through the snow and they all burst up into the clear blue slanting sunlight and a shocking, fearsome cold.

The snow covered everything, Thorfinn's hall somewhere beneath a powdery mountainous drift, scooped hollow around each of the holes in the roof where the smoke rose in dirty plumes. The horse pens had turned into a pattern of graceful glittering blue-white windrows. The horses were already pawing their way out of their shelter, and from all around, other people also were digging their way up out of the buried mounds of their houses. Their voices rose, laughing, singing, and across the snow they shouted to each other as if they were returning from far voyages.

Soon they were building a fire in the marketplace, a great stack of flame that crackled and leapt as if it were fighting its way into the air. The whole city seemed to be gathering around it, passing drink from hand to hand, not caring where one jug went since another would soon come from somewhere, and sharing stories about the storm. Most of the people were the Sclava but there were several other men who looked dansker, the crews of other ships, from other halls. Screeching children dashed around pelting each other with snowballs. Conn disappeared. Raef wandered around, glad to be moving, even if only in circles around the fire. Down through the happy mob the posadnik Dobrynya came, riding on a bay horse; slaves ran ahead of him to clear away the snow under the oak tree and he took his place there. The man with the white cloth on his head was with him and sat talking to him.

Dobrynya's golden hair was braided and strung with beads; Raef marked again how piercing bright his blue eyes were. As the posadnik spoke to the other man, his hands rose in a sudden gesture, like setting loose a flock of birds.

Raef drifted on. Some way away he saw Conn, walking with the pie girl, who was calling her wares. Even from this distance, by the way Conn walked and the way she looked at him, he knew his cousin had already sampled what she had. He turned away, his groin aching; he had no way with women, certainly not as Conn had. Yet he wanted one, not in the easy way that Conn had, over and done in a moment, but something more.

"Koljada!" someone shouted, near him. "Koljada!" All around, a cheer went up.

By the market there were people now grilling meat, and offering little oddly-shaped cakes. He went there, fingering his purse; he had lost his real money at dice, and all he had left was the little gold piece, which he did not want to give up. His mouth watered. He walked along looking at the meat, and a man hunkered behind a little round grill waved him over and held out a skewer with some beef dripping juices.

"No," Raef said, his belly yearning, "no money, I have no money," not knowing how to say this in Sclava, and the man laughed at him, his mustaches flaring up.

"Koljada!" He thrust the skewer into Raef's hands. "Eat! Eat!" Laughing, he went back to his grill.

Raef devoured the meat and licked his fingers. Around him, in the unsteady warmth of the fire, people were joining hands and dancing. He backed away a little to watch. Bjorn the Christian who had stood for Thorfinn at the council walked by and waved at him. Raef wondered where he lived—he saw him go up among some of the other Varanger. He saw the scrawny boy Vagn lingering at the edge of everything.

All around the fire they danced, men in their baggy leggings, women in aprons and shawls, shrieking red-faced children, first in a ring, and then the ring broke open and they danced in a snaky procession, singing and laughing, twining several times around the oak tree, and then off into the city. Conn was one of them. He watched his cousin dance away into the distance. Around the fire another ring formed. The man next to him turned to him and handed him a cup and he drank deep of the fiery wotka, liking the Sclava a lot better suddenly, all of them. Somebody leapt and gamboled by him wearing the horns of a goat.

Part of him wanted to join the dancers. He trailed this line of singing, leaping people around the oak tree and off across the marketplace; going down a lane, they went from house to house, singing and yelling, and people came out and gave them things. But he did not join them, not knowing the words of their songs.

A goat pulling a cart led another jubilant train of people down the street. One was holding up a stick with a yellow circle hung from the top, which he kept whirling by flicks of the wrist. Raef saw a dancer with a goatskin pulled over his back and head, the tail at one end, the horns at the other, and then a swarm of children with more spinning disks; all these things looked old, worn, as if they were kept in a chest somewhere and only came out at special times. One procession after another began at the fire, circled around the oak tree, around the fire, and set off through the city.

Raef steered wider of them, passed by the oak tree again, where many men crowded around Dobrynya; the man with the white headcloth was gone. Instead, behind Dobrynya stood Pavo, taller than anybody, bald as a pared fruit except for the long scalplock hanging down from under his cap.

Raef slowed down, going by, staring at him, and the big sleek head swung toward him, a narrow, warning glare. Raef looked quickly away.

He went back to the warmth of the fire. The sun was already lowering, the day draining away, as if the light leaked from the sky. He wondered where Conn was. He thought sadly of going back into Thorfinn's hall. They were still dancing around him, but now in their dancing he felt something desperate. Many people were thrusting the whirling disks up toward the sky, as if to show the sun what to do. The wind was rising, keen-edged, whistling in the branches of the oak tree. The cold began to bite, even near the fire. He trudged on back toward shelter, his head down.

⚓

Conn stared down at the chessboard, where his king stood helpless between Thorfinn's rooks; he said, "Why do you always win?"

"Because you always make mistakes," Thorfinn said. "You're learning. But you'll never beat me."

Conn reached out for the pieces and began setting them up again. From the far side of the table Thorfinn watched him with a gentle smile on his face. He said, "This clear weather should hold for a few days, and we're running low on wood. Tomorrow I'm sending the slaves down the river to get some more, and you're to go and stand guard over them."

Conn set his elbows on the table. "Who am I guarding against?"

"There are huns in the forest. Sometimes they try to pick off a wood gatherer. Other strange people. And Magnus, of course."

"What about Pavo?"

"Pavo won't interfere, outside the wall. That's why you have to watch out for Magnus."

"All right." Conn set out his far right pawn. "We'll go."

"Good. Janka knows where to go, and he can handle the team. We cut wood last summer, it's just waiting on the riverside to split and haul." Thorfinn picked up a pawn and turned it back and forth in his fingers, looking at the board. "That's an odd opening."

"I've got to try something," Conn said.

⭑

Janka was the short brown slave, sullen, with tilted eyes and not much dansker. Conn stood watching him hitch up the horses to the sledge, harnessing them in pairs and then leading each of the three pairs up to the cart tree, while Thorfinn gave everybody needless orders.

"You should take Einar and Helgi," he said, again. "In case." His gaze went off down the river shore, where some other people were leading up teams and dragging the flat two-runnered sledges out onto the ice. There was no sign of Magnus Redbeard.

"Raef and I can do it," Conn said.

"You're cocksure. I hope you know what you're doing. Bring home a good load of wood, is all." Thorfinn leaned his hand on Conn's shoulder again, as he often did. "Get going."

Janka drove the sledge, using a long limber stick for a whip. Shod with caulks, the horses pulled the empty sledge easily enough over the ice, sometimes even breaking into a trot. Conn and Raef sat on the seat in front beside Janka, and the other slaves sat in the flatbed behind. One of them had brought a jug and they passed it.

The river stretched away from them into the white distance. It was hard to tell where the banks were, the river blending imperceptibly into the snowy reaches on either side. Janka steered them northward along the western edge, where the wind had blown away most of the snow. The ice glittered in the low sun. Ahead the forest grew down closer to the river, like a wall on either side of winter-deadened trees.

The sledge stuck on a patch of rough and broken ice; Conn got down with a maul and cleared out the sledge runners, bashing the path smoother and wider. Behind them he could see the other sledges lumbering along in his wake. This pleased him obscurely, and he went along ahead of the sledge, making sure the way was clear for all these followers. He wondered if one was Magnus's sledge.

Around a bend of the river they came on a broad meadow, maybe a frozen marsh, piled up with cut trees and logs and branches like a range of small hills, all capped with snow. Beyond the clutter of wood, the forest hemmed the meadow's edge, dark and deep. Janka drove the sledge up onto the flat land, to the edge of the heaped wood, and the slaves all got off and began to throw in whatever wood they could lay hands on.

Conn bellowed at them and smacked a few of them, sending two to find good wood and leaving two to stack it properly on the flatbed, and taking the maul and a wedge he began to split big oak logs, which would make the best fires. Janka unhitched the horses and let them browse, and came to help. Raef had gone wandering off toward the forest as soon as the sledge stopped.

One by one the other sledges pulled up, and each time Conn looked sharply over, to see if it was Magnus's men, but they never appeared. The newcomers drew their sledges in on the flat ground and gathered some loose wood into a bonfire, and stood around the flames talking and drinking. Conn bent his back to the work of the maul and the wedge, his sledge already half full. Somebody yelled at him, from the fire, to come join them, and he waved back, and stayed at his work. Magnus wasn't coming, he realized. The hard waiting had backed up into his muscles; he felt clogged, stalled, frustrated. He smashed the maul into the wedge, splitting the log half its length in one stroke, and the wood gave up a squeal like an animal.

⚬

Raef walked through the forest, under old elm trees far apart, whose long straight trunks raised their leafless outstretched heads high over him; on the ground beneath the spread of their branches snow covered everything like a treacherous white plain. Every few steps his feet broke through to black frozen clumps of bracken. Sometimes what seemed level ground was a gorge filled with snow. Under the trees the light seemed watery, dim, blue in the shadows. Tall and straight, the trees ruled it all, rising from the castles of their gnarled boles into the soaring pale sky. No bird sang. The wind howled through the tops of the trees and stirred them wild, as if some great army passed by overhead. Underneath, as under water, only a little moved.

He looked eastward, searching through the trees, his eyes striving to see farther, as if somewhere out there lay the answer to whatever the question was. All he ever saw was more trees. He wondered if this was the edge of the world.

Away from the river, the elms yielded to stands of massive oaks and dense pines clumped together in thickets. He walked along the thick icy crust on the snow; once the crust broke under his foot and he fell in up to his waist. The struggle up out of the hole exhausted him, clawing through crumbling snow, his fingers and his feet going numb and his lungs gasping.

He went on, moving to keep from freezing. In the snow, paths of tracks wound, the signs of huge deer, mice and foxes, and smaller things with foxlike feet. He began to feel as if someone were watching him, but he thought it might be only the tall, overarching trees, aware of him in their ancientness like a passing wind.

From the edge of the trees he looked over and saw the bonfire blazing, and the men standing thick around it; beyond them, Conn was hard at work, and in no trouble.

Raef went back into the trees, circling the other way. Halfway to the riverbank again he glimpsed something moving ahead of him, a flicker of motion between the upright trunks, gone in an instant.

He knew at once it was no deer, no wild creature. He ran recklessly across the snow to where he had seen it, found the deep tracks of a horse plunging down a trail like a breath through the trees.

His heart bounded. The trail went eastward. There was something, then, beyond the trees. On the other side of the question. Something to find out. He stood staring along the blue-white line of broken snow, his heart galloping to match the horse.

Then behind him a shrill whistle sounded. He wheeled, and went to the edge of the woods and saw Conn there, with the sledge full, calling him in. Quickly he trotted back across the frozen meadow.

⟳

"We'll get back before sundown, this way," Conn said. Braced on the driver's seat, he was eating the last of the bread and cheese. Beside him the slave Janka hunched down over his reins and his withy whip. The load was stacked high behind them, over Conn's head; they had all had to put their shoulders to the sledge to get it moving, but now the horses were drawing it steadily along, leaning into their collars, their heads bobbing. The wind was behind them, and their own stable was ahead and they went along eagerly.

The road they had cut on the frozen river wound southward around the bend, the scoured ice gleaming like dull metal in the late day-light.

Raef said, "Somebody was out there watching us. In the for-est." He handed Conn the jug. "That's the last of it."

"You should get a bow from Thorfinn. Was it Magnus?"

Raef shook his head. "Somebody from east of here."

On Conn's other side Janka muttered something, his flat brown face aimed forward. They slid and scraped along; Conn was cold and tired and the motion of the sledge made him sleepy. Then Raef said, under his breath, "You know, I don't like the feel of this," and even as he spoke, a horse neighed, in the woods up ahead.

Conn jerked awake. They were rounding the bend in the river, halfway back to Holmgard; here the trees grew down almost to the road along the ice. He saw nothing but he knew to trust his cousin's foresight. He reached down under the seat, where the maul was, and to Raef said, "Go out—go around behind. Can you?" Raef slid off the sledge like water off a rock.

Janka said, taut, "What I do?"

"Keep driving," Conn said. He threw off his cloak, and pulled the maul up into his hands, standing up behind the seat; the sledge was creeping around the tip of the bend, and then abruptly men streamed out of the trees toward him.

Six of them. Eight of them. He stepped up onto the seat, the maul in his hands, and they circled around the sledge and stopped the horses.

One of them bellowed, "Well, there, worker boy, ready to fell another tree?" and everybody laughed, as if this were some huge joke.

Conn looked hard at this man, his bushy beard and barrel chest, thinking he had seen him before; out of his memory came a whiff of onions, and he smiled. He had beaten this man already

once. He said, "You want some more of the last time, hah, Big
Nose? Get out of my way, or I will hew you down."

Magnus's men let out a roar, all around him, and Big Nose
sneered.

"You know what? We'll just take this wood. You can walk
home, worker boy, if you get down and start now and don't bother
us." He smiled, showing a few scattered teeth. "You're alone, you
know. Your brother's not here, I see, and these slaves won't fight
for you." The slaves who had been sitting on the back end of the
sledge were already getting down and walking away. Janka sat unmoving on the driver's seat, his shoulders hunched.

"You can try," Conn said. "I've been splitting wood all day, a
few more knotheads won't stop me."

A ringing neigh sounded over his words; he swiveled around
to look toward the trees. Shrilling and kicking out, a horse
plunged out of the woods toward the river. A burning branch, tied
to its long flowing tail, bounced along behind, spitting sparks. The
horse bounded onto the river and its hind legs went out from under
it and it skidded twenty feet across the ice on its rump and propped
forelegs.

A yell went up from Magnus's men. Behind the horse with the
flaming tail half a dozen others burst from the trees, their legs
milling at a dead gallop; before they reached the river, the first
horse was up and running again, straight down the river toward
Holmgard, and the rest went all pounding after. The sledge team
surged forward in their harnesses, trying to go after them.

For a moment Magnus's men stood motionless, gawking after
their horses, and Conn gave a whoop of laugh. "I think it's you
who'll be walking home, Big Nose!" He reached back into the
sledge for a chunk of wood and hurled it at Big Nose, below him,
and knocked him flat.

The rest came at him from all sides. He swung the maul
around, the heavy head whistling through the air. They had to

scramble up the stacked wood, and that slowed them, so he got the first of them right away with a great broad sideways swing and swept him off the sledge. Behind that one two more men lunged toward him, trying to scale the shifting woodpile.

"Drive!" he screamed at Janka. "Drive!" He scrambled up over the back of the seat onto the very top of the stacked wood; a log rolled under his foot, and off-balance he drove an awkward blow at the men coming at him.

That was a mistake. One grabbed the maul handle, and the other dodged under Conn's outstretched arm, a knife in his fist.

Janka screamed something. Conn, wrestling for the maul, kicked out at the man with the knife. His foot hit flesh and bone. The woodpile moved under him again and he went down, and in a tumble of falling logs the man with the knife went rolling down off the sledge. The other man, still clinging to the maul, had lost his footing also, and Conn wrenched the handle out of his grip and knocked him down again and leapt up and kicked him in the head and fell again into the unsteady mass of wood.

"Help!" Janka was shrieking over, and over, and Conn wheeled around, and saw the slave standing in the sledge seat, beating with his whip at a man trying to scale up the woodpile behind him. Conn was to his knees in the wood, and when he tried to climb up the wood shifted underneath him. He waded through it, slipping and falling with each step, but he kept the maul swinging in great swishing rounds, and Magnus's man jumped free just ahead of it.

"Drive! Get us moving—" He wheeled around to take on another rush of men clambering up the back of the sledge.

"No move," Janka cried. He was thrashing at the horses with his whip; they were straining into the harness, their hoofs slipping helplessly on the ice. "It no move—"

Conn flung the maul into the face of the first man coming across the pile at him. That one staggered back, his face exploding

in a gush of blood, but behind him another man cocked up his arm
to throw a knife.

The sledge jerked forward suddenly. The knife thrower wobbled off balance, his arms flailing out, and suddenly Raef reared
up behind him. He caught Magnus's man by the hair and flung
him backward off the sledge.

Conn straightened, his chest heaving, a chunk of wood in one
hand. The sledge was sliding briskly off down the ice road again.
All Magnus's men were gone. Half the wood was gone, too; Raef
as he struggled up through it toward him was grabbing logs and
sticks to save them from falling off. "Stop throwing the wood
away!" The rest of the slaves came running after them, wailing,
and scrambled up onto the back of the sledge.

Conn lifted his gaze up, looking back along the ice road, scattered with chunks of split wood and with men, some sitting, one
sprawled out flat on his back, none of them still trying to fight.
Without horses they would have a long walk home before the cold
night set down, especially if anybody was badly hurt. Probably
the other sledges, coming later, would pick them up. He wiped his
sleeve across his face, realized he was still holding the chunk of
wood, and dropped it onto the pile.

"Stop," he said. "Let's get the wood."

"Crazy," Janka said, on the sledge seat, and the four slaves on
the back of the sledge lifted up a chorus of agreement.

"Stop," Raef said.

The sledge stopped and Conn shouted the slaves off to gather
up whatever wood they could reach. Magnus's men stood in a
clump, their heads down, talking. The maul lay out there on the
ice, closer to them than to the sledge. Conn got down off the
sledge and paced back along the track toward the maul. The men
stood where they were, watching him, not moving. He stared at
them, looked each one in the face. He reached the maul and
picked it up, and slinging it up on his shoulder he turned his back

on them. His shoulder blades tightened but he kept his gaze forward and his back straight as an elm. When he reached the sledge
he let his breath out in a little whoosh. With the slaves he pushed
the sledge into motion again.

The slaves got on the back; he jogged up to the front and
climbed onto the driver's seat. Raef was already sitting there,
wrapped in his cloak, on Janka's far side. "I hope they freeze," he
said.

Conn sat down on the seat next to Janka, and banged his arm
into the slave's. "Thanks," he said, remembering. The slave had
gotten them through that, he thought. Magnus's men would have
overwhelmed him, coming from all sides.

Janka grunted at him. He held the reins threaded through the
fingers of his gloves; with a flip of his wrists, he slapped the leathers
on the horses' rumps. "He say I no fight." His eyes gleamed.

Raef laughed. The whole left side of his face was bruising up,
and Conn said, "What happened to you?"

"There was somebody with the horses." Raef put his hand up
over his face. Twisting, he looked back. "We lost a lot of the
wood, damn them."

They got to Holmgard again just as the sun was sinking down
into the trees. A small crowd waited on the shore, among them
Thorfinn; when they drove the sledge up, with the slaves all suddenly shouting and cheering, he came up beside Conn, and said,
"What happened? A mess of horses came down here, just now, not
a rider with them. And half of Magnus's crew left at noontide." He
looked back into the sledge. "You can pile the sledge a lot higher
than that, you know."

Conn snarled at him. "Magnus didn't get any." The slaves were
all leaping off the sledge, shouting to anybody within earshot of a
great battle on the ice which they, somehow, had won. He glowered
at Thorfinn. "Next time, you come along and load it yourself."

"I told you to take Einar and Helgi," Thorfinn shouted.

"I had enough trouble as it was," Conn said. "Janka helped us more than Einar would have." He tramped up the shore toward the boardwalk, suddenly dead tired, and aching all over, and very cold. Behind him, he heard Raef laugh. At the edge of the board-walk he brushed past Einar and Helgi without looking at them and went on toward Thorfinn's red sun door.

CHAPTER FOUR

Conn said, "I want to get Magnus back."

Raef leaned against the wall behind them. Thorfinn had given them a little more money and they had come down to a house in the city that sold wotka by the cup. The house was smelly and small and crowded so they had come outside into the icy sunlight.

"He didn't win," Raef said. "Why push it?"

Conn grunted at him, angry. "You are an old woman."

Raef took a gulp of the fiery liquor. "I've known a few old women who would make you bend your stupid neck."

"You want to try?"

"You just want to fight."

"I want to get Magnus." Conn emptied the cup. "How much money do we have left?"

Raef shook out his purse; besides the little gold piece, he had some clips and farthings, and he gave them over to Conn. The gold coin he kept in his hand. Conn went inside and came back with another cup.

"Remember about Pavo," Raef said. "You mix with Magnus, here, you mix with Pavo."

"You think I can't beat him."

"I don't think you can beat everybody at once."

Conn looked away, brooding. Raef looked down at the gold coin in his hand, turning it over and over, the face on one side with the crown, the face on the other side with the halo.

In front of him, someone with a strange accent said, "We call that a basileus, where I come from."

Raef looked up, startled. Before him stood the man with the white cloth on his head, whom he had seen twice with Dobrynya. Closer up, he was even more odd. He wore a heavy fur cloak, the hood lined with some soft red shiny stuff; his smile was white against skin dark as old wood, and his curly black beard was trimmed and combed to a point just below his chin.

He said, "I am told you come from far to the west. May I ask you a few questions?"

Conn said, "Who are you?" and got up and went away. Raef leaned against the wall behind him, staring rudely into the stranger's face, the neat little black beard, the eyes large and round and soft. He seemed guileless, maybe a little stupid, like a child. Abruptly Raef knew this was not so.

He said, "Who are you?" unlike Conn, wanting an answer.

"My name is Rashid al-Samudi," said the dark man. "I am a guest of the posadnik. I would very much like to ask you a few questions, if I could."

"What questions?"

"Could we perhaps go inside? I cannot endure the cold."

Raef did not want to go inside, with the bad air and the dark, but the stranger interested him. He got up and led the way down the steps and through the door. At one end of the tiny room, below the one narrow end window, were some benches, where other men already sat, curled around their cups. Bjorn the Christian was one of them, and some other Varanger. Raef pulled an empty bench over by the door and sat as close to the open air as he could.

"Sit," he told the man in the white headcloth. "You're not from here."

"I am from far south of here," Rashid said. "Where men ought to live." He settled himself gingerly onto the bench, tucking his cloak carefully over his legs. He took a flat pouch from inside the cloak and laid it on his lap. His shoes were stitched red leather, soaked now from walking through the snow. His hands were small and soft and round at the tips, with short black-rimmed nails, the fingers smeared with black. "I had never seen a river turn hard as rock until I came here. Tell me your name, as I have told you mine."

"Raef Corbansson," Raef said, and put out his hand. "How do you know about me?"

"At the posadnik's table I heard that some men had arrived from the far west. I asked around." Rashid took his hand in a brief, soft grip, instantly released. Raef half-expected him to wipe his hand afterward on his robe. "I am trying to learn as much as I can of the world, and you can help me. Tell me where are you from?" From the flat pouch he took a sheet of pale gray birch bark and a stick of charcoal.

"West," Raef said. "As you said. Across a lot of water. It gets cold there, too. What's the name of your country? Where they don't like to shake hands?"

Rashid al-Samudi had been using the charcoal to make marks on the bark, but he looked up suddenly, and said, in a less considered voice, "Baghdad. It seems such a dirty practice." His eyes veiled, hiding his feeling, as if he withdrew behind some door again. "What's the name of where you came from, in the west?"

"It has no name," Raef said. "We were the first people to go there—the first people like us. There were other people, but not like us, and I never knew what they called it."

"Not England, then. Or Ireland."

Raef laughed. "No. Much farther west than that."

The man of Baghdad frowned at him, his eyes narrow. "I have heard of a place called Greenland."

"So have I," Raef said. He could win this game with no trouble.

The long grave face before him quickened in a grimace of frustration, and opening the flap of his pouch he removed another sheet of his birch bark and held it out toward Raef. "Show me what you think the world looks like. If you made a drawing of it, the whole world."

Raef stared at him, his jaw dropping open. It amazed him that anybody thought he could do such a thing; an idea of the whole world flashed through his mind, the endless sweep of the forest, and windblown ocean waves, the sky that went on forever, the countless beasts and people, and he gave a puzzled laugh. Then Rashid smiled, and laughed also, and said, "No. A chart. Just the shape. The outline?"

Raef laughed again, uncertain. He had never thought of this before, drawing the shape of the world, but as he considered it the notion appealed to him. He took the birch bark, and laid it on his knee, and thought a moment. Then he made a circle on the piece of bark, and put Denmark in the middle, with Norway above.

"Here is Hedeby." He put a mark for Hedeby in the center of the papery gray surface, in the south of Denmark. "Here is Rome." Another mark far down at the bottom of the circle. "Here are the ocean islands." He drew shapes, one for England, one for Ireland, and Orkney, and Iceland, and a few others because he knew there were others but not how many; he said the names aloud, and as he did, the world appeared in his mind like a jeweled circle. He said, not knowing how he knew this, "Whoever holds England, Denmark, and Norway holds the whole world, or all that matters."

The other man gave a muffled sound that might have been a laugh. He said, "And that's where you come from."

"No," Raef said. "Here is where I come from." He drew a vertical line at the far left edge of the circle, far beyond the islands, and put a mark there.

"Hunh." Rashid leaned keenly forward to look.

"Here is where we are now," Raef said. He put another mark midway between Hedeby and the right edge of the circle, and turned the bark around to the other man. "Show me this Baghdad."

Rashid's eyebrows were arched like church windows. He said, "I have never before contemplated Hedeby as the center of the world." He took the charcoal, straightened the birch bark carefully, and made a mark down below the circle, on the edge of the bark straight down below Holmgard. "Here is Miklagard."

"No," Raef said, surprised. "Miklagard—that's Rome, I put that on."

Rashid looked up at him, his hand poised, and his eyes shining with intense interest. "Miklagard, what you call Miklagard, is Constantinople, the city of the Greeks. Where your basileus, there, came from."

"I thought that was all Rome," Raef said. He shook his head, bemused. "It seems I'm very ignorant."

"Well," Rashid said, still looking at him, "what you say is true, however. In a way, Constantinople is Rome, also—Roumi, we call it." He studied Raef a moment, his lips pursed. "I have not been to Hedeby. Is it larger than Novgorod?"

"Holmgard," Raef said. "Yes. Much bigger. The houses are above ground. Better weather. Better food. Are you going there?"

"I would if I could," Rashid said. "I would go everywhere. It is my life's work to seek knowledge, and a high and noble way of my people, and the Caliph in Baghdad, may Allah give him every victory, enjoys my correspondence." His long, grooved face contorted into a sudden grimace. "Enjoyed it. But now there has been a . . . Anyway. I must go back to Baghdad, when the river flows again." He looked down at the birch bark sheets on his knees. "Well. This is much for me to think about. I hope we may speak again sometime." He slid the bark pieces carefully into the pouch and got up.

Raef said, "I'll talk to you." He wanted to ask him what Baghdad was like, and where else he had been. He felt suddenly there was something like him in Rashid. He put his hand out again, and Rashid looked at it, smiled at him, and put his fingers to Raef's fingers.

"Peace." Gathering his cloak around him he went out the door.

Raef sat thinking about what had just happened; almost at once somebody who had been sitting in the dark across the room got up and sat down next to him.

It was Helgi. He had one of the house's wooden cups in his hand, and he held it out. He said, "You know, I never liked Einar."

Raef drank deep of the cup; if he sipped the wotka it stayed in his mouth too long and burned his tongue and he had learned to toss each swallow back into his throat. He gave the cup again to Helgi. "Whatever you say." The wotka hit him like a wave of heat along all his nerves.

Helgi sat silent a moment, and then said, "Rashid, there, what did he want?"

"Where I came from. Like that. Who is he?" Raef got up, unable to bear the stinking air inside anymore, and went up the steps.

Helgi followed him, talking. "A friend of Dobrynya's. He's from somewhere down in the hot lands. You have to watch out, he'll get his hands down your drawers."

Raef wheeled toward him, startled. "Yours?"

"No! No. But I've heard." Helgi hitched around at his belt, pulling his drawers up more snugly. He sat down beside Raef, and offered him the cup again. "He's got some strange god he wants Dobrynya to follow. The La, he calls him. Where's your brother?"

"Chasing a girl," Raef said.

"That will get him in trouble here," Helgi said.

"Conn loves trouble," Raef said. He drank the rest of Helgi's wotka, remembering he had no more money. "Do you have any dice?"

Helgi drew back a little, wary; Raef had been picking him over with the dice for months. His eyes glazed a moment as he weighed making friends with Raef against the prospect of being picked over once again. Finally he said, "For drinks, that's all."

"That's all I want," Raef said.

⇒

The weather turned stormy again, shutting them back down into the sunken hall, close and foul as a nest. Conn listened to stories, got steadily trounced playing Thorfinn at chess, brought in wood, wrestled with the other men, and sometimes just sat on the sleeping bench by the door and looked across the room at the women.

Two of Thorfinn's women slaves were crones, shapeless and worn, but the third, Alla, was a girl of Conn's own age. She was the prettiest girl he had ever seen. Her face was molded smoothly over the curved shapely bones and her eyes were as blue as sunny days. Her full mouth always had a half-smile to it, as if at some secret happiness. Her hair was pale, not scruffy white like Raef's but shining and golden, braided neatly in two plaits down her back. He caught himself looking at her more and more, and more and more, he wanted her.

He wanted to cherish her, to hold her tenderly in his arms, and keep her safe from any harm; at the same time he wanted to tear her limb from limb and devour the pieces. This was like a war in his belly. All day long, with the other women, she sat at her loom and wove Thorfinn's wool into cloth, and Conn grew almost sick with longing for her.

She knew he was watching. She glanced up once and caught his eye and looked hastily away, and on her cheek the blush shone fair as sunrise on soft white snow.

There was no way to talk to her. Thorfinn kept all the women close under his eye. All Conn could do was look at her and ache.

The weather broke again, and just as before, all the people, Holmgard and Novgorod, rushed out into the snowy marketplace, built a bonfire before the great oak tree, and began to eat and drink and dance. The cold was so bitter they danced only around the fire, and two drunken men froze to death right under the oak tree while everybody else was still celebrating.

They went to the bathhouse, packed with other men, and sweltering from the fire, whacked each other with birch boughs, and rolled naked in the snow until their skin was red as fever. They diced and wrestled, fought and slept and drank. Raef walked around and around the place, trying to quell the restless itch to move, to get going again, to go anywhere else. Day by day, he thought, the year was turning, but the cold and the snow still covered them, and the river was like a rock in its bed.

⎯⎯

Conn said, "I keep dreaming somebody's trying to bury me. I think it's Thorfinn."

Raef said, "Thorfinn seems to be burying you pretty regularly at chess." They had come down to the shore of the river, just inside the earthworks. Ahead, on the broad expanse of the river, half a dozen men were gathered. "What are they doing down there?" In the long light the shadows of the men there stretched along the ice like long thin giants.

Conn said, "Those are Varanger. That's Leif, the Icelander from Marten's hall. What's that he's got?"

Down on the ice, among the little group of men, one stooped and picked up something in both hands. "Looks like a rock," Raef said. He pointed down the river. "See?"

Conn frowned, not seeing, and down there big-bellied Leif marched bent-kneed two steps forward and slung the stone in his hands onto the ice, so it slid smoothly off along the river. Its shadow was darker and bolder than the stone itself, easier to track. Some fathoms down the ice, it rapped smartly into another stone resting on the cleared surface, which spun away.

Conn grunted, seeing now. He yelled, "Leif!"

Out on the frozen river, the four Varanger paused at their game, and Leif called, "Hey! Come play with us."

Conn started eagerly forward. "Come on. This looks like fun."

"Not me," Raef said. He could see this would be harder than it seemed at first, with a high possibility of humiliation. He watched Conn bound down the filthy snow of the shore onto the ice, where for a moment he slipped and wobbled off balance, his arms wheeling in the air. The four Varanger whooped at him. Conn went in

among them as if they had always been friends. A moment later he
was picking up a large smooth stone from the pile on the ice.

Raef went on by himself, along the shore. He turned around to
see Conn with the stone in his hands step forward and hurl the
stone, lose his balance, and fall hard on his backside. The stone
slid only a few feet down the ice. The watching Varanger roared
derisively. Raef turned forward again and went on along the shore.

The ships were drawn up a little higher, eight dragons without
their heads, tightly covered with canvas, and a clutch of the
hollowed-out logs the Sclava used. He went around by Thorfinn's
ship, tipped on its side and wedged fast with blocks, its topside
swathed in striped cloth. The old snow crunched under his feet. He
put his hand on the gunwale by the steerboard, imagining the ship
alive again, and sailing; through the cold wood he struggled to feel
the rush of the sea under her keel, and the wind singing past.

Under his hand the ship was cold and still. He walked up
amidships, where the canvas cover was a little loose, and pulled
the lacing tight again.

When he touched the lace he realized someone else had been
there, had undone it, and then, under the ship, in a patch of loose
snow, he saw a single print, less than a day old, of a shoe with a
pointed toe. He stiffened, looking around. At once he thought of
Magnus, doing something to Thorfinn's ship.

There was only one footprint. He snugged the canvas down
again, thinking Magnus would not send only one man to do evil.
He felt uneasy here, still, as if somebody were watching him. Out
there on the river he heard a distant chorus of yells from the stone-
sliding game. Thinking about Magnus, he went on around the end
of the line of ships and almost walked into Pavo's horse.

He backed away several steps, looking up at the Tishats, sitting impassively in his saddle, watching him narrow-eyed.

"What you do here?" Pavo said.

Raef said, "I'm just walking around." The memory swarmed
into his mind of this man striking Conn down, and his back tingled,

every muscle tightening. "I'm not doing anything, Pavo, leave me alone."

The big Sclava did not move. His whip was coiled over the pommel of his saddle. He was bundled in a fancy fur-lined coat, a fur cap on his bald head, his feet in high soft black boots. His eyes glinted like chips of ice.

"Where Raven?" he said.

"Raven." Raef realized he meant Conn, with his thick black shaggy hair. He jerked his head back toward the river. "Playing some game."

Pavo grunted. He straightened, and the little horse under him moved neatly, swiftly forward and circled around Raef, so close its tail lashed his chest. "You no trouble. Hear?" With his coiled whip he tapped Raef on the shoulder. Then with a leap the horse was up the bank, past the ships, gone back into the city.

Raef backed up toward Thorfinn's ship again, watching him go. Big as he was, Pavo rode light as a hawk on the wing. When he was gone from sight Raef stretched his leg out and smudged away the footprint under the ship, and then went back, to watch Conn play the stone game.

Early the next morning he went with Janka to feed the horses in their pasture, and when he forked up a swatch of the hay he uncovered the scrawny black-haired boy Vagn, who had been sleeping underneath.

Janka screeched. Vagn made no sound, but dashed away through the horse pen. Janka threw a snowball at him, screaming after him in hunnish.

Raef bent back to the work of feeding the horses. Janka strutted around a moment, as if he had run off an ogre.

Raef said, "He was just trying to keep warm."

"My place," Janka said. "This my place."

"No, it isn't," Raef said. "It's Thorfinn's place. But he lets you go around however you please, mostly, doesn't he." Throwing the bundle of hay into the pen, he saw, where Vagn had run through the old snow, a new line of footprints, with pointed toes. The horses were gathering along the fence, snuffling and whisking their tails.

Janka said, "I keep horses." He thrust out his chest. "Thorfinn know I know horses."

"You could run away."

The hun grunted at him. Industriously he bent with his fork for more hay. "Now, too cold."

"In the summer, then," Raef said. "In the summer he isn't even here."

"Too far," Janka said.

Raef said nothing; he thought of the boy Vagn, sleeping in cold ships and hayricks. Janka was staring at him, his mouth twisted.

"Thorfinn good, he no whip, he feed me. Why go off?"

Raef heaved an armload of hay to the horses. "You're a slave here," he said.

Janka growled at him. "Better than him!" He waved an arm after the vanished Vagn. "Better than him, though!"

"No, you're not," Raef said. He stuck the fork down into the hay and went back toward the hall, leaving Janka snarling and muttering behind him.

—⊷—

With the weather still very cold and dry, they went out to get wood again. The stocks of wood nearby the city were all used up, and they had to go farther to find more, out onto the great frozen lake to the south. It took half the day just to reach the wood stores. They pulled the sledge up on the riverbank, built a roofless hut out of snow, and started a fire in the middle. Conn gave the orders and worked harder than anybody else, driving them all along. Raef helped him split the oak logs and load the sledge. He needed the work to keep warm and he caught Conn's worry that they were far from the shelter of Holmgard. The slaves hauled in small wood and broke up limbs of trees. Janka kept the fire in the hut going.

They brought the horses inside the snow fort, and, as the night settled over them, and the cold, they ate the bread and cheese Thorfinn had sent with them, told stories to scare each other, made the fire crackle and leap, and slept finally bundled up in their furs and packed in together like a litter of puppies. Raef could hardly sleep; all the night long, wolves howled in the forest and closer, and once he heard something snuffling along the outside of the snow wall, something big. He dozed, and dreamt of his mother, as he often saw her, tall as heaven, her head among the stars, her feet upon the mountains, walking away from him. He was too small. He could not keep up with her. He woke with an ache in his chest and a fleeting, immeasurable sorrow. Overhead, blue and silver curtains of the armor-light shimmered over the black arch of the sky.

He lay on his back thinking of his mother, her eyes gray like Conn's eyes, her hair long and thick and black; Raef with his pale hair and blue eyes looked nothing like her. Every time she saw him, she must have remembered his horrible getting. He did not understand how she could ever love him. The sky danced above him with the light of stars. The sky was the same here as it had been on the island, which reassured him. Nothing else was the same. He searched for Corban's stars, the wanderers, but saw none of them.

He dozed; when he woke again, just before dawn, snow was falling. Conn was hustling everybody up, his voice urgent.

The sledge was nearly full of wood and hastily they put on all they had already cut. The wind was rising, and the snow fell in whirls and sudden gusts, sharp-edged, whistling. Janka climbed onto the seat of the sledge. "Horses take us back," he said, over and over. "Horses take us back." They got the sledge moving and started off across the lake toward Holmgard, Raef and Conn crowded in beside Janka.

The snow fell thick and white, and the wind came roaring straight into their faces. The horses trudged along, their heads down, but as they pulled on they tried to move away from the wind. They drifted off the way to Holmgard, veering out toward the middle of the lake. In the white blast of the snow nobody could see anything anyway. Raef could feel they were off course, and finally he climbed down from the sledge and went up to the front horse, and led it along, forcing it around again to the north, into the wind.

"Horse take us home," Janka shouted. His teeth chattered. He was bundled to the eyes in his cloak, plastered with snow, crouched on the seat like a white boulder. Conn came up to walk beside Raef.

"We should stop."

"No," Raef said. "It's not that far. We can make it." He thought if they tried to stay out on the lake they would die.

The cold pierced him through, as if his flesh became ice inside his clothes, his feet solid and unfeeling. He clutched the horse's bridle and forced the team on toward the narrowing end of the lake, into the river. His fingers began to throb with pain and then turned numb. The wind shrieked around him, battered at him. He sensed nothing before him but the blank whiteness. They should have stopped. If they had stopped he would be asleep by now. He was walking into nothing, endlessly into emptiness. Every step heavier. His eyes were full of snow. He heard voices in the wind, laughter, hands pulling at him, his feet like weights at the end of his legs. A mocking whisper just below hearing. Lie down, give up. Conn appeared on the other side of the front team, head down, shoulders hunched, and plodded along with him. Raef dragged each foot forward with an effort that drained him. He could not stop or Conn would stop. On the far side of the front team his cousin just a dim moving lump. He hung on the horse to stay on his feet. He would not stop before Conn stopped.

Then ahead of them snow was cascading through a hazy yellow light, and a real voice yelled. They trudged up to the bank of

Holmgard and into the light of torches and a dozen men shouting. "You're alive! You've made it! We thought—we thought—" He plodded on, still filled with white and cold, into the hall, to the warmth of the fire there, and the red-gold warmth spilled into his mind, flowing light and heat into every corner of himself, until his frozen center thawed, and he could turn to Conn beside him, and laugh.

⸺

Coming through the storm had matted Conn's beard into a black thicket. The next day he had Raef cut it off, honing his knife before he started and a few times during. Raef was surprised at how much it changed his looks; Conn's whole face looked thinner and stronger. Conn rolled up the cut-off hair, twisted it and knotted it until it was a nub, and kept it in his purse.

Raef never cut his hair. He combed it out as much as he could, and braided it up, but he thought perhaps there was some essence of himself in every hair, and it would be a mistake to cut it. His beard grew slowly and thin, anyway, and he braided that too, to keep it out of his way.

CHAPTER FIVE

For three days they were penned into the hall, fighting the storm just to go out and piss, and then the weather grew kind again. Raef had gotten into the habit of helping Janka with the horses, to have something to do; he went out very early on the first clear morning, before the sun came up, to haul hay and water.

The dawn was just breaking. The night sky still blazed above him like a great crackling icy white fire. The fresh snow squeaked under his feet. The horses' lean-to, with its walls packed deep with snow, kept surprisingly warm, and the half-dozen shaggy little beasts who came plodding out of it at the sight of him turned the air around them into a misty steam, that caught the first light, so they seemed wrapped in halos. He smashed the ice on the water trough, and while they shuffled and plodded up to drink, nickering, he went around to the hay pile.

Janka was already forking out hay. Raef looked up into the sky, and there, at the edge of the horizon, above the top of the earthworks, was the great blue-white wanderer, Corban's favorite star.

A start of excitement went through him. "Here," he said. "You do this." He thrust the fork into the hay and went over to the earthworks and climbed it. There were trails all over it, like a net, and he followed one up to the top, where he could see the horizon better.

The sun was just below the edge of the sky. In the purple flag of light above it, the blazing blue-white wanderer shone like a crystal teardrop. As he walked, more of the horizon came into his view. He let out a gasp. Right next to the great blue-white star were two more of the wanderers, in a row, like steps of light leading down to the sun.

His heart leapt; he felt as if Corban had somehow reached

across the world and touched him on the shoulder. The wind slashed through his shirts and wraps, and to keep warm he walked on toward the highest part of the wall, behind Dobrynya's compound, where he would see best. Then, to his surprise, he saw someone already there ahead of him, hunched up inside a mountain of fur robes.

He knew, even before he reached him, who it was. He said, "Peace, Rashid. Have you come to see the wanderers?"

The man of Baghdad jumped, startled, and looked up out of his nest of furs. "Raef," he said. "Well, I'm glad to see you. Yes, I'm here to observe the conjunction, Allah be praised." His eyes were sharp. "Yet I'm surprised one of . . . that you know how amazing this is."

Raef sank down on his heels next to Rashid, not wanting to sit on the ice. "Sometimes one of us ignorant people just happens to notice things."

Rashid said, "I apologize. I mean to be courteous." His arm shot out, pointing into the east. "They are coming. Behold, the glories of God."

Above the pink edge of the eastern horizon the line of the wandering stars burned like lamps, half-veiled in the gathering sunlight. The thin edge of the new moon hung just above them. It was like something written in the sky in a strange language. Raef again thought of Corban, sending a message to him, some promise, some direction. He felt suddenly, unbearably, the urge to be home again. But he had no home.

"Zuhra," Rashid said, in a placid voice. "Queen of the sky." He held up a round metal plate at arm's length, laid the edge against the highest of the wandering stars, and then squinted toward the runes on the disk's edge. With the other hand he scribbled on a bit of birch bark laid against his knee.

"How beautiful she is." He lowered the metal disk and stared at the stars. "You see, she sits before her mirror, making herself beautiful for the day to come. And behind her, Mushtarie, the king, in his grandeur. And see after him Zuhal, the old man, hobbling along."

"How do you know all this?" Raef asked. He was watching the three stars fade into the daylight. Rashid was right, he, Raef, lived in a cloud of unknowing; he had never even guessed these stars had names.

"In Baghdad we have a palace where nothing is done but the translation of old writings by the wisest men of the past. And we have found the wisdom of the ages, which includes the working of the stars."

He cleared his throat, and Raef knew he was about to educate him. Rashid said, sonorously, "They don't really wander aimlessly through the sky, these stars. They travel in circles, as all objects must that move by natural motion. It seems as if they wander because their circles are connected at their centers to other circles, sometimes very many circles."

"Why?" Raef asked.

Rashid looked down his nose at him. "Because that explains how they move."

"There are others, too," Raef said. "What does it mean, that these three are so close together?"

Rashid turned back to the sky, his face tipped up, his eyes wide. The daylight grew steadily stronger; the stars were fading away. Everything seemed much more ordinary. Eventually, he said, "I don't know. Something."

Raef choked back a laugh. Rashid gave him a dark look.

"You are Christian, surely."

"Christian," Raef said. "No. I have no god."

The other man's jaw fell open. He shrank off a little, frowning. "That is blasphemy."

"Whatever it is," Raef said, "I see that there are gods, like the four faces under the oak trees, but none of them are mine. Who is your god?"

"There is only one god," Rashid said, straightening up, zealous, "and his name is Allah, and Mohammed is his prophet." He studied Raef a moment, very grave. "God chose Mohammed, peace be upon him, the holiest of men, to bring His last, final revelation into the world. What Mohammed has given us is God's plan for the whole world. Thus may all mankind be saved and perfected."

"What does God tell you to do?" Raef asked swiftly.

"Five things. To acknowledge Him as God. To pray to Him. To keep holy the month of Ramadan, when His word was revealed to Mohammed. To go once in every man's lifetime to Mecca, the holy city, where Mohammed received His word. And to give alms to the poor." Rashid held up five fingers, triumphant. "Very simple, very pure."

Raef said nothing, disappointed. Rashid watched him intently, and finally said, "What do you say, Raef Corbansson?"

Raef said, "I don't see why you needed a god to tell you this."

Rashid's cheeks flushed dark red above the graying strands of his beard, and his eyes glistened with temper. "You blaspheme. Every word from your ignorant pagan mouth is a blasphemy." He got up in a swirl of his white robes and heavy cloak and stalked off along the icy earthworks, toward Dobrynya's compound.

Raef stayed where he was. He knew he had hurt Rashid's feelings, but he had expected something more. Something new. He thought about the Christian god, the Father god, who wanted the same things, actually, as Rashid's god did—faith, prayer, taking care of little people. As if this were all a man could do. Building a nest of small dependable virtues, while the real world went roaring on outside.

Something in this reminded him of the basileus. He took the gold coin from his belt pouch and turned it over in his hand, looking at the face on either side, the one haloed, the other crowned; he was beginning to understand what it meant.

At sunset he went out with Janka again. The cold seemed to be breaking; there was no wind, and a little fog had gathered along the ground, knee-high. While Janka watered the horses Raef dragged the small sled down toward the river, where Thorfinn kept a great store of hay. He heaped the sled high with swags of the hay, cold and smelling of snow, but as he bent to pick up the towrope again, he looked into the western sky and stopped short.

Above the last purple stain left from the going down of the sun, two more of the wandering stars shone, the red one, which he had seen both brighter and dimmer than this, and the tiny one that never got too far from the sun at all. He thought that was all of them, the ones that appeared now in the morning, and these ones coming out at night. They were all together now, for some reason, hovering around the sun like an escort, some when it went down, and some when it rose. The moon, too, he remembered, as if all the great lights held council.

Rashid had not known this, even with his star measurer and his house of wisdom; for all his story of the lady with the mirror, it was just a story: Rashid knew no more than Raef did. It broke in on him that nobody really knew anything. He stood staring toward the horizon, and the immensity of the world overcame him. Through the eye at the center of his mind he saw the whole vast explosion, the myriad stars in their wheels, each one a life far huger than his own, millions on millions, and the presumption that anybody could ever understand them pierced him through like an invisible radiance.

Is this god? he thought, dizzy. Is this what god means?

His astonishment faded into the dull ordinary fatigue of the day. Into his usual fretful momentary self. The stars went down with the sun. He shook himself back to the now, bent and picked up the rope

of the sled, and went off to feed the horses. Within a few nights,
anyway, all the wandering stars had gone their own ways.

———

Every day now, the sun rose higher into the sky, and stayed longer,
and the snow began to melt, dripping off the roofs of the houses and
turning to filthy slush where people walked. The horse pen was a
swamp and Thorfinn had them move the horses to pasture just outside the earthworks. The frozen river groaned and the ice cracked
and heaved up, erasing Conn's sledge road, creasing the ice into
ridges of dirty chunks. The wind swept up from the south, warm as
love. One morning Conn noticed a green fuzz all over the branches
of the tall elm tree by Thorfinn's hall, tiny shoots coming up through
the thinning snow. He went into the hall, and found Thorfinn gone,
and none there but the three women, working at their looms.

His heart bounded; he went over by Alla, with her golden
braids, and stood watching her hands move with the shuttle. She
began to blush, although she never took her gaze from the work;
she reached out and moved the beater up, to tighten the warp, and
Conn put his hand out and touched hers.

"Alla," he said.

"Please." She licked her lips. Her voice was low. "Please."

He wondered what she was asking; she would not look at him.
Then the door opened, and Helgi came in, and it was all gone anyway.

"Come on," Helgi said. "Help me get these bundles up to the
pelt house." Conn gave her one last longing look and went away.

———

Dobrynya's pelt house, which Pavo's guardsmen watched over
night and day, was at one end of his compound, a square made of

thick logs, its door clasped in iron and always locked. When
Thorfinn sent in a day's worth of pelts, the guard made a great
ceremony of unlocking the door, and a scribe who sat always just
inside the door counted every pelt and made a tally on a stick; the
stick, which had a loop of leather around the end, hung on the wall
behind him with several other tallies. Thorfinn's tally, Raef saw,
was longer and more notched than any of the others.

The scribe took a clean tally, and on it made a replica of the
cuts he had just made in Thorfinn's master stick, and gave it to
Raef to take back to the house of the red sun. Raef stuck it in his
belt and went out, and the door shut behind him, and the lock
clicked shut.

The sun was lowering, but the courtyard was still full of
people, coming and going, the Sclava lords in their fancy coats,
each surrounded by his underlings, and Dobrynya's slaves. Near
the gate, where the guards kept a brazier for warmth, Raef found
Rashid, sitting on the ground, writing on a sheet of birch bark. He
had brought out a carpet from the hall to sit on, and a cushion for
his back, and was sitting close on the brazier, but still he paused
every few moments to blow on his hands to warm them up.

Raef sat down on his heels next to him. "You should wear
gloves." He himself thrust his hands inside his cloak, up under his
armpits.

Rashid said, "I can't write with gloves on." He stretched his
back and shoulders. "But soon, you know, the warm weather will
come again, praises to Allah." He smiled at Raef. "You've been
busy. It's been a great season for fur, I see."

"I don't know, never having seen another. But I suppose so."
Raef turned his head a little, to look at the little stack of birch-
bark sheets next to Rashid; writing seemed to him very useful and
he wished he knew how to do it. The marks on the thin gray sheets
were not like the runes he knew from Denmark, sharp-angled and
harsh, hacked hard-edged into stones with chisels. Rashid's script
was beautiful, with long curves, loops, coils. The charcoal gave

them a subtle shading. He watched the other man draw another swooping elegant line on the brittle gray surface.

"That's very nice," he said. "Like clouds, or the ripples of rivers."

Rashid laughed, looking quickly up at him, as if to catch him in a joke. Seeing Raef was serious, his laugh turned into a snort of disdain. "It is the writing of God. It is more perfect and beautiful than any cloud. You must lift your mind above the ordinary things of the world."

Raef shrugged. The ordinary things of the world seemed amazing enough to him. "What will you do with it all, when you're done? Will you ever be done?"

Rashid put his piece of charcoal down, and held his hands over the brazier. "When I get back to Baghdad I will transcribe it into a book, annotate it, and put it in the House of Wisdom."

"Aren't there already many books there? You said all the wisdom of the world was already there."

"Yes, the knowledge and measure of the center of the world. But of these borderlands, like Novgorod, and Hedeby, and the farther islands, we know little. In time to come, we will bring Allah into all these places. And by my study and writing, we will know more about them, and be better prepared."

Raef grunted. Suddenly he saw a different aspect to Rashid's work here. The urge came on him to take the birch bark and cast it into the brazier.

Perhaps Rashid sensed this. In any case he gathered up his sheets, stacking them, and slid them away inside the pouch at his side. He said, "Someday all men will submit to Allah, my young friend. Even you and yours. Toward that glorious day we all labor, even you, somehow, in your blind way are part of Allah's plan to bring the whole world under His will and His law and His justice."

"Most other people already have gods. What if they're happy with them?"

"There is no god but Allah." Rashid rubbed his hands together in the warmth of the brazier. He spoke as if to a child, his voice crisp with certainty, allowing no doubt. "Yet in His Mercy, which is beyond our comprehension, Allah the Compassionate, the All-Knowing, has ordained that there be no compulsion in religion. All must come to Him of their own will."

He gave a grave nod of his head, his eyes wide, the pure truth, the undeniable rightness of this idea shining in his face. He said, "There are evil people, of course, who willfully deny him, and they shall be killed. Or made slaves. We have a tax for people of the book, so-called, those people who have come part of the way along the path—the Jews and Christians—but who refuse to yield entirely to Allah. We've found this tax convincing to many. Also it is not permitted that any Muslim should own any other Muslim, because we are all equal in the eyes of Allah, and so many facing slavery see the truth by that means."

Raef could see a variety of problems with this. He felt the wicked urge to go angling for Rashid's temper. He said, "Oh. But you do have slaves in Baghdad."

The older man shrugged, his face drawn long in a deep judicious calm. He was still teaching. He did not see yet that the game had changed. "Of course—there is no great enterprise of men without slaves."

"Then the whole world can never submit to Allah," Raef said. "Or else you would have no slaves. That excludes a good part of the world. And you said something about others—evil people. So the world will never be entirely under Allah."

Rashid's eyes narrowed. Now he saw the bait. Raef waited, patient, like a good fisherman, the fish circling below the wiggling fly. Corban had shown him this as a boy, how to turn his wrist just a little, to twitch the fly, and fascinate the fish.

"There are always the ignorant and the savage, who cannot see truth even when it stands before them," Rashid said, biting the words off. "And some men are made only for laboring in the cause of others. You must see that. Allah orders the world, we all submit to His will according to our fate. None of us can know our fate, which is in the Mind of Allah."

Raef said, "My mother was a slave. She never submitted to that." He thought of her, wherever she was, whatever she had become. A bright blazing star. "She made her own fate. She was greater than any man."

Rashid looked down his long hooked nose at him, which meant cocking his head back, since Raef was taller than he was. "This is a sign of your delusion. Women are of no consequence, save as vessels."

"Men are of no consequence, without women, because without women, there would be no more men. Now you've excluded, oh, half the world from your Islam. At least."

"You think crookedly and narrowly, as befits your ignorant and savage condition."

"You don't seem to me to think at all, but only to recite something."

At that, Rashid snapped, and like a fish caught on a hook, he leapt violently upward. "Recite! Recite! You don't know what you're saying! God, what a fool!" Clutching his pouch he stormed off across the courtyard, shouting in his own language.

Raef laughed, satisfied. He wasn't entirely sure which of his hooks had set but he knew he had buried something barbed in Rashid. Off by the gatehouse, he heard another little burst of laughter, and looked up. Pavo stood there, just inside the gate, watching. He had been listening. He looked Raef in the face and made a gesture with his thumb, approving. Raef laughed again, and got up and went back out to the city.

———

Alla went out to the coldhouse, to bring in some cheese, and Conn cornered her there, just inside the door.

She rounded on him, not afraid, frowning. "Stop following

me," she said. She held the big slab of the cheese in her hands, wrapped in its cloth like an infant.

"I love you," he said. "I can't stay away from you."

"Well, you have to." She pushed at the door, but he held it, so that she couldn't get out.

"Tell me you don't want me," he said. "I've seen you look at me."

The girl's beautiful blue eyes were fixed on his. She gave a choked laugh. "What I want! What has that to do with anything? I am Thorfinn's slave. I belong to Thorfinn. He takes care of me, because I obey him—"

"You go to his bed."

"Whenever he calls me," she said, staring at him. "Which is often."

"For an old man."

"For any man. And as long as I do he will care for me better than otherwise. And if I have his child the child will be free, as long as he can be sure it's his. So leave me alone."

He saw in this a strange sense, that went crosswise of his purpose, and reluctantly, he stepped back, and she darted past him with the cheese. He pushed the door shut again and stood there with his hand on the plank. He liked the way she had faced him, unafraid, but he hated what she had said.

A sound alerted him; he looked around, and saw Einar standing there, at the edge of the horse pens. He stooped, gathering the nearest ice for a snowball, and Einar sprinted away.

—❦—

He and Leif the fat Icelander went down onto the river, and slid stones, trying to knock each other's stones farther and farther down the river. After they had moved the stones halfway down past the city Conn looked over at the bank and saw Pavo there, sitting on his horse, beside the ships drawn up on their blocks, and a little way down, Helgi, watching. He had learned how to give the stone a good smooth shove, the little push of the wrist as he let go spinning it to keep its course true, and he sent the next stone clipping down the ice of the river like a skimming bird.

The ice between him and the target stone was clear and smooth. His shot struck Leif's stone and knocked it off sideways, across some bumpy ice that launched it in quick jerks toward the far bank. Near the center of the river it fell into a patch of rotten ice and disappeared with a brief splash of slush. Leif grunted.

"Well, we can't have that happen too often," he said. "We're low on stones as it is." He nodded. "Here comes some of Magnus's men."

Conn straightened. The man he still thought of as Big Nose, whose name he knew now was Olaf, and half a dozen others of Magnus's crew were sauntering out onto the ice.

Leif said, "Likely they just want to throw some insults at you. I don't have any trouble with them."

He stooped, and whipped the stone away down the ice, running beside it to clear away obstacles and try with strange hand signals to coax it back on the path to the target. From the side, Big Nose Olaf bent down and got a rock and heaved it awkwardly out onto the river.

It was a short throw, but he got his stone directly into Leif's path, so he had to veer out of the way. Free of his influence the sliding stone curved off into some rough ice. Leif turned and yelled, "Olaf! You want to throw? Come join us!"

Conn circled off to collect the stone; once or twice the ice heaved a little under his feet. The river was finally flowing, down there somewhere, a hidden vein of free water. He picked up Leif's bad miss and walked toward the Icelander in the center of the river, watching for the crinkling in the ice that betrayed a soft surface.

Magnus's men were lined up opposite Leif, each with a fat stone or a chunk of ice in his hands. Conn said, "I thought you had no trouble with them." He set himself to drive the next stone.

Leif bellowed a warning, and he whirled around to see a slab of ice hurtling toward him from Big Nose, and he leapt into the air so the ice passed under his feet. He came down and glared over at Pavo, still there, on his horse, watching, making no move to stop this. Clearly Pavo's interest ended at the river's edge. On the bank Helgi was still not taking either side, but Vagn had leapt up and was running back into the city. Conn had a stone in his hand, and he let out a yell, and swinging around as hard as he could fired the stone at Big Nose Olaf.

⸻

Bjorn the Christian stared down at the tabletop, at the dice, his face graven with lines. "Double," he said.

Raef shook his head. "Just throw. I don't have much money, if you win it all at once, the game's over."

"You have that little gold piece."

"I'm not betting that."

Bjorn shot him a hard, scowling look. Cupping his hands over the dice, he shook vigorously, his lips moving, and flung his hands apart, so the bones burst down onto the tabletop like falling stars. He won. He swore, and scooped the money off to his side. "Double."

"Get us another cup," Raef said. He stretched his legs out, uncomfortable on the stump stool, thinking suddenly for no reason of Conn, who was probably mooning after Alla again. Bjorn leaned back. He was short, square, older than Raef by some years; he always rolled exactly the same way, shaking the dice the same number of times, whispering something into his hands.

"What are you saying?" Raef asked. Bjorn had signaled for more wotka. "When you talk over the dice."

"I ask Jesus to help me," Bjorn said, looking surprised. He touched the cross around his neck.

"You believe Jesus, the savior of the world, is interested in making sure that you win at dice?"

"Well," Bjorn said, "you're pagan. Of the two of us . . . but I see what you mean." He scratched his cheek, almost smiling. "You're not being smart, though. Something is going on, isn't it, between the gods. Some big war, and not just Thor and Jesus. A man can try to get on the right side of that." He nodded at Raef. "You aren't as smart as you think you are, Raef."

He reached for the dice again and shook them twice, as he always did, before he stopped, and said, "Double, now, damn it!"

Raef smiled at him. He tossed a farthing on the table. "Not now. Throw."

Bjorn threw, and won. "Double!" he said, pushing the farthing, and another two of his own coins, out into the center of the table. "Double, now! Put that gold piece out there and I'll match it, damn you!"

Raef gave a shrug, not meeting Bjorn's eyes, not feeling all that good about this. "You need to put a lot more out there." He fingered up the little gold coin and laid it down on the pile of money. He could not sit well on the stump, and he shifted around again, trying to get easy.

Bjorn pushed out half of his winnings, cast the dice, and threw the dead man. Raef drank the last of the wotka, and took the dice also.

Bjorn's face was red. When Raef reached out to sweep the heap of money toward him, the other man said, "Double again, damn you."

"If you want," Raef said. In his hand the dice felt warm, fat, like two sixes. Bjorn dumped the rest of his money onto the pile, leaning over it, whispering to it, calling in Jesus on a throw of dice. Raef tossed the dice; he did that always the same, also, but he just threw them down. The two sixes won.

Bjorn sat back. "I don't know how you do it."

"What?" Raef said, uneasy. He could see other people watching from around the room. "I don't do anything. You won more times than I did, just then. You can roll every time, if you want.

Here." He picked out his gold piece, and pushed half of the rest of the money back at Bjorn. "Get us some more wotka."

The door flew open, and Vagn came hurtling in. "Your brother's in trouble. Down on the river. Magnus's men."

Raef got up, realizing he had known this, had been ignoring this for a while so he could read the dice, and started toward the door. Bjorn said, "I'm with him. Ulf? You coming?"

"I'm here," said a voice in the dark, and they all went up the steps and out at a run after Vagn, toward the river.

＝◦＝

Leif leaned his head around the end of the stump, and shouted, "Magnus, I had no trouble with you, you had no reason coming at me, but now we have trouble, I promise you!" He sat down with his back to the stump, panting. "There are eight of them now. They can take us in one charge."

Conn said, "No, they won't. We can knock down half of them before they even touch us." Under a steady barrage from more and more of Magnus's crew, he and Leif had retreated behind this great stump, halfway frozen into the ice, which gave them plenty of cover. He had gathered up a lot of rocks. Nonetheless he knew that he had gotten Leif into this; although the Icelander so far hadn't said so outright, Leif knew it too. "We can beat them. If we run out of rocks we can break up chunks of ice."

Leif's eyes rolled. "I've got a better idea. You know that patch of rotten ice? It runs from just over there almost all the way back to the north beach. We run out around behind it, they'll cut across to meet us, they'll get caught in the bad ice. We'll get away easy."

Conn was watching over the top of the stump, across the short stretch of rock-splattered river where Magnus's men were having a little council. At the same time he was stacking up his rocks on a flat part of the stump, ready to hand. "Raef will get here pretty soon. Then we'll have them between us."

"Making it much worse," Leif said. "And getting Pavo into it. I like my idea a lot better." His voice wheedled like a woman's. "There's always another way, boy. See? Safer."

"Run, then," Conn said, getting angry. He didn't like mention of Pavo.

"I want you to run first," Leif said. "You're likely a lot faster than I am." He heaved his belly over his belt as he spoke. "And they'll waste a lot of their blows on you."

Conn faced him, knowing reluctantly that Leif was making sense, and also that Conn owed him something for getting him involved in the fight in the first place. And he was right: Pavo would move in if the fighting turned much worse, or lapped up onto the riverbank and into the city, and they would all get the whip.

He said, "Here comes Raef, anyway." Up past the brickstack of the forge, he could see tiny shapes of men running along the boardwalk.

Magnus's men had seen them, too. They turned toward him and charged across the stretch of rock-strewn ice between them.

Conn reared up and hurled all the rocks in his stack, as fast as he could, into the faces of the men rushing at him. He guessed he hit nobody. With Magnus's galloping herd halfway to him he wheeled and raced out of the shelter of the stump. He cut around a ledge of upthrust ice he thought marked the beginning of the rotten stuff, the slush above the deep now-moving gut of the river, and the surface seemed to bounce under his feet. Rocks skittered and pelted around him and one caromed painfully off his shin. He glanced back, and saw Leif pounding after him, head down, knees pumping, his fists going back and forth with each step.

But Magnus's men were doing as Leif had said, had turned their charge to cut him off, run out on the treacherous stretch at the center of the river, and now the leader stumbled into half-melted ice up to his knees.

He yelled, then staggered, trying to go back, and thrashing sank in up to his waist. The men behind him stopped in their tracks.

The trapped man screamed for help. The rest of Magnus's crew stretched cautiously out, gripping arm-to-arm, and finally one man lay down on top of the rotten ice to reach the one trapped. The rest, holding him by his feet, dragged them both away.

Meanwhile Conn and Leif, at a dogtrot, circled the end of the bad patch and came up along the bank, where the ice was still solid. They climbed onto the beach, close by Pavo, who had been watching everything. Helgi was there also, and half a dozen of the townspeople.

Raef had been standing somewhat down the beach, but he walked up to meet Conn. Bjorn the Christian ambled after him, and another of Marten's crew named Ulf, or Rolf, or something. Vagn had disappeared.

"I'm glad you got here," Conn said. "You almost missed the whole fight." He hung his arm over Raef's shoulder.

"You got out of it easily enough." Raef was looking past him, at Pavo. "I'm glad you didn't let it get any worse."

"That was Leif's idea. Smart one, too, actually." He turned toward Leif, his hand stretched out. "That worked."

Leif shook his hand. "You did a good job, boy. They'd have made hash out of me, except for you." He turned and they all watched Magnus's men hauling the half-drowned, half-frozen man away to a warm fire. Nobody wanted to fight any more, not even Conn.

The sun was setting, anyway, and the night cold descending. The red sundown spread its harsh bloody glow steadily higher across the sky, until the whole great bowl above them looked on fire.

"The red eagle," somebody muttered, behind Conn. The light spread out like great wings overhead, and then as the sun set they seemed to fly away into the west. Bjorn the Christian was crossing himself, his lips moving. Conn almost laughed. All these people spent too much thought on trying to figure out what everything meant, when it likely meant nothing, just the spinning out of the world. The red sky meant no more than that night was coming, and he was cold. He pulled Raef along, up toward the boardwalk. "Come on, let's go get the fire going." As if he had released them, they all went back into the city, to their hearths.

CHAPTER SIX

Every day Thorfinn sat at his place in the market, and from the outlands there came wild men with sacks of fur to sell him. Magnus also bought pelts, and the other Varanger in Holmgard, but the trappers came mostly to Thorfinn.

This was why Magnus had tried to force him out of Holmgard, Conn realized. Through Thorfinn's hands now was flowing the treasure of the north.

The trappers brought the long slim pelts of winter ermine and sable, thick and sleek, prized of kings, and fox and bear and wolf, heaping them up on the table until Thorfinn himself was almost hidden from sight. The only skins he would not buy were hares. "They shed," he told Conn. "You wind up with a piece of rotten leather." He did not pay in coin, but in cloth, the ells and ells of it that his women had woven all through the winter, and in salt and iron, amber, pottery, wotka. The skins were stacked neatly by their kind, and then bound together in bales, and carried off to the pelt house in Dobrynya's stockade, where Pavo himself stood guard over them, almost night and day.

The days hurried on into spring, each one longer, warmer, more thriving with life. Open water appeared in the great shallow lake just south of the city. Plates and sheets of ice rode up over the frozen surface of the river and made ridges taller than a man. The ice thundered and cracked and water gushed through the gaps, sometimes erupting up into the air in spangles of rainbows like the spouts of whales. Every day the sun stood higher, sometimes so warm they stripped off their shirts when they worked outside. The river rose along the bank, carrying up the sodden corrupted ice, drowning the shore, and Thorfinn had them haul his ship to higher ground.

Magnus, though, left his two ships there. Conn noticed this and thought he was a fool.

Then one morning, down the center of the river, a stream of open water flowed, dark and sleek as blood, and around it the sun-rotted ice cracked and floated and was carried off on the sudden torrent. Just down the river where the banks pinched down on either side, all the chunks of ice jammed together and held the water back and everybody gathered on the shore and talked about a flood, as the water climbed steadily up the edge of the bank, but at sundown the clog broke with a crash and a thunder and the hollow roar of water going fast, and the river sank swiftly back down where it belonged. By the next afternoon, the last of the ice was gone.

That evening, when Conn came into Thorfinn's alcove and sat down across the chessboard from him, Thorfinn said, "You know the girl Alla, here? Stay away from her."

Conn shut his lips tight. His belly burned with his anger and he looked up at his chieftain with a hot temper. Thorfinn was staring at him.

"You've done good work for me, ever since I first offered you my penny. And you've been loyal against Magnus, for which I'm very grateful. But stay away from the girl."

With an effort Conn lowered his eyes to the chessboard between them, stifling the beast in him, his arms already aching from the clench of his muscles. The black and white squares of the board swam before his eyes. He put out his hand and moved his pawn, and Thorfinn moved, and neither of them spoke for a while. Conn let the game take over his mind and his mood steadied.

He thought again that if he beat Thorfinn at chess, somehow he would make him give the girl to him as the prize. He remembered what she had said to him, and knew suddenly that she herself had spoken to Thorfinn. He began to wonder if he really wanted her. He liked Thorfinn. His eyes aimed at the board, he saw how Thorfinn had left him a little opening on the left, keeping two pawns side by side, and thought that over, looking for a way to turn it without doing what Thorfinn expected of him.

Then Einar came up to them, and said, "You know, Thorfinn— Magnus wants to talk to you."

Thorfinn stirred on the bench, his shoulders moving back, and his gaze rose to meet Conn's, his eyebrows rising. He said, slowly, "Well, then, send him in." He gave Conn a weighty, confidential nod. "See?" He turned toward the hall.

Conn kept his mouth shut. He turned away from the game, his hand on the table next to the board, but his body twisted around square with Thorfinn's. He cast a quick glance around the hall for Raef, who was not there. Magnus was strutting across the way from the door. On his arms and in his ears, he wore numbers of gold rings, and in the little clearing between his hair and beard where he kept his face, a fat false smile.

He held out his hand to Thorfinn, who shook it, and then to Conn, who shook it, and mouthed some words about the weather, and the spring, and the great number of pelts. Thorfinn put the cup down before him, and Magnus took his place at the table.

"Aha," he said, looking at the chessboard. "You play the master of this game, youngster. Learn well."

Conn still said nothing. Since he had cut his beard everybody had been calling him a boy. Magnus fussed awhile on the bench, settling himself, and drank wotka, smacking his lips after. Then he planted his elbows on the table and stared at Thorfinn.

"I'll get down to it, Thorfinn. You know me, I'm a man who goes to the heart of things."

Thorfinn said, mildly, "I know you."

Magnus wiped his mouth. "Well, we've been around together a long time, you and me. We know each other." He huffed a little more, and then abruptly, he said, "You know, they're planning something. The Sclava."

Thorfinn's smile spread across his face, his eyes crinkling.

"You're talking about Dobrynya, now. He's always planning something."

"This—" Magnus hunched himself a little closer to Thorfinn, and his gaze poked at Conn as if he could push him out of earshot with a look. His voice dropped to a murmur. "This is different. I've heard he means to throw down the old gods and take a new one."

Conn folded his arms over his chest. Talk of gods always bored him. His father had ranted sometimes about god but his mother's drawings and stories got more of a grip on his mind. Now with what Magnus had told him Thorfinn wasn't amused anymore, and his voice had a new sharp edge.

"I don't think so. They just put up all the new images of the Thunderer here, when Volodymyr took power. He said the Thunderer gave him the crown."

"You know that black man from the south? The Mahmet?" Magnus nodded portentuously. Conn had to think a while before he realized he meant the stranger Raef talked to now and then, who was dark-skinned but not black. "He has a new god. Very powerful."

"I don't believe it," Thorfinn said. "Dobrynya made sacrifices to the Thunderer just last summer." He formed the sign for Thor with thumb and forefinger. In a less certain voice, he said, "All our pledges here are so sworn."

Magnus said, "They mean to have us all out of here, and give Holmgard to the Jews and the Mahmettans. That's why the black man is here."

Thorfinn said nothing. Magnus was watching him fixedly, and now his voice sank to a whisper. "You and I, Thorfinn, between us, we can bring all the Varanger together. We could throw the Sclava out. Dobrynya, Pavo, the lot. Take over the city. Make it our city only." His eyes winked toward Conn. "Your boy there would like that, wouldn't he. Make him Tishats. And then we'd have Holmgard forever, and damn them."

Conn watched Thorfinn, whose face seemed to shrink and harden, beneath the shining dome of his head, his eyes narrow and his mouth thin. He said, between his teeth, "Get out."

Magnus grimaced in the thicket of his rusty-red beard. His eyes glittered. "You're a coward."

"I'm a man of honor," Thorfinn said. "Get out, before I have my boy here show you where the door is."

Magnus was already shifting sideways, off the bench. He said, "If you go to Dobrynya with this, I'll say you lie."

"Get out!"

Magnus slid off the bench and went to the door. Conn sat back, watching him go; as he went out, Raef was coming in, and he turned, curious, to watch Magnus tramp past him. Conn faced Thorfinn again, who was staring down at the chessboard, his lower lip outthrust, and his eyebrows knotted.

Finally, the chieftain said, "What do you think of that?"

Conn shrugged. He didn't like Magnus and everything he did seemed tainted to him. He thought Thorfinn had spoken like a free man, and he liked him even better than before. He was sure now he had been right to give up Alla. He said, "Ask Raef. He's interested in such things. And he's friends with the Mahmettan." He lowered his eyes to the pieces on the board, trying to get back into the game. "It's your turn, isn't it?"

Thorfinn said, "I guess so." He bowed his head over the board, still frowning, and his voice grated. "It's all a chess game, Conn. Everything."

"Then I'm glad I'm getting better at it," Conn said.

⟶⟨⟶

"Now that the river's open, we can get out of here," Conn said.

He was still brooding over Alla. He lay on his back on the sleeping bench, his head cushioned on a fold of fur; somewhere in this hall lay a beautiful girl he could not have, and his heart was sore. He knew also, like a voice inside his head, that he could not have her because she was Thorfinn's, and Thorfinn was an honorable man who had dealt justly with him.

In the dark beside him, Raef said, "Rashid is looking to go back wherever he came from. I'll ask him if he's found a ship." He laughed. "If he talks to me, dirty pagan that I am. When is Thorfinn making another voyage?"

Conn turned toward him, to keep the talk between them; the whole hall was quiet, the fires banked, the door barred, everybody else sleeping. "Thorfinn will go west again. I want to go on south." He pulled the bearskin up over his shoulder against the night chill.

Raef's voice came softly out of the close darkness. "They say it's rich, down there—rich and warm and fat. Big cities, a lot of people. A lot of kinds of people."

"If they're all like that black man we could rule the place in a month."

Raef laughed again. "I think you misunderstand him. But he is a very odd man."

Conn laid his head down on his folded arm, thinking of beautiful Alla. Imagining her in the chieftain's arms made him sick. He struggled against his temptations. Honor was just a chain to bind him. Thorfinn was a horrible old man, who would not move out of the way. Yet he remembered how Thorfinn had spoken to Magnus, and his admiration for the older man flared again.

Nothing else held him. He could forswear his pledge, that was easy enough. He could steal her. He imagined how he would carry her away, how she would love him for doing it. In spite of what she had said to him he knew she wanted him. Drowsy now, he thought of a new chess opening, and played it out in his mind. This passed into dreams, where he fought against half-seen monsters, and arrows pierced him. Then, from far off, he heard a horn blowing.

He struggled up out of sleep and opened his eyes, and the horn was still blowing, somewhere outside, short shrill panicky whoops.

Every hair on his head stood up, and he flung off the bearskins and slid off the sleeping bench, shouting, "Fire!"

Out in the muffled darkness of the hall someone bellowed, and several voices rose, high-pitched with fear. Something fell over with a crash. People were rushing back and forth, calling, and cursing, and somebody gave a scream of pain. Raef bounded off the bench beside him and they charged toward the bolted door, which already ahead of them somebody, he saw it was Helgi, was struggling to open. He lunged to help. Before they could pull the door wide the whole household crushed up behind them, screaming and clawing at their backs, and jammed the door shut again. Raef wheeled, shouting, and Conn shouted, their voices lost in the uproar, and then Helgi wrenched the door inward and they all rushed up the steps into the clear black night.

The fire was not in Thorfinn's hall. That rooftop was a cold black ridge behind him. But the air smelled of new smoke. As the household streamed up past him, Conn looked all around, and then yelled, "There!"

He flung his arm out, pointing. Off across the city, above the scatter of eaves newly stripped of their snow cover, a fountain of flames was rumbling up into the air, giving off sparks in gusts.

He ran that way, Raef at his heels, dashing across the open ground and in between the two other Varanger halls, into a space of flickering yellow firelight. It was Magnus's place that burned, he saw. A crowd had already gathered to watch, everybody's face bathed in the glow of the crackling, leaping flames, and he stopped at the edge of it, staring up at the towering blaze. Glowing embers drifted by him, and the smoke rolled off thick and black into the predawn sky.

The fire was enormous, eating up the whole thatch of the hall at once, so that no one could get near the door. Nearby, somebody turned toward Conn and said, "Didn't you have some feud with him?"

"We had a fight on," Conn said. "That doesn't mean I'd burn him up. Did they get out?" On the far side of the blaze he saw Pavo, painted in the firelight, riding up and down, his horse skittish and snorting. He was directing a line of slaves with buckets, trying to bring up water from the river, but they had no chance against the fire.

"Nobody's seen any of them," someone else said. "They must all still be in there."

Conn's gut tightened. He could think of no worse death. He said, "I don't hear screaming." He glanced at Raef, beside him, frowning.

"Maybe the smoke got them all already."

So low that Conn could hardly hear him over the roar of the fire, Raef said, "Nobody is dead, here. Nobody is here." His face twitched, he looked rattled, the way he did at his odd times. Conn tensed, trying to cast his mind more widely around this. A Sclava ran up into the light of the fire, his head turning, looking for somebody, and went panting over toward Pavo, waving his arms. The Tishats veered his horse toward him and bent down from the saddle to listen.

Several people in the crowd of onlookers were giving Conn sharp looks, and he turned and glared at them all again. "It wasn't me! I was in Thorfinn's hall asleep—"

A bellow from Pavo interrupted him. The Tishats's horse spun on its hocks and galloped away from the fire so fast its hoofs threw back chunks of dirt. The onlookers scattered out of his way, and a stream of the city guardsmen raced after. Everybody left behind slewed around to watch them, and one of the men who had just been eying Conn with such suspicion said, "What was that about the pelt house?"

"The pelt house," Raef said, loud, and Conn suddenly understood what was happening. The crowd was pushing off to follow Pavo. "Come on!" he cried, and turned and ran the other way, toward the river, with Raef on his heels.

The sun was just coming up, its first long rays shining into their faces, sliding its sheer pale light along the surface of the river. On either side the land was still dark and featureless. By the time Conn reached the shore, Magnus's two ships were already out in the middle of the river, in the ripples of the current, and past the northern edge of the earthworks. The oars rose and fell like wings, pushing them on. Conn gave a furious, wordless yell, and back from the longships came a derisive chorus of jeers.

"Damn him," Conn said. "Damn him. Can we catch him?"

Raef stood watching the ships glide away. His head jerked around, looking north, using whatever the crazy feeling was he had for water, and flung his arm out to the north. "Around the bend, there—maybe. Come on."

They ran north along the bank of the river; Conn was thinking, now, at last, Pavo would not step in no matter where he fought Magnus, and his muscles sang. They slopped through the shallow mucky water at the foot of the earthworks and up again onto the bank, out onto the pasturage there, where Thorfinn's horses were. The river curved away from them, trending northeasterly, its surface gleaming in the strengthening daylight. Far ahead, already nearly into the great bend to the west, Magnus's ships crept along like beetles over the water.

There was no time to catch horses. With Raef beside him he ran straight north, cutting across the open meadow, to meet the river beyond its broad loop back to the west. The flood had swept this flat ground clean; he could run full-striding, straight ahead, and he leaned into each step. Looking off to his right, he could not see Magnus's ships anymore, nor anything of the river, and he shouted, "Are they beating us?"

"Keep running," Raef cried. He tossed his head back, indicating behind them. "Look!"

Conn twisted to see behind him. Back there, a pack of horsemen was galloping out of Holmgard and following on their trail.

He faced forward again, his breath coming shorter; the ground here was slippery under the crust of dried mud, spiky with dead grass, and he skidded and caught his balance again and raced on. They had nearly crossed the open meadow. Ahead of him there rose a long heap of drifted brush and branches, marking the edge of the water. To the east he could just make out the river sweeping in broad and glittering from the right. It coursed past from east to west some way, and then swung north again, and he could see a good way of its length and there was no sign of Magnus.

He reached the wall of river drift and stood a moment, his chest heaving, catching his breath again, while Raef loped up after him. The horsemen were still far behind them. He scrambled up onto the heap of branches and trunks to look around.

What he saw made him bellow, exultant.

The great mass of the flood drift covered this bank all the way back to the bend in the river, and there, stretched out into the shallow water, was formed a tangled dam of branches and trunks and brush. Behind it the flooded river had piled up a shoal of gravelly sand that stretched in a pale angled curve almost to the eastern bank. Magnus's ships had run aground on this bar, and Conn could see them now desperately trying to work the hulls free.

He made his way along the top of the driftwood, slipping and sliding on the unsteady mass, jumping from trunk to trunk. Up there, Magnus's crews were throwing out their baggage, lightening their ships, and yet still they would not float.

Now, in the first ship, all the men ran back to the stern, so that the bow raised up; Conn heard a faint yell, and they all dashed forward again.

The stern tipped up and the bow went down. The ship slid forward on the shoal, and on the downstream side the bow began to float, but the stern was still stuck fast on the gravel bar. Conn gave a screech of delight at this. He was within throwing range, now, and he stopped running long enough to pick up pieces of driftwood and hurl them at Magnus's men.

"Run!" he yelled. "You bastards—I'm on you now—"

The crew leapt out to heave the ship into the water, and Conn saw Magnus among them and hit him in the legs with a chunk of wood. Magnus went to his knees in the river and when he rose Conn hit him again. Raef dashed past, scrambled over a fallen log, and headed for the other ship. One of Magnus's men—he thought it was Big Nose Olaf—hurled a rock at Conn, but it missed.

On the second ship, the men had rushed from stern to bow, trying to walk this hull forward also, but the keel was wedged into the shoal and would not slide. The ship teetered down and back again, sticking up like a bad tooth, and when the crew all ran back to the stern again for another try, the hull broke in half.

A wail rose from its crew. Conn bounded forward, wading through the loose jumble of driftwood, and snatching up the nearest branch for a weapon; he could see this ship was packed with cargo and knew it was the pelts. The other ship was still stuck on the downstream edge of the shoal, but the crew was poling and pushing it free, and now the men from the broken ship ran toward them, waving their arms.

Staggering across the piled driftwood ahead of Conn, Raef reached the open shelving gravel of the shoal and swerved off toward the broken ship, but Conn jumped down from the woodpile onto the shoal and, turning, charged into the stragglers of Magnus's crew as they tried to escape.

He laid one flat with his club before he could even turn to fight, and when another wheeled around to face him smashed him down too. A song of triumph rose from his lungs. They would not meet him; they ran, ahead of him, five men fleeing from one, splashed out into the icy river toward Magnus's ship, now floating away down the river. Finally they swam. Conn stopped in the shallows, panting, the club dangling from his hand.

He saw Magnus, in the ship, shaking his fists, and his voice came too faint for words across the water. The five swimming heads bobbed up beneath his gunwale, and at first he would not let them on board. Conn began to laugh. He guessed there was no room for the men unless Magnus tossed out more of the stolen pelts. Along the waterline of the longship the five men stretched their arms up like a stand of reeds, and in the ship, now, the other men were yelling at Magnus. Suddenly a bale of pelts came flying up out of the stern, and another. Magnus turned away, slumped. One by one the men were drawn up out of the water; the longship drifted along in the current, far out of Conn's reach, before the men went back to their oars.

"Well done, Varanger," said Dobrynya, behind him.

He turned, startled. The posadnik sat his fine horse on the dry shelving bank; behind him, the shoal was thick with horsemen gathered around the broken ship. Dobrynya waved his hand, and two horsemen galloped past him down through the shallows to try and retrieve the two bales of pelts, now slowly sinking into the river. Raef was coming toward them.

Conn said, "Not well enough done—he got away." He admired the winking jewels on the posadnik's golden chain. Raef came up beside him.

"I think without you two to chase him on like that he would have gotten away with everything," Dobrynya said. "Including my share." He smiled; he sat high-headed on his horse like a prince, and his clothes flashed in the sun. "You are Thorfinn's men, are you not?"

"We are our own men," Conn said. "We have no king. I am Conn Corbansson—this is Raef Corbansson."

"I am most grateful to you," Dobrynya said. "And if you are not Thorfinn's men, but free warriors, true Varanger, perhaps we could make some kind of arrangement between us."

Conn felt a start of eagerness; he glanced at Raef, and said, "What did you have in mind, Posadnik?"

"I'm not sure yet," Dobrynya said. "I'll have to know you a little better before I decide. But after what you've just done, I think I'll have a use for you this summer."

Pavo had ridden across the shoal behind them. He came within earshot as Dobrynya was saying this; he drew rein hard, so that his horse pranced, and said, "Posadnik."

Dobrynya wheeled toward him, head high. "How much did we recover?"

Pavo's face was hard and expressionless as a stone. He never looked at Conn and Raef. He spoke something in their own tongue, and Dobrynya nodded and answered in a crisp voice. Pavo bowed to him, but when Dobrynya turned back to Conn the Tishats looked around at him and Raef and his face twisted into a wicked scowl. He turned and rode away, shouting orders in Sclava.

Dobrynya said, "Will you come?" His smile widened in his sleek golden beard. "I promise you loot that Thorfinn never dreamed of."

"Do we have to learn Sclava?" Conn asked.

"Pavo is my commander," Dobrynya said. "But I'd like you to gather up as many of the other Varanger as you can." His lips pursed, thoughtful. "Especially sailors. Seamen, not just rivermen."

Raef said, "Where are we going? On the river, here?"

"We have to go to Kiev, where my nephew is the Knyaz. From Kiev . . . that will depend on how everything works out." Dobrynya nodded at him. "I promise you gold in plenty. If you win my battles for me. Do you have weapons?" He glanced at the club, which Conn still held.

"No."

"Come to my stockade. I'll see you are well armed."

He went off. Conn turned to Raef. "What are we obligated to Thorfinn for?"

"Let's go ask him," Raef said.

CHAPTER SEVEN

Thorfinn shook their hands, and said, "You're leaving me very short of men, but I can tell you have your own way to travel, and best be on it." He clapped Conn on the shoulder, as he often did, and said, "Keep your head about you, boy. Come back this way, when you're done conquering Constantinople." He shook Raef's hand and looked him in the face and nodded. He said, "You too," and then went off.

"He doesn't care," Conn said. "He's glad to be rid of me, I think." There was a bitter edge to his voice. He put his sea chest up on the bench and folded his cloak into it and his extra shirts, and the litter of useless junk he had won at dice or wrestling. "I was about to beat him at chess."

Raef gave a snort of laughter; he thought the slave girl Alla had something more to do with it than chess games. He said, "Well, now, though, we have to do something. Dobrynya said we should look for some others, make a war band. Leif will go."

"Leif is a lazy slug," Conn said. "There isn't one of those slackjaws and stoneheads at the wotka house that I would want to come with us."

"There isn't too much else in Holmgard," Raef said. He gave Conn a shove. "Let go see what we can get out of Dobrynya, first."

⎯⎯⎯

Dobrynya gave Conn a long sword, and Raef a two-bladed axe, and a bit of money also. They went down to the wotka house to drink it up and look over the men there for prospects for their company.

Half the other Varanger in Holmgard were there, sitting around

the crowded room; one was Leif, the big-bellied Icelander Conn
had already spurned, at least to himself and Raef. Conn and Raef
got a jug and sat down at their usual place by the wall, at the end
of the long board table, and Leif came over, bringing with him
Bjorn the Christian, who of them all Conn thought might actually
be worth taking, in spite of his misplaced piety.

Bjorn said, "That was a good lick you handed Magnus, you
two. I for one was glad to see it." He set a wooden cup on the
board, and Conn immediately filled it from the jug.

"Magnus had it coming," Conn said. "Now, anyway, Raef and
I are getting up a war band."

Leif settled himself on the bench. He picked at his face with a
dirty fingernail. He did not seem as excited by this idea as Conn
had expected. "A war band. Aren't you two a little young to give
orders?"

"Dobrynya doesn't think so," Conn said.

"Oh, that's it," Leif said, and gave Bjorn a nod. "This is one of
Dobrynya's plots."

Conn leaned back, annoyed at this. "Yes, in fact. What's
wrong with that?" The cup came by him, and he emptied it, and
filled it up again and handed it on to Leif. "You've been around
here awhile, haven't you. Have you fought for him?"

"The last time I took up the sword for Dobrynya and Volodymyr we spent the summer walking up and down in the heat and
burning villages. There wasn't any loot to mention and it was
damned hard work."

Conn said, "Hunh." Raef leaned his arms on the board, listening with a frown.

Bjorn said, "We did get a lot of slaves and cattle."

"And had to drive them all here to Kiev," Leif said. "For which
he gave us about three hrvnya each."

Raef said, suddenly, "Where was that?"

"In the north. Against the Yotving. Gloomy people, the Yotving,
and poor, and a long way between villages."

"What if we were heading south?" Raef glanced at Conn. "Thorfinn said that's where the gold is. And easy, too, he said."

Leif's head rose. Bjorn said, "That would be more interesting. But he's a hard man for gold, Dobrynya. That's why he keeps it all on him."

Conn said, "We'll go find out where exactly he wants to fight. Who else could go, besides you?"

"Well," Leif said. "Why should I go at all—I had it in mind to go west, to the English Sea, when Marten leaves. He pays well, Marten. Safe work, and Jorvik at the end of it."

"If this is a raid against the Greeks," Bjorn said, "that's different. The Greeks are rich, and worth raiding. There's Ulf and Skinny Harald, from Halvard's old crew. They've been here awhile, they'll be up to go viking. A couple of others."

"Skinny Harald was one of Magnus's men."

"No. He came in with Halvard, who died a couple winters ago, he had friends with Magnus's crew, but he's got nothing on with you. He'll be good, if he agrees."

"The trouble is," Leif said, "there are a lot of other choices out there. Going south, that's a risky trip, even if it is for the fat."

"We'll see what the prospects are," Conn said, getting up. "You get those men together so we can talk them into this. Come on, Raef."

They got up and went out of the wotka house. Conn said, "What a bunch of slackpots."

Raef said, "Maybe they know Dobrynya better than we do."

In the yard, outside the wotka house, the scrawny boy Vagn was standing under a tree, and as they went away from the door he fell in beside them.

"I heard—you want men?"

Conn stood and looked him up and down, a short, dark boy barely getting his first signs of beard. Not even dansker, somebody had said: an escaped slave. Conn said, "Can you row? Have you ever pulled an oar on a dragon?"

"No." Vagn gave a slight shake of his head. "I came here on a ship but I didn't row."

"Can you use a sword?"

The boy's face worked, and he looked elsewhere. His shoulders slumped. After a moment, he said, "No."

Raef said, "He spent the winter on his own, living how he could, without any help." He jerked his head toward the wotka house. "None of them can say that."

Conn gave him a piercing look, and turned back to Vagn. "Yes, then. Come. But you have to break your back for me."

"I will!" Vagn leapt slightly forward, his face suddenly bright, his hands rising, his fingers spread as if he wanted to grab hold of Conn. "I will," he said, backing off. He made a gesture with one hand, like saluting. Conn and Raef went past him, toward Dobrynya's hall.

⁓

"We aren't so young," Raef said.

Conn laughed. "Young enough not to be a fat-bellied slackpot who'd rather pull an oar than keep his sword sharp."

"Still," Raef said. "Leif would be a good one to have along, if he's fought here before."

His cousin banged him with an elbow. "If we accept him. I think we set the mark up there pretty high already with Vagn."

Raef gave him a hard sideways look. They were coming to the double gateway into Dobrynya's stockade. Pavo himself sat there, his back to the corner and one booted foot up against the wall, and watched them down his nose as they went by, and then got up and followed them. Inside the stockade a line of well-dressed Sclava men stood by the wall of the great hall, waiting to get in, but Conn went straight to the door and barged in, with Raef behind him, and Pavo behind that.

The posadnik was sitting in his big chair at the end by the

hearth, talking to the Southerner Rashid. He saw them coming and put out his hand to Rashid and scowled at them, but Conn walked straight up to him and said, "We have to talk to you about this. Now."

Dobrynya sat back. His hair was shining sleek and his beard braided with little blue beads. He wore the glittering golden collar, all sparkling with jewels. The crystals bothered Raef and he moved a little to one side, trying to get out of their influence. He noticed that Rashid had left his star measurer on the far end of the table, and he went that way, to look at it: a battered circle of brass, the edge notched and marked with signs. A narrow arm, fastened at the center, could swivel all the way around the disk.

He straightened, looking over at Conn and Dobrynya, who were staring at each other as if across a chessboard. Raef drifted back toward his cousin. Music was coming from the side of the room, behind a screen, and abruptly Dobrynya clapped his hands, and the music stopped, and Rashid stood up.

He spoke to Dobrynya in the Sclava tongue, which he seemed to speak as well as he spoke dansker, and bowed, and went off. The musicians filed out from behind the screen and left also. Dobrynya said, "Well, now, tell me what you want. I am a busy man, as you see."

Conn glanced over his shoulder. Raef followed his gaze, and saw Pavo standing by the door. Facing the golden Sclava lord again, Conn said, "Nobody will agree to go with you, because they think there will be nothing worth plundering. You have to tell us where you want to fight, so we can offer something more tempting."

Dobrynya grunted at him. "My experience is that you people have a fatal fondness for gold." His eyes traveled over them both, speculative. "Sit down. As long as you're here, I want to know more about you—start with your names, which I think are not dansker."

Conn glanced at Raef, who knew by the look which story he would tell, and they took places on the bench opposite Dobrynya.

Conn said, "Our father was Irish, our mother English, from Jorvik. So the names. We fell in with Sweyn Tjugas while he was in exile in Jorvik, and he would not be King of Denmark without our help."

"I have heard of Sweyn Tjugas," Dobrynya said. He made a sign with one hand, and a servant came from a dark corner and brought them carved wooden cups. "Along with your fondness for gold you people sometimes have a fondness for exaggerating your connections. If you were his friends, how did you come to pull oars for the likes of Thorfinn?"

"Sweyn and I had a disagreement. He tricked us into going with the Jomsvikings. We wound up in the water at Hjorunga Bay—"

"Aha," Dobrynya said, his eyebrows rising.

"And when Hakon let us all go, rather than stay with him, or go back to Sweyn, we came here."

"Hjorunga Bay. That was a very great battle. Hundreds of ships. Why didn't you tell me this before?"

Conn grunted at him. "Nobody is glad to be in a losing battle, Posadnik."

"Very well. Have you fought on land, as well? Can you ride horses?"

"No," Raef said, and Conn said, eagerly, "I have, a little. Not as well as Pavo."

From the doorway came a muffled, mocking laugh.

Dobrynya said, "When we go south to Kiev I mean to take several boats down the river, with some goods for my nephew and his court and markets. If you cannot find me crews for these boats I shall find Sclava. We are not babies on the water. After that—" He shrugged. "Volodymyr fights in the summer, and I fight at his side. With whatever men have the hearts and the arms and the balls to follow us."

"You mean to sail those log things," Raef said, with distaste.

"You'd rather fork a horse?" Conn said. He looked past Raef, down the hall, and then swung back to Dobrynya. "We will find you as many as we can. But I need gold. I need to prove to them there's something for them in the work."

"Gold," Dobrynya said, as if he spoke of some unpleasant smell. "I warn you of this once. You people will die someday of gold hunger."

"You said that we saved your share of the pelts. So far all you've given us for that is a sword and an axe and some pennies."

Dobrynya's face settled a little. His bright blue eyes were fixed on Conn. His hand rose to cover his mouth. Raef thought that he had a mind full of crisscrosses, ups and downs, boxes inside boxes. Nonetheless, he realized, Conn had learned something, playing chess. At last Dobrynya lifted both hands and took off the jeweled collar around his neck and tossed it down on the table between him and Conn.

Neither Conn nor Raef moved. The golden links with their light-catching crystals lay on the table. After a moment Dobrynya took some rings also from his fingers and cast them down.

"No more," he said.

Conn shrugged. "That's not much but it will have to do." Getting up onto his feet, he took the collar as if it were a handful of rocks and slid it into his purse. Raef took the rings. They went down the length of the hall, past Pavo, who was standing with his arms folded over his chest, and out the door of the hall.

Rashid was standing there, under the eave in the shade. Raef caught the sharp curiosity in his look. He thought, Yes, you would like much to know what we just said. He and Conn went on out toward the gatehouse.

"What do you think?" Conn asked.

Raef shrugged. He held out the hand with the three gold rings on it, not enough to tempt a crowd. "He gave us as little as possible. You notice he never answered you about where we're going. He steered all the talk around to what he wanted to say, he's good at that. But south—" They went through the cool shadow of the gateway. "They've taken everything north and east. I think south is the only way they still have to go." He slid the rings on and off his fingers, thinking. "The Sclava are river boatmen. Whatever he's planning, he needs seamen. The Greeks are across the sea."

Conn said, "That's not much to go on. We have to get Leif and Bjorn and all those others pledged to this." He stopped, and took the jeweled collar from his purse. He spread it on his hands a moment, looking at it; Raef stood away from the annoying prickle on his nerves. The collar meant nothing to Conn, except that it was gold. Conn lifted it in both hands and put it around his neck, fixed the clasp, and spread out the crystals on his chest.

"Come on," he said, and started toward the wotka house.

⟡

Raef was half-expecting to find nobody waiting for them at the wotka house, but to his relief when they came to the door he could see Leif and Bjorn inside, and in a far corner several other Varanger. At least they were interested, which was half the game. Vagn was standing tipping up against the wall beside the door, his head down. When Conn and Raef came in, the waiting men gave a roar of laughter.

"So that's the kind of warrior you're taking," Leif shouted, and banged the table with his fist. "You two aren't making a really good start to this, are you?"

The room was dim, with a low ceiling, the only light coming from a lamp hanging from the center post. Conn went over there and stood under the lamp, throwing his chest out, and turned slowly to show them all the golden collar.

Leif's voice stuck in his chest; the rest of the mirth died down. The light glinted and sparkled on the collar, and the shards of color spitting from the crystals stabbed Raef through the eyes and he looked away. He stopped just inside the door, beside Vagn, leaving this to Conn.

"You see," Conn said, sweeping his gaze over them all. "If you go about it right, you get what you want."

Leif gave a false harumph of a laugh. "Did you knock him down and steal it? Is Pavo on your trail right now?"

Conn said, "Come with me and Raef, and you'll get armfuls of baubles like this. All the Greek gold you can carry."

All around the room, the Varanger were canted forward, their eyes on the glittering collar; Raef remembered what Dobrynya had said. Bjorn cleared his throat. "Well, it's a lot warmer down there."

Leif said, "I'm still waiting for Pavo to show up." But he stood, massive in the dim light, and held out his hand. "I'm your man. You're a fighter, you've got a viking's heart, and I'd be interested to see what kind of fight you make out of this. I've rowed up and down this river and the big one south of here, paddle boats and oars both, and I've tasted salt water."

Bjorn said, "Me, too. I've always wanted to see one of those Greek cities."

All around the room the men were stirring, getting to their feet, and pushing forward. Their voices rose in an eager mutter. One by one they shook Conn's hand, and then came over and shook Raef's, and they said names, which Raef mostly forgot, and nodded and smiled. "When do we sail?"

"We'll go up and tell Dobrynya, and likely look at the stars," Conn said. "We'll know the best day to leave." He was grinning all over his face, back again in a war band, like the Jomsvikings, like Sweyn's, one of the pack.

Then he said, "Raef, bring me your axe."

Raef went over beside him, in front of the nearest of the drinking tables. Conn swept the dice and empty cups aside and lifting both hands to his neck took off the collar and laid it down on the battered wood. The men surrounded him, silent, intent. The lamp just overhead on the rafter turned the gold and the crystals into a glowing sun, as if they cast their own light. Bjorn whispered,

"What's this?" Conn took the axe and cut the collar into bits, carefully, to keep from hitting the crystals. When the beautiful thing lay in pieces on the table he handed one piece to Leif, and then another to Bjorn, and another to Harald, and so on, until every man who had joined them had a piece of gold in his hand. Finally he went over by the door and gave one to Vagn.

"That's how it will be," Conn said, turning around toward the rest of them. "What I have or Raef has you will have. We're all together, until the fighting's over, and we've won."

The roar that went up shook the room.

⭑

Even Helgi decided to go with them. Einar knew better than to ask Conn. The wind was rising, keen out of the northwest. Raef's hands and feet itched, as if now that they were finally leaving he could not bear to be here a moment longer.

They stood on the bank of the river and Dobrynya spoke in a long, singsong way, and then cast something out onto the water, money, Raef thought, or maybe bread. Then Conn went to the bow of the monoch and pushed it off, and Raef followed with the stern, and the voyage was begun.

CHAPTER EIGHT

Raef dug the paddle into the water, driving the boat on. He was setting their course close along the western bank, where there was no current pushing against him; the sun-gilded stretch of water sprawled out ahead of him in a twisting braid, winding through sandbars and clumps of brushy driftwood. The flood was just past and the water was still sand-colored, catching the sunrays in shafts like curtains hanging into the depths.

Here the trees grew down close on the eastern bank but on his right the oaks drew back away from the water, leaving an open glade, green with new grass. Up over the high edge of the bank he could see just the heads and horns of a herd of deer scattered along it. The river was alive with birds; as the boat wallowed by a stand of reeds, a white crane spooked up into the air, spreading its feathers like veils on the soft sweet air.

Raef hated the clumsy monoch, made from a single tree trunk, with its stubby bow and dead feel and smell of burned wood. It gripped the water like a fist, so that he needed all his strength and constant vigilance to hold it straight, and keep sorted out in his mind the complicated currents and eddies of the river ahead of him. He worked hard to set a course that avoided the downstream push of the water but still the boat sometimes scarcely seemed to move.

He was sitting in the stern. Conn, in the bow, and two other paddlers in between were working as hard as he was. He called to them, now and then, to go to one side or the other, to dig harder or slack off. The hull was packed with bales of fur and other trade goods, and exactly in the middle of it sat Rashid, with his birch bark and his charcoal, doing nothing useful. Raef dragged his paddle a moment, to ease the boat around past a fallen tree whose upper branches stuck up out of the water like a wooden flower.

Higher than his head, twisted with strands of grass, the spiky branches slipped by. He looked back over his shoulder to make sure the other four monochs were coming along after him, following faithfully in his wake.

They had left Holmgard and the broad lake south of it well behind them. The river looped wide and slow through flat lowlands where the elms grew down almost into the water. As they pulled steadily higher up the river the water was clearing out. In the slack by the bank the deep pools were turning still and green and clear. The long narrow shapes of fish hung in the deeps, and turtles sunned themselves on fallen logs. Now and again a fish leapt up with a splash into the sunlight. The river widened and spread out and the bottom shelved up and he maneuvered the boat through riffling water, past a collapse in the bank where thousands of hoofs had trodden out a muddy ramp. Beyond, the river narrowed, and the current came straight at him and he fought through it to quieter water out in the middle of the stream.

There was no sign of Dobrynya and the horsemen but he guessed they were well behind them. They were supposed to stop at a certain place, up ahead, to make camp for the night, and Dobrynya would catch up with them then. Because in the end they had gathered only eight more Varanger they had divided them up among the five monochs but the Sclava who took the middle paddles were good enough rivermen. He cut the boat across the current, pushing it back straight at each stroke, and found better water on the far side.

Wherever the trees grew back from the bank, and the sunlight showered over everything, the flowers grew high as a man, great hairy stalks that exploded at the top into masses of foamy white. In the midafternoon they came into a long reach between trees and meadowland where the river was running clear all the way to the bottom, green to blue. Once, looking down past his paddle, he saw a sturgeon in the depths that was almost as long as the boat.

In spite of the hard work and the bad-handling boat he was

enjoying this, the traveling, the moving along, the going somewhere else at last. The wind pushed at his back, as if it urged him
on, and he bent into the paddling, sensing calmer water ahead of
him near the west bank.

They came long before sundown to the place where they were
to camp—Leif knew it, and anyway, there was one of the Sclava
god images on the bank there, a post with four faces carved into it.

They hauled the monochs in against the shore and climbed up
a short steep bank. Under some scattered trees on the edge of the
grassland, old firepits dotted the ground. The ground was crunchy
with broken nutshells, and squirrels chattered angrily at them
from the high branches. Conn called out orders and the men went
off to find wood and stretch out their legs.

Raef gave Rashid a hand out of the boat; the man from Baghdad stepped gingerly down onto the damp sand of the shore, holding the hem of his long gown like a woman. When he straightened
up, he groaned and arched his back. Behind him, he left a space
among the baggage, and when Raef reached in to lift Rashid's
pack out for him, there in among the piles of furs, he saw a leg.

He reached down and grabbed the ankle and pulled, and
dragged Janka, Thorfinn's hun slave, out from under the cargo.

"I no go back," Janka was saying, even before Raef had slung
him up onto the bank. "I no go back. No back me."

Rashid was working hard at looking amazed. Conn walked
down the bank toward them, his hands on his hips, grinning. He
said, "No way back you, Janka, not now. I'm glad you're here, for
one." He stuck his hand out, and the hun gripped it in a single big
shake, smiling broadly.

Raef got Rashid's pack up onto the bank. "From now on he
can row like the rest of us."

Helgi had come up among them from one of the other boats.
He nodded his head toward the north. "Here comes Dobrynya."

The horses were galloping down along the bank toward them,
the riders whooping and cavorting. Raef went up to the camp,

where already somebody had laid out a fire, and went off a little way to piss and see better where they were. The trees were far apart, here; he thought there had been a wildfire once, that burned everything but the great old oaks.

An indignant yell turned him around. Pavo had ridden into their camp, and as Raef watched he swung down from his saddle and kicked the fire apart.

"Not there! There—" He pointed off, still bellowing. "Build where I tell you! There!"

Conn and the others were staring at him, and Conn started forward, his mouth open to argue, but Pavo leapt onto his horse and wheeled and galloped back toward Dobrynya. Conn let out a nasty oath, and kicked violently at the ground.

"Build it here!" He tramped around, using his feet to knock the scattered wood back toward the fire site. He flung a hard look over his shoulder at Pavo, who had gone in among the other horsemen. They were building their own camp. None of the Varangers went over to join them. Janka knelt down and relaid the fire, his head swiveling to cast his gaze first toward Conn, and then toward Pavo in among the Sclava, and back to Conn. Pavo did not come back to tear it up again. Conn tramped around swearing and swinging his arms.

Moments later a Sclava rider came over, with the forequarters of a deer slung across his saddle, and dropped it on the ground by their fire. "From Dobrynya," he said, in raw dansker.

"Thank him," Conn said. "And tell him that tomorrow we'll have the meat roasted and ready for him when he gets here." He fired another fierce angry look at the Sclava camp.

The Sclava smirked at him, wheeled his horse, and rode back. When he reached his own people, a burst of broad laughter went up.

Raef said, "Are we fighting them, or some real enemy?" He stretched his arms; his shoulders ached.

Conn slapped him on the chest. "We'll beat them tomorrow, too. You keep doing what you do."

Helgi and Leif were butchering the deer meat into chunks small enough to cook. The Icelander looked up and nodded. "You got us down here right quick, for sure, Raef. Likely you surprised Pavo, usually they have to wait for the boats."

Conn had gone down to the boat again, and came back with a jug. He said, "Not this time." He sat down by the fire, and unstoppered the jug, and everybody settled down to drink and eat. Janka, burning to be useful, had gathered up mushrooms, and even some birds' eggs, to make the meal more interesting. The Sclava were gathered around their own fire now, and dark was coming, and there was no more trouble that night.

—◦—

The next day Conn roused them out of their blankets before the sun was even up, and piling into the boats they clawed their way upriver again. The horsemen broke out of their camp only a little after, and ranged along the shore almost even with them. Although the current was clear the river still wore the fresh marks of the spring floods, its banks collapsed, and its course treacherous with sandbars and riffles and heaps of deadwood, the course shifting back and forth constantly. In the middle of the morning the main stream began a long bend around to the west, and with whoops and screeches of triumph the horsemen set off to gallop straight across the bight of the curve, so the boats fell behind. Conn cursed and raged and belabored them all to paddle faster, but soon the horsemen were out of sight.

"You can't find us a shorter way?" he said to Raef. "Look at all these channels."

Raef was following the deep water through a stretch of little eddies, where on either side new streams were running into theirs, and the sandbars were like teeth waiting. "No."

"What about there? Or there?"

"Those don't go anywhere. Sit down."

Raging, Conn sat. The river bent back again, and they struggled through a long stretch of shallows and rushing current; around noon, with the sun beating down on them from a cloudless sky, they had to get out of the boats and carry them one by one across a broad bar. While they were doing this, Janka went upstream a little, and fished, and brought back a string of narrow deep-bodied fish Raef had never seen before. They still had meat from the previous night, and devoured that; Conn kept the fish aside, to feed Dobrynya, as he had promised.

Rashid waded out to the boat, holding his gown up with with one hand, and his shoes in the other, and climbed back into his space with a grimace, and Raef said, "Maybe you should ride with Dobrynya tomorrow."

Rashid made a sour face. "Better the boat." He took his stack of birch-bark sheets on his lap, and got out a piece of charcoal. Everything was wet. He daubed with disgust at a smudge on his writing. He looked back over the bar, where Conn was furiously hauling the last boat across the gravel, and shouting and cursing the men helping him. "Your brother is a madman. What does it matter?"

Raef made no answer. His shirt was sodden with sweat and he peeled it off and went to hang it over the stern of the monoch. With Conn roaring at him he began to paddle again.

They drove on upstream; although the land seemed flat enough Raef could feel it rising under them, spilling the water down faster, and the river was slowly narrowing, so there was nowhere to go but into the current. The work was slow and hard, and when in the late afternoon Leif called out, hoarsely, "There it is!" and they pulled into the shore, they found Dobrynya, Pavo, and the other Sclava already in the camp waiting.

The bank was high. The Varanger got out of the boats and started up the short steep climb; the shouting, triumphant Sclava lined up along the top of the bank to keep them down on the river bar. Pavo rode up and down behind his men bellowing orders.

"Raven," he shouted. "You lose! You lose! Oolyoch! You lose!" Conn was red as raw meat. He wheeled toward his crews and shouted, "Everybody get a weapon!" But then Dobrynya was riding up, and calling the Sclava off.

"I want my dinner," the Sclava lord said, mildly, looking down the bank at Conn. "Did you bring it?"

Conn was biting his lip with rage. He could do nothing but nod, and scale the bank, and then make his camp where Pavo told him.

They built a fire, and cooked the fish and took it to the posadnik. Dobrynya sat on a carved chest in the middle of his camp, his feet on a splendid little rug. He accepted the fish with a nod, and gave it to his servant to put on a plate, but when Conn would have turned and stamped off, he said, "No, sit here with me, both of you. Is Rashid with you?"

Raef said, "He's off drawing pictures of birds." He sank down on his heels in front of the posadnik, and put out his hand and touched the softness of the little rug. The pattern in it seemed to him like the patterns of the river, twining and coiling. Conn was still standing, still angry.

Dobrynya said, "Sit down, Raven. You'll learn nothing in a rage."

Raef glanced up over his shoulder, and saw Conn's face alter into the set, hard expression he wore when he was losing to Thorfinn at chess. The servant came back with the fish on a golden plate and a fat little pottery jug. Pavo had drifted over to sneer at them, and Dobrynya gave him a single hard look that sent him off again. For a moment, he picked out bites of the fish, devoting all his attention to that, while Conn sat down, and Raef studied the rug.

Finally, the posadnik waved the dish off, drank of the jug, and handed it to Conn. He said, "You think you lost today. Nonetheless I'm pleased with you. Maybe we got here first but there have been some trips where the boats took days to travel this far. My compliments."

Conn grunted, swung the jug up, and drank deep. Raef laid his forearms on his knees.

"What do we do when we get to the top of the river?"

Dobrynya said, "This river runs out of a lake, up in the high country. We don't go that far. There is a place—maybe two days, maybe three—where we haul out and carry the boats over the hill."

Conn passed the jug to Raef. "Do we do that all ourselves, too?" His voice was harsh; he had covered over his temper, not put it away.

"We will use the horses to help," Dobrynya said. "It's not a hard portage, nor long." He wiped his mouth on a cloth and tossed it to the servant. "Then we come to another river, much bigger, south-flowing, which after some many days runs by Kiev."

Raef held the jug out to him, and he took it with a smile. "But let me warn you, soon we will come to the edge of the forest. This going on by yourselves is fine for a while, but the steppe is hun country, and you must stay close by us so that we can protect you."

Raef said, "I thought the Knyaz ruled this land."

"He does, and no question, but the huns come through in their yearly passages, and they have their own ways. And there are places where they'll attack boats on the river—there are rapids, where you will have to walk the boats through, while we ride on the bank above. So watch out." He passed on the jug to Conn; Raef marked he drank none himself. His gilded smile matched his mild voice. "A band of huns is no match for an army like this one, but they will take single boats, and I do not mean to lose these goods."

Conn said, "How far now to Kiev?"

"Seventeen, eighteen days." Dobrynya laid his hands on his knees. "You've sailed on the sea—are you as good at that as running rivers?"

Conn wagged his head at Raef. "He can go anywhere there is water."

Dobrynya turned his gaze directly on Raef; he had always

before spoken mainly to Conn, but now the full bright blue of his eyes fixed on Raef, like a bolt. He said, "So you are the navigator? There's truth in a name, then."

Raef did not ask him why; he had guessed at the meaning of the word he had heard the Sclava calling him. Instead, he said, "This big river, up ahead, it flows into the sea?"

"Into a certain sea. We call it the Greek Sea, because it is close by the land of the Greeks. The big south-flowing river we call the Sclava River, because it is ours. But the Greeks call it the Danapur."

Raef shook himself. Names meant nothing to him, and he knew only where this river went, ahead of them, but at the very edge of that knowledge he was beginning to sense something else, a fiery city, smoke, and blood. He felt himself suddenly covered all over in blood. His belly clenched, and the back of his neck prickled up; he started to say something and stopped. Conn and Dobrynya were staring at him as if he were an idiot. He got up and walked away, all his body tingling.

⸺⸺

Conn caught up with him before he had gotten halfway back to their own fire. They strode along together a moment, wordless, until Conn said, "What's wrong?"

"I don't know. Nothing."

"He's playing us against Pavo. Thorfinn said he was always scheming. I wish I knew what he was up to."

"I don't trust him," Raef blurted.

Conn's head swiveled toward him. "Why?"

Raef only shrugged. Darkness was falling. Ahead the red splash of their fire shone up on the faces of the men around it. Raef had brought up his bearskin from the boat, and now kicked it out flat into a place for them to sit. Leif turned toward them, holding out a slab of wood with some cooked fish on it.

"Here. I saved this for you."

They sat down, Conn next to him, and Raef reached for the fish. The skin was crisp and delicious. Conn was sitting next to Leif; he said, "How is Vagn doing? Is he worth keeping?"

Leif was slicing another fish down the belly, his hands quick and neat with the knife. He stuck his thumb into the fish and stripped out the guts in a ropy little pile. "He's trying hard. He's stronger than he looks. I'd say he's getting the idea." Raef handed him the wooden slab again and he laid the raw fish on it.

The other men were coming and going around the fire, getting ready for the night. Vagn came in with an armful of wood and laid it down and began to feed the fire. Leif said, louder, "When you're done with that, boy, haul some water up, quick now."

Skinny Harald laughed; he sank down across the fire, took out his belt knife and a piece of wood, and started to cut on it. "Anybody have a good story to tell?" Vagn vanished off into the dark with the buckets.

Leif turned to Conn. "You know, somebody told me you were at Hjorunga Bay."

Conn grunted at him. Raef glanced at him and went back to eating.

Harald said, "I heard something—they were going to kill you all?"

"We lost," Conn said, curtly. "I don't like thinking of it. Leif, tell me about this Danapur River."

Leif pulled the plank out of the fire with the cooked fish. "That's the big river south of here. It runs by Kiev. Here, you want this? How did you get out of that at Hjorunga Bay, anyway?"

"We were damned lucky," Conn said. He began picking out bits of fish with the tip of his knife. "They were cutting off everybody's heads, one by one. One of the captains. Thorun, his name was, I think."

"Thorkel," Raef said.

"That's right. His brother got killed in the fighting. He started with the wounded men who weren't going to live anyway. He got about nine or ten of us."

"What happened?"

"As he went along we were getting more lively, and everybody thought of an insult or a joke to make on him, as he was hacking us, and finally he lost his temper, and swung around and hit the man helping him, not the man he was supposed to be killing. And then he tripped and dropped his sword, and we all went for it, and one of us got loose and killed him."

Raef grunted. "What I remember most is hanging by the fingernails from that rock and watching Hakon's dragons coming for us." Vagn was back, gray-faced with exhaustion, lugging buckets of water.

Conn said, "One thing I can tell you. Dobrynya says we're going to fight the Greeks. This isn't going to be a little slave and cattle raid."

In the gloom at the edge of the firelight, Rashid suddenly lifted his head. Raef got a cup, and found some wotka, and ate more fish. Leif said, "The Greeks don't fight. And they're all rich. Even if we just take one of their ships, we'd all be rich." He gave a gurgling, luxuriant chuckle. Conn was bent over the food; Raef knew he wanted the conversation anywhere but Hjorunga Bay.

Vagn sank down beside him, on the far side of him from Conn. Raef said, "Did you get something to eat?" and pushed the planked fish toward him.

"I ate," Vagn said. "Why—" His eyes gleamed in the firelight, aimed at Conn. "Why doesn't he want to talk about it? It was a great battle."

Raef drank his cup empty. "Go get me some more wotka." He stood up, and went a little way off, and made water.

Vagn came up behind him, the filled cup in his hand. He glanced back toward the fire, and then turned toward Raef, his voice almost accusing.

"It was you and him, wasn't it. Who saved everybody there. It was a glorious deed. Everybody should know."

Raef wheeled toward Vagn, his voice rasping. "You know what I found out at Hjorunga Bay? That everybody loses. So there's nothing to brag about, either way."

The boy watched him steadily. He was filthy with dirt, and the hard work had worn him even thinner. "Why did you lose? Was it your fault?"

"No. It doesn't matter. Bad planning. Everybody loses sometimes. Where are you from?"

At that, Vagn looked away, and his feet shifted. Raef said, "Somebody told me you escaped from a slave pen."

The dark head swung sharply toward him, taking insult. Raef watched him steadily, saying nothing. Eventually he took the cup out of the boy's hand, and drank from it. Finally Vagn relaxed a little, and shrugged. "Well, that's so. It wasn't back in Cymry. It's been a long path." His face quickened. "When you die in battle, you Varanger, you go to the war god's hall. Is that only for you, or for all fighters?"

"I don't know," Raef said. "I don't really believe it."

"Well, I believe it. And I'm going to win my way up there." The boy's voice had dropped, confiding, fierce with his vision. "Why else are we tested? Except to be chosen. I'm going to be chosen."

Raef said nothing, and the boy went on, in the same soft, intense tone. "Everything that's happened to me has been leading me somewhere. Why haven't I died any of the times I could have died, in the raid in Cymry, in the ship, in the snow, the ice, except that something great awaits me? As long as I don't give up."

Raef felt himself a coward. He wished he could believe in anything as much as Vagn believed in this. Vagn took back the cup and drank. He turned toward the fire, the cluster of men gathered into its light, and Leif, spinning out a long funny story about how the Greeks didn't fight. Raef folded his arms over his chest, swiveled his head the other way, facing into the dark, the brush whispering and rattling in the night wind. He felt that inside him, that emptiness, where other men, even Vagn, had enormous palaces of ideas. He wondered if he should envy them, but it was all wind to him. Or maybe it really was he had no courage to believe. Eventually he went around the campfire and found his blanket and lay down to sleep.

CHAPTER NINE

Rashid said, "When I first came here, I did not believe these were horses."

His voice was still brittle with anger; they had been talking about god again. Raef had expected him to get up again and stalk off, after Raef said that he saw no difference between his god and Christ, but the Baghdad man stayed where he was, his face turned toward the meadow before them, where Conn was trying to ride a horse.

For two days they had been traveling through a sort of high-land, a stretch of gentle hills and rises, scattered with little lakes. They had left the river behind. Every day now instead of sailing they dragged the monochs along the deep dent of a much-used path. The work was hard and slow and hot. Old campsites and pieces of broken gear littered the trail. Twice they passed by shrines, with a four-faced post set into the ground, and a litter of old offerings around the foot. Great flocks of birds cluttered the many lakes and the hillsides and there was plenty to eat, easily killed.

The Sclava spent the long spring evenings in the camp play-ing horse games. This day, with an air of great condescending amusement, Pavo had invited Raef and Conn to join them; Raef hated riding, and had declined, but now Conn was out there in the middle of everybody, trying to stay on a shaggy dun horse that apparently had no intention of letting him do so. Now, as he watched, Conn vaulted up onto the dun's back again, and the horse squealed and bounded into the air, twisting and kicking, its head down between its forelegs. The Sclava all whooped and whistled, derisive, and with a terrific shuddering leap the dun horse cast Conn off.

"What don't you like about these horses?" Raef asked.

Rashid sighed. His fine hands lay in his lap; his clothes were ruined from the hard travel. He said, "Where I come from, the horses are beautiful. Elegant, even. Their skin is like silk, their thighs like a woman's. Their manes are as fine as a woman's hair. We call them our children." He heaved up another exhalation of longing.

Raef was used to the idea that everything in Rashid's home country was better than anything anywhere else. He watched Conn gather himself up off the ground and approach the dun horse again. The dun stood breathing in snorts, its ears back, and its forelegs planted hard against the dust. Conn took the reins again, and looped them up around its neck.

"Your brother should give up trying to do this," Rashid said. "The horse is clearly not ridable. You know Pavo means to see him humiliated. He's foolish to let it happen."

Raef said, "Conn has never minded looking like a fool if it meant he could do something new."

This time Conn did not get on the horse right away, but stood stroking its neck, and talking to it. Rashid said, "If he were going to ride he would know how already." His voice changed slightly. He said, "But of course Dobrynya isn't interested in him as a horseman, is he."

Raef smiled halfway. "Fortunate, isn't it."

Conn put his hands on the dun's back and leapt on again, and the horse immediately stuck him back down on the ground. The watching Sclava sent up a strident chorus of jeers. Pavo roared, "Let him ride you, Raven! You'd do better!" He shouted with laughter, his hands on his hips. He wore no shirt; his belly rolled over the belt of his trousers, massive as if he had swallowed a rock. Dobrynya was on the far side of the meadow, under the trees, too far away for Raef to see if he was watching.

Conn got up, and went back to the horse again. Rashid muttered something.

"He is persistent."

Raef said, "He will go on until the horse drops dead, or he does."

The dun was tiring. It gave a few lazy hops forward, and then abruptly spun around with a squeal, and Conn slid sideways around its barrel and fell into the dirt. Pavo howled more insults. Among the other Sclava, though, a few men clapped their hands, and somebody called, "Good going, Raven! Try again, Raven! You can do it." Raef looked over there and saw Janka there, in among the Sclava; obviously he preferred the horses to the boats.

Conn stood up, covered with dust, and faced the horse. The dun's shoulders and neck were dark with sweat; it watched Conn with a wary suspicion, and when Conn took the reins again, backed away from him, its ears pinned flat back. It was the meanest-looking horse Raef had ever seen. Conn went hand over hand up the reins and stood patting the dun's neck and talking to it, and then began to lead it around in a circle.

Rashid said, "Obviously you had no horses, where you grew up. On the other side of the ocean."

Raef shook his head. "I would sooner walk, anyway. A man wasn't made to fork a horse like that." He reached down between his legs to comfort his balls. Rashid laughed.

"You learn to keep them out of the way. But you certainly are excellent sailors. No wonder Dobrynya's taking you on this expedition." His voice altered slightly, silken. "You said this war is to be against the Greeks?"

Raef saw no reason to satiate his curiosity; he only shrugged. He didn't know very much anyway. Conn walked the horse past them in his circling; Raef could see in his face how tired he was, but his mouth was set tight, and he turned again to the horse as it walked along, and swung up onto its back again without stopping it. The horse kept on walking, its head down, carrying him along as if it hadn't noticed.

All around the watching Sclava there went up a yell. "Raven!

Raven!" Pavo grunted and moved off, swinging his arms. His long mustaches drooped.

Rashid said, "You know what they call you?"

"I've heard it," Raef said. "Oolyoch, something like that. Is it Sclava? What does it mean?"

Rashid smirked at him. "Goose," he said. "They call him Raven, and you they call Goose." He got up and walked away.

⎯⎯

The gentle rises of the upland began to slant down again. The trampled pathway coursed through stands of oak trees, through open meadows of waving grass. One morning as they hauled the monochs along, the trail took them into sight of the river, running like a winding strip of the sky south across a limitless treeless plain. That night they made camp on the bank. The air smelled different here, not soft and leafy, like the wind in the upland, but dry, tangy, like something wild and free. The long feathery grass rippled in sumptuous waves, streaming silver and green. Herds of wild horses mixed with great-horned cattle and deer grazed all across the far side of the river. In the cloudless sky vultures coursed in their sweeping enormous circles up toward the sun.

The only trees grew close down along the riverbank, just bursting into new leaf, their reflections lying on the calm water. These were not oaks, but trees Raef didn't recognize, the peeling gray bark swirling around the trunks, the ground underneath deep in crunchy spiky seed husks. Whirring insects sprang up from the grass ahead of him. The bank and the ground along the river were punctured with the holes of little animals. He sank down on his heels by one, where the earth was freshly dug up, and lifted a handful of the black soil.

He raised his head to look down the river again, and the vast distance drew him out of himself; he felt gigantic. He thought, I can do anything here.

Rashid said, "What are you doing?"

Raef stood up, not looking at the Baghdad man. He dropped the earth out of his hand. "Just looking around." He stared off to the south. The sun was going down, and its long slanting light picked out the river's meandering course, curving and curling along, sometimes not in one bed but in several. He thought if it had gone straight it would not have been half as long.

"You've been here before," he said. "How far to Kiev?"

"A long way," Rashid said. "There are a number of bad places, where we have to portage again, or if the river is slow enough, take the boats along under the bank."

Raef grunted. Finding the course would be interesting, and he felt his spirits lift, called to something, like the vultures rising toward the sun. He realized he had been low-minded since they left the other river. Now he yearned to get on the water again.

Rashid said, "You should come on to Baghdad with me. You and your brother. You'd find it a lot more exciting than Kiev, I promise you."

"I'd like to know more about Baghdad. Is it a country?"

"It's a city. Our country is the whole world. We have no such confusion and chaos as you do, everywhere another border. Baghdad is the most magnificent city in the world, as full of wonders as Constantinople, and filled with the true faith."

"It must be very old, then."

"No." The other man's voice lowered, a little, admitting this flaw in his city's perfections. "But it is built nearby to Babylon, which is the oldest city in the world. Or nearly." His hand made a gesture minimizing any qualification. "Babylon is ruins now, and Baghdad is the heart of the world, with places of learning, and great mosques, and the richest of palaces—Novgorod would fit into a single quarter of it, a poor quarter, even Dobrynya's palace is nothing by comparison."

"I'm surprised you bothered to come all this way to see it, then," Raef said.

"Yet I have seen it, and I tell you, you and your brother have seen nothing, until you come to Baghdad," Rashid said. His voice turned sleek. "And you will be rewarded there as you deserve. The Caliph will give you a place in his army, higher than anything Dobrynya can offer you."

"We have given our pledges to Dobrynya," Raef said.

"Pledges to an infidel. You know Dobrynya cannot be trusted." Rashid's voice was slick as fish meat. "We offer you everything you wish. Gold while you are on earth, and if you die in the service of Allah, the most wonderful paradise is prepared for you, every delight, every pleasure."

Raef thought of what Vagn had said. "Yes. And Odin has his Valhalla, and the Christ has his heaven. It's a wonderful place, the world after this one. Too bad you always have to die to get there."

Rashid's face clenched like a fist. "You are cursed. You are an evil thing, you can believe in nothing." He strode off, furious.

Raef watched him go. He thought that Rashid was right, in a way. He was cursed, as Corban had been cursed; perhaps his mother had cast him off even in that instant when his father forced him into her, so that he lived forever in some gap between. He lifted his gaze again to the river. Maybe that was why he loved the water, never stopping, never resting, always hurrying on to somewhere else, girdling the world. He turned away and went slowly back toward the other men, around the campfire.

⸺

In the morning, again, with his whole army lined up behind him, Dobrynya made a long grave speech to the river, and cast a handful of coins into it, and some salt. When they put the monochs back into the water everybody gave a cheer. The boats pushed off and Dobrynya and his horsemen rode along on the bank. On this river the current ran with them. The spring flood had subsided, leaving behind gravel shoals and impenetrable snags of brush, through which the course snaked along, sometimes over deep pools where the bottom was forty feet down, and sometimes over riffles so shallow the monochs struck and stuck and had to be pushed across. On the west bank, the land rose up into steep yellow bluffs, but on the east, the broad plain stretched off flat from the river's edge.

After some days of this, they came to the first rapids.

Raef had felt them coming for a long while. Even before they came around the curve at the top of the fall, they could hear the thundering water ahead, and Dobrynya had sent orders for the boats to stop and hold against the surging river.

Raef climbed up onto the bank, to see what lay ahead; the western bluff here was high, and the current cut in against it, foaming brown over the rocks. Soaked from the spray, he scaled up to the top and looked south over a long stretch of boiling water.

Conn had come up after him. "What do you think?"

Raef shook his head. "What does Dobrynya want us to do?"

"They say we can haul them along against the far bank. Leif says he knows how."

"Let's do that."

They went back down to the boats, still laden with their cargos. Along the east bank the river ran shallow and Leif showed them what to do—they waded into the water, which even here tugged and pushed and battered at them, and holding the boats by their gunwales walked them carefully along under the very overhang of the bank, down past the rapids.

Raef hated this. He loved to be on the water, not in it. The river roared by over the rapids so loud he could hear nothing else, bounded up in towers of spray and crashed and slopped and whirled along in a wild tumult. With his whole heart he wanted to ride through that, and not creep along up to his armpits in muddy water, nursing the monoch along step by step, or worse, heaving and grunting it over a sandbank. Twice they had to stop and clear brush and broken trees out of the way.

Dobrynya and his men were following them along on the top of the west bank, and got to the bottom of the rapids much ahead of them; it was after sundown before the Varanger managed to get the last of the log boats safely down and over to the western shore again.

When they went on in the morning they had clear running, and fast. The river plunged down through the plain, broke into several streams, curled back and forth and around again on itself, leaping with fish, crowded with white birds that rose shrieking and whirling at their approach. Scuds of foam billowed up behind the flood drift in the shallows. Here and there rocks broke up from the streamway, crosswise ridges like ribs, as if the water cut down into the corpse of the earth. Raef paddled hard, kept them all at a pace even faster than the river's. Ahead, he knew, lay another rapids, and this one, he intended to challenge.

⟞⟝

Conn sank down on his heels, looking out at the foaming, surging stretch of river ahead of them; from the high bank here he could see a long way south but he saw no end to the wild water. He gave Raef a keen look. "You think so?"

"Not in one of these hulks," Raef said. "In a boat like Pap's— the old one, the hide boat." His hands shaped a boat in the air before him. "They killed one of those giant oxen today, to feed us—tell Dobrynya we want the hide. Any other hide they have. Make them save the fat."

"We'd better get started," Conn said. He got to his feet, glad of the chance to fight something.

The bluffs here were high, pocked with holes and caves, and topped with close-packed trees. The flood, undercutting the bank, had toppled some trees downward, so it was easy to climb down to the river shore. There, and on a gravel shoal in the middle of the river, thickets of willow grew. They cut the longest withies they could find, bundled them up, and hauled them back up the bluff. Dobrynya's men brought the green hides of two oxen. All the other men, Sclava and Varanger alike, drifted over to watch what Conn and Raef were doing, even Pavo.

Conn had not built a boat in a while but he remembered it well. He and Raef worked quickly and almost without talking. They laid out the longest of the willow withies crisscross on the ground, sun-shaped, and lashed them together at the center with strips of hide, which dried quickly into a joint hard as a nut. Bowing these ribs up they bound them to a ring of willow, so the whole thing formed a bowl.

The rest of the army circled them, watching, but Conn let no one else help them. Only, after the dark fell he had them light torches and hold them, so that he could see to work.

When he and Raef had the round form of the boat, they turned it turtle, and stretched the larger of the green ox hides over it, with the hair out. It didn't fit very well and they had to cut pieces from the second hide and sew them on to patch the gaps. Raef cooked the few scraps of fat until they all melted together.

Dobrynya said, "You're mad. You can't do this. I'll lose two of my best men."

Conn laughed. "If you have to pull us out of the water, Dobrynya, I hope I am dead." He was carving a paddle from a piece of green wood with a nice natural curve to it. Raef was going around and around the new boat, smearing the seams with fat. Everybody else had gone to sleep, except Janka, who sat on his heels watching them, and holding the only torch.

They slept a few hours; in the dawn Conn woke, already too excited to stay still. He took off all his clothes except his drawers, because of the heat and the good chance they would have to swim. Raef, he knew, was less sure of this than he acted. Raef too was eager, his eyes shining, a constant smile on his face. Conn stowed his gear in one of the monochs, dumped everything out of his leather belt pouch, and brought that along to bail with.

The whole army came down to the bank to watch them put in. The monochs would go as before, creeping along the low bank. Just before they put the hide boat in, Janka came up to Conn's side.

He said, quietly, "Raven, watch." He waved his hand up toward the bluff. "Watch."

"Watch what?" Conn gave him a hard look.

Janka grimaced, out past the limit of his words, but he banged himself in the chest several times, and then pointed toward the bluff again. Saying nothing, he went back among the Sclava and the other Varanger.

Raef was watching them. Conn said, "You see that?"

"Let's get going," Raef said. He gave a snort, his mouth curling in the scraggle of his beard, contemptuous. "Nobody is going to make any trouble for us from the bluff."

They carried the hide boat into the reedy shallows and climbed in. Raef took the paddle. With a few hard strokes he sent them down past the gravel shoal, where the two streams of water rippled together. As soon as they were past the island, the current caught them. Raef nudged them out toward the center of the river, running clear and green past the first lips of the rocks. From this level Conn could see nothing ahead at first but the smooth breast of the water, and beyond that, some white spray leaping up, constant as a fence.

The boat rode high and light, like a leaf. Raef steered rather than drove it; Conn, in the front, felt every tug and jar of the current. The broad sleek water swept them along. Ahead lay another of the low willow-covered islands, a deep green thicket, streaming branches out into the water. On either side the river rumbled over shallows, crisscrossed with patches of leaping white. Raef managed them quickly out past the island, and then worked the boat neatly back and forth between sudden eruptions of rock. He yelled once and Conn leaned out to fend them away from a looming tree trunk.

The roar of the rapids ahead grew steadily louder. The river was narrowing, crowded toward the high bluff on the west. The boat bucked over a swell, and the water broke up over the side and sloshed in. Conn began to bail, first with his hands and then with the pouch. Raef yelled. Conn flung his arm out to grab hold of the side as a great crumpled rock loomed up over him, and the boat tilted up, and then abruptly slid away in a wild careening spin that tossed him sideways.

He caught a glimpse of Raef, poised at the back of the boat, the paddle cocked, his face wild, his eyes popping out, his mouth open, every hair on end. The boat struck a wave and skidded off the other way, and Raef suddenly was stroking madly downward into the river. They swayed past another huge lip of a rock and another wave crashed into them. Raef thrust down the paddle and the boat slewed around and swooped down and up again. Conn wheeled to look out, on his knees, clutching the willow rim of the boat.

All around them the water leapt up in glistening towers, crashing down in foaming white. On either side, in front and behind, the rocks burst up through the surface like the teeth of monsters. The thundering of the rapids was the roar of monsters. The boat climbed a slick green slope and for an instant stood on the crest of a standing wave and he saw all below him the wild water, studded with great rocks that flung it back and forth and churned it into shattered gusts of foam. He felt the air gusting in and out of his lungs and knew he laughed, exhilarated, part of this tumult, this masterless fury. Then the boat was sliding down so steep a curve of water he saw nothing ahead of him but swirling green.

He was kneeling in water and he bailed again, taking the gust of an incoming wave square in the face as he hurled out whatever he could of the last one. They surged close against the west bank, Raef getting them somehow around an enormous snag that stuck up from a nest of boulders, and high above his head, he saw people looking out over the rim of the land at him. Remembering what Janka had said he stopped casting out water long enough to throw his hand up in a taunting salute. Then the boat rocketed down between rising ledges of rock streaming slick green weed, smashed first into one side and then into the other, and bounced out onto a pool, where the current broke up to the surface in great spreading blisters, and a boulder dam shut them off from the on-rush of the river.

He bailed. The eddy carried them slowly around the pocket of water, toward where the river poured on over a half-submerged ledge. He looked over at Raef and saw him scrubbing his face with his hand.

"How do we get out of here?"

Raef gave a crow of laughter. He was soaked head to foot, his shirt plastered against him, his hair and beard matted to his skull. "Only one way—straight down. We have to get the right channel. It's worse, up ahead—watch out—" He took up the paddle again and thrust it over the side of the boat.

His first hard stroke sent them over the edge of the pool and down a narrow twisting run white from edge to edge with foam. The rocks loomed in close overhead like a tunnel. Streamers of slimy weed whacked them in the face. Abruptly their course veered right, and Raef leaning into the paddle swung them around out of the foam, out of the deep water. Conn wailed, hapless; they were losing the river, but where the river ran was a jumble of rocks.

An eddy carried them backward a few feet, and then Raef thrust the boat hard forward onto broad pebbly shallows, propping them along like a bird with one leg. They shuddered across a gravel bar, and then spun off again, bouncing down a ladder of rapids, turning so that when they reached the bottom Raef was in front. They passed under a fall of water that hammered down on Conn's head and shoulders so hard he could not breathe. Raef whirled them around again with what was left of the paddle, which had split its length, and got them out of the waterfall. Conn shook his hair out of his eyes and bailed. The boat dragged, heavy with its burden of water. It rocked up in front, standing almost on end, and he clutched at the rim and missed and fell into Raef and they grabbed each other, half-drowning, and then the boat was diving forward again and they rolled over each other up against the front, pitching down and down. A wave broke green over them. Conn swallowed river water.

Raef shouted something. Abruptly they were gliding smoothly out into the sunlight. Dazed, Conn realized the thunder of the rapids was fading. He got up on his knees, letting Raef squirm out from under him. His ears were still ringing. His hands were scraped bloody. They were wallowing along in a boat half full of water over a stretch of flat blue river, far from the bluff, the sun beating down on them from a hard blue sky.

"Are we through?"

Raef was leaning back against the side of the boat, his arms spread out along the rim. "For a while." He looked dreamily down the river, his face soft. "Until after the city up there."

Conn gave a startled look down the river, seeing no sign of any city. His gaze swept up the western bluff, where he had noticed the people watching. "Come on," he said. "Let's see what's over there."

"The boat's sinking, anyway," Raef said.

He worked the remnant of the paddle awhile, and Conn bailed. As Raef had said, water was leaking in fast through all the seams in the boat. Two of the ribs had broken and the hide was pouched inward. Still they kept it afloat, bailing and paddling, traveling slowly down the river until they reached the west bank. The bluff rose high over them, small trees sprouting out of it here and there; along the yellow shore, the willows grew dense as a hedge. They pulled the boat out onto the shoal, and Conn looked up at the bluff.

"How can we get up there?"

Raef shrugged; with his fingers he peeled his soaked shirt away from his body.

"You're no good at this on land, are you," Conn said. Raef laughed. Picking out a way along the face of the bluff, they started upward.

CHAPTER TEN

Scaling along the crumbling yellow face of the bluff, hanging on to bushes and the bare earth, they at last reached a deep runoff channel, and climbed more easily up through that to the top. The trees on the crest of the bluff were noisy with birds, rising in raucous gusts out of the branches. Conn walked away from the river, the trees thinning out quickly as he left the water behind, and came out on an open meadow. He wore nothing but his drawers, now drying out, and the sun burned his shoulders.

From the north came a distant shouting, and a dust cloud hung in the air, but he could see nothing else of what was going on up there. Raef came up beside him, raking his hair back; the sun was drying them both out, and his hair stuck together like clumps of white moss. He pulled up the tail of his shirt and wiped his face. "Dobrynya and Pavo," he said, nodding toward the north. "Chasing those people off. Janka's people, likely." He pointed off ahead of them. "See there?"

Conn turned toward the broad treeless slope running westerly away from him, scored deep and broad with another brush-filled ravine. He shaded his eyes with his hand against the blazing overhead sun. On the far bank of the ravine, he could make out a herd of horses, close held, which meant not wild, and some blocky shapes he thought were small houses.

"Come on," he said, and started at a jog through the high grass.

Raef followed him. As they drew closer to the ravine Conn could see people over there, too, now, standing in a little group on the far side of the horses, facing away to the north. Watching whatever was happening there. He reached the ravine and slid down the bank, sending a shower of dirt and stones ahead of him into the tiny pebbly watercourse at the bottom. Raef on his heels, he clambered up the far side, where some animals had worn a long slanting trail down.

They came up onto the flat ground again close enough to the horses that the herd began to shift and stir within their rope fence. On the far side of them, he saw the blocky shapes he had thought were houses were wagons, four of them, with high square covers. One of the horses let out a warning neigh that rang in the broad air.

Raef yelled something. Conn waved to him to stay where he was, at the back edge of the pen, and ran around the rope fence toward the far side. He wanted the horses to run north, not south. Ahead, the people out there past the wagons were turning around toward him, warned by the horses, and a faint scream went up. They were women, mostly, women and children. He reached the north edge of the pen and pulled the rope down.

The horses had shied back away from him, as he circled them, and the whole little herd was pushed into the center of the rope pen, but now at their back Raef bounded over the rope and charged at them, shouting and waving his arms. They needed nothing more. With another single shrill neigh, and then a whin-nying chorus, the horses plunged forward toward the opening in the fence.

Conn shrank back out of their way. Their hoofs tore at the beaten grassy ground, hurling up chunks of sod; their bodies rushed past him in a solid stream of bay and chestnut and dun. He could feel the pounding of their hoofs through the earth under his feet. At the very end of the herd galloped a little brown horse, a foal at her heels, and as she pattered past, he ran out, caught her thick black mane with both hands, and swung himself up onto her back.

He gave a whoop of triumph. He wrapped his naked legs around the mare's barrel, gripped her mane with one hand, and waved the other over his head, howling the stampeding horses along ahead of him. The herd swerved away from the wagons; they cast up a great pall of dust as they galloped. The mare was small enough that he could shift her course with his weight and his hands and he swung her out away from the others, out of the dust, where he could see.

He glanced quickly behind him; the foal was hurrying along behind, long stick legs in a furious blur, but he saw no sign of Raef. He leaned back, to slow the mare down, to go back and look for him. Then he saw, ahead of him, someone running down toward the herd, arms waving, trying to turn the horses back.

It was a woman, her long black hair streaming out behind her, her legs flashing bare as she ran. He veered toward her, pressing his hand on the mare's neck to keep her straight. The woman saw him coming and whirled to flee, and he caught up with her at a full gallop, leaned down, and scooped her up over the withers of the horse.

He nearly went off; the mare stumbled to her knees under the sudden weight. The woman screamed, facedown across the horse's shoulders, and Conn grabbed hold of her to keep her there and dragged himself back where he belonged. The horse herd had veered off to the west, out onto the broad open plain. His horse slowed, snorting, laboring under the weight, and he felt her shift her gait, trying to swerve to follow the herd. He kicked her hard in the gut to keep her galloping and pushed her head round straight with his free hand. The other hand had the woman by the back of her clothes. She squirmed around, trying to hit him with her fist. He let the weary mare slow down; now he could see Raef back there, running after him. The horse stopped. The foal raced up and immediately pushed its head up under the mare's flank to nurse. One hand on the woman's back, Conn held her fast, head down, and waited for Raef to catch up.

⟞⟝

Raef said, "What are you going to do with her?"

Conn glanced toward the woman, trudging after him on foot

with her hands tied together before her, and her hair all in her
face. She was crying now. She had tried twice more to run away
and he thought maybe he should have let her. She was not pretty,
not even very young, a round brown face, narrow little eyes like
Janka's, tangled dirty black hair. He said, "I don't know."

"Let her go, then," Raef said.

Conn said, not thinking much, "No." She was his, he had won
her, and he meant to keep her. He knew what this touched on with
Raef, but he put that aside to work out later.

The sun was lowering, and he was very tired. Ahead, glad, he
saw the first signs of Dobrynya's camp, two men gathering wood,
and beyond them, under the trees, the smoke of a campfire. He
kicked the little mare, which groaned, and plodded on, her head
bobbing, the foal going along close against her flank. Then ahead
of him one of the wood gatherers yelled.

It was Janka. Leaping and flinging his arms up, the hun slave
dashed toward him, his face joyous. Behind him, the other man let
out a shout. The horse stopped, and Conn slid down to his feet,
and Janka rushed up to him.

"You go! You make!" Janka hopped up and down; with his
hands he made great waving motions, illustrating the river. The
other wood gatherer was staring at them, and behind him, a few
more men appeared—Sclava, all of them.

"I think you die!" Janka was shouting. He saw the woman,
frowned an instant, and then turned with a bright face back to
Conn. "I think you dead!"

"We aren't," Conn asked. "Where's everybody else?" They
were coming up to the camp, toward the Sclava, all standing there
watching them approach.

"You men still—" Janka pointed down. "With logs." He
wheeled around and shouted, in Sclava, "Look! Raven and Goose!
Raven and Goose!"

The other Sclava burst into cheers. Conn waved absently at
them. He felt a lot better for thinking about the other Varanger,

stuck now with the long slow hauling of the monochs. Ahead, he saw the camp, a wide circle flattened out in the grass, the fires already laid out and the hobbled horses scattered over the pasture beyond the clearing. By the fire in the center, Pavo stood watching them, head and shoulders above the rest.

Conn lifted a hand in cheerful salute. Among the watching Sclava, now, somebody let out a whistle, and a general yell went up. "Raven! Raven and Goose!" Pavo turned away, putting his back to them. Conn gave a whoop at that, triumphant, slid down off the exhausted horse, slung his arm over Raef's shoulder, and strutted on into camp.

⸺∘⸺

"Raef, look!"

Raef had been gawking up at the bluffs along the river, at the rooflines and fences and towers showing through the heavy-headed trees that cloaked the slopes and heights. They passed a ravine like a yellow notch cut down to the river's edge, white water spilling from its foot. When Conn shouted, he jerked his gaze toward the bow of the monoch, past Dobrynya, who was sitting grandly in the middle, past Rashid in front of him.

Conn was leaning out from the bow, pointing toward the riverbank. Ahead of them, the tree-covered bluffs drew back a little, and a many-leveled bench opened out above the bank of the river, a set of old shorelines. These level lands were packed with people and buildings, colors and smoke, moving and shouting, such a confusion that it all rushed at Raef like an overwhelming wave. For a moment he could sort nothing out, the shops, the markets, the to-and-fro of so many people. Then he began to see the rows of rooftops, the open common at the center, and there, what Conn had seen first, standing along the top of the bank in their wooden cradles, six dragonships.

Warships. Raef gave a yell, and shot up onto his feet, almost tipping the monoch over. Conn hooted at him and Dobrynya grabbed with both hands for the gunwales. Raef ignored them. With the clumsy monoch rolling under his feet he looked at the dragons and felt a surge of lust.

He had not seen such ships since he left Hjorunga Bay. Low and lean, probably fifteen oars to a side, their long sweet lines looked as light as a bird's wingbone. Their bows and sterns swept up into swan necks. Even the trim lines of their strakes were elegant. Now they wore no dragon heads, carried no shields, raised no painted sails, but when they were dressed for war, they would be magnificent.

They were old, he realized, they had been sitting there on the cradles for a long while, weeds grown up around them, and the canvas covers green with mold. It would take work to make them seaworthy again. The monoch had steadied under him; Conn in the bow was pushing them in toward the landing, just before the first of the great dragons. Raef stood where he was, his gaze feeding on the ships.

In the middle of the stupid monoch, Dobrynya twisted around to speak to him.

"These are Sviatoslav's ships. We have kept them, as well as we can, since he died. Once a year, they sail along the river here, to honor him."

Sviatoslav was Volodymyr's father; this was most of what Raef knew of him. The rest he gleaned from the voices of those who spoke of him. Dobrynya was still watching him, perhaps to see if he understood all this. In fact all Dobrynya's interest in their sailing on the salt was making a lot more sense. He remembered the sea at the end of this river, the sea that led to the Greeks, and for an instant a wave rose high and blue in his mind, broke into a white crest, and flowed on.

If they sailed them only once a year, they could not sail them very well.

Dobrynya said, "He was the greatest of the House of Rurik.

Pavo wears his hair so in honor of him. The style has gone out of use among our Varanger." He said this with a kind of sneer in his voice.

He was staring in toward the shore, where a little crowd was gathered to watch the monoch come in to the shallows. Most of this crowd were ragged children, and a few women, and as he observed this Dobrynya in his place was turning dark with bad temper. His golden beard bristled, and he put his fists on his hips.

Raef and Conn jumped out of the monoch and led it in through knee-deep water to the shore beside the wooden landing, so that Dobrynya and Rashid could climb out dry-shod. The narrow wooden dock was empty. It ran out from the next higher level of the stepped shoreline, and a ladder of several rungs led from the water up to the landing. Dobrynya climbed up this ladder and Rashid followed him, and on the landing Dobrynya turned and glared around him.

"This is the welcome Kiev gives the posadnik of Novgorod!"

Rashid put a hand on his shoulder and spoke quietly to him. Raef glanced at Conn, who shrugged. They dragged the monoch on to the shore and made it fast to the first pier of the landing, and Conn went up on the bank a little and began to wave in the other boats as they came along toward them. Raef went up beside him, but looking the other way, at the city.

There were far more people here than at Novgorod, and the houses crowded thick together on the level ground. Above, on the hilltops, he saw other buildings, bigger, with heavy rooftops. The buildings were whitewashed, and many of them were painted. The people crowding through the market carried baskets of vegetables, drove pigs ahead of them, or out of their way, shouted and yelled and strode along at a city's pace; women with their hair bound in scarves, like the women in Novgorod, men in groups talking, here someone led along a string of horses, and there already came a gang of slaves, bound together at the neck, to unload Dobrynya's goods from the monochs.

There also Raef saw, pushing in through the bustle of the crowds in the market, a man in a blue coat with gold clasps, some kind of helmet on his head, on a horse, heading for Dobrynya. Behind him came a disorderly line of other blue-coated horsemen.

The leader drew up at the foot of the landing, where Dobrynya still stood, his hands on his hips, complaining loudly to Rashid about how he was being treated.

"Dobrynya!"

The blue-coated rider swept off his horse at the end of the landing and striding up to Dobrynya went down on one knee. He was tall, with long swooping mustaches. "Uncle Dobrynya," he said. "I apologize over and over at this greeting. No one told us you were coming until just now."

Dobrynya had his arms folded over his chest. He said, "Oleg Ivorsson, isn't it? I remember you. I sent my Tishats on ahead to tell the Knyaz I was coming. Pavo Borislavovich should have been here and given you ample forewarning."

"Yes, Uncle Dobrynya," said the kneeling man. "He finally got in to see the Knyaz, only just now. It was one of the boyars, Blud Sveneldsson, sir, Blud of Rodno. He held your man up at the gate. I came as soon as I was told—even before the Knyaz heard. I apologize over and over for this."

Raef glanced at Conn, to see what he made of the whole matter, but Conn was staring away into the city, looking bored. He turned and murmured, "Let's get out of here."

Dobrynya was saying, "I demand then that you take me to my nephew the Knyaz immediately." Rashid, beside him, had a hand on his arm, and was whispering in his ear. Dobrynya said, "Bring horses for my followers. Him—" With a gesture toward Rashid. "And them." He turned, and pointed to Raef and Conn.

Conn said, "I have my whole crew to tend to. I have to settle my camp." He turned his wide gray eyes on Raef. "Raef will go. He speaks for all of us." A wide grin split his short curly black beard, his amused gaze resting on Raef, and before Dobrynya said anything, he was turning away, calling out to Leif and Harald, giving orders. Dobrynya stared after him, frowning.

"I don't ride horses," Raef said. Rashid was already mounted, sitting neatly on a big crate of a saddle. Dobrynya turned to the mount led up for him and got on board, and they went off into the city.

⇒—

The crowd knew now who had just landed, and they gathered on either side of the little train that Oleg Ivorsson the chief guardsman led across the marketplace. "Dobryna! Uncle Dobrynya!" They called to him in Sclava, and he turned and waved and smiled with every step. Raef walked along at his stirrup. He stretched his legs and rolled his arms around him, getting used to being on land. The crowd pressed around so thick he could not see much of the market, which filled the open ground all the way to the foot of the bluffs.

They climbed an angling, rutted path to the top of the bluff, where they came out on flat ground large enough to hold a dozen or more houses. None of these was built down into the ground, like the houses in Holmgard, but stood square and proud in plots of gardens, little orchards, goats tethered in the dooryard and on the thatch. Their thick walls were covered white with plaster. Above the doorways were painted birds and flowers.

As they rode along, the crowd trailed along with them as well as they could, noisy and welcoming. On the bluff top, several women with their heads wrapped in scarves and their arms full of baskets rushed over toward Dobrynya, all talking at once. The guardsman Oleg tried to fend them off but Dobrynya called out sharply.

He stopped his horse and saluted them in Sclava, in his round, merry voice, and each one snatched something from her basket and offered it to him, fighting the others to reach him. He laughed.

He took a bit of bread from one, and a piece of cheese from another, and a fish from a third, and shooed them all away. The bread woman, the cheese woman, the fish woman went away glowing, all of them in a close babble of excitement.

"Dobrynya!"

They climbed a shorter, easier slope to another flat hilltop, girdled with trees, where a sprawling stockade, a wooden palisade, contained a dozen rooftops. But now blocking their way was another mounted man, with half a dozen riders behind him, and his voice rang out again with Dobrynya's name, not welcoming.

Dobrynya reined in his horse. The blue-coated guardsmen gathered up close around him; Raef drifted out of their midst to watch. Dobryna said, in a silky voice, "I am glad to be again in Kiev, Blud. Better still, to have your greeting."

The other man, Blud, nodded his head downward. The harness of his horse glittered with gold. A gold spur twinkled at the heel of his boot. "The Knyaz awaits you." He glanced past them. "Is this your whole army?" His lip curled.

"They are coming by land," Dobrynya said. "Probably they have already reached Kiev, and are exchanging greetings with your men at the great gate."

Blud smiled, showing peg teeth in his pale beard. "Perhaps this is so. I shall allow you to pass on to the Knyaz."

"You will allow me," Dobrynya said, violently, and kicked his horse into a sudden gallop straight down the path. Blud dodged out of his way. The blue-coated guards hurried after. Raef walked along behind them, watching Blud gather up his men and ride away.

⌖

The stockade of Volodymyr the Knyaz of Rus' covered nearly the whole top of the river bluff between two ravines. Inside the fortress wall, among the scattered towering trees, there rose the heavy thatched roofs of a dozen buildings, green with the summer grass. A double gate opened through the wall, and when Dobrynya rode up, the area just outside the gate was packed with horsemen, Pavo towering above them all in his red cap and long scalplock.

He saw Dobrynya coming; with a shout, he brought his Sclava into order, and they spread out in a line on either side of the entry. Dobrynya raised his hand in greeting to them. Through their lanes he rode toward the gate, paused a moment, and greeted Pavo. Raef looked around him. The gateposts were oak trunks, carved with lightning bolts, and the crosspiece was plated with gold. Blud was coming after them, at a little distance.

The courtyard inside, where Dobrynya and Rashid left their horses, was of beaten dust, but the wide-fronted building that faced them had doors with gold handles, and golden images of eagles on the peak of its thatched roof. Raef was looking all around, amazed at the number of people. Many of them wore the blue coats with gold clasps and clips of the guards.

They went up two steps into a hall, dark after the dazzle of the sunshine, where lanterns hung from the roofbeams and the floor rang underfoot. Gradually Raef's eyes grew used to the dim light. He followed Dobrynya into the center of the room. A lamp suddenly glowed ahead of him. He looked up, and saw a man high above him, watching him from the center of a hazy nimbus of light.

He stood still, startled. All around him, a great thunder of voices called out, "All hail Volodymyr Sviatoslavich, Knyaz of all Rus'!" And everybody bowed.

Raef saw no reason to bow; he kept his head up, so that he could look around, and he saw the black curtains there at either side, that had veiled the light and hidden the man until at some signal he was suddenly revealed. Everybody straightened, and the man up there in the center of the light came down the black-shrouded steps toward them; hanging by a chain, the lamp above his head descended also, so that he was always in the center of the light.

Raef glanced over his shoulder and saw Rashid standing there, smiling, not, for once, making notes. He stuck his hand into his wallet and fingered the gold basileus, wondering if they had gotten this idea from Rashid. He thought if Sweyn Tjugas had tried something like this, he would have been met with a shower of stones.

Dobrynya said, "My lord and Knyaz, son of my soul, Volodymyr Sviatoslavich, let me greet you as an uncle and a subject and an officer, laying my love and honor at your feet." He went on like this a little while longer. Volodymyr had stopped, in his descent, where he was still several feet higher than the rest of them. Raef studied him curiously. He was straight and slim, and dressed, to Raef's surprise, not in pounds of gold and jewels but in a plain black coat, only a little fur around the cuffs to show his rank. His lean, angular face was grave as if he never smiled; not handsome, but full of purpose. He had Dobrynya's piercing blue eyes.

When Dobrynya had done with his ceremonial greeting, Volodymyr made a gesture, and someone else walked forward and answered for him. This man talked a long while, in dansker, but with an accent so thick Raef could make little of it. At last, Volodymyr raised his hands to them all, and abruptly the lights went out and the curtain came down, and everybody turned to leave.

Raef turned gladly to go, but Dobrynya said, over his shoulder, "Stay where you are. You're coming with me. Rashid?"

"I am here, Lord."

"You should come also. Volodymyr will want to welcome you back."

"Lord, I long to see the prince, may Allah show him the true way."

They went on through the hall, out a back doorway, and through a covered passage to another building.

This one was well lit, smaller, warmer. Heavy cloths with pictures woven into the thread hung from the walls, and there were benches heaped with cushions, cushions on the floor, carpets spread on the floor. At one end was an open hearth, and at the other an intricate screen, floor to ceiling, of some carved wood fitted with gold. In every corner of the room, though, stood a man in a blue coat, a sword at his belt, so motionless they might have been stones.

Behind them, the door shut, and then Volodymyr appeared there in front of them, no taller than Dobrynya. He was smiling, which made him look younger. He took the little round cap from his head as he walked.

"What did you think?"

Dobrynya said, "It was better than the last time. It's good to have Sfengus do the talking, I liked that." He put out his hands and Volodymyr took them, and they kissed each other on both cheeks, and then embraced, standing there awhile with their arms around each other, and not speaking.

Volodymyr broke the silence and the grip, stepping back. "Yet the whole thing is still too simple. I want not just to be above everybody but to be finer—alone, separate." He circled his hand around, searching for better words. "And the light must be stronger. There must be more to do, more elaborate." He looked around him for the first time at the other people with his uncle. "Rashid!" His face lit, bright as a child's. "Let me remember—As-salaam! Is that right? Alekium!"

Rashid bowed over his hands, giving out a little patter of his own speech. "You honor me, Prince."

He put out his hands, and they kissed and embraced also. Raef thought this was the Sclava way, all this overworked welcome. The light, he thought, was some other thing, not Sclava and certainly not Varanger: maybe this was what they meant by Rus'. Then Prince Volodymyr clapped his hands. "I am glad to see you all, Uncle, and my lord Blud. Uncle, make this other man known to me."

Dobrynya waved a hand at Raef. "This is one of my Varanger."

Raef gave him a dark glance, and Blud came striding forward.

"Varanger! This limp piece of rope? What is he, Dobrynya, another Sclava done up to look like Sviatoslav? If you want to return to the glories of your father's reign, Volodymyr, you need to stop mixing the red wine of his blood with river water!"

The prince turned to Raef, his eyes sharp. "Who are you, stranger?"

Raef burst out, "Not one of his Varanger."

Blud roared, triumphant. Dobrynya wheeled toward the boyar, all his usual calm crackling into temper. "You backbiting little swine, I'm tired of your interference. You've humiliated me once too often, Blud!"

The boyar drew himself upright like a sail up the mast. Like Dobrynya he wore a fancy long coat, embroidered in gold, and his dark red hair all smoothly combed and curled. "We threw out Yaropolk, when he decided he was better than the rest of us, Dobrynya. Don't think we can't do all that over again!"

"I conquered Yaropolk," Dobrynya shouted.

"With my help, and don't forget that! My forefathers came here with Rurik—I am blood of Rurik on both sides." Blud held up both forefingers, like some kind of sworn oath. "What are you?"

Dobrynya almost lunged at him. "My family was here before Rurik!"

"Your sister was Sviatoslav's housemaid," Blud said, his lip curling.

Raef backed away; he was hungry, and still angry about the rope remark, and he had seen enough of this. The prince had gone back to his chair, by the hearth, and was watching impassively as the two men screamed at each other. Along the walls the blue-coated men stood like stones. Raef went to the door, where the guard captain Oleg stood. Oleg made no effort to stop him, and Raef walked out.

CHAPTER ELEVEN

Out on the apron of land at the approach to the Knyaz's compound, a fringe of oak trees grew along the edge where the land fell off into a ravine. Beneath the oak trees in a line were little images of the Sclava gods, each one with a scatter of offerings before it. Raef wandered along from figure to figure. Most were wooden, like the ones in Holmgard, but some were stones, carved and smoothed into human shapes, knees, jaws, eyes, and arms. Scattered around the feet of each one were a few nuts, a wooden bead, a bit of shell, an old apple. Under an image with breasts was a doll. A woman with a ragged scarf wrapped over her gray hair still knelt down before this one, to give her little gift of eggs. He remembered how the ordinary people had cheered Dobrynya on his way up here; these were the people who left pieces of fruit before these images. He wondered what they made of Volodymyr descending in a halo of light.

"Raef!"

He wheeled; Skinny Harald was coming up along the trail from the city, past the Knyaz's compound. He had a keg in his arms. Raef swerved over to meet him, guessing what was in the keg.

"That had better be wotka. Where are we camped?"

"Down there." Harald nodded ahead, where the trail led down the side of the ravine. "Your brother has us all set up."

"Is there anything to eat? I'm really hungry." They walked together onto the trail, and started down. The slope of the ravine went down in steps and shelves, and there were little thatches and the ruins of houses scattered all over it.

"Ask him." Harald nodded ahead of them.

The trail they were following was wide enough for two people, winding down through thick brush into the ravine, but just ahead, where the slope leveled off a little, a narrower path forked off to the right, and ten yards along that path the ledge ended under a great sprawling old tree. On the ledge beneath the tree was a hut.

The wooden walls had lost much of their whitewashed daub and the roof had fallen in along one side of the ridgepole, but Janka was balanced up there on the gable, holding with one hand and with the other laying bundles of old thatch back in place. The mare was hitched to one side of this house, her foal asleep on its side in the sun nearby, and Raef's and Conn's sea chests were standing in the narrow doorway. There was no sign of the hun woman, whom Janka had been supposed to bring down along with the horses. Conn and Leif the Icelander were standing in the open ground in front of the house, where a fire had been laid, and Conn saw Raef and shouted and flung one hand in the air.

"Where have you been?" He gave a quick, commanding glance at Leif, who went back up past Raef to the main trail, where Harald was waiting. As the Icelander went by Raef he muttered a greeting. Raef sauntered down onto the ledge and over to his cousin, who stood watching the other men stride off down the main trail. The hillside was so steep that now that Leif and Harald were descending on the main trail Raef was looking at the tops of their heads. He banged Conn companionably on the arm.

"How did you find this?"

"Just looking." Conn turned to look around. "What do you think of this? There's more houses down there. All empty. I just moved everybody in. What's going on here? Did you find anything out?"

"They had a war here, sometime, not too long ago, a lot of people left. Or died. When they drove out the last Knyaz. That must be why all these houses are here and empty. I saw Volodymyr. Dobrynya's little prince wants to be king of the world, but they don't even have control of Kiev. There are people here who think they are more Varanger than we are, but they aren't like us at all. They all speak dansker, kind of."

Conn grunted. "What about those ships? Are we getting those ships?"

"I don't know. Is there anything to eat?"

"I'm still working on that," Conn said. "But this is good, isn't it? Once we get the roof fixed." He looked very pleased with himself.

"Good enough," Raef said. He clapped Conn around the shoulders. "You did a good job." He stooped to pick up his sea chest, and went through the narrow door into the hut.

The roof of poles and thatch wasn't solid, but the huge overspreading canopy of the tree and the makeshift frame of the roof shadowed the room, and he was inside before he saw the hun woman, huddled in a corner, her knees and arms against her body. He lowered his sea chest to the floor, looking around. There were no sleeping benches, but against the wall was a stack of rugs, or blankets, which must have come from somewhere else, since they weren't dirty. The wall behind them was shedding plaster daub all over but the hut had been swept out, and behind this room was another, small as a cupboard, which Janka seemed already to have moved his own gear into.

Overhead, Janka had fastened up half a row of thatches, and now he climbed down off the roof and was gone. Conn came in with his chest. He looked at the hun woman as if he had forgotten about her. Raef went out again, looking around.

The vast tree was heavy with the long white strands of its blossoms and the air was sweet with their scent. He felt at once this was a good place. He walked across the ledge to the downslope into the ravine. Another ledge opened up some fifty feet below, this one wider, with six huts on it, and from high over their heads he looked down at Leif and Harald there, sitting by a fire bed. Vagn hurried past them with a bucket, from Raef's viewpoint only a brimmed hat with milling feet beneath. Down behind their huts, out of sight of the Varanger, Janka was sealing another row of their thatch. Along a lower ledge, farther down the ravine, a string of horses was tethered and he recognized Pavo's lanky chestnut among them. Across the blooming trees that filled the ravine were more houses, scattered where the land was flat, and down toward the river. Maybe this wouldn't be so bad, he thought.

Behind him, in the hut, the woman screamed.

He knew, right away. He could not have stayed out; it was as if his mother screamed. He plunged back across the yard, and into the hut, in the dimness seeing only the tangle of their bodies, and he got Conn by the shoulders and heaved him off. In one stride he put himself between his cousin and the woman.

She was sobbing, but she started up off the floor, and he pushed her toward the corner again. "Stay there."

Conn stood up, naked, the light from the doorway behind him, and said, "Get out of my way, Raef."

Raef said, "I won't let you."

Conn lunged at him, and they grappled together. Raef braced himself, his head down. He felt Conn gather against him, the smooth collected irresistible strength that Raef had always striven to match and never could, and couldn't now either, one knee buckling, his muscles groaning, giving way; his left arm lost its grip. Then abruptly, Conn let him go and stepped back.

"What's the matter with you?"

Raef was panting, his shoulders throbbing. He said, "I won't let you." He glanced quickly behind him to make sure the woman was still in her corner. "You'll have to kill me, Conn."

Conn stood quiet a moment, his arms slack at his sides. The sunlight through the door behind him kept his face in shadow. Finally, he said, "All right. You know I won't do that. Couldn't, ever." He wiped one hand across his face. "I'm going out and find us something to eat." He picked up his shirt from the floor. "And somebody more willing." He went out the door.

Raef stood still a moment, thankful; he knew he would never beat Conn. He looked at the woman again, crouching in the corner, staring at him. The edge of the sunlight reached her and he could see in her face what she thought, and he called for Janka. The hun came at once in from the yard. He had likely been watching everything. He said, "You brother fight?"

"No," Raef said. "I was just making a point to him. Tell her he won't do it again. Tell her I won't, either." He was on the edge of explaining about his mother, but he didn't want Janka to know that. "She can haul water and wood and do other work and sleep in here and we'll feed her. We'll protect her. If she runs away somebody else will catch her and he will rape her, and probably kill her, too, while he's at it."

Janka stared at him, his forehead rumpled, and then he turned to the woman and spoke, gesturing now and then, at some length. As he spoke the woman's gaze turned from him to Raef. The shimmer of fear in her eyes changed to a wary curiosity. Raef looked away from her; he thought she would run off, likely, no matter what he said. The memory of his mother trembled on the edge of his mind, what had happened to her, suddenly much more real. How he had come of that suffering. His muscles hurt from the fight and he was tired and still very hungry and he hoped this story didn't get around. He said, "Fix the roof, Janka," and went out of the hut into the long summer afternoon.

Conn brought down a haunch of meat, and they got a fire going in the circle at the upper house, where he and Raef were staying. Conn thought of this as his holding. He had never before ruled a hall of his own, but now he had one, even if it was only a hut. He got some stones set around the fire for people to sit on, and sent somebody for the wotka.

What had happened with Raef amused him. He had always known Raef had a soft place for women, because of his mother. The hun woman was ugly anyway. He sat on a rock with his arm hanging over his cousin's shoulder watching Leif cut slices of meat to roast. Then while they were eating the first half-raw strips, Dobrynya himself came down the trail, riding a trim chestnut horse.

"I've been looking for you," he said. He turned his horse sideways on the little path. Conn admired how effortlessly he mastered the horse. "If Pavo hadn't seen you I would not know where you are even now. I want you to come with me, I want the Knyaz to meet you."

The other men were gathered around the fire; after a few glances at Dobrynya, they ignored him. The steady loud eating went on. Raef looked up and said, "Is this going to be like the last time? All show and the odd insult?"

The golden Sclava lord grunted at him. His cheeks flushed. "No. This is merely with me and the Knyaz. I have something to . . . propose to him."

"Come on," Conn said, and started toward the trail. He wanted to see what this Knyaz was like, and he certainly wanted to hear what Dobrynya proposed to do. The six dragonships down in the market were never far from his mind. They followed the posadnik up the trail and across the height to the gate into the stockade.

Inside the gateway Dobrynya dismounted and a servant took his horse away. Conn looked around. The palace compound was much bigger than he expected. Men in blue coats stood at every gate, every doorway. Two people in the rags of servants were hauling wood into the great hall in front of them and he could hear axes ringing, just around the corner. He could smell bread baking.

They crossed the open ground inside the gate, but they did not go into the hall with the painted door; instead, Dobrynya led them around the side, and in through a gate into a courtyard, which lay between the back of the hall and two smaller buildings, also gleaming with whitewash, their walls painted with birds and leaping deer. A narrow roofed corridor led between the two buildings. In the courtyard, three or four men dressed as grandly as Dobrynya were standing around, each surrounded by a little circle of other, lesser men. One of these great men broke forward to meet Dobrynya as he walked in.

"Are you here to make plans with the Knyaz, Dobrynya?" he said. "Do you think you can keep me from finding out?"

Dobrynya did not stop. "Come, then, Blud Sveneldsson. Hear what you want to," he said.

They went up between two guardsmen to the door into the farther of the two buildings. The doorframe was all carved and gilded, and the door itself was painted with an eagle. Going through it after Dobrynya, Conn came into a room longer than it was wide, with hangings on the walls, and cushions and little tables. Just inside the door were more guards, one of them the man who had met Dobrynya at the dock. At one end of the room, on a big carved chair, sat a tall slender man in a dark coat.

He was talking to the Mahmettan, Rashid. Dobrynya went forward, and said Conn's and Raef's names, and the tall man stood and came forward, tall and high-headed.

"I am glad to receive you. I have heard much of you." He did not offer to shake their hands. This man was older than Conn by ten years; he had a manner that put Conn on edge, as if he expected them to bow to him. "Tomorrow we shall have a great feast, such as you must be used to, in the kings' halls in the north. Meanwhile, welcome to my court and to Kiev."

The red-haired lordling who had barged in with them stamped forward. "Knyaz, are these men guests? Or are they—as Dobrynya claims—"

Volodymyr said, "Blud, when we hold council, then you will hear everything. Wait until we hold our council."

The redheaded Blud strutted a little in the middle of the room. Conn looked around again, admiring the Knyaz's furnishings, and saw the latticework screen across the opposite end of the room, and wondered what was behind it. Blud said, "Just remember, you can do nothing without me!"

Conn turned around, drawn to the challenge in his voice. Volodymyr flung his head back. He flashed with righteous kingly wrath. "I can do nothing with you!" His voice poured out of him, furious. "Whatever I plan, you stand in the way. Whoever I command, you command to disobey me. If I am to be master here I shall be master over everybody, Blud!"

"The gods give power to those who respect them, Volodymyr. Well is it known you seek another god, that when you were a boy your grandmother Olga the Christian whispered in your ear of another god, a greater god than ours—"

"She spoke openly, to me, to my father. She was a holy woman, very deep-minded."

"But Sviatoslav knew if he abandoned the old gods, his men would not follow him. I heard this with my own ears! How can you do what your father dared not do? Do you think you are as great a man as Sviatoslav?" Blud gave a sneer, and tossed one hand up. "When have you even sailed beyond the rapids?"

Volodymyr's whole face twisted, dark, his teeth showing. "Would you follow me if I did? Do you follow me now? When I have put images of Perun in every village under my sway, and overcome the northern tribes?"

Dobrynya said sharply, "You use the gods for your own ends, Blud. And Sviatoslav himself did not sail on the sea."

Conn glanced at Raef, beside him. "Is this what happened this morning?"

Raef nodded. Conn turned his eyes toward the screen again; now for a moment a light shone behind it, as if a door opened. Then it was gone: the door shutting.

Dobrynya and Blud were shouting at each other again. Raef seemed somehow deeply interested in this. Finally, when it seemed the two might begin to hit each other, Volodymyr ordered Blud out, and the redheaded lordling flung himself away through the door. Volodymyr went back to his chair.

"Uncle. Blud is a boyar, he is my kinsman; someway, half the great men in the kingdom are related to him."

"I'll cut his tongue out," Dobrynya said, raging.

"Yet his tongue betrays him with the truth," Volodymyr said. "My grandmother told me when I was a child that to be a great king I must follow the god who can give me power above all other men, and every word from Blud's mouth, every deed of his, proves her true, that great old woman. As long as they can call on their own gods I am only one of them."

He nodded at Dobrynya. "And as you know, Uncle, I have been seeking for that god. I sent to the Khazars, and one of their rebbis came and told me about their Yahweh, and I sent to the Germans and they told me much, much about their Pope, and I sent to the Mahmettans and they told me about their Lah." He gave a little bow to Rashid, sitting beside the throne, who bowed stiffly back, his face gone rigid.

Conn remembered Magnus Redbeard in Holmgard saying something about this. But he was much more interested now in the screen, where he thought he saw an eye peeking out, and a little white hand, just for a moment, showing through the lattice. He nudged Raef, beside him, but Raef was intent on what Volodymyr was saying.

The prince was declaiming in a full round voice, proving something. "And as I look at the world I see what's there in front of me. There is only one man above all others in the world, and he is the Emperor, in Constantinople. All men know this. So it is his god I must seek, if I am to be supreme here. But I can't get him even to send me a messenger."

Conn nudged Raef a little harder, until his cousin's shaggy fair head swiveled toward him, and he nodded at him to look at the screen. Raef looked, and his eyes widened out like windows popping open.

He shot Conn a single, fierce, warning look, and turned back to Volodymyr, who was saying, "All others court me. Him only, whom I seek alone of them all, pays me no heed."

Dobrynya said, "My prince, you must capture his attention." He glanced at Rashid, sitting quietly on a cushion by the wall.

"My lord," Rashid said quietly, "I shall take my leave, as I see these are secret matters of the Rus'." His cheeks were red, and he went out the door. All around the room, the blue-coated guards stood motionless. Conn thought, briefly, that if Volodymyr and Dobrynya truly wanted this kept secret, sending the guards out would be a good idea too, but they stayed where they were. He glanced through the corner of his eye at the man by the door, whose name he thought he remembered—Ivor, or Oleg. The guard stood there utterly still, expressionless. Volodymyr was up out of his chair and pacing around. He went by the cold hearth and threw a twig on it, and came back toward Dobrynya.

"Capture his attention. How do you propose we do that?"

"I have an idea to force the Emperor to give you what you want," Dobrynya said. "I have brought here the men to make this idea work."

Conn turned toward the screen again, and Raef trod hard on his foot. Dobrynya stood in the midst of them all, saying, "This is what Sviatoslav realized, anyway—you cannot go humbly to this new god like a beggar. You must have signs from the Emperor that you are favored over all others." His hands came together, palm against palm. "The Emperor's own priest must baptise you, not some wandering monk."

"Yes," Volodymyr said. "But how?"

"And to show that you are above all others, the Emperor must give you his sister, a princess born to the purple, to be your bride, so you are brother to the Emperor himself."

"Yes!" Volodymyr stepped toward him, his face sharp, and his eyes glinting. "But how?" He gripped Dobrynya's hands.

His uncle smiled, as if he saw everything clearly as in daylight while everybody else fumbled through the dark. "My Knyaz, my nephew, if you want this baptism, and this bride, and all that comes with them, you must offer him something in return."

Volodymyr was watching Dobrynya steadily. "What can I offer him?"

Dobrynya said, "You will give him Chersonese, the heart of the Greek Sea."

Volodymyr's face fell a little, creases appearing like cracks between his eyes. "Chersonese! I don't have Chersonese!"

"But you will," Dobrynya said, and he swung out his arm, his hand aiming at Raef and Conn. "These men, and the rest of the Varanger, can get it for you."

"A walled city." Volodymyr's voice trembled a little. "A Greek city! My father never took a Greek city. But—" He glanced once at Raef and Conn and back at Dobrynya. "How do you propose we attack Chersonese? Not even the Khazars have ever taken it."

"Not by land," Dobrynya said. "Their wall is well fabled, high enough to hold out giants. But from the sea." His fist pounded into his open palm. "These men, here, can sail Sviatoslav's ships, and we can sweep into Chersonese harbor and storm the city from the water."

"Sviatoslav's ships," Volodymyr said, and raised his head, looking not at the men around him, but over their heads. "I will take my father's ships to war. I will sail on the Greek Sea, and force the Emperor to his knees." His voice was quiet, almost reverent. "I will make Kiev a new Constantinople!"

Dobrynya flexed at the waist into a bow. Raef did not move, nor Conn. Volodymyr wheeled around. His face was vivid with excitement. To Raef, he said, "Tomorrow, we will go down to the ships, and you can tell me what must be done to make them—"

He fumbled for a word, and Raef said, flat-voiced, "Seaworthy."

"Ah, yes. And you will have to teach us to use them again. But we are all river boatmen here from birth. It will not be hard." He swung toward Dobrynya. "We must talk."

Dobrynya rose from his bow as if on strings. Conn thought it was not he who was on strings. The posadnik said, "We will see you later, at the welcoming feast, all of you Varanger." He was shooing them out. Conn glanced once again at the screen and turned toward the door, Raef on his heels. For an instant as he went to the door he looked into the face of the blue-coated guard, Oleg, but the man stared straight ahead, no muscle moving. Conn went out.

CHAPTER TWELVE

Conn said, "I say we steal the ships. Why wait for them to con-
vince all the rest of their men? Especially that one, that Blud, he's
never going along with this. What was the name of that place—
Kersony?"

"Chersonese," Raef said.

"Have you heard of it before?"

"No."

They went through the courtyard, now empty of everybody but
a few servants hurrying around; one carried a platter of cooked
meat that left a mouthwatering trail in the air behind it. Conn
looked back at the building they had just left.

"There's your little black friend."

Raef glanced around. Rashid was at the far end of the building, talking to a blue-coated guard.

"I'll bet he knows all about Chersonese," Raef said. "I'll bet
he knows a lot more about all this than we do."

Conn followed him around the side of the great hall, looking
around; he thought of the screen in the Knyaz's palace, and the
murmurs and giggles behind it. The glimpse of a bright eye looking through it. They had to wait, at the gate, for a pack train of
goods coming in, three horses neck-roped together. Another
crowd waited just beyond for the chance to enter. Conn got into
the gate ahead of them and led the way out.

"Blud Sveneldsson. What kind of a name is that? They speak
dansker but they don't act like free men." Conn glanced around to
make sure nobody was listening. "They can't sail anymore. If you
ask me they're all Sclava."

Raef said, "They've been here awhile."

They went across the flat ground by the row of Sclava gods

and down the trail to their holding. The sun was midway down the western sky, shining into the ravine, gilding every leaf and flower. At the holding the rest of the Varanger were all crowded around the fire, passing a cup, and patting their stomachs. The food was gone. Janka sat in the doorway of the hut, and the hun woman was nowhere.

Leif was sitting alone on the big rock by the fire and Conn nudged him with his foot until he got up complaining and moved around to the ground. Conn took his place and moved over so that Raef could sit next to him; Raef craned his neck around toward Leif. "You said you'd been around here awhile. Who are these men in the blue coats?"

The cup came to Leif, who drank from it, wiped his mouth, and handed it up to Conn. "The Faithful Band. Volodymyr's guards. Their fathers all rode with Sviatoslav against the Khazars and the Bulgars and anybody else stupid enough not to run when they saw them coming. They were a tough bunch." Leif grinned. "What's it like, up there? Pretty fancy, I'm guessing. See any women? Volodymyr has lots of women."

"Sviatoslav followed Thor's way."

Leif grunted. "Who else? He was a viking, that one." He made the sign for Thor with his thumb and forefinger. "A lot of good men came down the river to join him."

"You knew him?"

"No, I came later, but I've heard the stories. Always at war. Always at the front of his men."

"Do you know somebody named Blud Sveneldsson?"

"I recognize the name. One of the boyars. From Rodno, west of here. He thought for a while maybe he could be Knyaz, until Volodymyr took it to him. Did you find out where we're sailing?"

"The Greeks," Raef said. "On the Greek Sea somewhere. What's a boyar?"

"They hold most of the land. Something like that. They all

claim they came in with Rurik, the first Varangian prince. There's some council where they all sit and try to tell the Knyaz what to do."

Conn noticed Raef hadn't mentioned the name of the city on the Greek Sea, which he himself had once more forgotten. Something red moved out on the hillside, and he looked off toward the trail up from the ravine.

"Here comes Pavo."

The Varanger all slewed around. Pavo was riding up the trail straight toward them, alone. His red shirt was dirty and scuffed at the hem and the cuffs. His scalplock was bound with a long strip of red cloth. He had his gaze pinned on Conn, and Conn sat where he was, his legs stretched out in front of him, and waited.

Pavo reined in on the trail at the end of the path down to the holding.

"Raven. You and me talk."

"Talk," Conn said. He did not stand up. Pavo's horse ducked its head and scratched its nose on its knee. The whip hung from its saddle pommel. It always burned Conn to remember that whip touching him.

Pavo said, "Someplace quiet."

"No," Conn said. "Here. They can hear anything I want to say."

Across the fire, Helgi grunted; he, Leif, Harald, and the rest sat there motionless, watching intently. Pavo swung down out of his saddle, let his reins trail, and paced along the path to them.

Conn still did not stand up. Pavo towered over him, his hands on his hips, and stared down at him. He said, "I no like you. You no like me."

"That's right," Conn said.

"Here, in Kiev, now—" Pavo shook his hands back and forth in front of him, flat. "No fight. Here, we like. Understand?"

Conn frowned at him; beside him, Raef was rigid, his arms folded over his chest and his long legs crossed at the ankles, as if he had tied himself in a knot, and his eyes looking anywhere but at Pavo. Conn said, "Truce, then. Is that what you mean?"

"Truce," Pavo said. He held out his hand.

Conn looked at him a moment, and then stood up and took it and shook it. "Truce. Why?"

Pavo lowered his hand to his side. "Blud," he said. He turned and walked back up the path toward his horse.

"Blud Sveneldsson," Leif said, and turned to give Raef a knowing look.

Helgi said, "What was that about?" The other Varanger began to murmur and talk among themselves. Conn sat down again, staring after Pavo, and lifted the cup to his mouth, but it was empty, and he put it down again.

Vagn said, "Don't trust him."

Raef gave a shake of his head. "What?" Conn said.

"He trusts us," Raef said. "I wish I knew what was going on here." His head swiveled toward Leif. "Somebody ruled here between Sviatoslav and Volodymyr. Another Knyaz. Some—" He struggled for the name. "Yaro."

"Yaropolk," Leif said. "I remember him. Volodymyr's older brother. Half brother."

"They threw him out?"

"Dobrynya and Volodymyr and a pack of Swedes Dobrynya brought in." Leif's forehead wrinkled. "Blud had something to do with it, too. They killed him. Yaropolk. Not in a battle—by treachery."

"Why?"

"He wanted to turn Christian."

"Hunh." Raef turned around and stared at Conn.

Conn said, "This gets more interesting all the time, doesn't it." He stood up. "I'm going to look around, I'll be back later."

Raef understood this, and scowled at him. He knew better than to say anything in front of all the other men, and Conn smiled at him and went on out to the main trail and back toward the palace.

The sprawling stockade with its heavy wooden wall covered most of the top of the bluff. He did not go through the gate, but made his way around the outside of the fence, trying to get somewhere that would be behind that latticework screen in Volodymyr's room. A long building blocked him, maybe a shambles since it stank of old blood, and he turned another way, and that pushed him off almost to the edge of the bluff, which ran here sheer down to the river.

He thought his own holding was well behind him, up the ravine to his left, maybe as much as a mile. The whole palace compound lay on his right. The wall came down here to the bluff and then turned right to follow the bluff's crumbling edge. Between that drop-off and the log wall were thickets of dusty brush. He made a way through them, following a path made by something much smaller than he was.

Finally the path ended at the wall, overgrown with vines. There was nowhere else to go, and he climbed up, pulling himself on the vines and finding toeholds on the logs, to the top.

The ends of the logs were hewn into sharp spikes. Directly below him anyway was a woodlot, with a gate opening inward, where anybody could walk through at any time; there was no one in sight now but an axe stuck up from a great stump in the middle and there were logs waiting to be split. He stayed down between two notches of the spiked wall to keep out of sight and looked as much as he could into the compound beyond the wood-lot fence.

There was the long thatch of the hall, the largest one, and beside it the two smaller rooflines, one the room where he had seen Volodymyr, the other the room from which the door had opened and closed, somebody had come in, not alone, and laid a little white hand on the lattice as she listened.

The sun was setting, but the summer twilight was almost like daylight. He crept along the outside the wall, staying below the top except every twenty feet or so, when he peeked over to get his bearings again. The bluff ran tight against the wall below him. If he fell he would fall all the way to the river hundreds of feet down. He moved carefully, feeling for each foothold, and sticking his knife into the wood sometimes for a handhold; the log wall was old, with knots and knotholes and chinks. Finally he came to a place behind that room, with Volodymyr's house beyond, and he peered between two logs, and saw a garden down there, with its own fence, nearly as high as this one, which met the fence he was climbing only a little way on from here.

Tall trees shaded it, and bushes made copses in it, among carefully tended patches of flowers. On the far side of the garden from him rose a white plastered wall, painted, like its side, with birds and deer.

He crept on a little way, to get past the garden fence, to where a huge tree grew up almost against the stockade wall. He climbed this tree much faster than the wall, and got up high above the garden, in among the leaf-shrouded branches.

One branch stretched out over the garden. He crawled out on it, and laid his head on his arm, smiling, because all around this sunny, secluded space, there were women.

Near the doorway through the Knyaz's wall, on a wooden platform, there was a fat woman in a glittering robe, surrounded by girls sitting below her, looking up at her, submissive. They were doing handwork, holding it up for the fat woman to admire, or poking through baskets for more thread. One of them was playing a kind of lute and singing.

Nearer to him three girls with long golden hair were throwing a ball back and forth. They wore only shifts of some thin stuff and he could see the curve of their breasts and their ripe sweet behinds when they moved. One stooped to pick up the ball, her back to him, and he murmured to himself, catching just a glimpse of fur beneath the hem of her shift. A baby cried somewhere, and up on the platform, some of the other girls began to sing along with the first. Two older women strolled by almost directly beneath him, talking; they too wore almost no clothes, and he looked down into the soft crevices between their breasts and longed to slide his hands in there, into that warm, motherly darkness.

Even this, just dreaming, was better than fighting the ugly hun woman. He waited until the two below him had passed by, looked carefully to see he was unwatched, and dropped into the garden, behind the flowering bushes along the foot of the wall.

He heard water running, and stooping behind the flowers he followed the liquid gurgle downhill a few steps, got down on hands and knees to creep under a bush, and froze.

In the clearing ahead of him, a spring ran out of the ground and filled a stone bowl. The grass grew lush and green all around it. A dense copse of bushes hid it from the rest of the garden. Sitting on the very edge of the pond, her feet in the water, was a girl, crying.

He sank down on his belly. He could not take his eyes from her. He had thought Alla was beautiful, with her golden hair and clear blue eyes. This girl before him was the very opposite—her hair was thick and black, her skin golden brown, her eyes dark as midnight. Beautiful as the starry sky at midnight. When she lifted her head, her huge eyes swimming with tears, all the grace in the world fit into that one gesture.

He dared not move. If she saw him she would scream, he would be finished. He lay on the ground and devoured her with his eyes. Her feet were bare—long, slim, brown feet with high arches, around the left ankle a thin chain of gold. He longed to stroke her ankle, to kiss her instep. To run his hand up the slender curve of her calf. He shut his eyes, willing the hard hot lance in his crotch to go soft.

When he opened his eyes, she was staring straight at him, through the leaves and flowers.

She said, "Who are you? How dare you come in here. You'll be killed if you're caught here."

He crawled out from under the bush and sat down on his heels before her. "Don't call, then. Just tell me why you're crying. You're too beautiful to cry." He smiled at her, glad to be this close to her.

Her eyes flashed, contemptuous of flattery; she sat up straight, her arms around her knees, and stared at him.

"I've seen you before," she said. She did not smile back, her face stiff and cold. She glanced over her shoulder, back toward the palace, and he tensed, thinking she would call for help. But she faced him again, her voice low. "I saw you today, with Dobrynya, in the council room."

Conn said, "I saw you there, too, through the screen. So I had to come find you. Tell me why you were crying, before."

Then tears spilled out of her eyes, and she sank down on the ground by the fountain and wept into her hands.

He licked his lips; she was too far away to touch, and he was afraid if he moved toward her she would run. He was battling the old urge to fall on her like a wolf and at the same time gather her up in his arms and cherish her. He waited until she had given up the first gush of her unhappiness. She lifted her head, her cheeks wet.

"Tell me," he said. He put out his hand to her, palm up.

She looked away, coming no closer. "Volodymyr. My husband. Not my husband. I have been here for more than a year and he has never called me to him since that first night."

"Then he's a fool. You are more beautiful than any of the others." He trembled to close in on her, but he kept himself where he was. He lowered his hand to his side.

She wheeled toward him, intense, leaning toward him. "You don't understand. You heard what he said today but you don't understand."

"Tell me, then."

She came a little closer, lowering her voice, almost within reach now. "Know this, then—I am Khazar. I came here to teach him to be a Jew, like us, but now, today, what you heard—he has rejected my god, and so he rejects me." The tears welled up in her eyes again; even in the deepening twilight he saw them glisten on her cheeks. "And I must live here all the rest of my days, with nothing. He never . . . no child, no love."

She buried her face in her hands again. Conn slid toward her, took hold of her wrists and when she flung up her head at his touch he kissed her.

Under his mouth he felt a sweet and ardent sudden longing, a woman awakened and left unsatisfied. He gave her back the hot promise of his lust, his lips parted, the tip of his tongue in her mouth. Then she was pushing him off.

"How dare you," she said, in a wooden voice. She turned away. "Go. I'll call out. Leave me alone."

He said, "You will have nothing, if you won't take what's offered to you. You are beautiful, and young, you should be loved, the way I can love you."

"Go. I'll call out." But she turned toward him, her eyes wide. Not crying now, her mouth soft where he had kissed it sweet again.

He said, "Call, then." He got to his feet. "I'll go. But I'll come back. Tell me your name."

Her lips trembled. Now she didn't want him to go. Her eyes brimmed with something eager, brighter than tears. He said, "Does Volodymyr remember your name?"

Her eyes blazed. She stood up, tall and slim as a wand, her body taut. "Rachel. My name is Rachel."

"My name is Conn." He turned to go, forcing himself, against all his desire, and looked back toward her and saw her leaning after him, her face naked with longing. He said, "Remember," and went back to the wall, jumped for the branch, and swung himself over.

The sun was going down. The tree shaded the outside of the

wall so that it was nearly dark, and slippery with moss. He made his way out going the opposite of the direction he had come in, guessing that the city was much nearer by this way, and after some patient groping along he found flat ground at the foot of the wall and walked around to within sight of the main gate, and the trails up and down.

He stood in the dark, collecting himself. He knew he would have her. She was beautiful, more beautiful than any woman he had ever seen, and she was royal, highborn, in every line of her the elegance of blood. And she was eager. A ripe, lusty woman had given him that kiss, eager for more. Rachel, he thought, like a prayer. Rachel. He did not want to go back in among the other men and he stayed in among the oak trees, remembering everything about her.

After Conn left, most of the other men got drunk and stumbled down the path to their huts by the time the sun went down. The long summer twilight began, the sky slowly deepening, darker and darker blue, the brightest stars glimmering overhead. A mist was rising from the ravine. Raef knocked the fire down and went toward the hut; he circled wide around the tethered mare, which kicked.

He went into the hut, expecting to find the hun woman gone, or sleeping with Janka, but Janka wasn't around, and the woman was sitting wrapped in a blanket in the corner. She watched him steadily. The long heavy rugs had been laid down in two piles against the two long walls, and cushions and blankets spread on them to make beds, his sea chest at the foot of one, Conn's at the foot of the other. The roof was better, also, almost completely thatched. In the middle of the room was a brazier full of coals, which gave a little reddish light.

Janka came in, carrying a bucket; seeing Raef, he looked around, and said, "No Raven?"

"No Raven," Raef said. "You have to settle for the Goose."

Janka laughed. He set down the bucket and went instantly into the little room at the back. Raef opened his sea chest, got out his fur cloak, and laid it on the bed. He kept his back to the woman in the corner. Stripping off his shirt, he lay down on the cloak. The rugs were softer than a sleeping bench, and he was a little drunk, and even with the stranger there in the room he began to doze. Then she was getting into the bed with him.

He wakened all over with a jolt. She was naked. She slid down beside him on the fur, the soft weight of her breasts against his chest, her thighs pushing against his. He said, "You're crazy, girl." He yanked down his drawers, cupped his hands over her rump, rolled onto her and fit himself into her like a key into a lock.

She groaned. Close to his face, she shut her eyes and turned her face away a little from him. He felt, suddenly, what she felt, the thrust up into her deep places, riving her open. Felt her pleasure in this. An ancient womanly itch scratched. All around his fierce pounding her softening fire. When he burst, he let out a howl for both of them.

She laughed, breathless, and said something he couldn't understand. He moved a little to let her out from under him, not tired anymore, wanting already to do it again. She was just as ready. She helped him pull the rest of his clothes off, took his hands and pressed them to her breasts. She slipped her knee between his thighs, her lips against his face, sucking on him. Drawing him into her. He launched himself into her again like an arrow.

After a good while of this, he slept, until Conn came in.

It was well into the night now. In the dark Raef heard his scraping footsteps come to a stop in the middle of the room. "What?"

Raef said, "It wasn't my idea." He had his arm around the hun woman and he pulled her in against his side.

Conn stood silent a moment in the darkness; finally he started to laugh. The woman crept closer to Raef, her head down. Conn's laughter filled the room, buoyant, and Raef began to laugh, too, under his breath. His cousin went across the room, to the other bed, and Raef heard him throw himself down, still laughing. A moment later he began to snore. Raef shut his eyes, the woman's scent in his nostrils.

CHAPTER THIRTEEN

Raef had had other women but never one who stayed, after, and tried to take care of him. He sat in the sun outside the hut, watching the hun woman drag out the bedding and shake it into the air. Under the ragged long shirt she wore, her legs were bare and brown. She planted her feet against the ground and shook the fur vigorously so that the dust flew from it, and she laughed.

Janka had been hauling in water for the horses, but now he swerved over past Raef. "I tell her you good. Raven not so good by her, but Goose good." He smiled. "She by you now. Make you wife."

Raef snorted at him. He understood this: If he protected her she would sleep with him and serve him. This seemed simple enough, a good bargain, and he said, "What's her name?"

Janka's eyes widened at this apparently unexpected question. He swiveled his head toward her and asked something in his blur of a language.

She answered, "Merike," and Janka said, "Merike," as if Raef couldn't have heard her without him.

"Tell her my name isn't Goose," Raef said. "Tell her my name is Raef."

Janka sent a flood of talk back over his shoulder, and the woman laughed again. She had a throaty, deep, lusty laugh. She was spreading the sleeping rugs out on the bushes so the sun would kill the fleas. Still holding the rug by one edge, she turned toward him, and said, "Raef."

He nodded at her. "Merike."

She broke into a broad toothy smile, her eyes shining, her face soft and round. She bent to gather the rest of the bedding, and he watched her backside swell her clothes with a new sense of ownership.

⸻◦⸻

Before noon Dobrynya came down and collected them all for the Knyaz's feast. They went up to the great hall in the palace, where already dozens of other men were gathered; Blud Sveneldsson was there, and some other boyars, each with his own following. They sat at great tables along the sides of the room, all the Varanger together on one long side, with Volodymyr on a higher seat on the short side to their right. Rashid sat on his right hand, but lower down, like an ordinary man. Even some of the blue-coated guards sat among them, on the short side opposite Volodymyr; other guards stood by the door and in the corners, as usual.

As soon as they were all gathered, servants brought around cups for all of them, and Volodymyr stood up and saluted them with a big golden chalice.

"We welcome the men from the land of our fathers! We welcome our brothers from the north!" He drained his cup, and everybody standing around the table gave a yell, and drank.

The servants came around filling the cups again. Nobody sat down. Volodymyr said, "I greet my brother Blud Sveneldsson! All honor to him, worthy son of his father!"

He drained his cup again. Raef realized they were going to have to drink to everybody here; he wondered if it would be an insult not to drain his cup at each salute, and certainly everybody else was, Leif on his left hand pouring the wotka straight down his throat, Conn already putting his down empty. Raef pretended to drink, but while no one was watching, he lowered the cup under the table and poured it out on the floor.

The servant came around again, filling up all the cups, all around the table. As this happened, a back door opened, and three women came quietly into the room behind Volodymyr, sat down on some cushions, and took up the tools for music—one had a pipe, and one a little drum, and one something that looked like an Irish harp but with far more strings, which she laid on her lap, and plucked with one hand, and tuned with the other.

He watched this with some interest, having always liked watching music made, and slowly he realized Conn was watching this woman too, but with a fierce heat. Raef kicked his cousin under the table, and Conn started a little, as if he had forgotten where he was. The woman was bent over her instrument; she seemed not to notice him.

Now Blud was on his feet, saluting Volodymyr, and they all drank, except Raef, who took one gulp, and then poured the cup out on the floor again. He hoped the carpet under him was thick.

They drank again and again, and now servants began to bring out platters of food, great dripping chunks of meat, baskets of bread, cheese in lumps and wheels. All around the room, the men lolled in their places, red-faced, shouting, laughing, and drinking more. A few got up and went outside and came back in again, walking unsteadily. Done eating, Raef set his elbows on the table, trying to hear the music. Then Volodymyr was on his feet again.

"We feast today in honor of our brothers from the north, but also to begin a new season of war."

That brought a yell from everybody in the room, even the guards by the door and in the corners, who shouted, and brandished their fists in the air. Volodymyr looked around at them all, smiling.

"We will conquer, again, as we have always conquered. We will bring glory to Kiev and to Rus' and to each other. And how better to start this than with a story of war? Who has a great story of battle and war to tell us?"

Somebody shouted, "Sviatoslav!" and someone else called out, "Rurik!"

Dobrynya stood up; he sat at the corner of the table where the Varanger sat, close by Volodymyr's left hand. He said, "Another tale! A new tale. We have all heard bits of news of a great battle in the north, last year, at a place called Hjorunga Bay—and some of these men fought there." He turned, looking down at Conn and Raef. "Tell us this story, you Corbanssons. Fire us with a tale of glory!"

The whole table fell momentarily silent, every gaze coming to Raef and Conn. Raef felt himself flushing, and he hoped nobody noticed the puddle under him. Then all around the table a call went up.

"Hjorunga Bay! Tell us what happened there!"

Raef turned to look at Conn, who sat there as these cheers rained down; Conn put his fists on the table in front of him, and waited until the uproar quieted.

He said, "I'll tell you about Hjorunga Bay, not because I want to make out that Raef and I were heroes, but because it was the end of the Jomsvikings, and they were the best men on earth."

All around the square of the tables, the men murmured, the words "Hjorunga" and "Jomsviking" going from lip to lip, and all eyes were fixed on Conn. Raef slid a little down the bench, putting more space around him, so nobody would be looking at him because of Conn. The music played quietly, so that Conn's voice was clear over it.

He said, "You all have heard of Sweyn Tjugas, the King of Denmark, who had a feud on with Hakon the Jarl, who ruled Norway. Sweyn thinks Norway should be his, and so he set a plot against Hakon, and the tools for his plot were the Jomsvikings."

A servant was coming along with more wotka, but Conn put his hand over his cup, and went on.

"The Jomsvikings were a brotherhood of warriors, who held all things equal and in common, and who fought together and never left any battle without the victory, and never left any Jomsviking in peril of his enemies. Only the best fighters could become Jomsvikings. They always elected their own captains, two for each ship, and after Palnitoki died, they didn't even bother to elect a new chief for all of them, but listened to each other and did what everybody agreed on."

Raef sat back a little. He did not remember this of the Jomsvikings, and he thought Conn had his own reasons for saying it. He could see Leif and Bjorn the Christian and Skinny Harald and the rest smiling and reaching out to each other. Even Vagn banged his cup with Harald's and Leif's and the others'. The Sclava lords, Dobrynya and Blud and the rest, sat still, listening, not smiling.

Conn went on. "They had their great fortress of the Jomsburg on a crag over the sea, in the territory of some little German king, but they had a connection with Sweyn because his foster father was Palnitoki, who called all free vikings to him in the Jomsburg, and gave the band its rule. So Sweyn called some of the Jomsvikings to a great feast he was having in Zealand, which is in Denmark, where he has a great feast hall, even bigger than this one.

"Sigvaldi went, and Bui, and some others, who the Jomsvikings sent in all their names. We were there, too, Raef and I, because Sweyn had given us ships, and honor, and called us his companions, since we had been with him before he was king and in fact he would not be king without us. But we didn't know he wanted us gone, and dead, if possible, because we would not kneel to him."

At that a growl went up from the Varangers. The Sclava made no sound, since kneeling and bowing was ordinary to them.

"So we all went into the feast hall, and we had good ale and mead to drink, and meat and bread, such as we have had here, and we feasted and drank until all of us were muddled. And then Sweyn got us into a contest, to see who would vow the greatest deed, and before anybody could stop him, Sigvaldi had sworn to take the Jomsvikings on a raid against Hakon the Jarl, in Norway."

He stopped and drank from his cup, and wiped his mouth. Nobody spoke.

"Then," he said, "like a drunken idiot, I agreed to go with him.

And Raef goes where I go, so we went off with the Jomsvikings to attack Hakon the Jarl."

Now some people were turning to look at Raef, and he lowered his eyes. He noticed that Conn had not mentioned the woman that he and Sweyn had been fighting with at the time, who was most of the reason; but they had been very drunk.

"So we raided along the coast of Norway, where there are villages and farms on every fjord. We had seventy ships and each ship was full of men. All the people fled as we came up but we burned homesteads and took every living thing away, cattle and slaves, and whatever we could find of gold and silver and fine cloth. Much of it we sent off to the Jomsburg, where it may be still, for all I know.

"But Hakon the Jarl heard we were coming, and he gathered all his men. Norway is a big country, and Hakon could call a lot of men together.

"We rounded the cape we call Stad, and put in on a little island, and someone captured a man from the shore. In return for his life this churl agreed to go find Hakon for us.

"Now among the Jomsvikings, no one lies, and we all counted it the best thing for a man to meet his enemies face-to-face and strike blows arm against arm, and maybe that's why we didn't think this churl would lie to us. Or maybe it was witchcraft. In any case, when we heard that Hakon was in Hjorunga Bay, just around the cape from us, without only a few ships, and a handful of men, we all got into our ships and sailed there."

Raef's hands had clenched on the table. He remembered how he had felt, before this battle, and how he had been afraid to tell anybody, for fear of what they would think of him. And even knowing what he knew, he had still gone. Had he told them, they would all still have gone, battle-mad and roaring. Better to die than waver.

"It was a bright, hot, sunny day, and many of us had our shirts off because of the heat. And we rowed into the bay, and there in front of us, and on either side of us, were hundreds of Hakon's ships."

"Now, no Jomsviking will leave the battle without the victory, as I said, and so we attacked them. Hakon the Jarl lined all his ships up before us and we tied our ships together with hawsers in a line, and rowed straight at the middle of them. First we threw spears and shot arrows, and when the ships lapped, we fought hand-to-hand, battling back and forth. And in the middle of Hakon's line, we fought so hard and so well that we cleared Hakon's own ship as far as the mast, and we were clearing the ships beside his, too, even though we were outnumbered.

"Then Hakon broke off the fighting, and pulled his ships back, so that he could save them. And we drew back also, to keep from being separated from our line, and the battle stopped for a while.

"Now, when this happened, the day was still fine, and the sun shone. We grouped our ships together, and all we Jomsvikings ate and drank and got ready for the battle to begin again. But Hakon the Jarl had other ideas.

"It's well known that Hakon has the favor of a certain ogress, whose shrine is in a forest not far from the shore of Hjorunga Bay. He went into this forest and called the ogress to him, to give him the victory. But she was angry with him. Maybe he had not been faithful. There was some talk he had let Harald Bluetooth sprinkle the water on him. He begged and pleaded with her, but she refused to help him.

"Then he offered her gold, all the gold he had, but she still refused.

"Then he offered her sacrifices, nine white horses, shod and bridled in gold, but she refused.

"Then he offered her greater sacrifices, nine men, whose blood he would spill here, in her own grove, and hang their bodies from the trees to feed Odin's birds, but still she refused."

Conn stopped. The hall was utterly still. Volodymyr was canted forward, his eyes blazing. Beside him Rashid had a frown on his face. Behind all the gathered men, Raef could see other people creeping into the doorways to listen—the women, and the servants. Conn looked all around at them, from face to face.

"Then," he said, "he offered her the sacrifice of his own son, his youngest boy, whom he loved dearest of all his children. And this she accepted."

A gasp went up, all around. Among the women, one gasped, and the music jangled out of tune. Conn nodded. "And so it was. Hakon's slave took the boy right away and cut his throat."

Another gasp, and a moan, and Raef thought, pleased, that this was a good revenge; ever after, these people would remember nothing of Hakon save this sacrifice.

"So then Hakon went back to his ships. And the battle began again.

"But now the sky was turning dark. Great black thunderclouds rolled up across it. The rain began to pound down on us. The two lines of ships joined, and we fought with spears and stones and hand-to-hand, striving to leap onto the ship in front, and drive all our enemies off. But when we threw spears the great wind turned them back into our faces, and when we shot arrows they came back into our faces.

"Then on Hakon's ship, straight before me, I saw the ogress herself. And she was twice as tall as a man, and twice as broad, and she had three eyes and three mouths, and a tongue sticking out of every mouth. She flung out her hands toward us, and from each finger arrows flew, one after another, so the men around me went down like mown hay.

"We fought on—I got onto the ship next to Hakon's, and Raef with me, and many other Jomsvikings, and we were forcing our way down that ship when in front of us suddenly there was another ogress, just as big and ugly as the first, and she stretched her hands out, and from each finger arrows flew, and shot men down.

"Lightning crashed, and the thunder was so loud nobody

could hear anything. After being so hot it was cold as winter now, and from the sky came hailstones the size of men's heads.

"We could not stand against the work of two ogresses. We backed up, we yielded, it humiliates me even as I say it, but we took all our men with us, not a Jomsviking did we leave behind us on that enemy ship, but got all back onto our own ships. Then Hakon charged us. We fought, Raef and I, back-to-back, against thirty of them, but then a hailstone as big as a horse hit our ship and holed her, and she went down in an instant.

"We swam to a rock. Many other Jomsvikings were leaping into the sea, as Hakon's men with the ogresses behind him swarmed over their ships, and as the hailstones smashed down. The rain pelted us. It was cold and I thought we would drown there.

"But Hakon came for us, and he dragged all of us—what was left of the Jomsvikings, maybe seventy men—up on the shore. They tied us all together in a line, and Hakon bid one of his men to cut all our heads off.

"This man's name was Thorkel Leira, and he was a base and evil man. He started by killing three men who were already dying of their wounds.

"The rest of us were still lively, and we all started in calling insults to Thorkel, for being such a coward, and killing wounded men. He did it thus: he got a slave to take a stick and wind it in the hair of the man he was going to kill, and thus stretch his neck out, while he knelt helpless on the ground, and then with his sword Thorkel sliced his head off. It was like killing sheep.

"All the Jomsvikings began to jeer at Thorkel; Hakon and his sons were looking on, his oldest son Eric, who was a Jarl also, and the rest of Hakon's best men. Hakon said, 'Kill these live ones, Thorkel, I want to see if they face death as bravely as they all say.'

"And the Jomsvikings now began to try to outdo themselves in bravery. The first two went straight up to be killed as if they were going to a marriage feast, while we waiting in line taunted Thorkel for his clumsy strokes. They were coming closer to me and Raef, but also, we Jomsvikings were all making such an uproar at Thorkel that I could see he was getting rattled. Even Eric the Jarl was laughing at him. He was still cutting off heads, but he stopped, in between, to bellow back at us, and his face was red and his hands shook. Twice he missed the blow, and struck the man he was hitting in the skull, or across the shoulders, and had to do it over again.

"Somebody called out if he was so bad with his sword he must be just as bad in bed, which was why his wife was so eager to have all of us. Then we all started shouting how we had fucked his wife, and added in some details of her and that, and how excited our long swords had made her.

"Now I was next, and they cut me loose from the rope to take up to Thorkel, but then Raef called out—" Conn turned and grinned at him. "Raef said he could not bear to see me die, and so Thorkel should kill him first."

Raef grunted at him. This part at least was true, although his intention had been only to stall against the inevitable. He sank his head down between his shoulders, feeling all the eyes in the room turn on him again.

Conn went on. "And then Hakon recognized us. He knew our father, see, and he had had some business with Corban, and now he called to Thorkel to watch out for us, and kill us quick, because we were wizard-wise. But Thorkel had already given the order to cut Raef loose, too, and lead him forward.

"So we were both loose from the other Jomsvikings, but nobody noticed, or tied me up again. Our hands were bound behind us but our feet were free. Then Raef—"

He grinned at Raef again, and Raef put his hands over his face.

"Raef has long beautiful hair, you see—" There was a general laugh at this; Raef's hair, he knew, was hardly beautiful, even if it was long. "And he said he didn't want it tangled up in that filthy stick—he can talk, you see, when he has to. Then someone of Thorkel's men came forward and offered to hold his hair out of the way, and Raef knelt down and the man took his long hair and pulled his head out, his neck stretched, like the others, and I thought I would see him dead in front of me.

"So as Thorkel's sword swung, I sprang forward. But as the sword swung, so also did Raef jump backward, and he jerked his neck out from under the fall of the blade, and pulled the man's hands in his hair under it, so the blade struck through both his wrists.

"Thorkel saw this happening, and tried to pull out of the stroke, but as he did I hit him from the side, so hard he went down and his sword fell. Then Raef and I were scrambling toward the sword, and I was loose and had the sword and killed Thorkel there before he even got to his feet."

A roar went up from men around the table. Many pounded their fists on the table, so that the cups jumped, and the knives bounced. Raef looked up out of his hands; to his relief he saw everybody was watching Conn now.

"Then Hakon's son Eric the Jarl said he thought Thorkel had got what was due him, and anyhow, he said, it was getting dark, and we should stop this. Then Hakon himself said that he was remembering that what had befallen him with Corban Loosestrife had not been all bad, and he offered to let us go, if we fought for him.

"Then we said we would not take our freedom unless all the rest of the Jomsvikings got theirs also. So Eric the Jarl offered them all to come into his ships, and be his men. They wanted us to join them, but we wouldn't, and we swore to Hakon we would not fight again for Sweyn Tjugas against him, and then we came east. And here we are."

Volodymyr said, "That is a story for a hall full of warriors, and for the beginning of a great war. You are great men."

"We are only men," Conn said. "It was all of us, the Jomsvikings, all together. We all made Thorkel die and got our freedom back. I just wielded the sword, by chance. But now the Jomsvikings are gone, there are no such men as them anymore."

He lifted his cup, though, and saluted the men of his band, and they all whooped and drank to him.

Blud stood up, swaying a little, flushed red with drink. He said, "In this tale I hear what power there is in our gods, and what evil befalls men who turn to the Christ!"

Volodymyr's head swung toward him. "What I hear is that when men stand together, and act as one, they can do anything."

Blud said, "Do you deny you want to overthrow the gods? Do you deny you favor the Christ?"

All around the tables of loud and drunken men, many paid no heed to this, but here and there, heads went up, and listened. The guardsmen opposite Volodymyr all looked up sharply, listening.

"The old gods are many, and they scatter everything among them. Christ is one," Volodymyr said. "As we must all be one, to make Rus' great." When Blud started to shout again he slashed his hand through the air. "I will talk no more of this. Let's sit and drink and eat and listen to music." He swept his gaze around the table, and they all quieted. The music went jingling on, strange and harsh. The servant went swiftly around again with the ewer, filling cups, and this time, Raef drank his down all the way.

CHAPTER FOURTEEN

Around sundown, the feast was over, and the Varanger all left the hall. Down at their holding, Conn set a fire and lit it, and everybody gathered around it, Helgi, Leif, Vagn, and the others. Vagn had brought a jug of wotka down from the hall. They all settled down, as the long summer night fell softly down outside the glow of the fire, and passed the jug. Raef saw the men watching Merike and caught her eye and jerked his head toward the hut, and she went in.

Conn poked at the fire with a stick, watching the flames burst up. "There is more going on here than we were told, coming into it."

Several of them grunted in agreement. Leif said, "Novgorod was always Volodymyr's city. But here, obviously, he has rivals."

"More than rivals," Bjorn said.

Skinny Harald sat across the fire from Conn, with his knees drawn up, his arms crossed over his legs. "I've been hearing a lot from the Faithful Band. They're all Thor's men, Perun they call him here, and they don't want to walk into the water. And they hate Dobrynya."

"The Faithful Band," Conn said. "You mean the men in the blue coats."

"The Knyaz's guards, yes. They're all around Volodymyr, all the time. When they're not they loaf around the wotka shops, down by the river, and I've run into a few. The local people don't like them much, either."

Black-haired scrawny Vagn said, "I've noticed that. But they're afraid of them. They all think they're Varanger still."

"They're not," Conn said. "Or they wouldn't stand in corners like servants. I saw how the local people love Dobrynya, and he isn't even from here. What about Blud Sveneldsson?"

Leif said, "You saw him. He wants to be Knyaz, that's plain. But if he could be, he would be already. He had some connection with this Knyaz's father, who was all Varanger, for all he had a funny name. But that's the trouble, likely—Volodymyr being half Sclava."

"Dobrynya's half," said Vagn.

Raef said, "There's more to it than even that, anyway. Volodymyr wants to be greater than Knyaz, and he will throw everybody else into a snake pit to get there."

Conn's nose wrinkled up. Raef knew this was too tangled and messy for his taste. Conn said, "Whatever happens, I swore myself to Dobrynya, and I'm keeping to that. That's the way to keep this straight." His gaze swept the circle of firelit faces. "Anybody disagree?"

Leif said, "No, no, we're all with you, Conn," and the others chorused in, nodding their heads, and Vagn clapped his hands together.

Conn said, "Good. Because there are six ships down there on the riverbank. That means, stuffed to the gunwales, three hundred and sixty men, likely considerably less. There's the nine of us. Pavo has another sixty, seventy men. The rest have to come from somewhere, and we'd better be sure they're on our side when our backs are to them."

The others growled and grumbled; Vagn said, "If our side is Dobrynya's side, I can tell you already one or two who are not."

Helgi said, "I'm not so sure of Pavo," and a couple of other voices agreed.

Vagn said, "That could have been another of his tricks, coming here."

Conn's brow wrinkled; he said, "I think Pavo's with us, at least while we're in Kiev and Blud's around." He turned toward Raef, his eyes disturbed. "Is he?"

"Pavo's good," Raef said. "He's nothing without Dobrynya."

"That's the trouble." Conn went back to stabbing and poking

at the fire, showering up sparks that crackled and snapped in the air. "Once you mistrust one you mistrust everybody. That's why we have to be together. Nine of us—that's a sign, isn't it? Nine's a lucky number. And all one in a fight."

He stretched his hands out to either side. Raef took hold of him, and reached out his other hand and took Leif's. He saw them all join hands, the ring unbroken, and for a moment no one spoke; they only sat there together. They let go, and the wotka jug came around again, and they talked about other things.

In the morning Conn went off to his prowling, and Raef sat in the sun before the hut, listening to Merike clean up inside. Rashid came down the path toward him.

He had gotten new clothes. His headcloth was white as salt, his flowing gown spotless. His pen case hung at his side. He came up to Raef and said, "Well, you are situated very nicely," not meeting Raef's eyes.

Raef moved off the stone, to give him somewhere to sit where he wouldn't get dirty. "Sit down. I haven't seen you in a while. Merike! Bring me the jug."

Rashid made himself comfortable on the rock. Raef sat on his heels next to him. The Baghdad man stroked his tidy little beard. "I have been at court," he said. "Hoping to change Volodymyr's mind." He sighed. "So blind the man who sees only what he wants to see."

Merike came out with the wotka; Rashid's brows flew down, and he watched her come and go with a frown. When Raef offered him the jug, he said, "No, no. That is forbidden me. You have a servant?"

"I have a wife," Raef said, thinking that funny.

Rashid did not; he snorted, disdainful, and looked down his nose. "God erred when he made women." He looked up finally into

Raef's face and said, "Heed me, my young friend, there's trouble. Blud is talking to the other pagans. Nobody wants the Greek Christ."

Raef said, "Really," as if he hadn't already known this. "What do you think will happen?"

"At the very least they will try to overthrow him." Rashid was looking around him again, not at Raef.

"When?" Raef said, wondering if he knew anything exactly.

The Baghdad man shrugged. "I hear only rumors. I am leaving soon, I have come also to say good-bye."

"Where are you going?"

"I am taking a ship down to the sea, and then to Baghdad."

Raef said the usual farewells, wishing him a safe journey, and the favor of his king. He said, "On the way, will you go to Chersonese?"

Rashid stiffened, resisting, as if he had something to protect, and his head tilted to one side, his eyes elsewhere. "Probably. I shall have to stop various places, surely." He swallowed. "Chersonese is a good place to stop, you see, being where it is."

"Where is it?" Raef asked.

He was watching Rashid intently; he saw how the Baghdad man wanted to say nothing, but it was not in him to say nothing. He said, "I am sure you have seen the chart that Volodymyr has. There is an island, a sort of island, Taurica, at the north edge of the sea, east of where the river here runs into the sea. And Chersonese is there, on the bottom edge of Taurica. The heart of the sea." He licked his lips. "I am telling you too much."

Raef laughed. "Why? Can there be too much knowledge? You could make me a little picture, like that other one."

Rashid said, abruptly, "Never mind. I shall say good-bye." He got to his feet to leave.

Raef thought of something. "Wait. I want to give you something." He fingered into his belt pouch for the gold basileus. Holding it to the sunlight, he spat on it, and rubbed it with his thumb, as if to make it shinier. Then he held it out to Rashid.

Rashid's face softened, seeing this as a gift. "Then I will give you something also." He pursed his lips, his cheeks drawn, and then took a ring from the little finger of his left hand, and offered it.

Raef accepted it with a smile, a gold circlet, cut with runes, like wearable money. Rashid said, "I know you are suspicious of my intentions, my young friend, but I think very kindly of you. I wish the best for you." They said good-bye again, not shaking hands, and Rashid went on up the trail toward the palace, white as a lily among the dusty green.

Janka came up. "You friend him?"

Raef shook his head. "Once. Not really. I thought he was. But he's a spy."

Janka frowned, puzzled. Finally, he went back to the start. "You not friend? Why give him that?"

"I'll get it back," Raef said. "When I find him again." He took the ring and studied it, wondering if it had some power. His mother would have known. He thought it was just a ring: for all Rashid's talk about his god, it was his king he served, in Baghdad.

He wondered if there was a god, anywhere, who was not someone's imagined thing.

"Find him again," Janka said, tentatively.

"Yes. In Chersonese." Raef held up the ring at arm's length, and looked through it up the hill; within the circle of the ring, the path, a few trees, some grass and sky seemed like a tiny world. He turned, saw Merike coming out of the hut, and put her face into the center of the ring.

He said, "Come," and beckoned to her, and she came to him, sturdy, brown, trusting. He took her hand and put the ring on her palm. "Here. Take. Yours."

She gave a little chirp of amazement. He got up and went up past Janka, onto the path up the slope, to find Conn.

⇒§⇐

In the cool of the morning, Conn went by his secret way into the garden. The woman Rachel was there by the pool, and he went to her without a word and kissed her.

She let him taste the sweetness of her mouth, her eyes shut, her body pliant in his arms, but when he tried to put his hands inside her clothes, she pushed away.

She said, "I will give you what you want, but only if you help me escape from here."

He sat back on his heels, disappointed. What had seemed easy and free vanished into the clutter of some bargain. He ran his gaze over her face, the perfect skin, the ripeness of her lips. Her black eyes were steady on his. Her hands rested on the thighs of her red trousers.

All she had to do was scream, and this was over; he could not force her. He said, "What do you mean?"

"Take me away," she said. "Take me back to Khazaria, to my own city there, and I will make you a prince among my people, and marry you forever. As I love Yahweh I promise this."

"I can't do that," he said.

She leaned toward him, showing him the round honey-colored tops of her breasts. "Please. I promise you, I can do everything I say. You will be rich. The Khagan is my uncle."

"I gave Dobrynya my pledge, that I would follow him," Conn said. He looked down the front of her clothes, and licked his lips, but then he raised his gaze to her face. "I can't, Rachel."

"He is betraying you!" she cried. "He is giving you to a brass-bellied idol of a god, that will burn up even your soul!"

"That doesn't matter," Conn said. "I gave him my pledge."

From behind the hedges, a girl called, "Rachel?"

He got quickly to his feet. Rachel rose also, her hands out, and her face suddenly softer, no longer bargaining. "Please—come back—"

"Someone's coming," he said, and went over the fence like a lizard up a rock.

He stood on the other side, his heart pounding, clinging to the wood with fingers and toes. He heard, in there, the brush rustling, and then a breathless unknown girl's voice said, "Were you talking to someone?"

"No," Rachel said, flatly.

"I thought I heard you say something."

"No. There's a sprite in the fountain. I talk to it sometimes."

"Ah. You silly." The unknown girl laughed. "There's no sprite." Rachel gave a muffled sob, or maybe a growl. Conn crept away along the wall and left.

———

With Dobrynya and the Knyaz Volodymyr, all nine of the Varanger went down to the marketplace by the river, to look over the new ships. It was a bright, windy day, and the market was full of sellers and buyers, a great bustle of a crowd going from stall to stall and basket to basket, trotting horses up and down, and looking over the slaves in their pen. When Volodymyr rode through on his prancing black horse, the whole crowd let up a whoosh of excitement, and bowed down to him.

He raised his hand and said some words to them. Conn kept his eyes away from the prince; he followed Raef around the ships. Someone had been keeping them well. They were caulked and scraped, every strake perfect against its neighbor, the keels broad and straight, their dragon heads and tails inside the stems. Raef could not keep his hands off them. There were no masts, although the ships were fitted for them. He doubted finding masts would be a problem here.

Conn was not thinking of the ships. He was watching Volodymyr, whose wife he longed to take in his arms. He had no such love for Volodymyr as he had for Thorfinn. And Rachel was not Alla.

He brought himself back to where he was standing, next to a

dragon, with Vagn beside him, and Raef farther down the row. "We made a ship like this once," Conn said to Vagn. "My father's ship. But that was an oceangoing ship."

Vagn scratched in his scraggly beard. "You made a ship?" He put out his hand to the steerboard in front of them. The broad blade, slightly curved at the outer edge, was mounted on a pivot on the ship's side, part of the third rib; the old wood was weathered silver-gray. The crutch for the mast stood up like a little idol in the middle.

A great cheer went up from the crowd; Volodymyr rode over closer to the ships and dismounted. One of his crowd of blue-coated guards came up to lead away his horse. Conn leaned on the dragon's hull, watching the Knyaz, thinking about Rachel again. A great mass of the blue coats stood around him, and Dobrynya beside him, the prince slender and straight as a mast in their midst.

He and Dobrynya stepped forward and climbed up the cradle into the first ship and walked toward the bow, talking. The blue coats moved to form a ring around the ships, standing with their backs to them, watching the crowds; many people had come over to gawk at the prince.

The Varanger wandered around the ships, inside the circle of the guards. Conn kept his eyes away from the Knyaz, whose wife he wanted so much it burned a hole through his mind and would not let him think of anything else. Volodymyr would likely kill him, if he found out, or try to. He played with the idea of letting him find out. Maybe then Dobrynya would release him, somehow, from his pledge.

Raef had gotten up onto one ship, going into the stern, and Conn followed him. The ship was a little tender in the cradle and rocked under his step. The floor looked like new wood. The oars were shipped in neat lines against the inside of the hull. Conn cast a glance over his shoulder. Volodymyr and Dobrynya stood in the forecastle, and Volodymyr thrust his arm out straight ahead of him. The wind blew his yellow hair out like a flag.

"What do you think?" Conn turned back to Raef.

"This ship feels good," Raef said. His face was bright, and he had his hand on the steerboard, as if he could sail through the air. Underfoot the hull of the ship trembled a little. Dobrynya was coming toward them, veiled in his usual smile. Behind him, Volodymyr turned and waved, and in the marketplace people cheered him. He came down through the waist of the ship, his long hair and his black coat whipping in the wind. Conn pushed into the very stern, and looked at Dobrynya, to avoid Volodymyr.

Dobrynya said, "You will be glad to know this. Volodymyr has said we will sail within the month. You shall each command a ship. I—"

Raef gave a bellow, and flung himself forward, throwing Dobrynya to one side; he crashed into Volodymyr, in the stem of the ship, and bore him down like a wolf on a deer. The crowd let up a many-voiced shriek of terror, and then a flight of arrows pelted into the ship.

Conn shouted, "Varanger! Varanger!" He had no sword; he turned to the steerboard and wrenched the tiller bar out of its socket just as blue-coated men swarmed up over both sides of the ship and leapt at him.

Dobrynya flung his arms up. "Hold!" he cried, and one of the blue-coated guards smashed him down.

Conn laid around him with the wooden handle of the steerboard, knocked one man flying over the side, and drove two more after. But they were coming too fast. Six feet from him, Raef had gotten up, looking around wildly for a weapon. Volodymyr lay at his feet. All around them, the blue coats were scrambling up over the gunwales, knives and swords in their hands, going for the Knyaz. Lashing out from side to side with the club, Conn bounded toward Raef.

"Goose! Goose!"

The crowd was shrieking and churning around him, many trying to get away, and others rushing toward the ship. Raef wheeled toward the sound of his name; Vagn hurled a sword hilt-first toward him, and he caught it out of the air.

Conn reached him in another step and they swung back-to-back. A helmeted head surged up over the gunwale directly in front of Conn, and he smashed it with his club. A wild ecstasy rushed through him and came out as a scream. With Raef behind him he could fight anybody. The ship rolled suddenly, so that he stumbled to one knee. Down the length of the ship he saw that Vagn and Helgi were fighting their way up onto the hull. Over his shoulder he saw Raef's long sword flash.

"Watch up!" Raef yelled.

Conn threw himself down flat, and another cascade of arrows rattled past him. Down in the stern Dobrynya still lay motionless. Beside Conn, Raef crouched, the sword low across his body; Volodymyr was at his feet, trying to get up, and Raef thrust him down hard with his free hand. Beyond him Vagn and Helgi together hurled a blue-coated guard over the gunwale.

The ship rocked violently back and forth, at each swing about to tip over.

Conn roared up onto his feet again, and leaned over the higher side as it swayed down again, and smashed with his club at the men around the cradle. He knocked one flying, but the others got their shoulders to the ship again and heaved, and Conn felt the hull rear up and then roll with a crash off the cradle. He fell backward into a mass of bodies. He twisted around out onto the ground and got up with Helgi on one side and Raef on the other and a solid mass of blue coats charging them.

The ship was behind him, standing on its side now like an incurved wall. Before him the guards came in a single lunge. He swung the club around him, aiming for knees, and the first rush faltered.

Volodymyr reared up beside him, a little belt knife in his hand, and his face dark with rage. "Come get me, you pig-hearted traitors!"

Someone was shouting in Sclava, over and over, the same

words. Two men in blue, with dusty helmets, rushed straight for the prince, and Conn swung his club around and laid the nearer one down like a chopped tree, but the other cried, "No—no—I'm with you—" He knelt before the Knyaz, offering up his sword. Before Volodymyr could take it, another blue coat, coming after, chopped an axe down into the kneeling man's back.

Conn bellowed, bounded forward, and drove the blunt end of the club into the axeman's chest. Blood spurted into his face. For an instant he could see nothing but the swarming blue, the helmets, swords slicing at him, everything through a mist of red. He staggered back into the shelter of the tipped-over ship.

Beside him, Volodymyr shouted, "Pavo! To me!"

Under Conn's feet the wooden hull rocked, and he wheeled around and saw a helmeted man scrambling up over the wooden wall above his head. One hand gripped the gunwale and the other hand held an axe. Conn swatted the axe away and laid the club against the side of the helmet so hard it flew off into the air. The body slumped down over the gunwale, arms loose.

"Pavo!" A dozen voices were yelling, all at once. "Pavo!"

A horn blew. Around either side of the fallen ship a torrent of horsemen galloped. Abruptly the mass of fighters before Conn was churning in the opposite direction. Half of them were running and the other half were chasing them. Conn straightened, panting. Volodymyr strode out from the shelter of the ship, raised the sword in his hand, and shouted something triumphant.

Raef knelt down next to Dobrynya. There was nobody left to fight. The broad marketplace before them was rapidly emptying. Pavo with his whip coiling out before him was galloping across it, sending his horsemen after anybody who lagged. In among the stalls, the shops and pens, people crowded tight as chicks, trying to hide. The whip cracked like a clap of thunder.

Volodymyr shouted, "Get them! Get them all!" Then he wheeled around, crying, "Uncle Dobry." He fell to his knees next to the Sclava lord. "Dobry!"

Dobrynya was rousing. He pushed himself up onto hands and knees inside the curve of the fallen ship, and heaved himself out over the gunwale. Still on all fours he vomited onto the ground. Raef stood back, his chest pumping, the sword hanging in his hand. Blood dripped down off the tip into the dust. He turned to Conn, and put his free hand out, and Conn reached out and gripped his hand, one strong hard clench of fists.

Pavo jogged up toward them and flung himself out of the saddle. "Lord." Volodymyr had gone to stand beside Dobrynya, who was slowly climbing to his feet, his face green, and not smiling. Pavo knelt down before them.

Dobrynya put one hand on the Tishats's head, and spoke into his ear. Beside him, Volodymyr suddenly thrust his sword up into the air.

"I have triumphed," he shouted. "I have won, here, again! Let no one doubt me!" He turned in a circle, as if he spoke in the midst of a great solemn crowd. Around him were only the battered, breathless Varanger, the bodies of his guards, the terrified people hiding in the crevices. "I am lord!"

A few of them knew to give up an answering cheer, no louder than the wind. Some began to creep bravely out into the open.

Conn climbed out of the fallen ship, braced on its side against the cradle behind it. At his feet lay the body of the blue-coated guard who had given his life to offer a weapon to Volodymyr. He stood there a moment, wanting to honor this, too tired to know how. Among the growing crowd cheering Volodymyr he thought were likely some of the men who had just tried to kill him. He took another step forward, and, startled, realized he had an arrow through his calf.

The other Varanger surrounded him, gripping each other's hands, and nodding and looking each other deeply in the eye. Raef draped his arm over Conn's shoulder; he struck Vagn in the chest with his other fist. "Thanks."

Vagn scratched at his beard, ducking his head down, red

around the ears, and muttered something. Helgi was staring up at Volodymyr, who had climbed up onto the fallen ship to shout and cheer with his people.

"We got them before Pavo got here; look, he's going to get all the shine for this."

Conn sat down in the dirt. He wasn't sure they would have won without Pavo. "Help me," he said, and took hold of the arrow. Leif squatted beside him with a knife, and cut his boot apart; Raef was still looking all around them, watching out for another attack. Conn gasped at the sharp bite of the knife, and Leif pulled the arrow out.

Volodymyr rode off in a swarm of Sclava horsemen. The wailing, restless crowd followed them, going up toward the palace. Bodies lay on the marketplace. Blood puddled on the ground. Raef bent on one side of Conn, and Helgi on the other, and they lifted him up between them on the chair of their arms and carried him away to their holding.

CHAPTER FIFTEEN

Raef's hun woman sewed up the slice in Conn's leg with an awl and some hairs from the mare's mane; he sat by the fire in front of the holding breathing evenly through his nostrils while she pushed the needle in and out of his skin. Every few moments Raef or Helgi or somebody else in the cluster of men standing around came over and poured wotka over the wound. The other Varanger had come through the fight with nothing but bangs and bruises.

"They were all going for Volodymyr," Leif said. "They didn't stop to try to kill us. They're a single-minded bunch. What do we do now?"

Conn said, "That depends on Dobrynya." He intercepted the jug of wotka and poured some down his throat. The sun was going down and he was hungry. "Get this fire built—Raef! Does this woman cook?"

Raef turned and gave him the broadest smile Conn had ever seen on his face. Helgi said, "I brought a boiled haunch down from the palace. Where's that grill?" Vagn and Skinny Harald were bent together over the firepit; Vagn snapped flint and steel together in the shelter of Harald's cupped hands.

"Hold," Leif said. "I think we're being visited."

Conn turned to look over his shoulder up the path. Down from the top of the bluff came Dobrynya, looking much sounder, Pavo on his heels, and three Sclava fighters behind them, carrying broadswords and big axes. Conn guessed Dobrynya would not be going around much without guards now.

He shifted his weight a little on the log he was sitting on and said, "Excuse me from getting up. My leg's a little sore."

Dobrynya came in among them. The sudden burst of firelight

glittered on his golden clothes. He said, "I think I owe my life to you, Varanger. Certainly Volodymyr's life."

The men around the fire muttered and shifted their feet. Conn said, "The Tishats saved us all, I think." He jogged his head toward Pavo, on the path. He looked back up at Dobrynya. "Sit down, will you, you're hurting my neck. Where is Blud Sveneldsson?"

Dobrynya laughed. "Nobody's ever taught you to talk gently, Raven. I will sit." He looked around, and two of his guards dragged up a log for him. The other Varanger went back to spreading the fire and laying down the grill. The jug came by, full again.

Dobrynya took a drink of it and passed it back to Pavo. "Blud is gone. He left this morning, he sneaked out of Kiev without anybody knowing. He has gone back to Rodno. Likely he expected to have a summons to come back, and become Knyaz, but that will not happen."

"What about the ship?" Raef said.

"The ship is sound. We got it back on the cradle before sundown. My news is this. Volodymyr believes this was a sign from God. There is only one way he had become truly master of Kiev, of all Rus'. We are setting sail against Chersonese as soon as we have the ships in the water and well rigged and the proper ceremonies conducted."

"You'd leave the place to Blud?" Raef said.

"When we come back victorious and with the Emperor's blessing Blud won't matter anymore."

Conn took a long pull on the jug. The smell of the roasting meat began to reach him and his belly growled. He said, "I'll be glad to be out of here," and Raef gave a grunt of agreement.

"I think so will Volodymyr," Dobrynya said. His gaze went around the fire, at the other Varanger. "You have all proven yourselves loyal, as well as fighters beyond match. I wish I had one thousand of you. When we have accomplished our desire I shall see you all rewarded beyond your most extravagant dreams. We'll take four ships. Each will have two of you—one, clearly, three. Choose captains among yourselves, in your way."

"Who are the crews?" Conn asked.

"Pavo's men. And some such of the Faithful Band as actually proved faithful." Dobrynya sucked his cheeks suddenly hollow. The fire leapt and crackled as the fat from the grilling meat dripped into it and the orange light flashed across the posadnik's face. "Yet I trust none of them anymore."

Conn remembered the man who had given up his back to the enemy so that Volodymyr would have a sword. They were Thor's men, he thought; maybe they thought Volodymyr had betrayed their loyalty, and absolved them of their oaths. He himself was thinking he had never sworn a pledge to Volodymyr. Dobrynya was leaning forward, his hand out to Conn. "I am honored to know true Varanger."

Conn shook his hand, and one by one, the other men around the fire did also, while Pavo stood in the darkness, his hands on his hips, saying nothing. After a while Dobrynya moved away up the path and his Sclava went with him. Conn's leg hurt and he poured wotka on it and down his throat. He glanced at Raef, who was busy cutting slices off the haunch and laying them on the grill.

Raef straightened up, chewing. He said, "I'm taking Merike."

Conn said, "You watch out for her." His leg throbbed all the way up to his hip and he reached for the jug again, to fight the pain.

───※───

Raef wanted more now than the bargain with Merike; he wanted to talk to her. In the dark, lying next to her, he touched her breasts with their small firm unused nipples, and he said, "No child?"

She murmured, half asleep, and took his hand and slid it down her body, using him to caress herself. He stroked her flat belly. "No baby? No man?" He knew he had not been the first with her.

She said, drowsily, "Man," as if she understood that. But she was drifting away into sleep. He could not talk to her, nor she to him, and she didn't even seem to care much.

He lay next to her and wondered if this were all there was to it, the rutting and grunting in the dark. He wondered if among her own people she had been a whore, and that was why she had come to him so easily.

When he thought that, he shrank away from her, as if she had turned to dirt in his arms.

He knew that was unfair. Whores had babies; in fact, when he considered it, he thought that whores should have more babies than most women. Maybe Merike was a widow. Or a barren wife. Or the husband had no seed. When he thought that, he felt better, and now he wanted to hold her again.

He shut his eyes, looking inward, into the black heart where everything turned into confusion; nothing was different about her, except the way he thought of her.

She had come to him of her own will, that was something. He knew she had her reasons for doing it; if she had not chosen him, somebody else would have taken her whether she wanted him or not.

He wondered what she thought of him. If she thought of him at all, aside from what he gave her. If she missed her own people. If she had left anyone behind.

He had already taught her some words—come, and go, and eat and drink. He had no idea how to teach her words like love, or trust.

He did not love her. He knew what love was, he had seen Corban and Benna together. He loved Conn. He loved his mother, who even in his dreams was out of his reach. He wondered if he could love Merike, if she learned the right words.

Or maybe leave it alone. Lies were made of words.

He knew Dobrynya was lying, or anyway that his honeyed praises to the Varanger were false, and that he had his own purposes, in which the Varanger were only tools. Volodymyr's whole rule here depended on pulling off this attack on a city somewhere in the middle of the sea, that nobody had ever taken before. He thought of Pavo, who hated Conn. He thought of Rashid, who would reach Chersonese ahead of them, and who knew their plans.

Ahead of him lay something tangled and dark and thorny, a test, a trap, water and fire and death. And yet at the center of it, something glowed. Something golden, like his basileus. Something he had to know. It was like before Hjorunga Bay. He could not turn aside; he felt drawn on like the river rushing into the sea.

Merike, also, was drawn into that wild rush, their lives wound together like streams flowing into the river. He wound his arms around her like the currents of the river. For now, maybe, he knew her well enough. He began to sleep, and dreamt of his mother, watching him from a great distance, suns shining through her eyes.

In Volodymyr's council room the prince greeted them all with solemn gestures, his hands lifted as if he gave them some blessing. He spoke about courage and loyalty but the words were round and empty; standing in among the Varanger, the few remaining blue-coated guards, and Pavo's Sclava, Conn knew that Volodymyr didn't even remember his name.

"You have proven yourselves to me," the Knyaz said, as if somehow he had arranged the battle on the ship just to find out who was loyal. "Tomorrow we shall sail for Chersonese. You see here." He pointed to the table, where there was a big piece of skin spread out, and drawn on with marks.

All the men moved forward, Raef pushing up closer to look at this skin, craning his neck to see over the shoulders of the men in front of him. Conn hung back, bored with all this. When they got to this Chersonese, everything would turn up different than what they thought and talked about now, and he saw no reason to worry

about it until he had to act. He looked over the remaining blue
coats, some twenty of them. One was Oleg, their captain, frowning down at the skin on the table.

Oleg said, now, "This is the coast of Taurica? So broken—it
will be hard just to find the city, in all those bays and inlets."

On the far side of the table, Dobrynya held up something that
flashed, a metal moon.

"This is a star measurer. It was a present to the Knyaz from
the Mahmettan king in Baghdad, and with it we shall sail straight
across the sea to Chersonese." He pointed toward the skin. "You
see, there, how it is marked on the chart."

The other men all gave a general murmur of amazement. Raef
crossed his arms over his chest, his mouth kinked down at one
corner; clearly this went against the grain with him. Conn glanced
over at the far end of the room, at the carved screen.

He heard nothing from behind it. The spaces between the
elaborate swirls and curls of the carving were dark. He backed up
slowly, until he came up against it, and sliding his hands behind
him laid his palms flat against the wood. The men around the table
were all bent forward, talking as if they knew what they were talking about, except for Raef, who stood impassive, saying nothing.
Dobrynya stood smiling and nodding, while Volodymyr behind
him watched everything with his quick, intense dark eyes.

Then, behind Conn, through a hole in the carving, a warm
fingertip ran over his palm and stroked his wrist where the pulse
beat.

He almost cried out, he almost turned around. He kept still,
his hands flat to the screen; for an instant nothing. Then he felt her
lips brush his palm.

The council was breaking up. Dobrynya beckoned to a servant
who came and rolled up the skin. Raef, in among the others,
turned to look around for him. Conn drew his hands forward; he
gave a quick glance over his shoulder at the screen and saw nothing. Quickly he went across the room to the door, to join Raef.

The next morning they killed a goat, and let it bleed into the river, and people gathered on the riverbank and cheered. One by one they put the ships into the river, and the crews into them. Volodymyr and Dobrynya each took a ship, and the third they gave to Pavo; Raef and Conn took the fourth. But they divided up the Varanger as Dobrynya had said, two to each crew; Vagn they made a great joke of not being a Varanger at all, and put with Pavo. They put almost all the remaining blue coats of the Faithful Band into Raef and Conn's crew, with Oleg leading them. Janka went with Conn and Raef also.

The Sclava, who were used to boats with paddles, learned to use the long oars quickly enough, rowing up and down Kiev's reach of the river. The guardsmen, who were horsemen, had to learn. Raef sat in the stern of the ship, by the steerboard, and Conn limped up and down changing men from side to side and oar to oar, to get them balanced, and whacking them when they faltered or cut the water and roaring at them to keep together. The day's heat was terrific and they were all half naked.

The first time they went downstream two oars clashed, and one man lost his oar entirely and the current pushed the ship around almost broadside. Conn shouted and kicked and beat them into pulling her straight again and then on the upstream leg they let the bow fall out of line and ran aground on an underwater shoal.

Conn showed them how to work the ship loose. When he came swearing and red-faced back into the stern, Raef said, "Move Oleg back here, where he can watch what's going on. He's got a better grip on them than you do, for now."

His cousin gave him a white-eyed glare. "He'd better not have."

He gimped off, the black-stitched wound on his leg looking like a grotesque ornament. But he moved Oleg back, to the last sternboardside bench, balancing him with another big guard across the ship.

They went down the current this time a little better, and got back up without incident, and then ran down well enough that Conn put them through a reverse, changing sides on their oars, so they could go back without pivoting. The maneuver was hard to do without tipping the ship over but they managed it, although it took too long.

"Good enough," Conn said, when they pulled into the shore. "We'll get better on the trip downstream. Go get ready. We leave tomorrow early. Do what you like tonight, but show up tomorrow at dawn, or I'll hunt you down."

The crew dragged themselves off, their bodies streaming sweat, their hair and beards soaked and matted, and trudged away up the bank. A crew of slaves had brought down the masts from some storeroom somewhere and Raef went over to look at them.

The masts were straight and long, their yards bundled to them with rigging, and there were enough for each ship to take two. Raef said, "We'll need extra yards, too. Poles, to bend the leech. I'll find out about those." He was rocking back and forth from heels to toes, smiling, excited, and Conn punched him lightly in the belly.

"There's the sails."

The slaves were spreading striped red canvas out on the bank, to check for rips and seams, and Raef and Conn went over to watch them. Raef said, "There's at least eleven. Make sure you get three for us."

"Where are you going?"

"To find the rest of the rigging." Raef smiled back at him. "I think I'll bring my sea chest down here and sleep here tonight."

"Oh, you would," Conn said, but he laughed. He bent absently to itch at the black-stitched mess on his leg. "Get going. I'll handle this."

Raef went down alone to the riverbank, to sleep by the ships, at sundown. The evening twilight stayed almost as bright as daylight for a long while, and before the sky had turned deep purple-blue the rest of the Varanger had come down to join him.

It was too hot for a fire. They sat in a circle anyway and told stories of wars and sailing and heroes, Harald Fairhair and Turf-Einar and Ragnar, Loki's tricks and Thor's strength. Raef was sitting next to Bjorn the Christian, and as the others were arguing over some name or another, he said, "I don't understand you, how you can follow the Cross, and still be Varanger."

Bjorn sat with his arms on his widespread knees, cracking nuts between his hands. He stopped to take the cross out of his shirt and kiss it. "Because Christ is winning."

Raef thought briefly of a footrace, all the gods running. "What do you mean by that?"

"Everywhere, the Christians have the most power. Maybe they're Roman, maybe they're Greek." He shrugged, looking down at the nuts between his fingers. "I want to be with the winner." He crushed his hands together with a crackling of shells.

Raef said nothing to that. He turned his gaze toward the rest of them, exploding into laughter at some joke Conn had just told, the firelight all around them, on Skinny Harald's face, on Leif with his peg teeth. Vagn was looking at Conn with a shy admiration. He thought, Some of these are going to die. A rabbity fear climbed his backbone. His hands and feet were tingling. He thought if he tried a little harder he would know which ones. I don't want to know, he thought, and realized he had spoken aloud.

"What?" Bjorn said, startled.

"Nothing," Raef said, and ground the heels of his hands into his eyes, rubbing out the visions.

The river wound south through flat reedy marshlands on the east, past low bluffs and pastures on the west, all the green fading into dusty brown in the late-spring sun. The shores were loud with waterbirds and on the grasslands herds of wild cattle and horses grazed. There were no trees. Sometimes in the distance they saw packs of the huns watching them from horseback. At night, they pulled out onto the shore, usually near a fishermen's settlement, where they could get some food. The fishermen often didn't want to give it up but Pavo took it anyway.

Although they were divided among the four ships, at night all the Varanger came to gather in one camp, and since most of the blue-coated guards were in Conn's ship they camped with them too. This was a problem, since Pavo gave the guards the worst of the food—the rotten fish, the moldy grain, nothing but water to drink.

Oleg, the guard captain, said, "I can see how this is going," and sent his men scavenging around the shoreline for eggs and birds and fish. Conn gave half of his meat to the guards; when they saw this, the other Varanger did also, and Merike found herbs in the wild pastures that she brewed into drink, heating up water from the river on a tiny fire in their midst.

After a few days they came to another rapids. From far upriver they could hear it, not only the roar of the water, but the screeching of birds. A wooden post, carved with faces, marked where they should haul the ships out, and the trail along the bank past the rough water was wide and beaten to dust. From the trail they could look out over the thrashing white water, jumping and tumbling over layers of rock in the river. As white as the foam on the water, clouds of birds soared and swept and squabbled over it all, pelicans with their long baggy beaks, and seagulls by the thousands. On the rocks the pelican nestlings huddled together screeching for food. Above them the seagulls wheeled on their black-tipped wings, waiting for a chance to steal the food or the naked baby.

It took a day to get all the ships past the rapids, while Pavo stalked up and down the line cursing them and threatening with his whip. But here even Dobrynya had to walk, since they had no horses. The great ships were like corpses on land, heavy as coffins. At the sight of clear water ahead, all the men cheered.

When they sailed, Merike rode along behind Raef, tucked into the stern of the ship. The other men cast looks at her but she kept her eyes always on the riverbank, or on Raef, and what he was doing. Nonetheless, one night, Leif asked Raef if he would throw dice for her.

Raef gave him a sharp look. Helgi, sitting on Leif's far side, burst out laughing. Bjorn the Christian sat up straighter, turning to watch them.

"I don't mean any disrespect," Leif said, grouchy. "I just think she's a fine-looking woman. One cast—one night."

One of the guardsmen said, "Yes, and it's a fine brotherly gesture for a man to share a woman."

Raef said, "When you have one to share, tell Leif."

Oleg, across the baked fire from him, lifted his head up and said, "Shut up, Roglod. It's obvious he's soft on her."

Helgi laughed again, slapping his thighs. Merike had picked up something of the way this talk was going and crouched down next to Raef, her arms around her updrawn knees. The dark was falling and some of the men were already stretching out on the ground to sleep.

It was a good time for a story, but instead Vagn began to sing; for a scrawny bitter-tongued boy he sang well, in some strange language not dansker and not Sclava. He taught some of the others the refrains and they joined in when they could. A few feet away down the riverbank, the Sclava camp was quiet, maybe sleeping, maybe listening. It was very hot, even at night. A mist rose from the river and clouded the rising moon.

Vagn stopped singing, and although the others begged and cajoled him he lay down. All but a few of the others were already bedded down. Raef had gone off modestly with Merike, and Conn sat by the cold fire waiting to be tired enough to sleep.

Helgi sat slumped across the ashes from him. He said, "How much farther is it?"

"Who knows?" Conn shrugged. "Every day we get nearer to it, is all."

"Those Greeks don't fight," said Skinny Harald, draped in his blanket in spite of the heat. "We'll walk right in their front gates."

The four men left awake crowded in closer, to talk without bothering the sleepers. Harald said, "I hope there are women," and smacked his lips.

Leif spoke with a hard certainty in his voice. Conn knew he had been around this country in the past. "Rich, it'll be. Good plunder—gold and jewels—Chersonese's just a stopover on the great road, all the fine things of the whole world find their way through there."

"What great road?" Conn asked.

As the night deepened around them Leif became just a thick shapeless lump in the darkness. "There's a great road that runs from one end of the world to the other. The center of it is Constantinople. Some ways go west, and some go east. From Constantinople to Chersonese, Chersonese to Tama-Tarkha, and then east to Khwarezm, and south to Baghdad, and east on to the silk lands, and south to the spice lands. But Chersonese's just a way station. I've heard of cities east of here where the rooftops are of gold, and the streets are paved with rubies and emeralds." He shifted in the dark, his voice changing. "And I've heard of monsters, and uncrossable desert, and men who will eat you, like a lion."

"Have you been to Chersonese?" Conn asked.

"No. But I've been out on the salt, down at the end of this river. The old Knyaz had a city down here for a while. It never amounted to more than a market and it's gone now. I've never been to Chersonese but I've heard a lot about it. They don't even have a wall on the seacoast because there's nowhere safe to land except the harbor. The city's tucked up inside and around the bend in a fjord, snug as a baby in its mother's arm."

"Interesting. What are the tides like on this sea?"

Leif's voice seemed to swell larger as he spoke, plump with this valuable knowledge. "There isn't much rise in the tide. Sometimes there's a big wave comes from nowhere. The wind gets pretty fierce. There are storms. Some of the Greeks call it the Bad-Tempered Sea, and it can get rough. We should make a sacrifice before we sail out on it, like they did at Kiev."

Harald grunted. "You're making too much of it. This will be easy." He yawned, and stirred around, settling himself to sleep.

Conn stayed up, listening to the night sounds. Helgi had lain down, and finally Leif got up and padded off to the edge of the camp to make water and then rolled in next to Harald. Oleg, the captain of the Faithful Band, was the only one awake besides Conn.

He said, abruptly, "I hope there is hard fighting. I hope I can die in the Knyaz's service. Prove at least I, I . . ." His voice fell off.

Conn kept his eyes on the dead fire. He thought Oleg had stayed awake to tell him this, waited patiently until everyone else was gone and only Conn would hear him. "I believe you," Conn said.

Oleg's voice came out in a spate, low and harsh. "I feel as if they dug out my heart and put a turd in its place. The Faithful Band! I love the Thunderer, what man does not? What fighting man." He shifted around, his hands at his throat, and held something out toward Conn in the dark. Conn could see only the stubby cross shape but guessed it was Thor's Hammer. "But my duty is to Volodymyr. It's hard, but it's clear. Isn't it?"

"It seems so to me," Conn said. "You pledge something, you do it, it seems to me."

"I want to die, and make up for them all. Volodymyr is my prince."

Conn said nothing; it seemed bad to him for anybody to want

to die, a bad omen for all of them, for the voyage. He didn't know
what he could say to Oleg to make him easier in his mind. Oleg
sat still a moment, waiting, but then with a sigh got up, and shuffled around getting ready for sleep.

When everybody was bedded down, Conn rose and stretched.
He went over near some rocks and pissed, and then he walked
once around his camp, making a circle of his footsteps around the
men he led, Oleg's guards, and the other Varanger.

Oleg's words weighed on him. He knew Oleg had told him
what he had for some reason, a man he hardly knew, and that
made him think of all the men around him, who hardly knew him,
and yet followed him. Followed him toward a battle that like
Hjorunga Bay could turn against them even if they fought their
hearts' own fights. He had to lead them well, which was more than
just making a pledge, and which he had no notion how to do.

Raef would help him. He knew Raef like the other side of his
own skin.

When he passed by the edge of the Sclava camp it was dark
and they all seemed asleep, but he saw someone stir. He slowed. In
there, in the middle of the Sclava, a smooth head rose and stared
at him; he saw the glitter of eyes, and stared back.

He remembered how Pavo was punishing the Faithful Band,
and he thought, Truce is over, you bastard. Over and gone. These
are my men now. Finally Pavo laid his head down again. Conn
walked on around in his circle, and then went to sleep himself.

⸺◦⸺

They came to a place where the river braided its way through islands, and rocks jutted up out of the river; they hauled on the bank
and dragged the ships along the portage. They carried the ship in
shifts along a rutted road. Conn saw that Pavo stalked the guardsmen, who were softer than the Varanger, huffing and groaning under the weight of the ship, and once the Tishats flicked his whip at

Oleg. Thereafter Conn took the same shift with Oleg and the
guardsmen and Pavo left them alone. But that evening while they
were camped Pavo caught Merike by herself.

Raef was down by the ships, helping to mend rigging. Conn
had found a comfortable place to sit beside the fire Janka was laying, and was thinking about cooking some of the river fish the hun
had caught that day, when he saw Raef's woman trying to sneak
into the camp from the steppe, where she had gathered bunches of
herbs.

Usually she was cleverer at this, and got to her own fire before
anyone saw her. But this time as soon as she came out of the high
grass Pavo leapt on her like a wolf.

Conn sprang up; the whole camp lay between them. Pavo had
the woman by the arm, although she twisted and thrashed, and
was dragging her away. Conn sprinted across the camp and without breaking stride hurled his whole body into Pavo, shoulder-
first, and knocked him flat on the ground.

"Leave her alone! You know she's ours!"

Pavo lunged up off the ground, red in the face, his arms churning. "You ask for this, puny Raven!" Merike bounded away out of
his reach; nobody paid any more heed to her.

Conn met Pavo's charge and stood him up, his arms twining
around the taller man's chest, his head pressed into Pavo's neck.
He felt the bigger man's power tighten and flex under his grip and
for a fierce moment he matched it, held Pavo still like a rock under
a waterfall. Then abruptly, he gave way, and twisted, and with one
foot tripped Pavo flat on the ground.

The Sclava went down with a roar. From all around the camps
men were running to watch, and other voices rose in excited urgent cries.

"Get up! Get up!"

"Kill him—kill him, Raven—"

Before Pavo could bound up out of the dust Conn sprang on
him from behind, wrapped one arm around his neck, and reaching

down into the back of his belt pulled out the looped brass weapon
there that Pavo had used once to lay him flat. He tossed the brass
away as far as he could, and sprang back. "More tricks? Pavo, any
more tricks?"

The watchers howled, laughter and rage. "Two hrvnya Pavo
wins!"

"Raven! Raven!"

"Five hrvnya!"

Pavo hurled himself at Conn, and carried him down onto the
ground, where they twisted and thrashed, each trying to get on top.
Conn leaned one way and lunged the other, locked his arms around
Pavo's waist, and threw them both backward. A fist smashed into
his side and he stiffened his muscles against it. Pavo rolled over
on the ground, trying to get Conn under him, and Conn wrapped
his legs around Pavo's waist and rolled with him, got above him,
got his arm snaked around Pavo's neck. He wrenched the big
Sclava's head back. Pavo was on all fours, and now reared up onto
his knees, slamming both fists into Conn's legs around him. Conn
felt a stab of pain up his thigh from the healing wound. He was
pulling Pavo's head back, his hands under his jaw, and when Pavo
flailed his arms out, Conn regripped with his legs and pinned the
Sclava's left arm.

Pavo went down hard, clawing with his free hand at Conn's
ankles, and then reached suddenly down toward his boot.

"Got a knife in there?" Conn yelled. He leapt up and clear,
landing lightly with knees bent, his arms outstretched, ready to
charge in again. "Get rid of it, or I'll get a bow!"

Pavo crawled away and got to his knees, sobbing for breath.
Conn stood still. He wiped his face with his hand, and said,
"More, Tishats? Hunh?"

Pavo's eyes were red and glaring; he straightened, wiping his
hands together. His bare chest was covered with dust and there
were red welts around his neck and his arms.

"Stop! I command this!"

Conn took a step backward, watching Pavo. The Tishats swayed slightly on his widespread feet. The fire in his eyes had dulled but his face was red; he knew he looked beaten. Then Volodymyr walked in between them, his hands out to either side.

His voice rang out, sharp and clear. "We cannot win if we are not all together, all one. No personal feuds!"

"Knyaz," Conn shouted, with a flick of a glance at Volodymyr. "Knyaz, he is abusing my men. I will not stop, until he stops."

Volodymyr wheeled toward him. "*Your* men!" His face was edged like a hatchet. "You are all my men!"

Conn glanced around him. The whole army had gathered around them. Behind him was Raef, and behind Raef were all the other Varanger, and all the blue-coated guardsmen. But the Sclava all stood behind Pavo.

Volodymyr turned slowly in a circle, looking at everybody.

"No," he said. "This cannot be. We will never take Chersonese if we are divided. We must be one. Whatever your differences, Raven, Pavo, you must give them up. We shall all be one, or we shall all die, because I do not propose to go back to Kiev without the crown of victory."

The watching crowd gave up a general sigh at this; even Conn to his surprise felt a leap of heart at what the prince said, mostly because he knew it was true. Volodymyr held out one hand to him, the long clean hand of a lord, and Conn reached out and took it.

On Volodymyr's far side, Pavo took his other hand. The crowd, again, cried out in one voice, and Volodymyr drew them together, and set their hands together in a clasp.

Above this knot Conn looked into Pavo's eyes, and he saw the red hatred there still. Conn smiled, seeing that. He understood that. He opened his fingers, and their hands slid apart. But they could give Volodymyr what he wanted.

The Knyaz was speaking on, talking of being one, of neither Sclava nor Varanger anymore but Rus', Rus' forever, and the crowd began to cheer, waves of cheers, each one louder. Conn moved back, and Pavo went the other way; they left Volodymyr alone in the middle, with the thunderous cheers all around him. Conn went by Oleg, standing with some other guardsmen, their gazes on their prince, their faces reverent.

Conn left the crowd behind, going back toward his camp. A little way on he saw Raef, standing separate from it all, silent, his arms folded over his chest. Merike was pressed against his side. Conn lifted one hand to him, and Raef waved back. Conn began to feel the bruises and knocks of the fight; the half-healed wound was aching and oozing. He had to take the stitches out, he didn't think it would heal completely with all that horsehair in there. He went wearily over to his fire and sat down with his knife to pick out the knots.

CHAPTER SIXTEEN

They reached clear water and rowed on. Just south of the rapids, they hauled out on a great island in the middle of the river, where stands of old oak trees grew. The villagers ran off as soon as they saw the army, and left behind bread and meat, so everybody ate well enough.

They made a big unruly camp along the shore that night, and the whole while, one person or another would leave the rest, and follow an old trail off through the oak wood to a certain tree. There they left offerings. Raef went along with Oleg, around sundown.

He said, as they started out, "I have my own reasons for going with you, as I suppose you know."

Oleg said, with a glance at him, "You want to know what I think of Volodymyr."

"Yes. Him and Dobrynya. Who leads?"

"For a long time, it was Uncle Dobrynya." Oleg laughed. "He is still the cleverest man of all the Sclava. But he does not have Volodymyr's largeness of idea. You've heard him speak of our greatness. I think now, most of the time anyway, Volodymyr leads. My prince."

"You follow him even if he goes Christian?"

"I won't turn Christian for him," Oleg said quickly. "But when he sees how I fight, he will honor me for it. He will see we don't need to take up Christ."

"You must think much of him, then."

"He is a very great man. Here, I must do this." They were coming to the edge of the forest, and Oleg stooped, and pulled some strands of the tall brown grass. Raef waited for him. He looked up at the broad blue cloudless sky, the sun higher and brighter every day, the year hurtling on in its wheel.

They walked on, no longer talking about Volodymyr. Oleg was carefully twisting and coiling the grass. He wound it into the shape of a horse, or a man, or something.

Then they came to the tree, and he bowed to it, said words, and laid his grass creature at its feet.

The tree was ancient, a bent and wrinkled crone, its trunk knobby with galls; from the branches bones hung, and chains of dead flowers, an old sword rusted to lace, shreds of decayed leather, part of a long wooden shield with the brass boss still attached. All around it on the ground lay newer things, like Oleg's horse of straw. Raef stood before the tree and felt the weariness and weight of its age, and nothing else. Even the offerings felt like a burden to it.

He had nothing for an offering, but he took his knife and cut off a few strands of his hair, and wound them around a twig.

Oleg watched him, absorbed. He said, "Some kind of charm."

Raef laughed. Stooping, he laid the twig down beside Oleg's horse. The big guard squinted shrewdly at him. "I have heard of Corban Loosestrife, you know."

"What," Raef said, and straightened abruptly.

"He was a very great wizard, do you wonder that his name is known? He summoned spirits, he visited other worlds. Hawks fed him, when Hakon the Jarl locked him in a tower for twenty years or more. He had a little ship, no bigger than a dragonfly, that he kept in his sleeve, and when he needed it cast it into the water, where it became as big as he required, and sailed anywhere, in any wind."

Raef could not keep from smiling. He remembered something else he had heard about Corban, that he had no power at all. Except the very greatest, she had said. He knows it when he sees it. He said, "I knew the ship. But Corban's gone now." He wondered also where she was, who had told him that, if her power were undiminished.

"If he were with us," Oleg said, and gave up a sigh, his gaze drifting off. They were in the dark oak wood, with night falling. "Then I would not fear anything ahead of us."

"Then you would be a fool," Raef said. "Corban spread trouble wherever he went, that's how he got his name."

Ahead, the noise and lights of the camp showed, and Oleg began to walk faster. "Nonetheless I hope some of the old wizard is in you. Don't tell me otherwise, for I shall not believe it." He waggled his hand at Raef, and walked away, back toward the camp on the north end of the island, where a big fire was already burning. Raef thought of Corban, who had gone entirely beyond his reach, who had fathered and not fathered him, crooked blood. The stars were coming out. He went on toward his camp, where the dragon was pulled up, Merike hidden in the hollow of the stern.

Below the island there were no more rapids. The river ran in its entwining courses between low reedy banks, under a sun-blasted blue sky. The guardsmen were better rowers now, understanding more how to work together, how to feel the ship's motion; Conn yelled at them endlessly. They came to a wide lake, which a sandy spit separated to the south from a vast blue water. The lake was of pure water, but the vast blue beyond was the salt.

They hauled out on the spit, and had another council. Volodymyr gave all the orders now, with Dobrynya sitting quietly beside him. They had brought bows, and Volodymyr told the men to go out onto the broad steppes and hunt, so that they would have enough meat in each ship for each man for six days.

"I guess it's good then the ships aren't overfilled," Leif said, the Icelander. "What happens if six days go by and we're still way out on the salt?"

"The sea is full of fish," Volodymyr said. He held up the star measurer on its stick; the brass flashed in the sun. "We have the Mahmettan circle, and the chart. They say four days from here to Chersonese."

"What do we find when we get there?" Pavo said. He stood up among the Sclava, his hands on his hips. "Will they fight?"

"Greeks would rather talk than fight," Volodymyr said. "They will be so surprised to see us rowing up their cove, they'll run like chickens."

Raef shifted from side to side; he was sitting on his heels beside Conn, his arms lying on his knees. He could see Conn was uninterested in this. Vagn as usual sat on Conn's far side, and he was listening, a little frown on his face.

Leif called, "Will they have the fire?"

Behind Raef, Bjorn the Christian muttered, "God help us if they do." All around the circle of men there was grumbling and whispers.

Volodymyr held up his hands, calming them. He turned to Dobrynya. "What do you think, Uncle Dobrynya?"

The posadnik stood up and walked forward. His voice spread soothingly over their jittery uncertainties. "It's said the Greeks have forgotten how to make the fire. In any case they hold the way to make it as a close secret and would not give it away to a mere provincial city like Chersonese. They won't have the fire there. They may have a city guard, no more."

"Can they chain the entrance to the harbor?" Conn said. He was paying more attention than Raef had thought.

Dobrynya nodded. "And likely will, if they have warning. So we are going to surprise them. The astrolabe will take us straight across the sea. The first they see of us, we will be rowing up the bay. They will have no time to rig chains."

Raef said, "Why do you think this will be such a surprise to them?"

Dobrynya swung toward him, golden, smiling as always. Behind him, Volodymyr was tipped forward a little, impatient. Dobrynya hardly heeded him. He said, "In the normal course of war we would march south by land through Taurica and they would have a long forewarning. But we will come straight to them, by sea, as I said."

He had not said it, but Raef let that pass. He said, "That may be true, and all." He shifted his gaze from Dobrynya to Volodymyr, behind him. "But the Mahmettan Rashid was in Kiev when you first told us this plan. Now Rashid has gone south and he will tell them in Chersonese you are coming, and there will be no surprise."

At that a ripple of comment went around through the men listening, and Volodymyr straightened, ruffled. Dobrynya's smile never wavered. He turned and exchanged a look with Volodymyr, as if to say, See how foolish these people are. Facing Raef again, he said, "Rashid is our friend."

Raef said, "Rashid is a spy for his Baghdadi king."

The listeners growled and muttered again, but Dobrynya laughed. "He is a spy for us. Where do you think I came by the star measurer and the chart?"

Volodymyr said, "But if he did go to Chersonese, even by accident he might let something slip."

Dobrynya shrugged, looking from one to the other. "Rashid is a bit of a fool, isn't he. He's only interested in plants and stars. He'll do us no harm, he's not clever enough to dissemble."

Raef bit his lips together, saying nothing more. Rashid, he thought, was clever enough to get Dobrynya to trust him. He felt the other men staring at him and when he did not argue any more they snorted and nudged each other. The rest of the talk was of how they would put on supplies. Afterward he walked back to his fire with Conn. Ahead of them, at the fire, he saw Merike sitting on the ground, the wind off the sea blowing her hair back.

Conn said, "Are you sure about Rashid?"

Raef shrugged his shoulders, not wanting to get into any explanations. He said, "Yes."

"What about the chart and the star measurer?"

"Maybe the chart is wrong. It looks like a bad coast, down where the city is, a lot of fjords, hilly, windward. A star stick like that, you have to really know the sky, the sea, the stick, everything."

"Can you find this place?"

"I don't know." He remembered his basileus, in Rashid's wallet, rubbed with his spit, which he had hoped would lead him there. He had long since lost any sense of where the basileus was. No better than the star measurer. "I can try. But this isn't our sea."

He turned and walked out over the low sandy spit, toward the surging blue water that stretched out toward the edge of the sky. All across it like a herd of leaping white horses the spume sprang from the waves. He loved the sight of it, after the long muddy confines of the river; he longed to sail out onto it, the real world, infinite and unconquerable, the bits of land only places to stop. The wind rushed over his face; the little purling waves sang in his ears. "It doesn't even taste the same. But it connects with our sea, even so, by some long crooked way."

"You can do it," Conn said. "Don't worry about anything else. Just get us to Chersonese." He swung his arm over Raef's shoulder. They went on to the fire, and the other men, and Merike hiding in the dragon.

The Sclava were great hunters. They brought in a lot of meat, which they cut up and soaked in brine, and wrapped in hide. They filled hide bags with water from the lagoon. After three days they sailed out onto the salt. After they had gone south out of sight of land, Dobrynya made a big show with the star measurer, standing amidships of his dragon, and moving the disk back and forth. He went on smiling but Raef guessed he found it harder to use the instrument on the tossing waves than on the ground. They rowed due south, across a steady westerly wind.

The crew thought they had learned how to row, but the sea was utterly unlike the river, and now they had to learn all over again. All the first morning Conn walked up and down the ship, trying to get them to row at one beat. Janka was hopeless at it and finally

Conn took over his oar shuffling the men around so that he sat on the bench across from Raef, on the backboard side of the stern. By sundown at least they knew the commands, and could work together a little.

That night a sudden squall blew up, and scattered the ships, but the next day Conn set up the mast and sent Janka up to the top. Raef told him where to row, and zigzagging back and forth they sighted the other ships one by one and gathered them all together. As soon as the first stray ship, Pavo's, was within calling distance, one of the men dove straight into the water and swam over to Conn's. It was the scrawny boy Vagn, and Conn took him in and put him on the oar he had been using.

Seagulls in flocks hovered around them, as if they might throw food overboard. Far to the east, a faint shadow of a point of land appeared, and slipped away to the north.

On the second day Bjorn the Christian contrived to go overboard from Pavo's ship, and Conn picked him up, although it meant they lost the race they were having with the others. Volodymyr's ship was winning the race, although they left behind a wake as ragged as the scar on Conn's leg.

They went racing on, each ship striving to pull ahead of the others. Conn's ship had fallen far behind to pick up Bjorn and nobody waited for them, but by nightfall Conn had caught up again.

When Conn said, "You can go back over there when you want," Bjorn shook his head.

"Something's ugly in that ship," he said. "I'll stay here."

Raef sat in the stern, his hand on the steerboard, but they were going due south and so he had nothing to do. Conn watched him; on Raef's face was the same soft, distant look as when they had gone down the rapids. Conn wondered how he knew about the sea. Maybe he watched the seagulls and stars, the clouds, the changing color of the water, felt the currents and the winds, just as other men did, only better.

He knew this was not true. He knew he cast this net of reason-

able explanations around Raef just to soothe himself. He remembered, once long before, thinking Raef was no use, and he would
be better without him. This, he thought, was a reminder of how
stupid he could be. He sat by his cousin in the stern, the mast
crutch between them and the great ocean of the stars overhead,
and no word passed between them.

The next day, they raced again, and this time, Leif and Harald
fell overboard from Dobrynya's ship, and had to be picked up.

"This is a poor bunch of sailors, I think," Oleg said, with a
wide grin. "Do you think Helgi, Bos, and Ulf will lose their footing soon as well?"

Conn grunted. "They're winning all the races." His ship had
more men now than any of the others; that meant they could
switch off rowing more often, but also that there was less food and
much less water. And the meat was going rotten, even in the brine.
But in fact that day all three of the remaining Varanger managed
to get themselves onto his ship.

⟢

Merike was sick all the first day and the next, moaning and limp
over the gunwale; when she was not throwing up she was huddled
into the hollow of the stem, behind Raef's sea chest, crying. When
he tried to comfort her she struck at him and snarled at him in her
own language, tears all over her face. Once she knelt and clung to
his knees and begged and pleaded with him incomprehensibly,
pointing back toward the land, and he laughed at that, and she hit
him and crawled back into the hollow of the dragon's tail. He took
his turn at the oar when it came, and then saw her begging and
pleading even with Conn, who also laughed at her. Of course this
meant she didn't need much food, either.

She was no use. He wished he hadn't brought her; he couldn't
remember why he had ever thought it a good idea.

The sea around him was sharp and harsh, shallow, and full of fish. It was blue as the bluest cornflower, darker, laced with spume. The wind worked it into an unpredictable chop that made rowing even harder. As they rowed they were drifting a little eastward, but still they were heading nearly full south. Then near noon of the fourth day he felt the bottom changing under them and stood up at the helm and said, "Conn. We should be going east now."

Conn gave him a swift look, and called to the oarsmen to change course a little, so they could come within hailing distance of Volodymyr's ship. Cupping his hands around his mouth, he called, "What's the course?"

Dobrynya's ship was just beyond Volodymyr's. The helmsman on the prince's ship turned and relayed the question to Dobrynya, and the answer came back, "South—due south!"

Raef said, "South, the sea's much deeper. Colder. The wind's bad. We're over some kind of ridge here, and I think it runs all the way to the land over there."

Oleg was staring at him. "What land?"

Raef waved vaguely eastward, and all along the two banks of oars, the men looked over their shoulders. The sky was broad and blue, the wind mild and from the west. Nothing marked the perfect circle of the horizon, not in any direction. But Raef felt the ridge under him, and the rise of the land east of him, as if they were carved into his feet.

Volodymyr called to Dobrynya, "What if they're right?"

Dobrynya swung around to face him, and for a moment, between them, an open anger crackled that Raef had never seen before. He started, "We need to have—"

And Volodymyr spoke over him, crushing his voice down. "Why did you bring them, if not to trust them on the sea?" He lifted his gaze to Conn, a ship's width away. "Where should we go?"

Raef said, "Due east. With the wind."

Between him and Volodymyr, Dobrynya wheeled around, not smiling, his face red with throttled rage. "If we get into the wind we'll be blown all across the sea. We'll die on the salt. You yourself mentioned this risk."

On the far ship, Pavo straightened, groaning. He had a greenish look about him; like Merike, he was not sailing well. But Conn was already wheeling around, his voice high and clear. "Up mast!"

Vagn and Bjorn lifted the mast straight up off its crutch, stepped it down into the hole, a lance to the sky, and chucked it. All around on the other ships, howls of rage and panic went up. Pavo bellowed, "No water!" He was pointing off to the west, sometimes, the north some other times. "Go ashore—"

"Up oars and stow!" Conn shouted.

Volodymyr himself was bellowing. "Follow them. Uncle, obey me—I am the Knyaz!"

Dobrynya clamped his mouth shut. Raef could see him clearly, from where he stood up by the steerboard, his hand on the tiller. He turned and looked east, and his forehead rumpled, but he turned, and called, "Up mast!" In his own ship, Volodymyr stood like an idol, pointing.

The tiller in Raef's hand was just a piece of wood, not carved yet, and he had no knack for such things and it would stay uncarved. Through it he felt down into the living sea beneath him. The rows of oarsmen lined their oars up along the inside of the hull, on the floor, and Bjorn had made the mast halyard fast; Vagn was hauling the sail up, and Bjorn went to snug the sheets fast on either side. Raef settled down to keeping the ship in the belly of the wind. From the hollow of the stem behind him, Merike crept forward, and looked out over the gunwale by his knee.

She said something to him, and then, "Home? House?"

"No," he said. "Land. Solid land. One day away." He held up his finger. "Not home. But land. Understand?"

She glanced around for Janka, who was at the far end of the ship, and faced Raef again and held her hand flat and still. He nodded, with a laugh. "Yes. Land. Not—" He waved his own hand

up and down, and then brought it hard against hers and held it still.
"Solid land."

She said something that might have been a prayer in her own
language, and gave him as dark a look as Dobrynya's. He reached
out to touch her, to comfort her, and she bit him. He whacked her
across the head. She crawled deep into the hollow, glaring at him.
He put his back to her, wishing there were room to do what he
wanted to her.

—⚬—

Conn helped Vagn and Bjorn trim the sail; the wind filled the red
and white striped canvas sail with a snap. At once the feel of the
ship changed, as if she rode higher and lighter, leaping forward, a
great swan of the sea. The wind sang in the rigging, and the sound
of the sea whispering against the hull was like music. Bjorn
crossed himself, looking up at the sky.

"The wind's rising," he said.

"A wind like this lasts for days," Conn said. "This is the way
to sail." He clapped his arm around Vagn's shoulders in an ex-
huberant hug and went along from man to man, telling them what
to do.

From the other ships came volleys of shouting and curses.
The Sclava were having trouble getting their masts up, their sails
set. The loosed dragon sped away from them, coursing into the
east, and Conn did not look back. When he had the crew settled he
sat down finally on his sea chest next to Raef, his hand on the gunwale, and ordered another ration of the water for everybody.

"Don't forget her," Raef said, jerking his head back over his
shoulder. Conn looked into the hollow of the stem, where the hun
woman crouched like an animal.

"Maybe we should make her row," Conn said.

"I'm not letting her out of there," Raef said. "Nobody would
row." He was watching the eastern horizon. The water skin came

along, Conn drank first, and passed the skin over. The water was
sour but Raef filled his stomach with it. After a moment's hesitation, he handed the skin back to Merike, who yanked it away.

"Sometimes I think we should just throw her overboard."

Conn laughed, and gave her another look, to see if she understood that. She looked just as sick of Raef as he was of her.
"There's still some meat on her, save her for when we get really
hungry."

Raef laughed.

＊

By sundown, with the other ship's hull down somewhere behind
them, they had raised a low cape. Raef had been steering them
slightly to the south, when the wind let him, not enough that they
had to rig up the leech-beater, just dumping off some air now and
then. Now with the point of land rising due east of them he
turned the ship out of the wind, set his hands on his thighs, and
cast a brief, derisive glance back to the west. Conn ordered the
sail rolled up for the night, and sent Janka to the top of the mast
with a lantern.

Oleg said, "How can you be sure this is Chersonese? None of
us has ever been here before. What if when they bring the chart
everything's wrong?"

Conn grunted. "The chart is false." He was watching the dark
coastline ahead of them, fading into the night. "Look." He pointed.

Vagn had hung the lantern to the top of the mast, where it
bobbed and swung as the ship moved. And now, suddenly, on that
coastline, another light appeared, and moved from side to side.

"See?" Conn said. "That's a beacon. They're calling us in."

The light on the coast flashed once, twice, and then three
times quickly. Conn said, "Except there's an answer, and we don't
know it."

Behind Conn, Raef laughed. Everybody on the dragon was

watching, silent. The light shone on again, once, twice, three quick gleams, and then abruptly went dark.

"No, not a friend," Conn murmured. "Not somebody you want in there. Is there any water left?"

"Not much," said Oleg, in the dark.

"Pass it around," Conn said. "We may have a long wait for Volodymyr."

⇒⊕⇐

But in the morning the other three dragons came sailing up from the southwest. Oleg gave a bark of a laugh, and all up and down Conn's ship, the Varanger and the guardsmen sent up hoots and jeers and long whistles. They brought all the ships together and threw out a sail for a sea anchor, so that they could hold another council. Conn and Raef went into the middle ship, which was Dobrynya's, where they also had the last of the water.

Dobrynya said, "You're sure this is Chersonese."

Conn shrugged. "Look at the smoke. How many towns do you think there are on this coast?" Lashed together gunwale to gunwale, the ships were bucking and thrashing and everybody had to yell to be heard. "Smell that? That's a city, over there, beyond the point."

On the next ship over, Pavo grunted at what Conn had said. "It stinks," he said. He looked hollow around the eyes and mouth, a horseman far from his saddle.

Volodymyr sat amidships his big dragon, on the weather side of the council. His face was sunburned, and his beard salty. His eyes shone with excitement. He said, "This is Chersonese. Even the chart agrees—only the signs for the star measurer were wrong, Uncle, or we read them wrong. But see here—" He took the chart on his knees, folded over against the lashing wind. "There is the cape, and there—" He twisted to look back eastward. "—the shape of the coast seems the same."

"You have good eyes," Conn said. Raef, beside him, nodded.

Volodymyr said, "That bay, there, that's the entrance. If we sail up that opening, there, we will come to Chersonese."

He leaned forward as he spoke, his hands in front of him; what he wanted was almost in his grasp.

"We have to do it soon," Conn said. "Nobody on my ship has eaten today."

"Now," Volodymyr said. "We shall do it now. And I will lead the way." He nodded to Dobrynya. "Uncle, you follow me. Then Pavo. Then the Varanger."

He held out his hand, and Dobrynya clasped it, and seeing what was supposed to happen Conn laid his hand on theirs and then Pavo's like a horny paw closed over them all. They looked at each other hard, and drew back.

Conn and Raef climbed back over the stern of Dobrynya's ship and swung around into their own. Conn went the length of the ship, talking to each of the men. Raef broke open the chests of weapons. The guardsmen and some of the Varanger also had helmets and leather armor and their own weapons, and Raef gave something out of the chest to anybody who didn't. They had a lot of bows, but very few arrows; they had spent most of them hunting game back at the mouth of the river. The wind was fair for the mouth of the fjord, the sun just climbing up into the shoulder of the sky. Volodymyr's ship hauled in the drogue. Raef settled into the stern of their ship, his hand on the tiller, Merike huddled into the space behind him, whispering to herself. The oars ran out. They stroked on toward Chersonese, across the frolicking wind.

CHAPTER SEVENTEEN

They rowed northeast, to clear the cape; beyond the fringe of white water the ground rose slowly up toward low green hills. Raef, feeling the currents under him roll and surge around the interference of the upthrusting coastline, watched the sky above the lowland and smelled the wind thrashing off it and thought they were burning something bad, in there. The back of his neck prickled up.

The mouth of the bay above the cape was far too wide to be chained and Volodymyr's ships glided smoothly on into it, with Dobrynya behind him, and then Pavo. Last in the line, Raef was thinking of Hjorunga Bay; suddenly this was the same thing, all over again, sailing up that gut toward disaster. Conn was walking up and down their ship, talking to the rowers, keeping them on their strokes, several lengths behind Pavo.

In the windbroken wavecrests at the mouth of the bay, seagulls were bobbing, resting out of the wind. The curve of the northern edge of the cape was a comb of fjords. Ahead, the bay narrowed rapidly, the northern shore a white ledge of stone rising sheer above the surf.

From Volodymyr's ship came the blast of a horn. That made sense, Raef thought: if they knew already up there that the ships were coming, be loud about it. The land was closing in on them, and all along the nearer shore to his right, he could see people running. Up ahead, Volodymyr's ship was pivoting, a hard steerboardside, headed for a narrow southerly inlet in the shore.

Conn called out sharply, and the rowers on their ship began to work harder, moving wide of Pavo. The wind was blowing stiff out of the west; when they all turned, he wanted not to have Pavo under their lee. Raef had nothing to do; the oars managed the ship; he stood up on the steerboard side of the crutched mast and peered ahead of them, at something bobbing in the water just at the mouth of the inlet. If it was part of a chain, it was too low. Volodymyr's ship stroked smoothly past it, and then Dobrynya's.

Raef saw two other similar things floating and bobbing out there in the inlet's mouth; his eyes followed the curve they made with the first, and marked a square wooden rig there on the wide ledge of the shore, cradling some kind of wheel. He shaded his eyes with his hand; he was looking almost due east now, and abruptly realized it was a capstan.

He shouted something to Conn, but then they too were gliding over the chain—he felt the narrow iron links go by, well below their keel, hard and cold against the bones of his feet—and over on the white ledge of the east shore, half a dozen men suddenly leapt out of hiding and rushed toward the capstan, threw themselves on the spokes of the wheel, and began to crank it up.

Conn yelled, "They're drawing up the chain!" He had seen it too.

"Go for shore," Raef yelled. He reached for his axe. It made no difference if they stormed the town. Ahead, along the southern and western shore of the cove, he could see the mossy rooftops now, the dingy air, the smoke, even the crowds rushing along the waterfront. There were no other ships, not even fishing boats. Volodymyr's dragon was halfway to the beach and he could hear the Knyaz's men cheering themselves on. Then, from the packed waterfront, something whizzed up into the air.

"Fire!" someone yelled, down near Conn, and Conn turned and whacked him. Raef wheeled around to look behind them; the turning wheel of the capstan had drawn the chain up out of the water, and it was stretched across the opening to the cove from one edge to the other. Along its length there were three bobbing little barrels, which were leaking thick and shiny ooze onto the water.

"Fire!"

Raef turned forward again. Volodymyr's ship was rowing hard toward the beach but Dobrynya's ship was slow in turning, and

Pavo's was running up alongside, too close. On both those ships some rowers stood up, to look toward shore, and then from the beach another volley of objects flew up into the air.

These were burning. They gave off a faint eerie screech. Smoke trailed after them. The first few dropped tamely into the water, but then several hit the dragon prow of Volodymyr's ship, burst, and splattered fire all over.

Shrill screams rose from Volodymyr's ship. The oars clashed together, and a man leapt overboard, and then another. The ship slowed, drifting. Raef threw his axe down, which was no use in this, and bounded up toward Conn. "Look—they have big slings—" Volodymyr's ship was wallowing, off course; they were trying to put out the fire, which was spreading down the dragon's head and back along the gunwale. Raef pulled Conn's attention from that to the beach.

On the white sandy slope below the first houses a clot of men were loading something into a big wooden arc, like Corban's sling gone large enough for a giant, and another spray of the burning objects hurtled up into the air.

Even Conn froze, for a moment, staring at the balls of flames hurtling toward him. Just in front of Raef, Vagn was still rowing hard, but most of the other oars were still in the water and Raef grabbed the young man's shoulder to stop him. From Volodymyr's ship, out in front of them all, a bray of terror went up. Half the crew leapt for the water, swimming for the next ship behind them, which was Dobrynya's.

Third in line, Pavo had had enough. Conn and Raef were a ship's length behind him; Raef saw the big Sclava fling one hand up and heard him bellow, and his steerboardside oars all went up and down at once, flaying in the air like broken wings. He was trying to pivot his ship. Conn shouted, "No—you idiot—" and then Pavo's ship lurched hard into Dobrynya's, and the prows crossed and with a crunch of wood and a splintering of oars Pavo's ship went up and tipped sideways, its stern going under water.

The burning shots fell thick all around them. Several men screeched in pain and terror. All around Raef's ship, men were leaping up, abandoning their oars. One smoking ball shattered on the floor of the ship at his feet and splashed the fire over his legging.

He gasped; a searing pain shot up the outside of his leg. Vagn was still beside him. Leaning over the side of the ship the boy scooped water with his hands to throw on the flames. Raef slapped at his blazing legging; he saw the bits of flame leap up, like a fiery liquid, and in his mind, he heard, *"It burns underwater."* He grabbed Vagn by the shoulder before he could throw more wet onto his legging.

"No—" He ripped off the legging from his hip to his ankle, taking the flames away with it, and cast it overboard like a burning flag. "Bury them." He pulled off his shirt and dropped it on the nearest little puddle of fire and crushed it under his feet.

Conn shouted, "We have to get out of here!"

"Reverse," Raef said. He put out another little flame, just catching on the wood of the ship's floor. Vagn was peeling off his own shirt. The young man knelt down and crushed a fire, and then jumped toward another.

"Reverse," Raef shouted, again, and went back along the ship. On his way he grabbed each of the guardsmen, half stunned still in their places, and turned him around to face the other way, making him duck under his oar, guiding him with a hand on his head. He reached the steerboard, now the bow of the ship, just as Oleg got there.

Oleg was stripping off his clothes. "We have to get that chain loose," he said, and dove into the water.

Raef howled wordlessly; he saw no use in this, one man swimming to the chain, but then Conn was at his side.

"Cover us! Get the bows!" Conn leapt into the water after Oleg and began to swim after him toward the point of land where the capstan stood, and where now the Greek defenders were clustered.

Raef began to swear, a stream of filthy, pleading words; in between, he bellowed, "Oars! Everybody row!" and lunged into the
hollow of the ship's stem. Merike scrambled out of his way. She
shouted something at him but he had no time for her. He dragged
out the chest with the bows. The men at least were rowing now, the
Varanger among them keeping some order, and the ship began to
stride back toward the chain. A few feet from him, Vagn on his
knees was putting out the last fire on the ship with his bare hands.
In the water between the ship and the capstan, Conn and Oleg
were only heads moving steadily along the surface.

The men by the capstan were shooting at them; one shot a
burning arrow, well wide, which startled Raef, until he saw it land
in a patch of the stuff leaking from the barrel floats. The flame
flickered there awhile, slow to ignite.

In his mind he saw them ignite, saw the fire spread, and burn,
all across the cove, until everything inside was smoke and ash. A
searing pain flared in his leg, deep as the bone.

He grabbed a bow. He was no good with this weapon and they
had only a few arrows but he nocked one; the ship was gliding
swiftly forward now, closer to the point of land, and maybe he
could hit something from here. Then Janka snatched the bow from
his hands.

"I do this," the hun said. "You steer."

Raef bounded back into the middle of the ship; he cast a quick
look over his shoulder, back into the cove.

Out in the harbor Dobrynya's ship and Pavo's were still fouled,
and Pavo's ship was swamped. The water bobbed with swimming
men, patches of slick smoldering stuff, and unbroken glass balls
trailing fumes and sodden rags. The slings on shore were loading
up again. Volodymyr had somehow gotten control of his ship, and
was pivoting it out around the two wrecks, putting them between
himself and the beach, coming after Raef's ship. Fire fluttered
from the prow of his ship. The scattered oars rose and fell wildly,
out of order.

Raef stood up on the gunwale to see better. Up ahead, Conn
and Oleg had almost reached the point where the capstan stood.
Janka had picked off two of the Greeks by the end of the chain,
and as the ship drew closer the rest of the defenders crouched down
behind the capstan frame. Some of the puddle of slick stuff in the
water was burning; the flame was spreading slowly but steadily.
Oleg and Conn plowed their way past it. Oleg reached the shore.

This was a sheer white ledge of rock, layered like a sandbar,
ending in flat grassy ground six feet over his head. The first time
he leapt up for a handhold he missed and splashed back into the
cove. A Greek with a sword was running down toward him from
the capstan and Janka shot him through the chest. By the capstan,
the remaining Greeks wheeled and ran.

Below Oleg, Conn gripped the rock with his hands, and the
guardsman put his feet on Conn's shoulders and climbed up. He
knocked Conn down as he did, sending him all the way under
the water, but the guardsman clawed his way up the white rock
bank onto the land. Wheeling, he reached down and pulled Conn
up after him.

Voldymyr's ship was ranging up just behind Raef's, the dragonhead still burning; all around it were swimming men trying to
climb on board. Ahead of them the chain blocked their way out. A
sudden hail of rocks and more glass balls pelted down around
Raef, and he flinched into the scant shelter of the hull. Bursting
near his feet, a ball scattered shards of glass and chunks of rock
all over, and but no fiery stuff. He saw Helgi go down, socked in
the head by a stone.

Over on the point of land, Conn and Oleg had reached the
capstan, were struggling to loosen the wheel, both leaning on
the bar. The weight of the chain held it fast. Between them and
Raef, floating islands of black ooze drifted by the ship. In one, a
glass ball floated, leaking fire, and around the ball, the ooze was
sending up thick black smoke. Janka had another arrow nocked.
The blazing dragonhead on Volodymyr's ship was nudging

closer, the men trying to get the head loose from the prow without burning themselves up doing it. The prince was screaming his oarsmen to their work, pacing up and down among them, trying to force his ship in between Raef's ship and the white ledge of rock, using Raef as a shield against the missile barrage. Raef picked up an unburst glass ball and threw it at the other dragon.

"Stay back! Damn you! Stay off me!"

At the capstan, abruptly, Oleg was wheeling around toward the chain. He took hold of the chain and began to pull, trying to lift its weight off the pawl, so they could unbrake the wheel. Raef roared, amazed. Impossibly heavy, the chain never budged, but Oleg bent himself to it, set his feet, lunged back, as if he could drag the world around. Conn leapt to help him, three feet higher on the chain, beside the capstan bar.

Another rain of missiles pelted down on Raef's ship and slammed painfully into his shoulders. They were bringing the sling closer. Now they were firing barrages of rocks. He guessed they were out of the fiery stuff, whatever it was. Then Oleg let out a shout like a tree limb ripping loose, and up ahead, on the point, the chain crept up off the capstan pawl.

By the capstan, Conn kicked something free, below the wheel, and letting go of the chain he yanked the bar out of the socket. The wheel began to rumble, the chain flying back of its own weight, dragging Oleg in a wild dive into the water with it.

On Volodymyr's ship a harsh ragged cheer went up. They had finally thrown off the burning dragonhead. The stumpy bow of the dragon pushed in between Raef's ship and the shore, headed for the open water. Volodymyr stood in the prow, his arms folded over his chest. Raef bellowed, "Oars up!" to let him pass. Wheeling around again, he looked back at the two wrecks.

Pavo's ship was flooded to its gunwales, dragonhead showing like a sea monster, but Dobrynya had gotten his ship clear. His hull was drifting, half its oars gone, most of its men. The slings on

shore were hammering everything with rocks and the few men left
on board were cowering down on the floor. Raef yelled, "Reverse!
Reverse!"

In front of him, Leif, still bent to an oar rowing forward, gave
him a white-eyed look. But he stood up, turned around, ducked
under his oar, and sat down again the other way, and the rest of
them followed him. Raef shouted again, and the two banks of oars
dipped down and into the water. The dragon shot smoothly forward, back to the drifting ship.

Dobrynya still stood in the stern, a bow in his hands, loosing
arrows in a steady stream. He saw Raef coming and one arm went
up like a flag. Through the foul smoldering smoky water Raef
closed with the crippled hull; he shouted, again, "Oars up!" just as
they glided up alongside Dobrynya. Then: "Grab on! Grab on!"

Before Raef gave the orders, the Varangers saw what they had
to do. They rode up over the few oars left on the backboard side of
Dobrynya's side, and Leif and Harald grappled the amidships
gunwales together. Ulf and Bos and Bjorn leapt across into the
drifting ship and found oars to run out on the far side. When Raef
screamed again, "Reverse! Reverse!" they rowed, and the men still
on his ship rowed, and linked together the two hulls pulled slowly
toward the chain.

Raef spun around, looking for Conn, seeing him nowhere.
Volodymyr's ship was past the chain. Flames slithered along the
water between. On the scummy blackened flickering surface two
bodies floated. He shouted his cousin's name. Janka had climbed
up onto the dragon's head, a bow in his hand, but no more arrows.
The two bound ships were sweeping toward the sunken chain and
in a moment would pass over it. "Conn!" Raef leaned out from the
gunwale, scanning the water, filthy with black muck.

Then, laughing, Conn rose up over the gunwale near the steerboard, and he pulled himself inside.

Raef let go his breath in a long sigh. He was hoarse, his throat
raw, the stink of the burning stuff deep in his lungs and on his

tongue. His leg hurt. He watched Conn pull Oleg up after him. Oleg's head was scummy with the black muck. The ship had crossed over the chain. They stood out to the middle of the bay, over deep water, beyond reach of the land.

The space between them and the cove crept with swimming men. Some were already scrambling up out of the water onto the ship; without orders, the oarsmen had put her around, to wait for all the swimmers. The black ooze covered them so much a few looked like seals. The Greeks sent up another volley of rocks, but they splashed harmlessly short. Raef thought of Merike, and wheeled toward the stern.

She sat there on his sea chest, watching him, her face slimed with tears. Her arms were around Vagn, who leaned against her, the life going out of his eyes. The boy's hands were blackened and burned and raw, and a great wound had laid open the side of his head. A rock had hit him. Before Raef reached him, he was dead.

Raef sank down beside her. He was thirsty and there was no more water. She turned to him, tears streaming down her face, set Vagn gently down, and bent over his leg.

The skin of his thigh was the color of a bad sunburn and all the hair on his leg was burnt off. Little blisters had risen all along his shin where the fire had first hit him. When she tried to touch him he pulled her hand away. Volodymyr's ship, in the center of the bay, turned and came back toward them. On Dobrynya's ship, Pavo sat down heavily on the floor and put his head in his hands.

Raef got onto his feet, his leg throbbing, and his knees going back and forth. Back behind them, all through the cove the black smoke rolled. If they had still been there they would have been catching fire. He went to Conn, standing amidships by the mast gallows. He wiped his face as he went, feeling nicks and sharp things all over himself, his hands, his chest, his cheeks, chips of glass in his beard. He was naked except for one leg and his drawers, and bleeding all over. Conn faced him, put both hands on his shoulders.

"That was not what I expected. Nothing. When I saw you pulling away from us I thought you'd gone crazy. You are crazy. You saved everybody."

Raef hugged him. "Not me. Oleg. You. Opening the chain." He glanced down the ship, where the men sat wearily on their sea chests, their shoulders slumped. Helgi lay stretched out on the floor. He said, "Vagn is dead."

"Yes, and Helgi, and some others. Not many. We came through." Conn draped an arm over his shoulder. "Are you hurt?"

"Not bad," Raef said. "Watch out." He pulled a shard of glass out of his hair.

"Was that Roman fire?"

"Not the real stuff, I think. Something else, something not as good, but good enough. But they ran out of it." Raef shook his head. "Even so I don't want to try that again right away. We have to get water. Food. Here comes Volodymyr."

The prince had drawn his ship up beside theirs, and stepped across the gunwales as if he stood on dry land. There was a bruise on his cheekbone and his clothes were filthy with blood and black smoky soot. He came toward them, and shook their hands, looking deeply into their eyes.

Dobrynya sat in the stern of the next ship, watching them. "We need to get onto the land," he said, and beyond him, Pavo growled like a sick dog. "If we can land farther west along the cape, out toward the sea, we can attack them that way."

Volodymyr turned to glare back at the city. "If I have to stay here three years I will take this place. I swear this on a handful of earth, and I shall take the earth from Chersonese."

Dobrynya said, "Three years is too long. Once the Emperor hears, he'll send a navy to drive us off. We have to do this quickly." His blue eyes turned toward Raef and Conn. He looked older, somehow, tired, his solid assurance cracked. He said, "We can't let them get word to Constantinople."

Raef said nothing. Conn said, "Then somebody has to watch

this way out. If they can't send a ship, it will take them months to get help."

Volodymyr said, "You two, and this ship, you are the gate here. Don't let another ship through, in or out. Uncle, where can we put our men onto the land?"

Dobrynya nodded toward the cape. "That looks flat enough, out there. And there's some little beach."

Raef gave a grunt of a laugh. The whole sea ran against the westernmost coast of the cape and it was a gnashing of riptides and rocks. He knew the inexperienced Sclava would have trouble managing the ships there. The Greeks would be waiting for them. His leg hurt and he wished he had some wotka. He nudged Conn, who said, "We have our orders, then. You don't need our help from here." Raef went back to sit on his sea chest and watch the other men get Vagn and Helgi ready to throw overboard into the sea.

They were wrapping the bodies in cloaks from their sea chests. There were a lot of rocks in the ship and they bundled them into the dead men's cloaks to weight them. Conn squatted down beside Helgi, and helped Bjorn tie the shroud. Coming next to Vagn, who was already wrapped up, he pulled the cloth back from the mess of the boy's face, and bent suddenly and kissed his forehead, and then folded the cloth back. Beside Raef, Merike gave a sob, and Raef reached out to her, and she let him comfort her, leaning her tear-scummed cheek on his arm; he guessed the battle had shaken her utterly. She would think differently of Raef now. Conn rose.

"Let's go get some water."

"Oars out," Raef said. He reached for the tiller bar.

CHAPTER EIGHTEEN

Volodymyr and Dobrynya were already rowing off along the western finger of the cape, and Conn followed them out to deeper water. On the shore they could hear faint cheering from the Greeks, who likely hoped anyway their enemy was giving up. But when they had cast the dead men overboard, Conn turned the ship around, and they rowed back up the fjord toward Chersonese.

Smoke was still rolling up from the water of the cove; the dragonship had sunk entirely. Along the point where the capstan was, three men were hauling at the wheel, trying to pull the chain above the water again. When Conn sent his ship swooping down toward them they all darted back into the high brush like birds from a hawk. Conn did not turn in to the cove; he rowed across the mouth once, looking into the harbor, and then went on a little way up the main fjord, around the stony knob at the end of the capstan point, which sheltered a little white beach.

Here Raef climbed over the side and waded in to the shore. Merike scrambled after him, her face frantic, and he had to take Janka, because they only had two arrows left. He took Leif, also, to help carry whatever they found. The Greeks, if they were still on the point, were hiding.

Merike ran up onto the land and flung herself down on it full length and laughed and rolled on the sand. She leapt to her feet and threw her arms up and sang. Raef looked up and down the tiny wedge of white beach, and saw no sign of water; he started inland and the others followed. As if the touch of the earth gave her new life Merike was joyous. Every few steps she came over and bumped into Raef, pushing her breasts at him, wiggling her hips.

He understood how she felt; the change from being on the

ship was wonderful, as if he had been set free from some tiny cage; he felt loose and lively all over, in spite of his hurts, and very hungry. The country was pretty, too, the rising slope, with its outcrops of white rock, studded with thickets of deep brush, spikes of yellow flowers, white roses and little red blooms like cups. The air smelled delicious.

He fended Merike off with one hand, his body aching, and his leg sore and stiff, and went toward the trees, where there might be water. In the first crumpled hillside they found a patch of brackish swamp, and followed the trickle of a stream up to a clear freshwater spring. They all drank for long moments. When they had filled the skins in the spring, he sent Janka and Leif to carry them back to the ship, pulled Merike in behind some thorny, red-flowered bushes, and laid her down on her back.

She was eager, sweet, tender with his cuts and his bad leg, babbling to him in her own language. He understood none of the words but the way she spoke them made him feel good. Her caresses and the thunderous release of his orgasm made him feel even better. He lay down on his back in the sun, his eyes shut, thinking about nothing.

She went off; in a little while she was back, excited again, her hands full of berries and leaves. He started to sit up and she pushed him back down. She gave him the berries, and while he ate them, she began to peel the leaves in half. The sticky stuff inside she daubed on his leg, and then on the cuts all over his body. Twice she stopped to worry bits of glass out of his skin.

He did sit up, hurting less, his leg no longer throbbing. He gave her a kiss in gratitude. The berries had hardly taken the edge off his hunger. The old fruits of the thorny brush lay all around, hard and yellow. When he tried to bite through the waxy skin the hard tart flesh inside puckered his mouth like a cramp. He heard Janka whistle, and stood up. The sun was nearly to the horizon, and he was too tired to look for food now and he went down with Merike to the shore, to go back on the ship.

In the morning two Greek ships ran for the open sea. Conn had warning, because they had to lower the chain, and he was waiting in the fjord just off the north point. The dragonship ran down the smaller Greek double-ender before she even reached the open sea. Conn was in a hurry, with the bigger, faster ship slipping by, and as soon as he caught the double-ender he stove a hole in her and left her sinking and her crew swimming for shore.

The second ship, bigger, with a high square stern, was stroking fast for the open sea. She had at least a dozen oars to a side and her rowers were pulling hard. Conn thought they would turn with the wind, once they weathered the cape, and set sail, but the ship kept on rowing to the west. Conn got his oars working in a good rhythm, letting four men rest every hundred strokes. By midafternoon they were close enough to the Greek ship that he could see the men by the sternboard up there looking back over their shoulders.

The freeboard of the merchantman towered over the dragonship; as the Varanger were swarming up over one side, the Greek sailors were diving off the other. Conn grappled on, and set his crew to looting the Greek ship, carrying off everything they could pack onto the dragon, casks of wine and jugs of honey and stacks of flat bread for the sailors on their journey. The rest of the cargo, much of the food, but also stacks of furs and wax and pottery, they left on board. When this was done, as his own men gorged on the food, Conn let the Greeks back onto their ship and broke their oars, so that they could only sail with the wind back to Chersonese.

The Varanger dragon harried the big ship along like a shepherd with one sheep. Conn could tell the Greeks thought they were going to get safely home; he kept the dragon just off their flank to discourage them from any other course. The Greek sailors were good enough at managing their sail to get the merchantman up to the mouth of the bay, and there Conn stormed their ship again.

This time the Greeks leapt off and swam toward the shore,
leaving the big ship in the hands of the Varanger. Conn and half a
dozen oarsmen from the dragon took over the Greek, bringing on
oars from the dragon, which did not fit. Nonetheless they were
able to coax and angle the strange ship back out westward again,
toward the western edge of the cape, where Volodymyr and Dobrynya and Pavo had put ashore. Raef with the dragon sailed
lightly along beside the Greek.

When they came up close to the western, windward shore Raef
made a growl in his throat. There on the rocky coast the wreckage
of the the two dragons lay in the surf, the two hulls already shattered into a hundred pieces; one of the great dragonheads lay up
against a rock at the foot of the seacliff. When the sea rose there to
dash itself against the cliff the curled surface carried dozens of
bits of the ships.

On top of that cliff, several men were waving their arms and
jumping, and more were running up from the inland side to join
them; one took off his shirt and began to shake it in the air. Whenever a wave carried the dragon high enough, Raef could see onto
the flat land behind them. The great mass of Volodymyr's army
was lined up behind shields before the clumped boxy houses of the
city. They had gotten up onto the city plain, and probably attacked
that first line of houses, but now the Greeks were fighting back and
had them pinned where they were, with the seacoast behind them.

Conn and his little crew were struggling to get the big Greek
merchantman far enough along the coast that the waves would carry
it in onto the foot of the cliff below Volodymyr's men. The sea ran
back and forth here, circling and plunging along the cliff face, and
Raef could feel the water trying to drive him in onto those rocks. He
had been managing the dragon with the sail and the wind, but he
had the other oarsmen ready, and now he had them row them farther
out to sea. Volodymyr's men were already climbing down the seacliff to meet Conn on the Greek ship.

Conn wasn't taking the ship any farther himself. At a yell from him his crew cast their oars overboard on the windward side and leapt after them. A moment later, the tiller pulled, Conn jumped into the sea, and started trying to swim out toward Raef's dragon.

The waves and the wind pushed the abandoned Greek steadily onshore, and Conn and his sailors could not swim out against the force of the sea. Their heads showed among the hurtling waves. Raef pivoted his ship, and rowed down to pick them up. Each heave of the sea carried the dragon farther toward the rocks and the cliffs and the miserable pieces of the other ships. Raef got Conn and Oleg up easily enough, but Skinny Harald and Leif were struggling farther inshore, and by the time he had pulled in the first three, the others were well east of them. Bjorn, the farthest, was also closest to the rocks.

Soaking wet and shivering, Conn stood in the stem of the dragon, watching his men bob helpless in the sea; he said, "Volodymyr could likely use some men."

Raef grunted at him. "Get a cloak." He got up and walked back along the rows of oarsmen; with the steerboard now in the front of the ship he could adjust their course better by the pull of the oars. Screeching off the halyards, whipping the sheets back and forth, the wind was luffing the sail in a useless flutter, but it pushed the ship on faster, and he swooped quickly down on Leif and Skinny Harald and hauled them up almost without stopping.

The Greek ship now was almost into the surf. The sea had turned her sideways to the shore and was rolling her madly from gunwale to gunwale, the waves breaking up over her fat hull. Bjorn, clinging to a floating oar, was only a dozen yards from her keel. He wasn't a good swimmer; he looked tired, and Raef imagined his lips were moving even faster than usual. Raef shouted orders. He could feel the ship drifting hard on shore, and the wind fighting to get it broadside. He got some of the oars pulling backward and some forward, to keep the ship trimmed to her course, and used the wind to gust them down toward Bjorn.

Leaning past the dragon's tail, he shouted, "Leave the oar! Leave the oar!" The sea carried him up with a sickening lurch into the sky. He looked over his shoulder, and on the far side of the dragon, only a few yards away, he saw Volodymyr's men reaching the Greek ship just as she began to break up. The white spume of the surf leapt high behind them. With a roaring cheer two Sclava stood up on the ship's flank and rode the hull in over the breaker and up to the foot of the cliff. Swiftly the men waiting in the shallow wavesurge began to haul off the casks and bails of cargo and heave them up to others waiting on the cliff above.

Bjorn was stroking wildly toward them down the slope of the wave. Raef bellowed, "Reverse!" and leaned down as the dragon swooped downward, and got Bjorn by the outstretched arm. With the ship tipping under them in the first rise of the next wave all the crew stood in unison, leaning to hold her upright, and turned around and sat again to their oars. The ship stroked up across the wave and out to sea, fighting the rake of the wind and the pounding of the crisscross currents. She skimmed along like a seagull, out of danger. Raef wrestled Bjorn aboard, with Conn holding him by the belt.

꘎

Conn bundled himself into the cloak Thorfinn had given him, thinking warmly of the old man. Once they were out of the reach of the inshore riptides, he got Raef to sail across the wind, past the seacliff again, so he could see what was going on.

Volodymyr's men were hauling supplies up the seacliff. The Greek ship was already matchwood. Several Sclava were wading out into the waves to catch floating cargo. They had gotten the bread, he saw, in its great sacks, and at least one cask of the wine.

The sea carried the dragon upward, and Conn saw, on the plain there, Volodymyr's shield wall, and beyond, men digging. They were trying to raise a fortification. As he watched, from the packed houses of the city, a spray of rocks came hurtling out against the workmen. One of the Greek slingers. Beyond the tiled rooflines of the houses rose the round top and upthrust cross of a Christian church. There was a row of white stone pillars, like statues of trees with flat tops, on the slight slope below.

Raef stood beside him, and shook his head.

"What are they doing? Building a defense? That's crazy. They should just attack."

Conn shrugged. "Not much we can do." He thought he had better chances, anyway. He pulled back into the mouth of the fjord. After a few days another Greek ship tried to escape, this one at night, and Conn burnt it to the waterline at the mouth of the cove, to show Chersonese what was going on.

⇒

Raef went inland again, to fill the water skins, and look for food, and because he wanted to see the inland side of the city. There were no villages, no sign of other people living around the city, no fields or pastures or flocks. He left Janka and Leif setting snares in a meadow and pushed on steadily up the rising ground, following the spine of the ridge.

From a height he looked out on the cove of Chersonese, on his right hand. There were three merchant ships hauled out at the farthest southern edge of it and a little flock of much smaller boats, maybe fishing vessels, along the western beach. Most of the city seemed to cluster along the ground just behind this beach. A high stone wall rose at the southern edge of it. Nearer the water, on a rise, was a little squat building with a cross on top. People walked back and forth along the beach, too far away for him to see what they were doing, and through the streets. In the blue water he could clearly see the sunken dragonship, and he could even make out the line of the chain, draped across the mouth of the cove, the barrels now sunken down under the water. Inside the chain, the water was smoother and calmer.

On his other hand, the great blue fjord reached back between this ridge and the next, deep into the higher ground, a magnificent harbor, as good, he thought, as Hedeby's.

The wind stroked over the trees, so they tossed their branches; the slopes were tangled masses of flowers. Insects shrilled in the trees, fat grasshoppers with transparent wings. On the far ridge he saw two deer come up from the water, angling through the brush, and vanish in among the trees. He found berries as he went along, and looked for nut trees and birds' nests.

Beyond Chersonese he could just glimpse the dark blue sea; a cloud of smoke hovered just inside of the coastline over where he thought Volodymyr and Dobrynya were trapped. Probably he and Conn would have to supply them, eventually, although they seemed to have taken part of the town. South, the land rose to a sheer cliff face like a wall.

He worked his way on down to the marshy low ground at the head of the cove, now well beyond the city, and slogged through half a mile of muck, sometimes knee-deep, spooking strange russet-colored ducks and setting birds to screeching in the trees. On the far side, the land rose again, open in places where the layered white rocks broke through the grass and brush. He passed a scattering of old bear shit, heavy with seeds. He climbed to the high point of this rise, and looked down at the city wall, now between him and the water.

It was solid as the cliff face, with a round tower at one corner, and a massive double gate. The road that led away from the gate was small and empty. He realized that this wall wasn't here to let people in and out but to fence the city off from the wild world; everything reached them from the sea. They were Greek; on the outside was not. He started down toward the wall, climbing over outcrops of rock, and came suddenly on a long wooden tube lying on the ground.

It was wet, and overgrown with moss, and brush grew all around it; he had put his hands on it to climb over it before he realized what it was. He pulled some of the brush and long green swags of moss away. The wood was dark from years of soaking in water, streaked with a crumbly white mold. He looked up the hill and saw the pipe vanishing into the brush near the top, and then turned his gaze down and saw it curving away into the brush toward the wall. He remembered there had been no water on the low ground. Inside that wall was lowland.

They had overcome that. He stood still a moment, admiring how they had overcome it. Then he felt his way along the tube until he came to a joint, and with his axe, broke through it. Water gushed out, a pure, steady stream. He directed the top end of the tube well away from the bottom end, so the water couldn't somehow still find its way in, and then cut across the slope looking for more of the pipes. He found another four, and broke them all. When he was sure no more water was going into Chersonese, he went back the way he had come, toward his ship.

Janka had killed a deer, and the crew had built a fire on the beach to cook it. The sun was setting when Raef arrived. They had brought in a cask of the wine and opened it and everybody was already raving drunk. The ship floated at anchor just offshore. He found Merike hiding out in the gloom, her face streaked with tears. She clung to him, sobbing, but he felt her over for hurts, even got her to let him look at her woman's part, and decided nothing bad had happened to her; she was just frightened. She was glad to have him back, at least. He took her out on board the ship, got his fur cloak and spare shirt out of his sea chest, and made a bed for them inside the stern, where they coupled sitting up, which he had never done before.

⸺⸻⸺

A day later a little cargo ship came down from the north, coasting along, and put into the bay. Before the captain realized his mistake Conn had laid up alongside him. He threw the sailors off, took the cargo of wine, and hulled the ship. Raef watched the sailors swimming off toward Chersonese, and wondered how much water the city had left.

Merike would not let him leave her alone anymore. She followed him everywhere, went around picking mushrooms and looked for plants while he roamed along the land across the little cove from the city. He took to sitting on the high point of the ground, near the start of the wall, looking toward Chersonese. Something was poking at the edge of his mind, like a pearl inside an oyster, slowly growing from just a small irritating pinch to a bright golden glow. Gradually he realized that it was his basileus, somewhere inside that city.

He wondered what he would say to Rashid, if he caught him. If one of the others caught him first, there would be no way to save him.

He thought, oddly enough, of Rashid's little red slippers, perhaps soon spotted with blood. He did not want Rashid to die and decided to offer the basileus to anybody who brought the Mahmettan to him alive. But he could not think what he would say to him.

Merike came up beside him, and leaned on him. "What?" she said. "What?"

He tried. He said, "Remember Rashid, the Mahmet who came to see me?" He took her hand, and turned the ring on her finger. Her fingers curled around his and she kissed him.

"Rashid," she said, in a voice that said she had no idea what he was talking about. "That?" She pointed across the cove, where the drowned dragon was clearly visible in the blue water. Raef was surprised to see they had gotten all the black scum off. The place beyond, with its crowds of buildings, its thronged street along the beach, looked as busy as ever.

He said, "No. That is Chersonese, remember?"

"Chersonese," she said, and her accent made it a different word. He shrugged. He said, "Rashid is in Chersonese."

She laughed, looking away, leaning on him, holding his hand. "Rashid," she said, with a little laugh.

He guessed it seemed as useless to her as it did to him, to talk. He put his arm around her, and thought about what he could possibly say to Rashid.

⸻

Janka killed every time he shot, and retrieved his arrows carefully. He set very clever snares, so they had a constant supply of meat, and now lots of wine. They took to coming onshore every afternoon to eat and drink, and going back on board the dragon at night to sleep. Every night, fewer of the crew made it back on the uncomfortable ship, and one night they all stayed off, even Raef and Merike.

She was tired of the ship, and complained and whined every time about going on board.

Raef felt itchy about them all being on the beach like that, with nothing around except the darkness of the night. He thought they ought to set out sentries, but they were all too drunk to talk to, especially Conn, dancing around the fire, his hair flying. The other men swooped joyously after him. They were all Varanger now, Oleg's guardsmen as well. Raef took Merike off higher on the slope, to a grassy place, and lay down with her.

Still he could not sleep, even after he had glutted himself on her. The moon rose, half eaten, and the woman slept deeply beside him, but he could not shut his eyes. He felt something creeping along inside his brain, like a worm in his skull.

He got up, went off to piss, looked down at the beach, where the fire had died. The men were sleeping around it, lumps in the pale moonlight, silent. But on the slope above them, like the worm in his head, something was creeping along.

He yelled. He was too far away, he would never reach them first. "Get up! Get up!" He ran with long bounding strides across the slope and tripped and fell headlong, and rolled with one motion back to his feet and running. "Get up!" But the men creeping up over the top of the slope heard him, too, of course, and they charged down on the sleeping camp.

—⚬—

Conn heard Raef's voice through a bleary fog of wine, and wanted not to heed it; but he pushed himself groggily up on one arm. Somebody crashed into him. He screeched, struggling up, scrabbling around him for his sword. Something pounded on him between the shoulderblades, driving him down. He bellowed again, knowing what was happening, seeing everything gone, everything lost, in a single stupid drunken moment, all this flying through his mind in an instant, and then he got his feet under him. He stood up, flailing around him barehanded, dodged a long lance, and with his fist knocked the lancer behind it flying.

That settled him. He leapt toward the lance on the ground and snatched it up, and seeing nothing before him but strangers pounding his sleeping crew he stabbed into a back and then into another back, wading forward into an ocean of enemies. They wheeled toward him. He swung the lance around waist-high at them. Then Raef charged in from behind them, bellowing, and the enemy circle broke.

Leif suddenly leapt in front of him, throttling a man down with his two hands. Just beyond the fire, two Greeks in white shirts were beating with swords at something limp on the ground, and Conn dashed at them, got one through the body, lost the lance, and ducked under the wild sword stroke of the man left standing.

The return stroke whistled by his ear. He dove forward, drove his shoulder into the swordsman's waist, and flung him down on his back. Something slit his side. Still lying full length on the twisting body, he reared up and got the sword arm, smashed it down on the ground, and with all his strength bending it over drove the sword through the chest under him.

Turning, he saw it was Oleg they had killed. Oleg lay there on the ground, torn with bloody wounds.

He let out a howl. He swung around, looking for somebody else to fight. The Greeks were running away. They were racing back up the slope toward the ridge between this beach and the cove, some limping, some carrying other men. Raef had stopped to help one of the Varanger; a lot of the crew were sitting on the ground. Conn bellowed, "Come on!" and charged after the Greeks.

Leif followed him, Leif and Bjorn the Christian. They went puffing up to the crest of the ridge and across the broken rocky ground there toward the capstan. The Greeks were already halfway across the cove, rowing in a pack of little boats; they had left two or three other boats on this shore, just below the capstan, their oars sticking up like wings.

Conn's chest was heaving. He realized he was bleeding down his side, and looked down. In the slanting moonlight he saw the gash along his ribs, a layer of shirt, a layer of skin and then a black layer of blood.

He pointed toward the little boats below them on the beach. "Go get me one of those boats," he said.

Bjorn was bent over, his hands on his knees, breathing hard. The cross around his neck dangled under his chin. "No use," he said, between gasps. "They're gone."

"Get me the boat," Conn said, with a few other words for emphasis. He went over to the capstan.

The bar was solid, immovable. He remembered heaving at it with Oleg, and a hot terrible grief came up into his throat. He had made a mistake. Raef had known, had not told him. No: he remembered, painfully, Raef saying something. His mistake. So Oleg had died. Oleg, and others.

He leaned his shoulder against the capstan and pushed. Nothing happened.

The base was buried under a pile of rocks. He began to throw the rocks aside. Leif came up beside him to help, and then Bjorn.

"I said to get me the boat."

"We did," Bjorn said. He picked up a chunk of the white rock. Some of the guardsmen came up to help them. They were uncovering the frame of wooden timbers that held the capstan wheel. More of the men came up and they cast away rocks. Raef came up.

"Harald's dead," he said. "Oleg, I guess you know. Three other guardsmen. Four Greeks."

"Help me," Conn said.

"Stand back," Raef said.

He had his axe, and he began to strike at the timbers of the frame; the other men gathered around him with swords and axes to bash in turn at the wood. The chain clanked. The capstan began to tilt. There were so many men trying to strike the frame that they had to line up for it, on one side, but on the other, Raef went the whole time at it with his axe. Finally the chain clanked twice, two timbers popped apart, and the capstan wheel shrieked, tore free, and sailed off into the cove.

Nobody cheered. Conn was not looking at anybody. Leif, Bjorn the Christian, and a guardsman named Vyorek carried off the fishing boat down toward the beach. The others went wearily along in the same direction.

He knew they all blamed him. He knew it was his fault.

Raef stood beside him, silent, his long body slack. Conn said, "He told me once that he wanted to die for the Knyaz."

Raef laid one hand on his arm; he said nothing. Maybe he blamed himself too. That was perversely comforting. Conn started down toward the ship, his cousin at his side. The moon was sinking down behind the ridge to the west, and the sun was rising. The men with the four-oared boat had just reached the beach. He watched them carry it out on the little waves, light and nimble.

He said, "You think you can take this cockleshell in to bring off Volodymyr and Dobrynya to meet me in the dragon?"

"Probably," Raef said. "Are you all right? Merike can maybe do something."

Conn felt the pain in his side for the first time, and laid his hand against the wound, slick with blood. "It isn't bad. Just a slice off my ribs. Let's go get Volodymyr."

Dobrynya said, "We took several houses, and a fountain, but now that's gone dry. They're pounding us day and night with arrows and their slings. I'm trying to build a wall, but the ground's all rock, and we can't find any more water. Or any more food, other than the paltry amount you were able to get us. We got into a granary in that first rush but we're running out of that, and there's no meat." His hair was pulled back and tied with a cord and his skin was ruddy with sunburn, his lips cracked.

Volodymyr said, "We have to attack them again. That solves everything."

"If we succeed," Dobrynya said, forcefully; this was a old argument with them, now, Conn guessed. The affection between them had worn to grit, that rubbed them both raw, and yet neither one could stop and let the other lead.

He glanced down the ship at Raef, who was staring moodily toward Chersonese, as if he could will himself there. The fishing boat lay in the lee of the dragonship. The rest of Conn's crew was transferring skins of water from the dragonship into the littler boat, along with some of the wine, the rest of the bread, the honey, and two forequarters of the deer. Every time Conn looked at the little boat, he thought of Oleg, and his chest hurt.

Dobrynya said, "We can't attack them yet. We have to get

closer—build the wall closer, to get us some cover to attack. They'll cut us down like sheep if we charge across the open ground."

Conn said, "I want to attack them now."

Volodymyr reared up, his face shining. "Yes! From both sides."

"Take the food back in," Conn said. "Feed your men, get them ready, and head for the city. I'll go back up and go in through the cove."

Volodymyr said, "You are a true Varanger. We'll do it. Uncle, agree to it."

Dobrynya was staring at Conn. "You're mad. They'll have made more fire by now. And we can't signal each other, with the city between us. We're losing men, too, and there's bad talk. They think the gods have turned on us. Even Pavo may not obey us."

"I don't need a signal," Conn said. "I'm attacking. You two can do as you please." He thought of Oleg and his throat swelled painfully. Volodymyr was already climbing over the side of the dragonship, into the fishing boat. Dobrynya hesitated a moment, staring at Conn, and followed after. With the cargo there was room only for him and Volodymyr and two other Sclava, and they all set to the oars and started off, the prince and the posadnik bending their backs with the others.

A big wave lifted the dragonship and rolled on. The boat rocked up sideways over it and slid away, already nearly in the grip of the crashing surf there. At the foot of the cliff, on a pebble beach only a few inches wide, half a dozen Sclava waited. Conn hoped they had managed to offload the cargo without losing much of it. He turned to Raef.

"What do you think?"

Raef was still watching distant Chersonese. "I want to get there. I want to see that place. Let's go."

Conn clapped his shoulder. "Your turn to row, then."

CHAPTER NINETEEN

Conn rowed out to sea, into the teeth of the wind, zagged back to the north to pick up the right approach into the fjord, and sailed down toward Chersonese. The sun was past the height of the sky when they set the mast. Raef sat then at the helm, and Conn beside him.

"Do you think Volodymyr will attack?" he said, eventually.

Raef shrugged. "Whatever happens will happen." He had not taken his eyes from the direction of Chersonese all morning. "Once they've had some of that wine, they'll come."

He was sitting easy there, Merike behind him, but Conn could not stay still and walked up the length of the ship, going from man to man, making sure they were ready, armed, brave, eager. He said all the names of their dead to them, Oleg's first.

He said Vagn's name and realized he was standing almost where the boy had died, putting out the fire on the ship. That had saved them, really, that boy's sacrifice, and yet everybody had already forgotten him. Ahead, the dark mass of the coastline rose above the churning white foam, and the fjord opened up before him, a gap of blue water in the surf. He felt the ship shiver under him, and knew the wind was changing. The world pulsated around him, all alive.

He turned toward the stern, toward Raef, who nodded at him. "Down mast," he said, and went to the bow to unlash the stay.

They swung the mast down into its crutches and brought out the oars. Conn, looking back from the bow, saw how smoothly and quickly they did this, saw also there were only twenty-eight of them now, and went back through them moving them around to balance the work. Raef came up to the bow with him afterward, and they took the two front oars. Janka climbed up onto the drag-onhead with his bow.

They stroked across the deep indent of the mouth of the fjord and through the mouth of the cove; on the point, some men were milling around where the capstan had been, and these Greeks saw the ship coming and began to scurry around with purpose, dragging something forward.

Raef said, "One of those slings. Pull hard and to backboard."

Conn shouted, and the dragonship shot ahead into the gap, going left more than straight, angling toward the town. Janka cried out sharply, "They load! They load!"

"Is it fire?" Leif cried, two benches upship from Raef. Somebody else wailed. The oars rose and fell as even as music.

"Pull," Raef shouted. "Backboard, damn it, pull hard!" Conn bent to the long stroke of his oar, waiting for the shot to come.

"They shoot," Janka cried, above his head.

There was a distant shout, and another stroke, with his head bent, waiting for the burst of fire on his back. Then a pelting hail of little sharp scraps and dust. Another stroke, and he looked up and back across the gunwale between Leif and a guardsman's brawny bare back, to see on the point the Greeks struggling to turn their clumsy weapon around. No fire. He laughed. And now they were out of range. He was afraid of nothing now. "Pull," he shouted. "Pull backboard, up steerboard."

The steerboard oars rose in a kind of salute; the backboard side dug in, and the ship turned neatly to the south. "Pull!" He shipped his oar and stood up, looking forward past the jaw of the dragon head, toward Chersonese.

On the white sand there a line of men was forming, with lances and big shields. Helmets. They had two more slings, one at either end of the line.

"Oars up!" He wouldn't even need to say that. The ship was gliding forward under its own weight now. Raef was beside him, his hand on Conn's back, his head pushed up beside him to look. The first sling fired, a clatter of rocks, and they hunched in against the ship for cover. Then the keel of the dragonship touched sand,

Raef struck Conn once hard in the back with the flat of his hand, and they charged.

⚬

Raef had a leather shield, which he held over his head as he plunged through the shallows. The second barrage from the slings rattled down around him, splashing all around him into the water and hitting the shield hard enough to jar his arm. Conn was a step ahead of him, going for the middle of the shield wall.

He knew two things about these battles, which were to keep his feet moving and Conn on his left side; nothing got through him. The tall shields locked ahead of him, and he chopped with his axe. A sword blade pierced right through his leather shield and he jerked it wide, shield and sword and all, hacked with his free arm at the arm behind the sword, saw another sword jabbing at him from knee level, and slashed wildly at it, hitting nothing, off-balance, his mind a clutter of shields and blades.

The guardsman on his right staggered backward, blood gushing from his face, and the Greeks pounding him swung toward Raef, two men at once, stabbing high and low together. He had to back up. His shifting feet dodged them as if he had eyes on his toes. Somewhere a horn blew, over and over. The Greeks were calling in more men. Frantically he parried off the high blow and dodged the low blow and stayed hard by Conn.

The guardsman next to him was down, and dying, and the hallooing Greeks plunged over him toward Conn. He slashed out wide with the axe, a mistake, and fended off the incoming spear with his bare forearm. They were pushing him back. He anchored himself to Conn's side; there was nothing behind him but the sea. He pushed with his legs, his feet paddling the ground. The horns whooping off somewhere distant. He hacked down through a tall shield and saw the face behind it twist, driving the spear at him.

Then on his left he felt more than saw Conn lunge forward,

and followed that way, blindly crashed after him through a gap in the line. Suddenly there was space around him. For a moment then he stood toe-to-toe with the man with the spear, stabbing and hacking at each other; another part of the Greek's shield went flying, and then the other man whirled and ran. Conn was running; Raef raced after him, up onto the broad street at the top of the beach.

There some of the Greeks were trying to stand again, shield-to-shield, shouting to each other, waving their arms to each other. The horns were still blowing, somewhere on the other side of the town. Raef gave a bellow. He realized Volodymyr had attacked. Maybe that was what the horns meant, that Volodymyr was attacking. Or maybe, when the horns blew the alarm over Conn and Raef, Volodymyr had realized his chance.

Conn bellowed, "Gather! Get together!" Behind the little knot of Greek shields across the street people were running screaming from the nearby houses and away. The Varanger charged the standing Greeks in a mass and smashed them back, crowding their own shields back into their faces, and some fell and the rest broke and ran.

Raef yelled, pointing; on the far side of the hill, beyond the rooftops, a thick black cloud of smoke rose. Conn flung one arm out to stop him. They stood, panting, looking around.

Conn gave a wild whoop. The main street was empty except for the Varangers, and the people in the side streets were all running away. There was a terrible yell in the distance. The smoke billowed higher. "I told you they'd attack," he said. Some of the men were breaking into the houses along the beach, and he veered over toward them. Raef thought of Merike, and turned back toward the dragonship, floating in the shallow water.

She was wading ashore. Janka came with her. Raef turned around to face the city again. At the corner of his mind something twinkled and gleamed. It had been shining bright as a lantern there since he came ashore but he could only now heed it. With

Janka and Merike behind him he crossed the main street and went into a narrow uphill lane, following that golden gleam.

The street beyond the beach was deserted. The wooden-slatted doors hung open in the stonework block of rooms on either side. He looked in one opening and saw a shop, a square workspace with stools and benches, pottery on the shelves, a counter. He looked into another and saw rugs and cloth. He could hear somebody screaming, in a nearby building, somebody fool enough to stay put, and then the scream abruptly cut off.

He walked straight toward the brightening glow of the basileus. On the next street, this course brought him to a blank wall, over-grown with white roses. Midway along the wall was a broad wooden gate sheathed and studded with iron. He tried the hasp and it was solid, moveless, barred on the inside. He took his axe, and hacked a hole in the wood panel by the hasp until he could reach in and push the bar out.

The gate opened easily, well balanced for its weight. He went inside, with Merike, and turned to Janka and handed him the axe.

"Stay here. Let no one else inside, except Conn. I'll handle this."

⸻⸺

Conn pulled Leif, Bjorn the Christian, Ulf, and a handful of the guardsmen away from the looting and followed the fleeing people. They were all going in one direction and he was content with that. Whenever he saw anybody stopping he ran at them, howling like a wolf, and the Greeks fled away. Leif swerved into an open door-way and came out with a skin half full of wine, and they passed it around as they walked up the street. Ahead of them, a few people burst out of a house and fled, and Conn chased them half a block to harry them along.

Ahead of them rose the round top of the church, with its cross; that was where these people were fleeing, to that sanctuary.

The smoke billowed up beyond it and he heard a great crash like a roof falling in. Suddenly, on the street ahead of him, Pavo appeared, and a dozen of his Sclava behind him.

Conn slowed, one arm out, holding his men back. From here he could see the masses of people packed around the church, too many to fit inside; the wailing of children and the sobbing of women sounded from them in a great mournful, single cry. Sclava walked around the outside of the crowd, their hands on their swords. The wind was rising, and the sky was full of white billowing clouds. There was still a lot of day left before the sun went down.

Then from the church came a blast of horns. The Varanger stopped, on the free side of the Sclava ring. The two doors of the church swung open and several men came out onto the flat porch. Among them was Volodymyr, who lifted a hand up over his head in salute.

Conn yelled; the Sclava and the other Varanger all shouted in response. The captive people moaned. Among the men behind Volodymyr was one in the long gown and domed hat of a Christian priest and he came forward to the edge of the porch.

His voice carried weakly out across the crowd. He was speaking Greek but with his hands he was signing to them to sit down, to be quiet, to accept what was happening to them. Behind him Volodymyr stood straight and proud. As Conn watched, Dobrynya came up behind him, and stood behind the prince. The quavering voice of the priest dissolved in the wind into an empty twittering.

What mattered was that they were surrendering. Conn turned to the other men.

"This part's done. Let's go look for loot."

—⚬—

Raef went in through the broken gate in the wall, and across a strange little garden laid out in perfect squares, trimmed in white rock, all the growing stuff thorny and rank and dried up. The hall ahead of him was of stone, blank except for the door. He went in through the door, and it was like walking into a different world.

He knew at once there was no one living in the place. The air felt hollow, old, long unbreathed. He stood in a room with a floor of mottled green stone, whose walls were painted with pictures of fish, and ships, and a city on a seacliff. In the middle of this first space was a stone basin, in the center a naked green woman, half the size of a real one, with her feet inside a metal wave and her up-lifted arms curled around a shell. The basin was empty, but he saw a dark stain a foot deep on its stone side and knew it usually flowed with water.

Beyond was an open courtyard, with stone blocks filled with dead flowers, and several figures of stone, painted like real people. People also were painted on the walls around the courtyard, each side pierced with several doors. He stood looking at the image of a woman, her large lovely eyes pointed at each end, her hair in ringlets, her red lips slightly pursed, as if she were thinking him over.

In the middle of the courtyard was a stool, overturned, and a woman's hairpiece, very pretty, made of shell and gold. Even the stool was beautiful, with smooth curving legs, and a little leather cushion. A stone table stood next to it.

On the table was a piece of birch bark, and in the center of the birch bark was his basileus.

He picked up the basileus, warm from the sun. Merike whispered, behind him, "Where all go?"

"They left," he said. "As soon as they knew we were coming." Including Rashid. He went on through the courtyard and out another door.

Here was another garden, square on square of white pebble pathways, all the plants inside the squares gone gray from lack of water. These looked like kitchen herbs, and when he went into the smaller building behind the garden, it was a cooking house.

A huge hearth took up half the wall, well built of brick, with spits and pothooks of iron. Along the south wall were two stone basins; on a counter next to them he found a chunk of mouldy bread, and a knife, much used, the edge honed white. Half a strange fruit, the coarse red husk filled with little jewels of seeds. Two big stone jars stood at one end of the room, and he took the seal from one and found it full of wine. The other was already opened, and gone to vinegar. On a shelf above them were goblets made of glass, and bright colored clay cups.

Merike poked at the hearth with a stick. She said a word in her language and then struggled with it in dansker; finally she shrugged. There was wood beside the hearth in a box and she laid out a fire, as if it were a cold day, and went around opening casks and cases. On a shelf Raef found some cheese in pots, little packages of crushed herbs, a jar of some syrupy stuff, astonishingly sweet. There were baskets of round red apples. The Greeks had had plenty of food, even salted meat, and grain. At least, some of these Greeks. At the far end from the wine, Raef came on a little side room behind a curtain.

As soon as he pulled the curtain, he knew by the smell what this was. The box stood before him, a comfortable height for sitting, with a hinged lid. Next to it, in its own little box, was a stick with something dry and white and lumpy as a wasp nest on the end. He opened the lid and looked down, far into the dark, and saw a gleam of water.

He stepped away, letting the curtain swing. He said, "They didn't even have to go outside to shit."

Merike spoke a rattle of hunnish; on the counter she was making something out of grain and the sweet syrup and apples. Raef went out the back of the cookhouse.

There, under a roof covered with flowering vines, was another big basin, made of stone. It had benches along the insides and a hole in the bottom with a wooden plug. In a hollow directly beneath the floor was a space full of charcoal and ashes, the ruins of

old fires. He stood there a moment imagining people cooking to
death. Beyond this, across a pavement, was a long low barn,
maybe for horses, maybe for slaves. It was empty now.

He went back around the outside of the cookhouse, and into
the hall, with its great open square in the middle, and the doors
opening into rooms on either side. He went from one room to another, looking at everything. The rooms were small, some with
long cushioned sleeping benches, a few still covered with silk
sheets. The floors were the hard mottled green stone but over them
were mats of thick cloth, plush and colorful, with intricate patterns of flowers and animals. In one room a wooden chest stood
against the wall, the hinges and hasps of gold, its top inlaid with
nacre in a scene of helmeted warriors carrying spears, captive
women with their heads bowed and hands bound. On the top of
this chest lay a scattering of little bits of gold—hoops for ears, a
few rings. Above it, on the wall, in a polished disk of glass, he saw
his own face.

He stared at himself, startled; he saw himself so seldom his
first sense was curiosity, as if he looked at a stranger. The glass re-
flection softened the lines of his face. Made his long sun-bleached
hair white as sand, his beard like a nest his mouth and nose and
eyes rose out of. A streak of dried blood ran down the side of his
face. He looked younger than he thought he was. He stood a long
while, staring at himself, in the midst of all this wealth.

In the next room, the bed was neatly made up; in the corner,
on a little wooden stand, was the golden image of a prancing
horse, only two hands high, the most beautiful thing he had ever
seen that he thought had been made by a human being.

He went into each room, and came out of the last one and
went into the center of the courtyard. Turning over the stool, he
sat down. He still had the basileus in his hand, and he put it into
his belt pouch, and looked at the square of birch bark.

It was the map he had drawn of the world, with Hedeby at the
center.

He wondered what Rashid had meant by this. If anything. Somehow Rashid had known he would come here, if he didn't die first. He remembered the Baghdad man saying that he wished him well. He looked up into the open air above him. Smoke was drifting across the sky. The sun was gone down out of sight behind the high wall. It was very quiet. He did not feel like rising. Presently Merike brought him a little cake. He felt the walls around him like a shelter. He reminded himself the walls had not saved the people who had been here before. Yet everywhere he looked was something beautiful.

Merike stood beside him, holding out one of the green glass goblets full of wine. Her hand rested on his shoulder. She said, "Who?"

"Mine, now," he said. He drank the wine, already uneasy about that.

—⊷—

Later, with evening falling, he went around looking for a torch, noticed the little burnt wick in a pot of oil in a niche in the wall, and lit it with a splinter from Merike's kitchen fire. It sent up a little yellow glow, not as smoky as a torch, not as much light, either. He went all around the open space, finding more pots of oil and lighting them, and while he was doing this, Conn came in, trailed by the rest of the Varanger, each carrying a bulging sack over his shoulder.

"Well," Conn said. "How did you find this?"

Raef blew out the splinter, and sat down on his stool. Leif and Ulf and Bjorn the Christian had thrown their sacks of booty down and were walking around the courtyard, ogling the pictures, and stroking the stone people. "There's room for everybody," Raef said. "Everybody we like, anyway. Take a room. That's mine, over there." He waved at the room with the golden horse in it, where he had also put the birch-bark map.

Conn found another stool, and sat beside him. Merike came silently from the kitchen with more cakes and a big ewer in the shape of a swan. The other men went quietly around the place, with only an occasional yell of surprise.

Conn said, presently, "This is nice."

"You haven't seen half of it." The wine was making Raef muzzy-headed. "Where's Volodymyr?"

"On the other side of the city. The Greeks have surrendered. Apparently they've been out of water for a while. They're sending to Constantinople with our terms." He finished his glass of wine and filled it again from the swan. "Dobrynya says we should take care of this end of the city. Let the local people come back if they want, he says. Don't steal too much." He glanced after the other men, with their sacks of loot.

"They'll come back in when we bring the water flowing again," Raef said. "We'll likely have to set up some kind of law-giving."

"You can fix the water?"

"Probably. Are you still thinking about Oleg?"

Conn shrugged. "Not so much. We did this for him. Maybe it makes up somehow. Everybody dies." He drank deep of the wine. "We could name the city for him. Chersonese is a stupid name anyway."

The lamps filled the space with half-light; the other men had chosen one or another of the rooms, dragged his loot into it, and gone out to the cookhouse to eat. Raef sat thinking about how they had come here. He remembered the fighting on the beach, when the Greeks raised their shield wall, their last chance to keep the Varanger out. He remembered again how he and Conn had broken the wall. Without Conn he thought he would have died there. The whole attack would have died there, and if they had fallen back, maybe Volodymyr would have failed too.

He reached his hand out between them and Conn took hold of it, and they sat there a while in silence, having no words that said

more than the hand clasp. In the shadowy lamplight the pictures
on the walls were like people watching them.

The little birds who had been twittering around the eaves of
the courtyard had gone away with the sunset, but now abruptly,
out in the garden, another bird began to sing, a long peal of pure,
rippling notes, as sad as death. Raef sat drinking, Conn silent beside him, and listened to the endless, almost weeping song of the
bird, as if the night itself sang for him, and for the first time in all
his life, it seemed, he felt no need to move on.

⟶⟸

Volodymyr called his guardsmen around him again, leaving the
lower part of the city to Conn and Raef. They sent out their men to
walk the streets and chase off looters. Raef took Leif up out of the
city to the broken water pipes, and they mended them back together. When he got back to his house, water was spurting up
from the shell in the arms of the little green woman and flowing
into the basin.

The people of Chersonese had all gone to hide in the church
and its yard, and in the stone-lined pit in the ground just beyond it,
where the white stone trees were. Volodymyr told them they could
go home but for a few days no one did. When the first brave ones
started back, they fought over whose house and shop was whose,
and Conn dragged them all down onto the beach and listened to
their complaints and settled them as best he could. Raef thought
he did surprisingly well and justly. He let nobody question his
judgments; he knocked down the first man who tried, and after
that they all did as he said.

They understood this, Raef saw. They submitted to power and
order, whether Greek, or somebody else's.

The shops began to open again. A bakery in the next street
down from Raef's house gave off delicious smells of bread.

Merike found wonderful clothes in the cupboard in the room

she and Raef were sharing, tunics of red and blue cloth so fine her body showed through, and little pots of scent, and she danced before him, teasing, smelling like roses, poking her breasts at him, thrusting her crotch forward, letting him nuzzle her there, until he bit her womanhood through the sheer cloth and dragged her down on the softness of the bed.

The part of Chersonese that they held seemed to be the oldest section of the city. What lay outside their reach was mostly a big vineyard, the broad pit with its benches, the stone trees, and the church and the houses around it. Raef wandered around the old city, looking into the shops and the market, walking up the narrow lanes.

He came to the wall, high and solid, made of squared-off rock set perfectly together, and laid his hand on it. Even the Danewirk was not built as well as this. The whole city was made to last. Now it had changed owners, but it was still a Greek city, and it went on as it had before, according to the ways and plans of the Greeks. Here and there, on a corner, a little fountain ran again, drenching the dried mosses in their old basins. As the people came back, the shops began to sell goods in them, people took up their crafts again.

Whenever he came into a place, everybody stopped still and stared at him. Since he knew no Greek, all he could do was look around. He thought they expected him to loot them; they looked puzzled when he turned and left, empty-handed.

A woman with painted eyes rushed at him from a doorway, chattering. She reminded him so much of the woman drawn on the wall of his house that he stopped, and she seized his hand and turned the palm up.

"You be wise," she screamed, in garbled dansker. "You king! You son be king!" He realized she was pretending to see his future. Her free hand stretched out, begging for payment. But around her neck was a big crystal that flashed and sparkled in the sunlight, as she shouted at him, and in it, for an instant, he saw her, older, with a man behind her, his hands on her neck, choking the life out of her.

He jerked his head up, and saw, through the open door behind her, that same man, sitting at a table, cutting a slice off a cheese. He jerked his hand free and strode away.

Back near the wall, at the marshy end, he found the ruin of a house, and decided Chersonese had once been larger than it was now. Only a few stones were left of the walls, only the traces of the rooms. A big leafy tree grew up in the middle of it, so it had been years and years before that anyone lived there.

He wondered if some day trees would grow up through Hedeby. Through the Coppergate at Jorvik. Trees would grow through Thorfinn's hall, through Corban's house on the island, through every holding and building of men, bones of the earth, gathering them back in, and even the walls of Chersonese would be only stones under the ground, hidden away under the enormous red and mossy trees. He shook his head free of that, not knowing what it meant.

He went along the wall, made of square stones fit perfectly together, made to last throughout time. He thought, These people believe they will be here forever.

He watched the glassblowers and the people who made ear hoops and rings and pins of gold wire. They used all kinds of magical stones, too, but just for the glitter. Here there seemed to be no magic, only wealth. Maybe that was the bargain here; maybe that was what forever meant. Mirrors, and not crystals.

In a dim shop stacked with bolts of cloth, an old man in a cap suddenly gave him a fancy red tunic, and waved off his fumbling try at buying it. Bowed to him, over and over, and said words he didn't understand.

The more the local people came back, the louder the place was, the streets always full, singing and shouting and arguing, children and their games, old women shrieking at each other from their upstairs windows, people selling hot sausages and wine by the cup, and the air drifted with the smells of food cooking. He passed Leif and Ulf sitting out in front of taverns playing dice. When they saw him, Ulf made a great show of hiding the dice from him, and all three of them laughed.

Ragged beggars sat around the edges of the market, their hands out. He took to carrying bits of bread around in his wallet for them. He put bread also on the roof of his house, for the birds.

After a while, people called something to him, as he went by in the street; he supposed it was the Greek equivalent of Goose.

The fishing boats went out and brought back fish. A big Greek merchantman put in from the east, and unloaded crates and sacks and earred jugs of wine and sold them on the beach. In the place of these goods the ship's crew carried bales of furs back onto their ship, some of them even sealed with the mark of the Novgorod pelthouse. A few days after that ship left, two more came in. Local merchants came down to the beach to buy and sell these cargoes, and the whole city sold the sailors bread and drink and good times while they were on shore.

Conn took to watching the merchants trade their cargoes; he spent a lot of each day on the beach, telling people what to do. When he began taking a little bit of each shipload, mostly food for the Varanger, the merchants acted as if they had expected it.

In the goldsmithing shop, Raef noticed that the workmen were shackled to their benches by iron rings around their ankles. The naked men who loaded and unloaded ships were all slaves. He looked around his house and realized, uneasy, they would need slaves, to live here, to clean, to carry.

The local girls liked Conn; there were always a few of them around Raef's house, waiting for his cousin, or just finished with him. Ulf brought in a woman from the street, who helped Merike in the cookhouse. Merike started wearing ribbons in her hair, the way these Chersonese girls did.

The moon waxed and waned and waxed again, and a ship came in from Constantinople.

Volodymyr ordered everybody out to meet it. Conn and his Varanger met the prince, Dobrynya, and all the Sclava as they marched down from their end of the city and walked with them to the Varangers' beach to greet the newcomers. Conn and Raef stood on the side of the street above the beach and watched the big galley put in. The high beaked prow carried the image of a woman with snakes for hair. The hull was painted black, with gold along the gunwales and around the oar ports, and a cross stood on top of the mast. Beside the lone remaining dragon, now anchored quietly in the cove, the Greek ship was immense, shiny, important-looking.

They had brought horn players, who got out first and lined up on the beach, and played blasts of sound through their brass tubes while a little parade of men came ashore. Conn was too far away to see much of them. He could tell by the way they clustered around one man that he was the leader—a tall, gray-headed man in a long red tunic.

This man walked up the beach to Volodymyr, and they both bowed, and many words were said, and they bowed again, and the watching people gave a dutiful-sounding cheer, and then they all went home. Volodymyr took the fancy Greek back with him to the church, which he had made his headquarters.

Raef said, "I was hoping this would not happen."

Conn was walking beside him up the street, toward the little church; just ahead was the cross street that had become the boundary between their town and Volodymyr's. Conn said, "What do you mean?"

"Now they're going to give it all back," Raef said. "Remember? That was the plan—to take Chersonese, and exchange it for a Greek princess."

Conn let out an explosive curse. "No, they're not," he said, and lengthened his stride, and they went up the street toward the church.

CHAPTER TWENTY

Somehow the Sclava had found themselves horses, and now, mounted, carrying lances, wearing leather armor sewn with iron rings and iron helmets on their heads, they rode around and around the church. The crowd of townspeople had mostly disappeared. When Conn and Raef walked up to the front porch, the big double doors were closed. Pavo himself came down the shallow steps toward them, a great breastplate on him, and a plume in his metal hat.

"No in. Only Knyaz and Emperor's man."

Conn's neck swelled, his head sinking down between the muscles of his shoulders. "You think I can't get through you, Pavo?"

"No." This was Dobrynya, coming swiftly down the steps from one side. "You two leave this behind you." The golden Sclava lord was polished up again, his clothes clean, his hair and beard combed. His blue eyes were piercing, confident, certain again. He wore an even more splendid collar of gold and crystals than the one he had given Conn. He came up between them and Pavo, and said, "I will talk to you, Corbanssons." As if this were some great gift.

Conn followed him off a little way around the church wall. It was an old building, Raef saw, and birds flew in and out of nests along the top, under the eave. A long graveyard stretched away on the opposite side. Before Dobrynya had stopped and turned to face them, Conn was arguing with him.

"You're giving this city up for nothing. Don't you realize what this is—we could hold this place ourselves, all the wealth going in and out—"

Dobrynya swung toward him, massive, his face set. "Volodymyr will be the brother of the Emperor. Chersonese, surely, is worth a princess."

"Not to me!" Conn's fists clenched. Behind him, Raef was

watching Pavo, up on the porch behind them, through the corner of his eye. "Dobrynya, you made a pledge to me, when I made one to you."

"You will get gold," Dobrynya said, harsh. "Volodymyr will make a hard bargain, I promise you."

"Gold! You promised me treasure. Now I've seen real treasure and you want to buy me off with baubles. Dobrynya, we can be greater here than in Kiev. Keep the city. We can defend it—give them back their woman, keep this city."

Dobrynya's face was rigid, icy. A hot red patch shone on his cheeks. He said, "Volodymyr will have what he wants. And you did give me your pledge. And you will obey me. For once."

"I have given you all this."

"You've been very useful. You'll be compensated. That was our bargain."

Conn was giving off a steady heat of rage. In the corner of his eye Raef could see Pavo watching them intently from the porch. Then abruptly the doors behind him opened.

A yell went up. The mounted Sclava galloped up before the porch, and Dobrynya turned away from Conn and swiftly joined them, climbing up the steps so that he was not beneath the riders' heads. Conn and Raef went after him and stood a step behind him, on the ground.

Two lines of guards came out from the church and made a lane. Down this corridor came Volodymyr, and beside him, the gray-haired Greek.

The Sclava roared the Knyaz's name, and he advanced alone out onto the edge of the porch, his arms raised, as if he blessed them. He called out, "Greetings to you, my Rus'! My children, for whom I do everything!"

The roar that answered hammered off the stone wall of the church. Raef put his hands over his ears. Conn glanced at him; they said nothing.

Volodymyr cried, "I swear in the name of God I shall build a

new church here, in this place, to make memorial of what we do
here now. Because on this day begins the true glory of Rus'. The
glory of Rome is now the glory of Rus'!"

The Greek stood behind him, in the shadow of the doorway. His
hands were folded in front of him. All that Raef could make out of
his face was that he was smiling. Volodymyr was shouting again,
calling himself the Emperor's own brother. Saying he would, when
he was baptised, take the Emperor's own name, Basil, before the
Christian god. And henceforth—

Conn turned, going, and Raef followed. They went down the
steps into the mass of the Sclava and pushed through, roughly,
crowding even the horsemen out of the way. Nobody tried to stop
them. Raef glanced back to make sure of Pavo and saw him standing beside Dobrynya, staring after him and Conn, but not moving.

Leif had seen them walk off, and he was coming after them,
from one side, and Bjorn the Christian was following them out from
the other. No one else walked away out of the crowd now cheering
Volodymyr's every word. The Varanger met together on the street,
below the church. None of the guardsmen had come with them,
only the dansker. Conn led them away, back to their own end of
the city.

⸺⸱⸺

Raef stood by the fountain, watching the water splash down the
green woman's shapely body. Conn was sitting out in the sun of
the courtyard. Raef put his hand out, and let the fountain's water
trickle over his hand.

Conn said, "We could hold this part of the city, at least, against
them."

Leif said, "There are five of us."

"We took Chersonese," Raef said.

Bjorn said heavily, "Now it isn't just Volodymyr against us,
it's the Greeks, too."

"They're Christian," Conn said, frowning at him.

Bjorn shook his head. "Not my kind. They cross backwards."

The door flew open, and Janka came bursting in, round-eyed. "Empor here!"

Conn grunted. "Nobody comes in without I say so. It's not the Emperor, you blockhead, it's some Greek. Tell him to go away."

Janka swallowed, turned, and went out.

Raef said, "It will be a while, anyway, before they get it all confirmed in Constantinople. Months. We can do something."

"Loot the place down to the stone," Ulf said.

Raef was thinking more about talking some of the guardsmen into joining them. Overthrowing Volodymyr. The pledge had to end sometime. Janka came rushing back in.

"Him say, him have you something." He looked from Raef to Conn. "Him say him come in quiet, no sword, only slave to carry it. Slave and me."

Conn stood up, and came over to stand beside Raef. After a moment, he said, "All right. Send him in."

Janka left again. Raef said, "A bribe?"

Conn shrugged. "I'm getting something out of this."

Once again the door swung open, and Janka and another man lugged in a chest the size of a sea chest, which they brought down into the foreyard, and set before Conn and Raef. After them came the Greek.

It was the gray-haired man. Seeing him close up, Raef, in spite of himself, felt his jaw drop open.

The gray-haired man met Raef's amazed stare with an easy smile. He came into the foreyard room as calmly as if he belonged there. His voice was gently apologetic. "Thank you for admitting me. My name is Michael Lecapenus. I am a logothete of His Imperial Majesty. I know—knew the former owner of this house."

Raef blinked at him. He had never seen even a woman as finely made as this. He might have stepped down from one of the pedestals around the courtyard, a stone man come to life, smooth

and white and beautiful. His skin was pale, indoor skin. His im-
maculate cloak, embroidered around the hem with red and gold
designs, hung in exact folds. Under it he wore a long sleeved shirt
and soft loose trousers, in spite of the heat, of stuff as fine as the
tunic, shot through with gold thread. His graying hair was immac-
ulately combed into rows of little curls, trimmed at the ears and
the back of the neck. Above the wiry beard that just traced his
jawline, his cheeks were smoothly shaven, his mustache as perfect
as if every hair were drawn on. His white, long-fingered, elegant
hands wore gold rings with red stones in them and his belt was
stitched with gold. He stood letting Raef gawk at him, a look of
mild self-deprecating amusement on his face.

Raef looked down at himself, at his new leggings filthy already from tramping in the streets, his bare arms, grimy, heavy-
muscled, sticking out of his frayed tunic, his fingers and palms
callused from the oar; he saw his beard tangled on his chest,
his hair hanging down over his shoulders. He remembered the
face in the glass on the wall; a wild, bloody boy. He stared at
Michael Whatever His Name Was again, his mind crowded with
thoughts.

Conn said, "Who the hell are you? And how do you speak
dansker?"

The Greek Michael seemed as at ease here as one of the birds
that fluttered in and out of the courtyard. He said, in a mild voice,
"May I come in?"

Conn said, "You're in, aren't you. What's this about?"

Michael walked toward them. He even smelled good, a kind
of dry woody aroma like a pine tree. He smiled as happily as if
they were old friends. "You left something behind today," he said,
and beckoned to the slave, who went up, knelt by the chest, and
unlatched it and turned up the lid.

From behind Raef, in the courtyard, came a soft collective
gasp from the other Varanger. The box was filled to the brim with
gold pieces. Several of the coins on the top of the heap trickled

down, fell off, and rang on the stone floor. The Greek Michael
stood behind him, his face calmly expressionless, his hands
folded in front of him.

Conn stepped forward, leaned down, and upended the chest,
so that the whole great golden heap of money casacaded across
the floor, chiming on the stone and rolling off into the sunlight. He
stepped back. He said, "That doesn't cover even a little bit of
Chersonese, does it."

Michael was looking around, at the magnificent pictures on
the wall, the fountain, and the courtyard beyond, now littered with
clothes and gear of the Varangers. He said, "I passed one of the
most interesting evenings of my life here once, discussing
Homer's understanding of fate and honor. That was with Stultius,
the previous owner. He was quite the scholar." He faced Conn
again. "I understand your anger. I have heard stories, since I got—
in fact, before I even got here—of you men—of you two, you
Corbanssons, especially. You won this city for them. That was
why I came, to see such heroes." He stepped forward, his hand
out. "I came to shake your hands."

He put out his hand to Raef, who almost refused, not wanting
his dirty palm to touch something so clean and white, but then,
slowly, laid his fingers against the Greek's. To his surprise, the
touch was firm and strong.

Conn shook the offered hand without hesitation. He said, "I
am Conn Corbansson, and this is Raef."

"I have heard wonderful stories," the Greek said, again. "How
you got them here across the trackless seas. Saved them from the
fire. How you stormed the city like a pack of wolves. You'll be famous for this. You'll be talked of from Constantinople to Novgorod and beyond."

"We killed nobody in this house," Raef said. He did not know
why this seemed important. "Nobody was here when we came."

"I believe you," Michael said. "Stultius would have fled at the
first warning of any unpleasantness. Probably he went to Sinope.

He has a villa there. Please let us sit. All of you." He looked around at Ulf and Bjorn and Leif. "I have a proposal for you all."

Conn waved him toward the red leather stool, and sat down on the other, and Raef went to the side and brought back a bench and put it beside his cousin. Ulf, Bjorn, and Leif came slowly up and sat down on the ground around them. Janka had come to the edge of the courtyard, and Raef made signs at him toward the cook-house. All around the courtyard, people were peeping out of doors. Janka skittered by on his way out the back.

Michael Whatever His Name Was had settled himself calmly on the stool, his hands on his knees. He said, "I must explain. Among my duties for His Imperial Majesty are the oversight of the Imperial Guard, which is made up of a good many men like yourselves—Norse, Danes, Swedes, even some Icelanders. And so I speak your language passingly." He said "His Imperial Majesty" in Greek, as he had before, as if there were no other way to say it. On the other hand, Raef thought, they probably had all immediately recognized what it meant.

He imagined himself trying to speak Greek. The sensation was so odd he stirred around on the bench, turning away, and watched Merike come in with glass cups and the big swan ewer. She set the ewer down, gave each of them a cup, beginning with Raef, and then went around to fill the cups. This time she started with Michael the Greek. He gave her the same warm, eye-crinkling smile he had given to Raef at the first, welcoming as the sun coming up.

He said, "I see you are divinely attended. Thank you, my dear."

Merike mumbled, her eyes shining as if she understood, her ears turning red, and scooted away back into the kitchen. Halfway out the bedroom door behind Michael, Conn's latest woman was staring at them, her mouth ajar.

Conn said, "Whoever this house used to belong to, it's ours now." His voice had a hard edge.

Michael said, "Well, you're here, aren't you. It's very beautiful and comfortable, and you've earned it. 'Leading your host like a consuming fire!' " He flourished with his hand. "Believe me, it sounds much better in Greek."

"Has Volodymyr agreed to everything?" Conn asked. "How certain is this, that we have to give Chersonese back?"

"Well, he has," Michael said. He drank some of the wine. "Excellent. Stultius always had the best. I'm sorry to tell you, but he has indeed acceded to all the terms, including the city as part of the wedding gifts."

"He gave in, just as if he had lost!" Raef leapt up, and circled around once, turning back to face Michael again, his temper simmering. "So, that's why you came walking all over here to see us? To tell us you beat us anyway?"

Michael did not try to smile this down. His face was open, serious, smoothly handsome, his eyes candid. On their side. He said, "No, not at all. I came as I said because I heard the stories. I wanted to meet you. Especially you two." He sat forward a little, looking from Conn to Raef and back again.

"Besides, you didn't really lose. That's a lot of money, among five men. You'll be justly famous for this, as I said." He paused a moment, and then said, in another, harder, voice, "The deal is done, and you can't really fight it, can you. The five of you." His eyes switched from side to side, where creeping in like dogs Ulf and Leif and Bjorn were picking up the farthest-scattered of the gold pieces. "The two of you," Michael said, looking back to Conn and Raef.

Conn grunted. He stood with his mouth clamped tight. Raef thought, We could murder him. Right now, just the two of us, we wouldn't need any help. He saw no use in that. He realized they had just seen this Greek somehow bribe their own men under their eyes and there was nothing they could do.

Michael was talking again, in his open, easy voice. "This should never have come so far, anyway. The Palace has known for a while Vladimir was ambitious. I warned the Emperor myself a year ago to take more heed of him. But His Imperial Majesty has other things on his mind." The smile returned, ingratiating, irresistibly friendly. The clear eyes candid as a baby's.

"In fact part of the agreement with Vladimir is for a Rus' army to come to the Emperor's support in his current difficulties. That is my proposal to you. Come to Constantinople. Become part of the Guard. I promise you wealth and honor beyond anything Volodymyr ever dreamed of."

Raef had heard this before, somewhere. He drank the wine in a gulp. He let his gaze travel over the house around him again, with all its beauties, which now he had to give away, and go shuffling again off into somebody else's war.

Something in his mind cracked like a bone. He stood up suddenly and went off, getting away from this. Michael, behind him, said, "Did he misunderstand me? I meant no offense, certainly—you'll be given very high rank in the Guard, your names known everywhere." Raef went out a door, into the little garden.

He wondered if this were how it felt to be a slave, passed along from hand to hand. He moved out to the warmth of the sunlight. The church bells rang, one, two strokes. The water running again had brought the garden back to green, and there were even some little blue flowers in the prickly herbs. He could have made this all work, he thought.

But he knew better than that. He stood looking around him, at the walls, the buildings. He thought again how long this place had been here. Years, he thought, and remembering the huge old tree in the ruined house: hundreds of years. Years past hundreds. Forever. He struggled to get his mind around what that meant, the sons upon sons upon sons, gone in and out of the house, the ships in and out, the buildings raised, and lived in, and fallen down. The layers of men's lives laid down here, maintaining what was there, adding more. That was what made this possible, that a man here could have clothes and furniture and beautiful pictures around him and good food and talk, comfort, something to build on.

He understood, now, why the Greeks had not fought to the death; they had known all along, if they could endure, the empire would come and restore them. In the end, Chersonese would be here, but Volodymyr would be gone. He and Conn, gone, tramping through the world living in holes in the ground, fighting other people's fights. He felt the huge lie under Michael's serene and transparent honesty, talking to them as if they were equals. Probably he had learned that with the dansker, how to talk like that, like a free man. He remembered thinking Michael might have walked down off one of the pictures in the hall. His massive assurance. He belonged here. And Raef never would.

Nor his sons. For the first time in his life, he thought that he might someday have sons of his own, and he wondered how they would live, in caves like Thorfinn's, at the oars of somebody else's ship, dying in somebody else's battles.

Conn had come out to the garden behind him. Raef stood ruffling the blue flowered herb branches with his hand, making the savory aroma rise up.

"He's gone," Conn said.

"Good."

His cousin came up beside him, into the sunlight. "Do you want to do this? Take up arms with them?"

Raef blurted out, "You want to fight for these people? Conn, look at this. We won this city. But somehow the Greeks won the war. How did they do that? Why is Volodymyr giving them everything back, and us, as if we were a bunch of pieces on a chessboard? They outtalked him, and outthought him, just the way that"—he nodded after the departed Greek—"outtalked us, just now."

"I didn't believe him," Conn said. "He didn't outtalk me."

"Oh? Why didn't we just kill him, then?"

Conn's eyes widened, and he said nothing. Raef went on. "Because it's really Volodymyr and Dobrynya who agree to all this, not us. It's the kings. All we do is carry the swords. And now people like this Michael will come to Kiev, and probably even to Holmgard. And those people will talk their way into running everything. And you and I will have nothing more than they care to throw us, like a scrap to the dogs."

Conn said, "If we go with them, to Constantinople, maybe we can have this. Something like this."

Raef crushed up a handful of the herbs and threw the broken leaves down. "Do you think you could be Emperor? More likely we'd stand around all day like statues, in corners and at the doors. Get a knife in the back, as soon as we're not useful anymore. You heard him. They let us have Chersonese because they were too busy doing something else. Something bigger, wider, in languages we don't know, with people we've never heard of. Do you want that? You want to hear yourself called some other odd name? Some new joke? All for a few gold rings, and some stories?"

The Greek girl sauntered out of the hall, and went by them, going toward the cookhouse. Her black hair was curly as Michael's, caught up in a blue ribbon. As she walked by Conn she gave him a sideways look, and her hips swayed. Conn ignored her; she would be gone by nightfall.

He said, "What do you want, Raef?"

"I want to go back where we belong," Raef said, not knowing until he said it that it was true.

"Where we belong." Conn's eyes widened in shock. "You mean—back to the island?"

"I don't think we can ever get back to the island. I don't think even Corban is there anymore. Somewhere that could be home to us. Hedeby. Denmark. Jorvik. Where we speak the right language. Where we know how things go. Where the people look like us. Where we belong." He figured this into words as it came up, like the water rising in the fountain and spilling out. He remembered the birch-bark map, with Hedeby at the center. "The old woman was right, the world is a ring, but there are a lot of rings, one after another, maybe going on forever. And each ring thinks it's the only

one. And it is, in a way, to the people in it. We have to get back to
our own ring, or nothing we do is going to come to anything. Not
for us, at least."

He looked around at the hall and the garden, aching for what
was already lost, for what he had never really had. "I want this. I
want to live like this. If I can't have it here, I want to build it. Start
building it. And if I have to fight and bleed, it's going to be for my
own sake, not some king's."

Conn said nothing; building was not something that interested
him. Raef could feel his cousin's uncertainties like an unraveling
in his mind. Raef said, "We have a good ship, sweet, and lucky. We
could follow this sea back to our sea. It would take a long while."

Conn faced him, knotted up again to some purpose. "I want to
go back to Kiev. There's a woman there—"

Raef stood up, angry. "You and your cunts."

"You dragged that stupid hun bitch all this way—"

Raef clenched his fist. Conn looked calmly down at that and
raised his eyes again. "Do you mean that? Because I'm of a mind
to beat the shit out of somebody."

Raef looked away, and let his hand open. The cookhouse door
swung wide and Merike came out, and called, "Food. Meat. Come."
She gave the two of them a startled look and went inside again.

"All right," Conn said. "She has her uses."

Raef said, "We'll go back to Kiev."

Conn smiled at him, and lifted one hand up to his shoulder;
Raef suddenly gripped him into an embrace. They stood holding
each other a moment, head beside head, Raef thinking as long as
he had Conn with him, he could get through anything. He could
give up this house. It was only a house. It wasn't really the house,
anyway.

They stood apart. Conn said, "We should have killed him."

"If we had," Raef said, "there would only be another one just
like him, right behind him." The smell of the roasted meat reached
them and they went in together to eat.

He lay that night with Merike in his arms and thought about Rashid. He had liked Rashid, and then disliked him, and now he thought he liked him again. He didn't know why. Merike snuggled close to him in her sleep, murmuring something in hunnish with his name in it, and he kissed her and stroked her hair back and went to sleep.

A month later, as the summer waned, the Greek princess arrived.

The orders came down from Volodymyr even before the ship carrying the Emperor's sister appeared off the cape. All the Rus' army would meet her; the Varanger would stand on the edge of the market street where it ran along the beach, with guardsmen on either side. Along with the orders came bales of new clothes, and chests full of swords and gold armrings and earrings and finger-rings.

"They don't want us talking it over," Raef said. He was watching Conn hand out the gold to the other Varanger; there was enough for everybody to have his choice. Raef guessed also Michael had reported back to Voloydmyr and Dobrynya that the Corbanssons were less than happy with the overall arrangement.

Conn said, "I don't care. I want to get out of here." He had found some gold ear hoops and was poking one of them in through the soft part of his left ear. A little blood dribbled down his hand. Below them the beach spread out its broad white apron, dimpled with footprints and dappled with trash. Pavo and his Sclava were already milling around on it, taking food from the sausage vendors and shouting at the packs of running children. The Sclava were all wearing fancy body armor, with metal studs and plates. Pavo was watching Conn narrowly, his head turning constantly as he strolled up and down the sand, stopping every once in a while to bellow something to his men.

Conn fixed the first hoop in his ear, and began to worry the second through the other. He had gold bands on his upper arms, too. Raef sniffed, to see if he smelled like a Greek.

The princess's ships came into view, and the whole crowd roared. The Greeks came pouring down from the city, shouting and waving their arms. Raef thought, She is their salvation. He looked down to his left and saw the last of the Varanger and thought, idiotically, Still, we could take them.

He wanted only to get out of here. He felt the cross-purposes of the Greeks and Volodymyr meshing around him like the work of spiders and he knew the prince no longer trusted them, if he ever had. What he and Conn had done for them was nothing, now that it was done. The prince had sent down no body armor for them, and when the soldiers lined up to welcome the princess, the Varanger stayed at the back, along the street, and out of the way.

There were three Greek ships, each as big and black and shiny and ponderous as the ship that had taken Michael the Blabbermouth away. Volodymyr had brought carpets down, and laid them along the beach to give his new bride a pathway up to the litter that would carry her to his church. A little barge, also stacked with carpets, went out to carry her in from the Greek ship.

Raef folded his arms over his chest. She was not young, this princess, not even as young as Merike, and not pretty, either. She was tall and stoutly built; she wore a headress so spangled with pearls and jewels he could not see the color of her hair.

She rode inward on the barge, and among the men and women who accompanied her she stood so that no one could have doubted who was born to the purple. She had a way of carrying herself that drew everybody's eyes, and brought everybody to an awed silence. The Greeks all knelt. Lined up on either side of the carpet-way, the Sclava, one by one, began to kneel also. Only the five Varanger, shoulder-to-shoulder along the market street, stood where they were, their feet widespread, their hands at their sides by their weapons.

She came up the beach along the carpets, glittering from head to foot, magnificent as a walking, living idol. Volodymyr met her, with his uncle behind him, and reached out his hand.

He bowed first, in spite of himself. Dobrynya bowed from the waist. The princess made an elegant inclination of her head and chest. They spoke—her in Greek, him in Rus' dansker, but it made no difference, since they already knew all the words. She stepped to one side, so that some of her followers could come forward and be made known to the prince.

One was the high priest, who would douse Volodymyr with water. Sheathed in splendid robes, he said more lengthy incomprehensible words. The sun was high and bright, the waters of the harbor glittered, all around, and the people cheered when they were supposed to. Finally the princess and her retinue, with Volodymyr, walked up the trail of the carpets and were carried off to the church, where he would be made Christ's man, and marry her.

An hour later, the seagulls screamed over the empty, rumpled beach, the big ships were anchored out in the cove, and nothing seemed changed at all.

CHAPTER TWENTY-ONE

The Greek ships carried the Sclava, Dobrynya, the princess and Volodymyr, and all their followers back up to the mouth of the Sclava River; the Varanger went in the dragon, with the guardsmen who had sailed to Chersonese with them to fill out the oars. They all rowed the whole way, but the Varanger got to the lagoon first, and were roasting an ox over the fire when the Greek ships finally arrived.

There, Volodymyr and his bride went by horseback and litter, with Pavo, the new leader of the Faithful Band, and all the Sclava who now were the Faithful Band, and rode along the riverbank to Kiev. But the Varanger rowed the dragon ship, and carried it around the rapids, and still got to Kiev first.

That night Volodymyr held a great feast in his hall. The walls were draped in thick new velvets from Constantinople. The floor was laid with wonderful new carpets. The two big chairs at the dais were carved and gilded. His new bride sat beside Volodymyr, her shoulders square as a rule. In the center of the room were Volodymyr's boyars, some of whom, apparently, were entitled to sit when the prince sat. Around the three sides of the hall stood the soldiers, most of them Sclava, who could not sit. None of the Varanger were there save Raef and Conn.

Raef, standing midway down the long wall, opposite the door, watched the new princess closely. The hall had been made over this way especially for her, the ceiling hung with banners, the torches screened with golden sconces; the crowd of women who attended her wore silks and jewels, and her husband had a crown of gold, and a new name, Basil, like the Emperor. But the carpets hung on log walls and the floor was of wood and the table she ate from of wood, and many of the women were Volodymyr's old wives.

Raef thought she would flinch, her proud mouth would pucker a little in distaste. But she sat like a lily among reeds, this woman, every gesture graceful and gracious, smiling, utterly composed. Volodymyr leaned toward her always, put his hands on her, kept his greedy eyes on her, always.

Raef lowered his gaze; he longed to be free of this place.

In among the princess's women, he saw, there was one who watched Conn. She served as the princess's second cupbearer, to bring the ewer to fill the cup; she had curly black hair, and her eyes turned ever toward Conn, who stood a few feet down the wall from Raef, his hands behind him.

Watching her, Raef lifted his head, alarmed. They were talking to each other with glances and looks all across the crowded hall, careless who noticed. This was the woman Conn had come back for. Raef's back tingled up. The prince already distrusted them. This was not over yet.

Volodymyr saw nothing; Volodymyr saw only his Imperial bride.

Then the prince was standing, and raising his drinking horn high overhead. It was said this was his father's horn, all chased and bound in gold, and that no other man had ever drunk from it. Volodymyr brandished it up, and the whole hall fell silent, the men lined up all around, the nobles in the center, and the foreign woman on the high table, all still.

"Now," Volodymyr said, "let us give all honor to those who served us incomparably well. First, to the dead!"

A roar went up. The boyars hoisted their own cups. Boys in bright tunics came down the line of the soldiers, standing along three sides of the room, and gave them each a cup and filled it, and all drank.

Volodymyr lifted his cup again, and all hushed.

"Then Pavo Sclavovich, who held the line at Chersonese!"

Another roar. Raef had not joined in the first and he did not join in this one, nor glance at Conn. When the boy came to refill his cup it was still full. At the head of his rank of soldiers, the Tishats strutted around, drinking and tossing his scalplock.

"To the Faithful Band, who won us the city!"

This time Raef looked down at Conn, and saw his lips drawn back in which Raef thought at first was a smile. And when Volodymyr, at last, said, "Conn Corbansson, who will lead our men to the aid of our brother Basil Emperor," and the shout, tired now, went up, Conn stepped forward, flung his full cup to the floor, and shouted back.

"Not me, Volodymyr, you traitor!"

Raef jerked, alarmed, and shot Conn a warning look. But Conn wanted this, he strode forward as far as he could, pushing boyars out of his way, his voice bull strong.

"We took that city with blood and death, and you gave it back for nothing! Don't expect anything from me, you traitor!"

Volodymyr reared back, his face flushing. Beside him, the princess was rigid as an idol, but her eyes were aimed straight at Conn. Volodymyr cast his empty cup aside. "You think so much of yourself, viking, here's what I think of you. You'll be first into the river tomorrow, to take my new god, and we shall name you Basil, like me, and you'll lead my men to drive anybody who hesitates down into the river too!"

Conn stood square before him, his head back. "I won't. My pledge is over to you and yours. I'm a free man, Volodymyr, and I'll stay that way."

Raef started forward, reaching for his belt knife, wishing he had a real weapon, that more Varanger were here. He took one step, and something sharp poked him in the back. "Stay still, Goose, or I slit you up and down," said Pavo's voice, behind him.

He stiffened. Volodymyr was shouting again, but this time giving orders. From all sides the Sclava were jumping at Conn, who wheeled around, barehanded, to fight them. Raef spun, dodging away from the knife behind him, desperate, and something struck his head, and he was gone.

He woke, lying on his side like a dumped cargo, his arms out in front of him, shackled at the wrists. Conn faced him, their wrists clipped together with four links of iron chain between the iron bands of the shackles. More chain led down to his ankles, which were shackled.

"They were ready for us," Raef said.

"They're afraid of us," Conn said.

Raef shrugged. "You're the one who told them about Hjorunga Bay." He shook his head, still aching from whatever had put him out. At least his eyes were clear. He looked around him at the narrow, cluttered space.

Conn was staring at him. "I'm sorry. If I'd listened to you, we'd be sailing home by now."

Raef said, "Never mind. Let's get us out of this." He felt around the chains, looking for any weakness, breaks, loose links. They were in a little room, half full of wotka casks, with a tiny slit of a window at the top of the blank wall. The floor was covered with mouldy straw and rat droppings.

There were chunks of fresh bread in the straw. Whoever had cast them in here had thrown in also bait for the rats.

"Hold still," Conn said, presently.

Raef froze. A beady nose, fringed in long twitching whiskers, was poking in through a chink in the log wall. Conn lay with his legs drawn up. The rat sniffed around a while, and then crept out, nosing in the straw, making for the bread. Much of the bread was gathered up in a heap, Raef saw, between Conn and the wall: Conn had spent some effort shoving it together with his bound feet.

Its whiskers trembling up and down, the rat found the bread. Conn lashed out with both feet and smashed it against the wall. The rat squeaked and splattered, but it dragged itself off through the chink, leaving blood behind on the straw.

Raef felt over the chain connecting his wrists and his ankles. He found a few cracked links, but also he noticed a loose bolt in the hinge on his ankle. The door rattled, and a key turned in the lock.

He lay still; Dobrynya came in.

The golden Sclava was as smooth and polished as ever in his embroidered robes. He sank down on his heels in the doorway, out of reach, and said, "You are fools, you two. This is your choice. Tomorrow all the Rus' take Christ. Either we open your chains, and you walk into the river of your own will, or we throw you in, chains and all."

Conn spat at him. "Get out of here. Leave me alone."

Dobrynya did not go. Raef inched a little closer, getting some slack in the chain so that Conn could creep within range. The posadnik said, "I want you with us. I don't see what the difficulty is. Christ is the highest god—in the end, he will be not just the greatest but the only God. The Emperor himself bows to him. You have never seen the glory of his rites, how they carry us up to heaven. I have seen that the gods of my childhood are only steps to him. We are men now, and Christ is a god for men." His hands lay together, palm against palm, his voice earnest. Raef thought, He's already learned to pray like a Greek.

Conn said, "Dobrynya, my father was a far-voyager, who wandered out beyond the reach of Christ and Thor and all the rest. My mother made worlds with her hands. What god do you have even as great as they? And they were only people."

Raef said, "This god, this Christ, he's just a puffed-up king. He tells you what to do like a king, he takes your money, like a king, and makes the laws for you, like a king."

Dobrynya growled, "His curse on you, then." He rose up, and went to the door, but he looked back, curious, and made them a light bow of his head. Then the door shut, the lock turned again.

Raef worked furiously at the bolt on his ankles, got the shackle hinge apart, and pulled one leg free. The heavy iron ring

still encircled the other shin. Conn said, "Damn!" He was watching the rats again. "There was one right there, looking out, and
you frightened it."

"You idiot," Raef said. The light was fading, the room gloomy,
soon it would be dark, the rats' hour. He was struggling with the
other ankle shackle when, again, they heard somebody outside.

Conn glanced at him and they hitched forward together, getting close enough to the door that Conn could pound whoever
came in. He drew his feet up, and Raef gathered himself to lunge
after him. The door opened. A woman came into the room.

She carried a lamp before her, and lifted it as she came in, so
the light swept up around her. It was the black-haired woman from
the feast hall, and she set the lamp carefully down and fell on her
knees beside Conn and kissed him.

"You alone spoke pure and true. You are the greatest of men.
I honor you, my dear one, my darling." She kissed his cheeks
and forehead and his mouth. Then she sat back and produced a
key.

Raef sighed. "Not as dear as you to me, right now," Conn said.

"I gave poppy to the guards," she said, working the key awkwardly in the lock between his wrists. She wore a short silk jacket
over a tunic, and her full breasts fell forward when she leaned over
to open the bonds. She had skin like honey. "But somebody could
come around any moment. We have to hurry."

The key clicked, and the lock sprang open; Conn yanked his
arms free. Raef worked apart the other half of his ankle shackle.
The woman was kneeling by Conn's feet, opening his ankle bonds.
She said, "When you spoke, I saw so many who agreed with you—
who dared not speak—oh, you were so brave."

"You're so beautiful," Conn said, free, and took her by the
shoulders and kissed her again.

"Come on," Raef said. "Let's get out of here."

They went out into a narrow dark space, where two men snored
like drunks against the wall. The woman with the lamp led them

on to another door. Dark was coming. When she opened this door, with another key, they looked out on a shadowy garden, stretching away through tall narrow trees, and a wall down the slope in the distance.

She doused the lamp, turning toward Conn. "You know where this is. You can get away from here."

Conn took hold of her hand. "What about you? What will happen to you? You'll get in trouble for this."

She set the lamp down on a shelf by the door. With that same hand she brushed her hair back. She had a long, straight nose, full lips, that trembled; she was very beautiful, Raef realized, beautiful and sad. She said, "I am in trouble already. I will not take the Christ. I am going to refuse to serve the princess. He will find a way to end me."

Conn said, "I'll take you back to your home." He turned to Raef, his face urgent. "We can't leave her here."

Raef said, "I have to find Merike."

Conn had the woman's hand tight in his own. He was already standing beside her, and not beside Raef. He said, "When I've gotten her to safety I'll meet you—back at the old holding?"

"No, no, they'll watch there." Raef felt a nagging, growing pressure to get moving, to get out of there, before they were found and this all came to nothing, and they were back to the cell and the rats. "That tree—on the bluff south of the city, you can see it from the river, that big chestnut tree. When the sun sets."

"It may take me a couple of days," Conn said. "Make it three days from now."

Raef said, "I'll be there when the sun sets, every night."

Conn whirled and drew the woman after him, running down the long slope of the garden. Raef went off along the closer side, looking for a gate, and eventually climbed a tree, and swung over the wall that way.

He stood by the foot of the wall, looking around him. It felt strange not to have Conn there. Dark had come to Kiev. On his right hand, Volodymyr's hall blazed with torches, and all across the ravine behind it, little housefires glowed. Raef walked along the wall, staying in the dark, to the trail down into the ravine, toward his old holding, on the first ledge.

Nobody was there except Bjorn the Christian, who sat outside by the fire toasting pieces of bread on a stick and taking long pulls from a jug. When Raef came up to him, Bjorn looked blearily up at him.

"So, you gave in," he said. "I told you Christ would win."

"Where is everybody?" Raef asked. He went to the door into the hut and looked inside. It was empty. His sea chest was there, but the lid was open, and everything gone from it. Conn's sea chest was gone utterly; they'd had to have something to carry the gold.

"Everybody else took off—Leif, Ulf. When they heard what happened to you." Bjorn jabbed his thumb at the room. "They took your gear, too, and all. For safekeeping, you know. Likely they'll go south. Accept that nice offer from the Greeks."

Raef came back toward Bjorn. "Where is my woman?"

"She left too. With the other hun. There's a camp of their people somewhere south of here and they went to find them."

Raef wiped his hand over his face, cold, and scared. Now he had nothing, not even a good weapon. He felt Conn going farther away with every moment. He had no way of keeping hold of Merike. Bjorn said, "Although who knows if the Greeks still want us, after what you did."

"Now probably they want us even worse," Raef said. "Here, I'll take some of that body." He got the biggest chunk of the bread. "And a little of the blood won't hurt." He took the jug and drank deep of it, until his head reeled. Throwing the vessel back at Bjorn, he wiped his mouth on his sleeve and turned and started walking south.

Rachel sat in the stern of the monoch, her hand on the gunwale; Conn rowed. He had taken the smallest boat he could find, but he needed all his strength to muscle it across the stream of the river. In the night the river purred along beside them, the dark city far behind.

She said, "There is a Radhun caravan stop two days' east of here. If we can get there, we will find Khazars. My people. They will take us on to Samkarsh, my city."

"Can you ride a horse?" he asked.

"Am I Khazar?" she said, with a toss of her head. "There will be horses, on the other bank, here. I have some money. But we have to be gone by daybreak." Her voice was strong and proud. "Don't fear. I will keep up with you."

The day was still far off. The moon had just risen, washing out the stars around it. The river rushed around them; he could see nothing beyond the water, where now the moon laid down its silver trail. Head east, toward the moon. He leaned hard on the upstream oar, trying to wedge the boat sideways across the current. The water felt dead to him, implacable, like a river of stone, and he thought of Raef and felt a sharp momentary twinge of grief.

She said, "I am more grateful to you than you can know, Conn. You have saved my life."

"We're not through this yet," he said.

"I never expected this of you. I have never met a man who would do this for such as me."

He looked up at her, startled; he said, "What else could I do— when you saved me?"

She reached forward, then, and kissed him, and he let the boat drift a little, kissing her back.

Reeds brushed against the side of the log, and then the hull rammed hard aground on something; yet they were far from the bank. He let her go and sat back on the stern thwart, and worked with the oar to get them off the sandbar. Raef would not have let that happen. He got them into deeper water and pushed toward the bank again. Rachel lifted an oar, and helped him sound the bottom, and they nosed their way slowly into a marshy cove, and then to a beach.

She was strong, and not afraid to act; he liked her more all the time.

Just up the river a single lantern showed, a couple of furlongs away. That would be the ferry stop, directly across the river from Kiev. He climbed out of the boat into waist-deep water, and gathered her up in his arms and carried her to the beach. The bottom was uneven and sandy and he went carefully along. She lay trusting in his arms. When he kissed her she tipped her head back and gave her mouth to him, letting him kiss her as deep as he wished. He took her to the beach, and then up a little bank, under some trees, where the grass was deep and soft, and set her down. He stripped off his fancy new tunic, watching her, to see if she drew back now; but in the dark he could see her pulling off her clothes. She stood up, naked, before him, and he put his arms around her and kissed her again, her breasts against his chest, and then laid her down on his shirt and embraced her.

In the gray before dawn, she said, "I love you. I won't let you go."

He had been dozing, a little, sated. He nuzzled her throat. Her hair smelled of wild lavender.

She ran her fingers along his chest. "Come with me. Come to Samkarsh. Then send for your brother. My father is tudun. Men are free there, and we all love freedom. The Christians' god and the god of Islam are just children of the Jews' god. You can live there as you wish—you and your brother. I will marry you, and make you a prince of our people."

He pushed himself up on one arm, listening to her, and looked east, where the dawn was coming. He felt cold, as if his skin had come off. He felt like a different man, without Raef around. A stranger. Rachel came to him again and kissed him again, and her mouth was sweet with promises. She was brave, and strong, and he wanted her again.

"Let's go," he said. "We've got to get some horses." He took her by the hand and they started toward the wharf on the river shore, across the rushing water from Kiev.

⸺◦⸺

Raef was still walking when the sun rose across the high grassy steppe, a great orange blob that seemed to swallow the horizon. He was exhausted; he would have to stop, soon, to rest.

If he didn't find her, would he walk forever? Conn, he knew, was far away, and going farther with every step, and he felt an ache deep in him like something uprooted that he might never again see his cousin.

The day warmed around him, birds flying up, and the mists rising from the ground. He was looking for someplace safe to stop and rest, when he saw a horse galloping up the steppe toward him.

He stood, swaying a little with fatigue, wondering if this were an enemy. The horse trotted up and wheeled neatly on its hocks.

Janka held the reins, and Merike was up behind him. Raef gave a wordless yell of pleasure, and she slipped off the back of the horse and came running toward him and flung herself into his arms.

"Merike," he said. "Merike." He buried his face in her hair.

The horse tiptoed nearer. Janka said, "I see you, before, long way, I go get her."

Merike, in his arms, was sobbing. "I think you dead. I think you kill. Them kill you. My goose. My good." She wept against his neck.

Janka said, "Where is Raven?"

"Conn. He went somewhere else," Raef said.

Janka looked back to the north. "I want see him. Now never." He sounded wistful.

Raef took Merike's face between his hands and kissed her. He said, "I'm going home, Merike. Back to where I belong. Come with me."

She kissed him again, her body pressed against him, her hands on his hips, and then she stood back. She glanced up at Janka, and faced Raef again.

"No. Here stay. I home here."

Janka said, "You stay with us, maybe, hah, Goose? Then Raven come too." He laughed. "You be hun, like me. Belong here."

Raef caught Merike's hand. "But I'll love you. I swear it."

She was crying, tears running down her brown cheeks, and she pushed his hand aside. Not hard. But away. "Someone else," she said. "Someone—" She tugged her thick black hair. "Not me. White hair. White skin. White eyes. When you home again. Not me. I home here. My people glad I home. What we do—I glad of that. All I see and do with you." She smiled at him, even as she wept. "But now I home."

He stood there, bereft. She came to him and kissed him again, firmly, and lifted his hands and pressed her face against them. "You good. You more good of all I know. Go home, Goose. My wild goose." She turned and went to Janka, who gave her an arm up behind him, and they galloped away.

—◦—

He slept, a little, and then walked back. From the top of the river bluff, that afternoon, he watched Pavo's warriors drive the people of Kiev into the river to be baptised.

First they hauled down the stone and wooden Peruns, who had stood under all the trees in the city, and cast them into the river; the biggest of these Volodymyr himself dragged along by a rope, through a steep streambed to make it easier. The local people all wept, and some followed along after the fallen idol, begging and pleading for it to be saved. Then Pavo's men closed in.

They rode horseback, and carried whips, and from every corner of Kiev they pushed the people out and down. Wailing and
crying, the people went the only way they could, down the long
steep hillsides to the river, and then out into the water. There the
priest said words, and sprinkled them. When they walked up out
of the river again, they were Christians.

Raef stayed by the big chestnut tree on the river bluff until
well after sundown, but Conn didn't come.

⸺⸱⸺

The next sundown followed, and Conn wasn't there, and the next.
This was the day he had promised he would come. When dark had
fallen utterly, Raef went down into the city to find something
to eat.

He felt alone, an old dry bone; he thought that the beautiful
princess with the black hair, who had freed them, who had after
all saved them, had taken Conn for her reward, lured him out beyond reach, snared him in some other ring. He felt a spreading
cold grief in the middle of his chest.

All the houses of Kiev were shut tight against him. But under
some of the trees, where the print still marked the ground of the
old gods, he found bread, and dried fish and meat, all fresh. Some
of the people at least were still bringing their offerings. He had to
fight some dogs for the food but there was enough to fill his belly.

He went back up to the top of the bluff. From the foot of the
tree the steep slope led down to the river, a path pounded zigzag
into it from hundreds and years of feet going up and down. The
shoulder of the bluff rose up like a grainy yellow wall, pierced
with rain gulches, and deep holes; some of the holes wound back
deep into the bluff, led into caves and tunnels. He found a little
sheltered opening to sleep in, where someone else had been: a few
stubs of candles lay at the mouth. He lay down looking out east,

where Conn had gone. The rising moon shone in his eyes, and he dreamt of his mother, lying with the whole world round in her arms.

—◦—

The next sundown, as he loitered by the big tree, he realized someone was following him.

He drifted away down toward the river, down the steep gritty slope of the bluff, which was gouged with little caves. When he looked up, there was still enough light in the sky to show him the man coming after him, enough to see the smooth blunt head, and the scalplock.

He went down fast toward the river; if he got to the water, he could escape. The path led around the shoulder of the hill, steeper with each step, and then behind him something whistled.

He felt the whip wrap itself around his ankles, and then he was flying out and slamming into the sloping ground, face-first, his arms out in front of him, so the skin peeled off up to his elbows. He struggled around, reaching for the tight hold on his ankles, and Pavo came scrambling down after him, laughing in the dark.

"You think I let you go. I kill you first, Goose—"

Raef broke free, and lunged forward, trying to get past Pavo, get behind him, into the darkness. Pavo reared back, and the whip cracked out again.

The thin leather lash burned around and around Raef's chest and waist and back, coiling around him like a snake that bit with its whole length. He lay on the ground again, smelling blood, his body stiff with pain.

"I kill you and hang you in the tree for Raven to find," Pavo said, in his ear. "Then I kill Raven, because he think him so good, so much better than everybody else."

He stepped back, ripping the whip away. Raef got up onto all fours, gasping for breath; he hurt all over, his chest sliced to ribbons. He struggled to stand up, heaved himself onto his knees, and the whip cracked again and this time it wrapped around his neck.

He gagged, choking, clutched at the thin cord with both hands, his breath sealed off. He sank to his knees, violent color spinning in his eyes. Pavo was laughing at him, somewhere close by. He felt the whip jerk tighter; sparks shot through the darkness of his vision.

Then something smashed into him, and rolled him over flat. Somebody howled. He clawed at his neck, loosened the whip and dragged in a deep breath, and nobody pulled it tight again.

Conn roared, "You want to fight, Pavo?"

Pavo lay sprawled on the ground in front of Raef; he reared up, and Conn pounced on him with both feet and drove him down again.

Raef unwrapped the whip from his neck and threw it away. He crawled off, still sobbing for breath, his throat raw, his legs gone soft. When he tried to stand up he fell down on his knees again. He saw Pavo leap up off the ground again, and Conn closed with him, and they wrapped their arms around each other and stood together a moment, locked together, their voices snarling, each trying to throw the other down.

Then Pavo flinched away, and went to one knee. Conn stood over him, hit him in the side, cocked his fist to hit him again, and Pavo wheeled around. In the moonlight Raef saw something metal flash in Pavo's hand, and he drove it deep into Conn's ribs.

Raef shouted, and staggered up, sagged down again, helpless, and saw Conn reach out and grip Pavo by the scalplock. Saw him drag the knife out of his side and thrust it into Pavo's neck below the ear, and wrench.

Raef let out all his breath in a rush. Pavo's body sagged down, his head still in Conn's grip, and the blood streamed out of him.

Raef struggled forward. Conn let go the head in his hand, and began to sway, and Raef reached him just as he fell.

"Conn," he said. "Conn." Everything he touched was slippery with blood. He gathered his cousin into his arms, the body shuddering in his arms, a fountain of blood.

Up on the top of the bluff, a horn blared.

Conn whispered, "Get out. Go. Damn him. All tricks." He sobbed for breath. The air was whistling out of the wound in his side.

Raef picked him up and reeled away on wobbly legs across the slope to the bluff face, the nearest of the caves. He dragged himself and Conn into the slot in the rock. For several feet it was only a chink, traveling steeply downward, between the damp-smelling gritty walls. He crept along it, cradling his cousin against him, his back scraping along the rock, eased himself and Conn around a hard corner, and then stood in some wider space, pitch dark.

He could hear Conn breathing, slow and hard. He staggered along under his weight, blind in the dark, brushing along the wall of the cave, and then saw, ahead, the faint yellow glow of a light. He went toward it, following the tunnel around a curve. Ahead, the tunnel curved again, back into the darkness, but a light was shining out of a little room, dug into the stone on one side. He went in that archway. The room was only a few feet deep, round-ceilinged as the doorway was arched, a burrow in the raw stone. A candle burned in a niche on the far side. He went into it and sank down on his knees, and held his cousin in his arms, his head against Raef's shoulder.

"Conn," he said. "Conn."

The light lay gentle on Conn's face. It glittered on the blood covering them both. Conn moved, his eyes opening, looking around at him, and he smiled. "Late. Day late." He whispered, "Better . . . I loved you . . . always only loved you . . ."

Raef said, "Conn." The light shimmering in his eyes.

Conn drew a ragged breath, and sighed it out. Raef felt trembling all through him, bubbling in the blood that poured out from the wound. Raef waited for another. There was no other. He clutched Conn tight in his arms, falling down into a pain so terrible and deep he knew it would kill him before he reached the end of it.

Drowning in grief, as if from the bottom of a well he looked up, and saw someone standing beside him, in a long hooded robe, head bowed, so he could not see the face.

The monk said, gently, "May I help you?"

Raef could hardly move, or talk. He leaned forward, laying his cousin down on the ground as gently as a newborn baby. He bent over him, bracing himself up on his arms, and wanted to weep and could not. The monk knelt down, and began to straighten Conn's body, laying him flat on his back, his legs straight, and then folding his arms over his chest.

"If you allow it," the monk said, "I will pray for him."

Raef hung there, unable to move, seeing the kindness in the monk's touch. He could not endure to think or move or act. He said, "What good will that do? Why do you pray at all?"

The monk said, "It comforts me."

He passed his hand over the dead man's face, shutting his eyes. A look came over Conn that Raef had never seen on his face before, a kind of peace: he looked much younger, like a boy, handsome, unspoiled, perfect.

The monk said, "You loved him. But you must leave here. This is a place of the dead, here, and you are still alive, and will be so for many years. I will take care of him. Here he will never rot, nor be eaten by beasts and vultures. His enemies will not touch him any more. He need never fight again. He will lie here in peace forever."

Raef stood up. He was covered with blood. He gulped down the hard lump in his throat. He said, "Who do you pray to?"

The monk lifted his head. "What does that matter?"

Raef looked into the monk's eyes, black as time. He drew in a ragged, shattering breath.

The monk said, "The candle is going out. You have to go."

Raef turned, stumbling out of the room, and abruptly he was in darkness. He said, "Help me." No one answered. He stood a moment, hoping someone would come show him the way, but finally he started off on his own, feeling his way along the wall of the cave.

He wandered a long while in the cave, in the dark. He never found the niche again, nor the monk. For once in his life, he had no sense of what was around him; he walked into the walls, and smashed his hands and feet. He saw Conn before him everywhere. He thought endlessly of Conn, how Conn had always been beside him, how Conn had always saved him. At last he saw a pale gleam down the tunnel, and went toward it, and came out into the sunrise, on the bluff.

He stood a moment, one hand on the stone, gathering himself. He had come out the same way he had gone in. There was a lot of blood all over the ground in front of him, and Pavo's whip lay there, but the Tishats himself was gone, head and body both. Raef went slowly downhill, toward the water, to wash off the blood. Conn's blood. He bent down over the water, and now, at last, he wept.